The Inked Reaper

Book One of Ink Stains

Mayson Kukwa

FOR THE ONES WHO DESPITE ALL ODDS, ARE CREATIVE

DISCLAIMER:

Hello, readers.

Mayson Kukwa here, the author behind this novel. If you're unaware, this book is adapted from the script for the first season of a screenplay I call *Ink Stains*. Every bit of royalty I earn from this novel is poured directly into the dream of bringing this story to television. It's a vision that lingers in my mind like a shadow, growing stronger with every reader who picks up these pages.

A warning: you are about to enter a world where the darkest elements of human nature come alive—where murder, assault, child trafficking, and dismemberment twist their way through the narrative, exposing the worst of society and the minds trapped within it. Mental illness is not just mentioned but delved into, peeling back layers of human psyche you might find unsettling. I've written these pages to disturb, to haunt, to make you look closer at what we sometimes choose to ignore.

If, at any point, you find yourself queasy or uneasy, remember: this is only fiction. But I've crafted it to feel real, every disturbing detail honed over time to create an experience that's both captivating and horrific. It is a story meant to linger, a story that might just stay with you long after you've closed the book.

So, let's not waste another moment. Dive in if you dare—and remember: in the end, it's just a story.

Or is it?

Just remember. If you feel sick repeat this saying:

IT'S JUST A BOOK...

IT'S JUST A BOOK...

IT'S JUST A BOOK...

IT'S JUST A BOOK...

IT'S JUST A BOOK...

IT'S JUST A BOOK...

IT'S JUST A BOOK...

IT'S JUST A BOOK...

IT'S JUST A BOOK...

IT'S JUST A BOOK...

IT'S JUST A BOOK...

PROLOGUE

The room was still, almost suffocating in its quietness. Dusty air hung heavy, disturbed only by the faint buzzing of a single desk lamp. Its pale, flickering light cut through the darkness, illuminating a simple wooden desk. On the desk, a blank notebook lay open, the crisp, untouched pages stark against the gloom of the room. Seated before it, Tyler Grayson, his long, dark hair falling in lazy strands over his face, held a pen in his hand, poised to write. His hand hovered just above the paper, each movement deliberate and precise, as though the weight of his thoughts demanded perfection before they could be committed to the page.

At just eighteen, Tyler had already lived more than most would in a lifetime. A published author with a mind as sharp as his pen, his words had captivated readers, pulling them into his world, keeping them glued to the pages he crafted. But there was something else, something darker that lurked beneath the surface. The faint light of the lamp barely concealed the shadows creeping into every corner of the room, giving it a sense of foreboding.

Tyler's hand finally moved. The scratch of the pen against the paper echoed in the silence as his thoughts began to spill out, measured and controlled, each word forming with an eerie precision.

"My name is Tyler, Tyler Grayson. I'm eighteen years old, a published author, and by all accounts, I have my entire life ahead of me. People say I have a gift, a way with words that pulls them in, keeps them turning pages, hungry for more."

He paused, tapping the pen gently against his chin. His blue eyes glinted in the dim light, reflecting a calm surface that concealed a brewing storm. A faint smile touched his lips, but it wasn't warm, it was cold, detached, and far too calculated for someone so young. Something stirred beneath the mask he wore, something far more sinister.

Tyler leaned back in his chair, letting the thoughts simmer as he contemplated the truth that no one else could know.

"But what they don't know, what they can't know, is that I write more than fiction. My stories... my characters... they live in these pages, but they breathe in the real world too. I control them. I create them, and I destroy them."

His gaze drifted to the notebook. He flipped to another page, revealing rough sketches and notes. To the untrained eye, they could be mistaken for plotting just the work of a dedicated writer mapping out his next novel. But to those who knew better, they resembled something far darker. The images on the pages looked disturbingly like crime scenes. There was an artistry to them, yes, but there was also something chilling in the details. Each note, each line, seemed to carry a hidden weight.

Tyler ran his fingers over the pages slowly, reverently, as though he were touching the edges of a secret only he understood. His smile deepened, but it was not one of joy, it was the smile of someone who knew what power felt like.

"There's a hole inside me," Tyler mused, almost as if trying to make sense of his own thoughts. "An empty piece of myself I don't remember how I lost... maybe I never had it to begin with. All I know is it's there, this constant, gnawing emptiness."

His pen hovered over the paper again, but this time, the movements were quicker, more urgent. The tip scratched against the page with increasing intensity, mirroring the tension that began to rise in the room. His heart rate quickened, his mind spiraling with the need for release.

"But when I do what I do,when I hunt them, punish them,it fills that space. For a moment, the emptiness isn't so heavy. It's the only thing that makes sense anymore."

As the pen moved across the pages, Tyler's world began to take shape. The camera of his mind zoomed in on each thought, each word forming an intricate web that led to only one conclusion: control. Power.

The notebook was filled with more than just ideas for stories. It held detailed accounts of lives he had touched,lives he had ended. His victims, though they lived on the fringes of his imagination, had felt his wrath in the real world. Every kill, every "punishment," was meticulously documented, hidden beneath the guise of fiction. What readers saw as suspenseful storytelling was, to Tyler, a form of justice.

"You see, the world is full of stories, dark, twisted stories that most people never get to read. Stories that deserve an ending. Deserve justice."

He spoke softly, his voice no longer filling the room but instead settling into the air like a cold breeze. These were thoughts not meant for others, not meant to be shared. Yet they thrummed inside him, demanding acknowledgment.

He paused for a moment, allowing the weight of his thoughts to settle. There was a strange calm in his mind now, a clarity that came only when he embraced the darkness he had kept hidden for so long.

"But justice doesn't always come through the law. Some people escape it. Some people... like the ones I hunt. The ones I punish. To them, I'm not just an author. I'm something much worse. I am their reckoning."

His pen scrawled the final words with a sense of finality. The ink glistened under the faint light of the desk lamp as he stared at the line that now stood as both a confession and a promise:

"I am the Inked Reaper."

"They say every story needs a hero, and a villain, I suppose I'm both."

Tyler closed the notebook slowly, his eyes lingering on the closed cover for just a moment longer. The room, once again, fell into silence, but the air was heavy with tension. His thoughts raced, his pulse quickened, but on the surface, he remained calm, too calm.

He leaned back in his chair, the world around him fading as his mind lingered in the darkness of his own creation.

THE CALM BEFORE THE STORM

Morning light filtered through half-open blinds, casting thin beams across the meticulously organized space of Tyler Grayson's bedroom. Every inch of the room was in perfect order, from the bookshelf lined with novels and notebooks, to the desk that held only the essentials,a laptop, a few pens, and an open black notebook. But this notebook wasn't ordinary. Its pages were filled with detailed sketches of crime scenes, so disturbingly precise that they could easily be mistaken for the work of a seasoned detective.

Tyler stood in front of the mirror, brushing his long, dark hair back to reveal piercing blue eyes. His reflection stared back at him, calm and unreadable. His movements were slow, deliberate, each stroke of the brush adding to the illusion he had perfected.

"I blend in," Tyler's thoughts began, the calmness of his inner voice betraying the chaos hidden beneath. "That's the trick. Appear normal. Unremarkable. It's easy when no one expects anything of you."

He set the brush down, running his fingers through his hair one last time before turning toward his desk. His eyes lingered on the notebook, its pages filled with plans and sketches, plans that detailed the end of Darren Holt. Holt's name, circled in red ink, stood out like a beacon, calling Tyler to action.

"But inside... I'm always calculating. Always planning. I've been following Holt for weeks now. Tonight, he'll pay. I'll make sure of it."

With calculated precision, Tyler packed the notebook into his black backpack, along with a small vial of chloroform and a piece of folded black cloth. The movements were practiced, methodical, leaving nothing to chance.

"It's been a month since my last kill," he thought, the emptiness inside him gnawing at his insides like a hunger that could only be satiated in one way. "A month since I felt anything. But tonight, that changes. Holt will scream... and the emptiness inside me will disappear, at least for a while."

Tyler's hand paused briefly on the door handle, savoring the silence of the room before stepping out into the world, where he would don the mask of normalcy once more. The city was alive with its usual bustle as Tyler walked down the crowded street, his presence barely registering among the mass of people. Cars honked, conversations blurred together, and the distant hum of traffic provided a steady soundtrack to the world outside. It was a world Tyler had learned to blend into with ease. Beside him, Emily walked with her arm looped through his, her bright laughter cutting through the city's noise.

They walked hand-in-hand, the perfect picture of a young couple in love. Her hazel eyes sparkled as she looked at him, her affection clear in every glance. She nudged him playfully, her voice teasing as she spoke. "Come on, you can't honestly say you didn't like the movie. You were totally into it!"

Tyler's lips curled into a faint smirk. "It was fine," he replied, his tone casual. "Entertaining, maybe. But the plot? Completely predictable."

Emily rolled her eyes, tugging him closer as they continued down the street. Tyler's outward appearance was relaxed, even happy, but beneath it all, the darkness stirred. The real him,the part that Emily could never know,was already miles ahead, planning for the night that lay ahead.

"With her, I can forget for a little while," he thought, his gaze sliding to Emily as she smiled at him. "Pretend I'm normal. Pretend I'm just some guy, not the one planning his next kill. Not the one waiting for night to fall."

They paused, Emily turning to face him, her expression softening. "You know, sometimes I think you're too smart for your own good. It's like nothing impresses you."

Tyler's blue eyes studied her for a moment, a brief flash of something unfamiliar stirring inside him. The way she looked at him, with such complete trust, stirred something, though it wasn't enough to stop the plans already in motion.

"Well, you do," Tyler said quietly, his voice steady. "That's enough for me."

Emily blushed at the compliment, leaning in to kiss him lightly on the cheek. Their lips brushed, the moment passing quickly as they continued walking, Emily still blissfully unaware of the storm brewing beneath Tyler's calm surface.The small café they found themselves in was warm and inviting, the rich scent of coffee filling the air. Tyler sat across from Emily, the two of them surrounded by the soft hum of conversation and the steady whir of the espresso machine. Emily stirred her coffee absentmindedly, her hazel eyes flicking to Tyler, who gazed out the window in deep thought.

"You're distracted today," she noted, her voice laced with concern. "Everything okay?"

Tyler blinked, snapping back to the present as he gave her a faint smile. "Yeah, just thinking about my next book. Trying to figure out where the story goes."

Emily smiled softly, admiration clear in her expression. "You're amazing, you know that? I don't know how you manage to write so much and still make time for me."

Tyler chuckled, the sound almost genuine. "I guess I just have my priorities straight."

"She has no idea," he thought as he took a sip of his coffee, the warmth doing nothing to touch the cold emptiness inside him. "No clue what's really going on inside my head. And that's the way it has to be."

No amount of coffee or conversation could fill the growing void within him. But tonight, when the clock struck eight and Darren Holt left his office, that emptiness would be satisfied.The sun hung low in the sky as Tyler and Emily walked back down the street, the evening casting long shadows over the city. Tyler's gaze flicked to his watch. 6:45 PM. His expression didn't change, but his mind was already calculating.

"Two hours. Plenty of time to drop Emily off and get ready. Holt leaves work at eight. He won't see it coming."

Beside him, Emily smiled up at him, still oblivious to the plans taking shape in his mind. "So, what do you want to do tonight?" she asked, her voice light and carefree.

Tyler smiled back, his tone easy. "Whatever you want."

"Whatever she wants," his thoughts echoed as they continued walking. "But first... I have something to take care of."

Tyler's face remained calm, the mask firmly in place. Inside, the clock was already ticking, counting down to the moment when the Inked Reaper would strike again.

THE BURDEN OF THE BADGE

The air inside the small-town police station felt heavy, almost oppressive in its stillness. Sunlight struggled to break through the grime on the windows, casting a dull glow over the room's worn and tired furniture. The flicker of a fluorescent light above buzzed intermittently, as if it too was on its last legs. The room smelled faintly of old coffee and papers that had been handled too many times. In one corner, rusted filing cabinets stood crookedly, barely holding together under the weight of decades of unsolved cases and bureaucratic clutter.

At the far end of the room, William Grayson sat at his cluttered desk, the weight of years etched into his lined face. His once broad shoulders now sagged slightly, evidence of the burdens he carried. His sleeves were rolled up, exposing his forearms as he leaned forward, scrutinizing a stack of crime scene photos. Dark circles ringed his eyes, a testament to too many late nights and not enough sleep. His thinning hair, now speckled with gray, lay matted to his forehead from constantly running his hands through it. Papers and files were scattered around him in chaotic disarray, but he knew where everything was. In front of him, an especially thick folder sat, its edges worn from frequent use. It bore a label in bold black letters: INKED REAPER.

William's tired eyes drifted over the haunting images,photographs of crime scenes that seemed too surreal to be real, each more grotesque than the last. The scenes haunted him, their brutality etched into his mind long after he'd put the photos down. He flipped through them methodically, one by one, his fingers moving with practiced ease, though his hands trembled slightly with fatigue. There was a chill in the air, or perhaps it was the weight of the case itself that made the room seem colder than it actually was.

The door creaked open, the sound startling him from his grim reverie. Kate Miller strode into the station, her expression one of mild frustration, though her eyes softened when they landed on William. Dressed in her usual casual attire, jeans and a faded jacket, Kate was a stark contrast to the dour atmosphere. She had that unshakeable quality about her, someone who'd seen too much but still managed to keep a spark alive. Her presence brought a faint warmth to the otherwise sterile room.

"Still here, huh? Should've known," she remarked, crossing the room with confident strides. She placed her hands on her hips, eyeing the desk and the disorganized chaos that was William's workspace.

William barely glanced up. His mind was too immersed in the details before him, each photograph demanding his attention as if it held some clue he hadn't yet uncovered. "Yeah, still here," he muttered, his voice hoarse from disuse. He flipped another photo, the image showing a young woman, her lifeless eyes staring blankly at the ceiling. Blood pooled beneath her like spilled ink.

Kate sighed and moved closer, her gaze shifting between William and the papers. "You've been at this for, what, twelve hours now? Didn't we talk about leaving at a reasonable time for once?"

She waited for a response but knew better than to expect one. William rubbed his eyes, fatigue settling deep in his bones, though he remained steadfast in his concentration. He was close, or at least, he felt like he was.

Somewhere, buried in these pages, was the key. The answer that would finally break the case wide open. He just had to find it.

"I'm almost done with this," he said, though both he and Kate knew it wasn't true. There was always more. Always another lead to follow, another theory to explore. "Just need a little more time."

Kate pulled out a chair and sat across from him, crossing her arms and giving him a look that managed to be both concerned and exasperated. Her auburn hair, streaked with early signs of gray, fell around her shoulders as she leaned forward. "Will, you know you can't solve this thing by not sleeping, right? You look like hell."

William sighed, leaning back in his chair as he ran a hand through his thinning hair. He knew she was right. He was burning the candle at both ends. But he couldn't stop. Not when they were so close. Not when every piece of evidence could be the one that made the difference. "It's not about that, Kate," he replied, his voice heavy with frustration. "I need to get ahead of him."

Kate raised an eyebrow, watching him carefully. "And you think skipping meals and staying here all night is going to help with that?"

Before he could answer, she stood and reached over to grab his jacket from the back of his chair. She tossed it at him, the fabric landing squarely in his lap. "Come on," she said, her tone leaving no room for argument. "You're not doing anyone any good by working yourself to death. Let's go grab something to eat."

William hesitated, looking back at the stack of photos, then at the pile of reports that lay unopened. His instincts told him to stay, to keep pushing forward, but his body was screaming for a break. Reluctantly, he stood, shrugging on the jacket she'd thrown at him.

"Fine," he muttered, "but I'm not staying out long."

Kate smiled, her eyes softening with relief. "Deal. You can go back to being obsessive after we eat."The sun had dipped low in the sky, casting a burnt orange hue across the sleepy town. The streets were nearly empty, save for the occasional car rolling by or a pedestrian hurrying home before nightfall. The diner stood at the corner of Main Street, its once-bright neon sign now flickering sporadically. The word DINER buzzed faintly, the letters glowing and dimming as if caught between life and death, much like the town itself. The place had a certain charm, though,it was the kind of spot where the locals came every day, more out of habit than hunger.

William and Kate pushed open the door, a small bell jingling overhead. The inside was just as run-down as the outside, but it held a warmth that the police station lacked. The walls were covered in old black-and-white photos of the town's heyday, and the red vinyl booths had been patched more times than anyone could count. The smell of frying grease and brewed coffee filled the air, mingling with the faint scent of something sweet,probably pie. In the corner, an ancient jukebox hummed a tune no one was listening to.

They slid into a booth near the back, where they could have some privacy. A waitress, Marge, probably in her sixties, sauntered over with a knowing look, her gum snapping as she dropped two menus in front of them. William barely looked at his, though Kate flipped hers open, scanning it with a raised eyebrow.

"So, what's the special again?" Kate asked, though the choices were always the same.

Marge barely looked up from her notepad. "Meatloaf," she said flatly.
Kate smirked. "One of those, then."

Marge turned to William, but his mind seemed miles away, eyes still locked on some invisible point in front of him. Kate nudged him under the table with her foot. "Earth to Will. What're you getting?"

He blinked, snapping out of his trance. "Uh, burger. I'll have a burger," he mumbled.

Marge scribbled down the order and walked away, leaving them in the quiet hum of the diner. The distant murmur of conversation and the whir of the coffee machine filled the silence between them.

Kate leaned forward, resting her elbows on the table, her eyes studying William carefully. "You've been working yourself to the bone over this case, Will. You need to take a step back. Maybe if you get some sleep, things will start making sense again."

William sighed, running a hand through his hair again. "Every time I think we're getting closer, something slips through my fingers. I can't shake this feeling that he's always one step ahead of us."

Kate looked at him for a moment before shifting the conversation. "Speaking of things slipping through your fingers... have you talked to Tyler lately?"

That seemed to pull him back to the present. William looked up, his face softening just a little. "Yeah, he's been busy with the new book. And the screenplay deal. Kid's doing great. Just bought a new place too."

Kate smiled, amused. "How's Emily? She still sticking around, or has she figured out how much of a pain in the ass he is yet?"

William chuckled, the sound rare but welcome. "Not yet. She's a good girl. They're good together."

Marge returned with their plates, Kate's meatloaf and William's burger, both looking as greasy and unappealing as expected. They dug in, the food doing little to improve William's mood but at least filling the gnawing emptiness in his stomach.

Kate chewed her meatloaf and grimaced slightly. "God, I love these small-town diners," she said sarcastically. "The food's terrible, but you gotta appreciate the character."

William managed a small smile, taking a bite of his burger. It was greasy, tasteless, but he didn't care. It was fuel, nothing more.

Kate leaned forward, resting her chin on her hand. She studied William's tired face, the way the lines of worry seemed etched into his skin like deep scars that would never fade. "Anyway, back to Tyler. You think he's ever going to slow down? Maybe give you some grandkids one of these days?"

William chuckled again, this time with a bit more life in it. "Honestly, I wouldn't be surprised. He's got his head on straight. I think they're serious."

Kate's eyes softened at the thought. "That's nice. It's gotta feel good seeing him succeed like that, huh? Especially after everything." There was no need to explain what everything meant. The years of hardship, raising Tyler alone after his wife had passed, juggling fatherhood and a demanding career that never seemed to give him any room to breathe.

William nodded slowly, his eyes distant but warm. "Yeah. He's worked for it. He deserves every bit of success. Sometimes I don't know how he turned out so well, all things considered." His voice was filled with quiet pride, but there was also a lingering sadness, one that only someone who had known him as long as Kate had would be able to detect. The years of sacrifice had been worth it, but they had also taken their toll. Tyler was a grown man now, thriving, but William still carried the weight of all those lost years.

Kate gave him a small, knowing smile. "You did good, Will. You gave him the best parts of yourself." She took another bite of her meatloaf, chewing slowly as the silence settled between them once again, though this time it was comfortable, a shared moment of quiet reflection.

William looked down at his plate, pushing a fry around with his finger. "I just wish…" He trailed off, unsure how to finish the sentence. He wasn't even sure what he was trying to say. There were always regrets, even when things worked out. Moments he wished he could get back. Time he could've spent differently. But life didn't give you do-overs, and he knew that better than anyone.

Kate didn't push him to finish the thought. Instead, she shifted the conversation again, knowing when to let things lie. "Well, at least one of us is doing something right," she joked, her smile returning. She grabbed her glass of water and took a sip, letting the cool liquid wash away the heaviness of their conversation.

William leaned back in his booth, gazing out the window at the dimming sky. The orange glow had faded to purple now, and the first stars were beginning to appear, twinkling faintly against the encroaching darkness. The town was quiet, as it always was at this time of night. It was the kind of quiet that could either bring comfort or drive a person mad, depending on what was weighing on their mind.

"You ever think about what comes next?" Kate asked suddenly, her voice soft but pointed.

William turned his gaze back to her, his brow furrowing slightly. "What do you mean?" She shrugged, leaning back in her seat. "You know, after all of this. After the case is finally over. What's next for you? I mean, you've been chasing this guy for how many years now? What happens when you catch him?"

William frowned, considering her words. He hadn't really thought about it. The case had consumed him for so long that it had become a part of him. The idea of after wasn't something he could easily grasp. "I don't know," he admitted, his voice low. "I guess I haven't really thought that far ahead."

Kate's gaze softened as she watched him, her concern deepening. "Will, you can't let this be the only thing in your life. You've got to start thinking about the future. What happens when the Inked Reaper is finally behind bars? Or worse, what happens if you don't catch him?"

The question hung in the air like a dark cloud. William didn't want to think about that possibility. He didn't want to consider a world where the killer got away, where the victims never got justice. It was a thought too unbearable to entertain.

"I'll catch him," William said, his voice filled with quiet determination. "I have to." Kate watched him for a long moment, her expression unreadable. "And then what?"

William didn't answer. He couldn't. He didn't know what came after, and maybe that was the problem. Maybe he'd become so wrapped up in the chase that he didn't know how to live without it.

Marge returned to their table, refilling their water glasses and dropping the check without a word. William absentmindedly pulled out his wallet and dropped a couple of bills onto the table, enough to cover the meal and then some. He pushed his plate aside, no longer hungry, though he hadn't eaten much to begin with.

Kate slid out of the booth, standing up and stretching her arms over her head. "Come on," she said, her voice lighter now, trying to shift the mood. "Let's get out of here. You're looking like you're about ready to fall asleep in your fries."

William stood as well, though his movements were slower, heavier. The weight of the case, and of Kate's words, hung on him like a shroud. But he managed a small smile as he followed her to the door, the bell jingling softly as they stepped out into the cool night air. The town had settled into its usual nighttime rhythm. Streetlights flickered to life, casting soft pools of light onto the pavement. The roads were mostly empty, the occasional car rumbling by, its headlights cutting through the darkness like blades. In the distance, a dog barked, the sound echoing down the empty streets.

William shoved his hands into the pockets of his jacket, the chill of the evening creeping into his bones. Beside him, Kate walked in easy silence, her breath forming small clouds in the crisp air. They had known each other long enough that words weren't always necessary. Sometimes, just being there was enough.

As they walked, William's thoughts drifted back to the case, as they always did. The faces of the victims flashed before his eyes, each one a haunting reminder of why he couldn't stop, why he couldn't let it go. The Inked Reaper had left a trail of bodies in his wake, each one marked with the same gruesome signature: intricate, disturbing tattoos carved into their flesh post-mortem. It was a pattern William had come to know too well, one that had kept him up at night for far too many years.

But Kate's words lingered, gnawing at him in a way he couldn't shake. What did come next? What would happen when, if, the case was finally over? Could he go back to some semblance of normal life, or had he already given too much of himself to this pursuit?

They stopped at the corner of the street, the diner now a distant glow behind them. Kate turned to face him, her expression soft but serious. "You'll catch him, Will. I know you will. But don't forget there's more to life than this. Don't let him take everything from you."

William met her gaze, his eyes reflecting the same determination they always had, but there was something else now. A glimmer of doubt, or maybe fear. "I won't," he said quietly, though whether he was convincing her or himself, he wasn't sure.

Kate gave him a small, reassuring smile, and for a moment, the weight on his shoulders felt just a little lighter. They stood there for a beat longer before William finally broke the silence. "Thanks for the dinner, Kate."

She shrugged. "Anytime. And next time, try to actually eat something."

William chuckled softly, the sound fading into the quiet of the night. As they turned to walk their separate ways, the cold air nipping at their heels, William couldn't help but think about her words. What happens next?

ABYSSAL PASSENGER

The night was still, the silence broken only by the faint chirping of crickets in the distance. Tyler crouched low in the shadows, a predator waiting for his moment. His eyes never left the figure of James Holt as the man locked his apartment door, his casual posture betraying the ease of someone unaware they were being watched.

"I've been watching you for weeks, Holt. Every move. Every lie. And now, your time's up."

Holt started down the sidewalk, his steps relaxed, while Tyler remained behind, hidden by the dim glow of the streetlights. A quiet force, he moved like a shadow, always just out of sight, following at a calculated distance. His hands flexed, ready for the confrontation he had been planning for so long.

Holt walked without urgency, his mind likely occupied with trivial matters. But Tyler knew better. He knew Holt's routine, the lies he told to others, and to himself. As Holt reached his car, Tyler's heart rate remained steady. He watched Holt throw his bag into the passenger seat and climb behind the wheel, none the wiser.

The engine roared to life, headlights cutting through the darkness for a brief moment before the car rolled down the street. Tyler allowed himself a quiet exhale, his hands tightening around his keys as he approached his own car parked just down the block. There was no need to rush. He knew exactly where Holt was going. He'd been mapping out every detail for weeks.

"Work. Home. The lake. Always the same routine. But tonight, it's different."

Tyler's grip tightened on the steering wheel as he tailed Holt's car through the empty streets. The city was a maze of dimly lit roads and flickering street lights, all of it leading to a single destination. Tyler kept his distance as Holt's car weaved through the nearly deserted streets of the city, the glow of his taillights the only beacon in the darkness. The buildings became sparser as they moved closer to the industrial district on the edge of town. Here, the air smelled of rust and old machinery, and the few remaining street lights flickered like they were on their last breath.

As Holt turned into a rundown lot, Tyler slowed his car to a crawl. He watched Holt park near a decaying brick building, his workplace.

The building was a relic of a different time, crumbling and forgotten, much like the man inside it. Rusted machinery sat idle in the dark corners of the lot, abandoned vehicles slumped against cracked pavement, and broken windows stared back like hollow eyes.

Tyler parked a block away, slipping out of his car with the ease of someone who had done this before. The night wrapped around him like a cloak as he moved in silence, each step calculated. His boots barely made a sound on the gravel as he approached the building. He kept to the shadows, his body pressed close to the cold brick walls, hidden from view. From here, he could see Holt through a grimy window, gathering tools for the night shift.

"One last shift. One last night. And you'll never see another sunrise."
Tyler waited, his breath steady, his heart beating with a calm intensity. In his jacket pocket, the bottle of chloroform felt heavy against his ribs, a constant reminder of what was to come. He watched Holt move inside the building, methodical but oblivious to the fate closing in on him.

Tyler moved to a better vantage point, crouching low as he studied Holt's movements.

The man was following his usual routine, tools, equipment, a quick check of the workspace. It was predictable. Holt's life had become a series of patterns, patterns that Tyler had come to know intimately. But tonight, everything was different. Tonight, the careful order of Holt's world would shatter.

Minutes passed, the quiet night only interrupted by the occasional creak of old machinery in the building. Tyler's patience was unshakable. He had all night, and Holt had nowhere to run. The lake was waiting.

When Holt finally left the building and locked up for the night, Tyler was ready. He watched as Holt crossed the lot toward his car, a fleeting sense of finality in his step, though the man himself seemed unaware of it. Holt paused before getting in his car, glancing around, but the gesture was routine, not suspicion.

The engine growled to life, headlights flashing once again before the car rolled toward the lakefront. Tyler watched, then slipped into his own vehicle, his fingers flexing around the steering wheel, knuckles white with anticipation. His mind was quiet, focused, like a predator stalking its prey.

"You think you're safe in your routine, Holt. But you're no different from the others. You hide behind your job, behind your charm. But the truth always bleeds out."

The drive to the lake was short, the road familiar. Trees loomed on either side like dark sentinels, their branches clawing at the sky. The moon was high now, casting an eerie glow on the world below. As Tyler drove, he could see Holt's car in the distance, nothing more than a pair of red taillights fading into the woods.

By the time Tyler reached the lake, Holt had already parked his car near the dock. Tyler cut his engine a few hundred yards back, not wanting to risk alerting Holt to his presence. He stepped out of the car, the cool night air filling his lungs, and moved with the same silent precision as before.

Tyler stood at the edge of the trees, hidden by the shadows, and watched as Holt walked toward the dock. The old wooden planks creaked beneath Holt's footsteps, the sound carrying across the still water. The lake stretched out before them, dark and endless, like a mirror to the sky above. It was isolated, quiet, a place where secrets could disappear forever.

Holt was lost in his thoughts, unaware of the figure lurking just beyond the reach of the moonlight. Tyler moved closer, his footsteps soundless on the damp grass as he followed Holt to the end of the dock. The lake was calm, but there was an underlying tension in the air, something primal, waiting to erupt.

Holt stood at the edge of the dock, his back to Tyler, staring out at the water. Tyler's heart slowed, his breath steady and deliberate. His footsteps were soft but purposeful as he stepped out from the shadows.

"James Holt."

The name cut through the silence like a knife. Holt froze, his shoulders tensing before he turned sharply to face Tyler. His eyes widened in shock, his body stiffening in an instinctual response to danger. He was unarmed, vulnerable.

"What the hell? Who are you?" Holt's voice cracked, the words tinged with panic.

Tyler stepped forward, his face emerging from the darkness, cold and unyielding. "Someone who knows what you've done. And someone who's here to make you pay."

For a moment, they stood at opposite ends of the dock, the distance between them narrowing with each passing second. Holt's gaze darted around, searching for an escape, a weapon,anything to defend himself. His hand settled on a nearby metal pipe, the only thing between him and the man who had come to end his life.

With a desperate yell, Holt swung the pipe, his movements wild and erratic. Tyler dodged easily, his body moving with fluid precision, sidestepping the attack. His eyes never left Holt, calculating every move.

Holt's desperation grew. He swung again, but this time Tyler was ready. He lunged forward, grabbing Holt's wrist and twisting it sharply. The pipe clattered to the wooden planks, and Holt cried out in pain, stumbling backward. But he wasn't giving up. Holt pushed Tyler away, his breath coming in ragged gasps. The fight had only just begun.

Tyler advanced, his expression unchanged, his body a coiled spring of controlled violence. "It's too late for you to back out now."

Holt threw a punch, wild and uncoordinated, but Tyler ducked under it, countering with a quick jab to Holt's ribs. The blow landed hard, and Holt doubled over, gasping for air. He tried to grab Tyler, his fingers clawing at the man's shirt, but Tyler twisted out of his grip and delivered a crushing uppercut that sent Holt reeling.

The night was alive with the sound of their struggle, the thud of fists against flesh, the sharp grunts of pain, the creak of the old dock beneath their feet. Holt's punches were frantic, driven by fear, but Tyler's movements were precise, each strike landing with cold, methodical intent.

"You can't do this!" Holt's voice was frantic, desperate. "I won't let you!"

But Tyler wasn't listening. His mind was a razor's edge, focused on the task at hand. He ducked another punch, grabbed Holt's arm, and twisted it behind his back, forcing him down to his knees. Holt groaned in pain, but still, he fought back, throwing a wild elbow that caught Tyler on the jaw. The hit was glancing, more out of desperation than skill, but it gave Holt enough room to scramble to his feet.

Holt stumbled back, his breath coming in ragged gasps, eyes wide with panic. His gaze darted around the dock, desperate, searching for anything to fend off Tyler's relentless approach. His fingers closed around a nearby wooden plank, thick and splintered at the edges, as he raised it with trembling hands. His knuckles whitened as he gripped it tightly, holding it like a makeshift weapon.

"You stay the hell away from me!" Holt's voice cracked with fear, but Tyler didn't flinch. He watched with cold detachment as Holt swung the plank, his movements wild, lacking precision or control.

The first swing missed, slicing through the air just inches from Tyler's face. Holt screamed, his voice high-pitched and hysterical, as he swung again. This time, the plank connected with Tyler's shoulder, the impact resonating with a dull thud.

Tyler staggered but didn't fall. His expression didn't change, his eyes locked on Holt like a predator toying with wounded prey. He wiped his mouth with the back of his hand, blood trickling from the corner of his lips where his teeth had cut into the flesh.

"You're only making it worse for yourself," Tyler growled, his voice low, devoid of emotion.

Holt swung the plank again, but his aim was off. The heavy piece of wood clattered against the dock as Tyler dodged to the side, then lunged forward with terrifying speed. In an instant, he was upon Holt, grabbing the plank mid-swing and twisting it out of his hands with brutal force. The wood splintered in his grasp as Holt's grip gave way, and Tyler hurled it across the dock where it landed with a loud crash.

Holt barely had time to react before Tyler drove his knee into his gut, folding him in half with the force of the blow. Holt's breath exploded from his lungs in a pained grunt, his body crumpling as Tyler's fist came down hard against the side of his head. The impact sent Holt sprawling to the ground, his cheek slamming into the rough wooden planks. Blood flowed out of his lip, painting the dock in a slick crimson smear.

But Holt wasn't done. Even as his vision blurred, he scrambled on all fours, crawling desperately toward the edge of the dock. His body was trembling, the fear so thick he could barely keep his limbs from shaking. He reached for anything, some means of escape, some shred of hope. His fingers grazed the cold, wet wood of the dock's edge as he tried to pull himself up, but Tyler was on him again, this time grabbing him by the collar and yanking him backward with a ferocity that sent him crashing to the floor.

"You can't run, Holt. You never could." Tyler's voice was a whisper now, filled with a dark, chilling calmness.

Holt whimpered, rolling onto his back, hands raised in a futile attempt to ward off the inevitable. He kicked out, his legs thrashing weakly as Tyler's shadow loomed over him. His voice was hoarse, desperate, as he gasped, "Please… please don't…"

Tyler didn't answer. His eyes flicked to the anchor lying nearby, a heavy, rusted thing with sharp, jagged edges. The cold iron gleamed in the moonlight, its weight promising an end to the struggle. Without a word, Tyler bent down and gripped the anchor's chain, dragging it toward Holt with slow, deliberate steps.

Holt's eyes widened in terror as he saw the weapon, his breaths coming in shallow, panicked bursts. He tried to crawl away, but his body was failing him now, the adrenaline draining from his system, leaving him weak and defenseless.

"No… no, please… I'll do anything, just,"

Tyler swung the anchor in a wide arc, the heavy metal whistling through the air before it connected with Holt's side with a sickening crunch. The impact sent shockwaves through Holt's body, his ribs shattering under the force of the blow. A strangled scream tore from his throat as he writhed in agony, his hands clutching at his side where the skin was already bruising, blood pooling beneath the surface.

Tyler didn't stop. He brought the anchor down again, this time smashing into Holt's thigh with a brutal thud. The bone snapped like brittle wood, the jagged edges jutting out beneath the torn fabric of Holt's pants. The scream that followed was inhuman, raw and guttural, echoing out across the still lake.

"Shut up," Tyler muttered, his voice dripping with contempt as he lifted the anchor again. "Just shut up."

The next blow came down on Holt's chest, caving it in with a hideous cracking sound as ribs splintered and organs ruptured under the force. Blood sprayed from Holt's mouth in thick, choking spurts, his lungs collapsing with every breath, drowning him from the inside.

Holt's hands flailed weakly, his fingers twitching as he tried to defend himself, but it was useless. Tyler swung the anchor like a hammer, each strike more savage than the last. His face was set in a grim, unrelenting mask of rage as he pounded Holt's body into the dock, the wooden planks beneath them slick with blood and chunks of flesh.

The anchor came down on Holt's head next. The skull didn't stand a chance, there was a sharp, sickening crack as the bone shattered, fragments of skull flying in all directions. Holt's face, already swollen and bruised, collapsed in on itself under the force of the blow, his features disappearing into a mess of blood, bone, and brain matter.

Tyler didn't stop. He swung the anchor again, driving it into Holt's skull with unrelenting brutality. The sound was nauseating, a wet, crunching noise as the metal sank deeper into the ruined mess that had once been Holt's head. Blood sprayed across Tyler's face and clothes, coating him in a slick, sticky film.

By the time he finally stopped, there was nothing left of Holt's head but a pulpy, unrecognizable mass of gore. The dock was soaked in blood, the planks stained dark red, and the air was thick with the metallic tang of death. Holt's body lay twisted and broken, limbs askew, his chest a caved-in ruin, his head little more than a puddle of blood and bone fragments.

Tyler stood over the corpse, his chest rising and falling with slow, deliberate breaths. His hands were slick with blood, the anchor heavy in his grip, but his expression was calm, almost serene. He let the anchor drop to the dock with a dull clang, the sound echoing out across the silent lake.

He knelt beside Holt's mutilated body, pulling out his Polaroid camera. He framed the shot carefully, ensuring the gruesome aftermath was captured in all its horrific detail before snapping the picture. The flash illuminated the scene for a brief moment, casting long, eerie shadows across the dock.

As the photo developed, Tyler stood, wiping the blood from his hands with a rag. He wrote something on the back of the photo, the pen gliding across the paper with precise, deliberate strokes. The words were simple, a final testament to the justice Holt had been denied for so long.

Tyler stood over Holt's lifeless, broken body, his eyes fixed on the gore-streaked remains of the man who had begged for his life just minutes earlier. The dock was slick with blood, the moon casting a cold, silver light over the scene. In the air, the thick scent of iron mingled with the dampness of the lake, clinging to Tyler's clothes and skin.

His breath was slow, deliberate, as though savoring the moment. The dock creaked beneath his boots as he crouched down, his fingers brushing against Holt's blood-soaked shirt. For a moment, Tyler paused, staring down at the mangled mess that was once Holt's head. What had once been a face was now a hollowed-out ruin, with shards of bone and ragged bits of flesh clinging to the pulpy remains. Blood still trickled from the collapsed skull, pooling beneath the body and seeping into the worn wood of the dock.

Tyler stood and moved toward the shoreline, his boots squelching through the mud and reeds at the water's edge. He scanned the ground, his gaze settling on the large, jagged rocks scattered along the shore. Without hesitation, he bent down and began gathering them, his hands now wet with more than just blood as he picked up stone after stone, feeling the weight of each one. The rocks were heavy, sharp at the edges, some flecked with dirt and algae, others smooth from the water's wear.

One by one, Tyler piled them into the boat moored nearby, the quiet lapping of the water against the hull the only sound in the night. The boat rocked slightly under the increasing weight of the stones, but Tyler worked without pause. His mind was focused, his movements methodical. Each rock was carefully selected for its heft, for its ability to ensure Holt's body would sink deep into the lake's black depths, where no one would ever find him.

With the boat prepared, Tyler turned back to the dock. Holt's body lay sprawled, limbs twisted at unnatural angles, his clothes torn and soaked through with blood. Tyler grabbed Holt's ankles, the flesh still warm beneath his grip, and began dragging the corpse toward the boat. The sound of Holt's body scraping against the wood was wet, nauseating, a mix of squelching blood and the dull thud of flesh against the planks.

As Tyler pulled Holt toward the boat, the broken bones in Holt's body shifted beneath the skin, creating sickening pops and cracks. The limp body offered no resistance as Tyler lifted it and tossed it into the boat with a heavy thud. Holt's head flopped awkwardly to one side, what was left of his skull sagging as brain matter oozed from the shattered cranium.

Tyler wiped his hands on his shirt, smearing blood across the fabric, and retrieved the plastic sheeting he had stashed beneath the boat's seat. With practiced efficiency, he laid the sheets out on the boat's floor, ensuring the plastic would catch every drop of blood, every stray bit of flesh. This was not his first time.

Tyler reached into a metal toolbox at the front of the boat, pulling out a set of surgical tools,sharp, glinting instruments that were disturbingly clean. A scalpel, a bone saw, a pair of heavy-duty shears. These were the tools of dissection, instruments designed for precision, but Tyler had no intention of being gentle.

He rolled up his sleeves and knelt over Holt's body, grabbing the dead man's arm by the wrist. The skin was still pliable, though rapidly cooling, and Tyler felt the weight of rigor mortis slowly creeping in. Time was of the essence.

He started with the scalpel. The blade was small but wickedly sharp, and it sliced through the flesh of Holt's wrist with ease. Blood oozed from the incision, sluggish and thick, the deep red liquid pooling in the plastic sheeting beneath the body. Tyler's hand was steady as he worked the blade deeper, cutting through muscle and tendons with a surgeon's precision, though there was no care in his actions, only cold efficiency.

As the scalpel tore through Holt's skin, the muscle fibers separated in long, sinewy strands, peeling away from the bone like shredded meat. The deeper Tyler cut, the more grotesque the sight became. Blood and tissue oozed from the wound, a mix of dark red and sickly yellow fat glistening under the moonlight. Tyler's face remained expressionless as he continued to work, his movements mechanical, almost detached.

Once the muscle had been sufficiently severed, Tyler reached for the bone saw. It was a small, hand-operated tool, but its serrated edge was perfect for the job. He positioned the saw against the exposed bone of Holt's wrist, where the skin had been peeled back like the flesh of a fruit. Tyler began to saw back and forth, the sound of metal grinding against bone a harsh, grating noise that echoed out across the silent lake.

The bone was thick, but Tyler was patient. The saw bit into it with each stroke, sending small fragments of bone and dust flying into the air. Holt's hand twitched involuntarily as the saw worked through the marrow, a final, reflexive gesture from the dead man. Tyler ignored it, continuing his gruesome task.

Finally, the bone gave way with a loud crack, and Holt's hand came free, dangling loosely in Tyler's grasp. He tossed the severed limb into one of the plastic-wrapped trash bags, where it landed with a wet squelch. Blood dripped from the stump of Holt's arm, but Tyler paid no mind. He still had work to do.

Next came the legs. Tyler rolled Holt onto his back, the body flopping limply as the dead weight shifted. The anchor had done its job, Holt's ribs were shattered, his chest caved in, making it easier for Tyler to maneuver the corpse. He gripped Holt's thigh, feeling the sharp protrusion of the broken bone beneath the skin.

With the scalpel, he sliced through the flesh of Holt's thigh, the thick muscles parting with a sickening tear. Blood gushed from the wound, pouring out in thick, viscous streams. Tyler worked quickly, cutting deep into the muscle and severing the tendons that held the leg together. The stench of blood and death was overwhelming now, a nauseating mix of iron and decay that hung heavy in the air.

Once the flesh was sufficiently cut, Tyler grabbed the bone saw again and went to work on the femur. The bone was dense, but Tyler's arm muscles bulged as he applied pressure, the saw slicing through the marrow with agonizing slowness. Each back-and-forth motion sent waves of vibration through the boat, the metal teeth grinding against the bone with a sickening screech.

The bone gave way with a final crack, and the leg came loose in Tyler's hands. He tossed it aside with the same lack of ceremony, the severed limb landing in the pile of plastic bags that were now filling with pieces of Holt's dismembered body. Blood soaked into the plastic, pooling beneath the discarded limbs.

Tyler repeated the process on the other leg, his motions robotic, his mind detached from the grotesque reality of what he was doing. Each cut, each severed limb was another step closer to the end. The dismemberment was brutal, efficient, and horrifyingly thorough.

By the time he finished, Holt's body was nothing more than a collection of dismembered parts, each limb neatly wrapped in plastic, ready for disposal. Blood soaked the floor of the boat, pooling in thick, sticky puddles, but Tyler paid it no mind. He wiped his hands on the plastic, smearing the blood away before grabbing the trash bags filled with Holt's remains.
With a final glance toward the shore, Tyler stepped into the boat and pushed off. The quiet slosh of the lake water against the hull was the only sound as the boat drifted out into the inky blackness of the lake, the dock fading into the distance behind him.

As Tyler reached the center of the lake, he stood, looking down at the bags of dismembered flesh. The rocks he had gathered from the shore sat next to them, their jagged edges gleaming faintly in the moonlight. One by one, Tyler tied the rocks to the bags, ensuring the weight would be enough to drag them to the bottom of the lake, where they would never be found.

He lifted the first bag, feeling the weight of Holt's remains inside, and tossed it overboard. The splash was loud in the stillness of the night, the water swallowing the bag whole as it sank beneath the surface, disappearing into the depths. Tyler watched it go, the black water rippling before returning to its calm, mirror-like stillness.

One by one, the bags followed, each splash a final punctuation to the gruesome task. And when the last bag disappeared beneath the water, Tyler stood in silence, staring out at the vast, empty expanse of the lake.

Nobody would find him.

Nobody would know.

BLOOD ON THE WATER

The morning was still and cold, the horizon just beginning to fracture with the pale light of dawn. A layer of fog clung to the lake, as if nature itself was trying to obscure the violence that had taken place here. The police cruiser crept down the narrow gravel road, its tires crunching softly over the rocks. The worn wooden dock jutted out over the water, its surface weathered and splintered from years of exposure to the elements.

William stared out the windshield as the dock came into view, his mind already racing. He barely noticed the cold. The scene, though eerily quiet, hummed with the weight of the crime that had occurred. He could feel it, like the place was tainted now, a scar that wouldn't fade.

Beside him, Kate shifted in her seat, her gaze fixed on the yellow tape fluttering lightly in the wind. It was too calm for the kind of brutality they were about to witness. Neither of them spoke as they got out of the car, their breath visible in the chilly morning air.

William's boots thudded softly against the wooden planks as they made their way toward the crime scene. His steps were deliberate, each one a reminder of the countless times they'd walked into situations like this. His jaw clenched, his body tight with frustration. Another scene, another body by the water. Always by the water.

"Another one," William muttered under his breath, breaking the silence between them. His voice was low, rough. "Another goddamn mess by the water."

He crouched down, his knees creaking slightly as he lowered himself near the large pool of blood. The dark, dried stain had seeped deep into the grain of the old wood, a permanent reminder of the violence that had taken place. His stomach churned as he studied the splatters, the patterns. His mind raced through the possibilities, trying to piece together the final moments of the victim's life.

Kate remained standing, her posture rigid but composed. Her sharp eyes swept the area, taking in every detail. The scene was chaotic, signs of struggle everywhere. She could see the twisted and bent remains of a metal pipe near the dock's edge, a wooden plank splintered into jagged pieces. This wasn't just a murder; it was a frenzy. A message.

"Except this time, the mess is worse," Kate said quietly. Her voice was steady, but there was an edge to it, a weariness that came from seeing too much. "Whoever did this wanted to send a message."

William didn't need to hear it to know it was true. The whole scene screamed it. He forced himself to his feet, eyes moving to the twisted metal anchor lying near the body. His jaw tightened further as he approached it, his hands reflexively curling into fists. This wasn't just about killing; this was about power. Control. The killer had wanted to make a statement, one that was impossible to ignore.

"This was a slaughter," he said, his voice hard.

Kate moved beside him, crouching near the weapons. She didn't touch anything, her fingers hovering just above the bloodied anchor, the crusted metal streaked with dark red. Her face remained impassive, but William knew her well enough to catch the slight flicker of disgust in her eyes. It was hard to remain unaffected when faced with something like this, but Kate was always better at hiding it than he was.

"Anchor. Metal pipe. Wood plank," Kate listed, her tone clinical, detached. "He used whatever was around to beat this guy to death."

William's body tensed, the muscles in his shoulders knotting as he imagined the sheer violence it would take to do this. He didn't need to picture it, the evidence was right there in front of him. Whoever had done this had taken their time. Made it personal.

"They didn't just kill him," William said, his voice low and full of barely restrained anger. "They tore him apart."

He turned away from the scene, trying to control the rage boiling beneath the surface. Kate continued her silent analysis, moving toward the edge of the dock. The wind shifted slightly, carrying with it the faint metallic tang of blood and the cold, earthy scent of the lake.

She crouched again, this time near the water's edge. The dock creaked softly under her weight as she peered into the still water. A few inches below the surface, something dark swayed gently with the current, a blood-soaked piece of fabric, barely visible through the mist curling over the lake.

"Looks like our guy might've fought back," Kate said, motioning to one of the officers standing nearby. "He put up a struggle."

The officer hurried over, carefully retrieving the cloth with an evidence bag. William barely registered the exchange. His eyes were locked on the Polaroid lying in a pool of dried blood near the body. Something about it drew him in, a sick feeling settling in his stomach. He stepped closer, crouching down again to pick it up.

The image was still developing, the colors slowly bleeding into focus. At first, it was a blur,a mass of indistinct shapes. But as the image sharpened, William's breath caught in his throat. The victim's face was unrecognizable, a grotesque mess of shattered bone and caved-in flesh. The brutality of it was staggering.

Flipping the Polaroid over, William found a poem scrawled on the back in neat handwriting. His heart pounded as he read the words aloud, his voice barely above a whisper:

"For every soul that walks free,
The lake will claim its due.
Pain repaid with blood and bone,
The righteous carve their truth.

I'll be the hand that deals the blow,
Where justice falls apart.
You thought you'd walk away, unscathed,
But your end began at the start."

William's hands trembled slightly as he read, the words burrowing into his mind like a curse. He could feel the killer's presence in them, mocking him, taunting him. His anger flared, hotter now, more intense. He threw the Polaroid down onto the dock, his breathing ragged.

"It's him," Kate said, stepping up beside him. "The same guy. Same calling card."

William's chest heaved as he struggled to contain his fury. He felt like a failure. They were always one step behind, always arriving too late. And this killer,this bastard,was playing with them, leaving them scraps to pick over while he moved on to his next victim.

"I'm sick of this," William growled, his voice shaking. "We're always one step behind. He's mocking us."

Kate didn't respond immediately, watching William pace furiously along the dock. She knew him well enough to recognize the signs. He was on the edge, his control slipping. She had to tread carefully, but she couldn't let him spiral out of control.

"William, we're doing everything we can," she started, but William cut her off, his voice rising.

"No! Everything we can isn't good enough! He's out there, laughing at us while we find pieces of what's left behind."

His voice echoed across the lake, the stillness of the morning amplifying the raw emotion behind it. Kate stayed calm, her own frustration mounting but hidden beneath a layer of professionalism. She stepped closer, her voice steady but firm.

"I get it," she said. "This isn't easy. But losing it here won't help anything. We need to stay focused."

William stopped pacing, his fists clenched, his jaw tight. He turned away from her, storming toward the end of the dock, his movements stiff with anger. Kate watched him go, her own patience wearing thin. She knew this case was tearing him apart, but she couldn't let him fall apart now. Not when they were so close.

"William. You need to calm down."

William stopped, his back to her, his voice low but filled with fury. "Calm down? You think I can calm down with this happening over and over again?"

He turned to face her, his eyes burning with anger. "Another body, Kate. Another sick bastard who thought he could get away with it. And we're just... standing here."

Kate took a deep breath, forcing herself to stay calm. "I know it's frustrating. But if we let it get to us like this, we'll make mistakes. We can't afford that. Not now."
William stared at her, his breathing heavy, his chest heaving. Finally, he turned away again, his eyes fixed on the distant horizon, the water lapping quietly at the shore.

"It's not just frustration," he said quietly. "It's failure. We're failing."

Kate stepped up beside him, her voice soft but resolute. "We're not failing. We're close. We just need to keep our heads on straight."

William didn't respond, his eyes locked on the water. The weight of the case, the constant dead ends, and the killer's taunting messages were wearing him down. He stood there, fists still clenched, his body trembling with pent-up rage.

Kate placed a hand on his shoulder, her touch gentle. "Let's go. There's nothing more we can do here right now."

William pulled away from her touch, his shoulders tense. "You go ahead," he muttered. "I'll catch up."

Kate hesitated, watching him for a moment before nodding. She understood that he needed space, needed time to process everything. With a sigh, she turned and walked back toward the squad car, her mind racing with thoughts of the case and the toll it was taking on William.

William remained at the end of the dock, his eyes trained on the water, which sparkled faintly under the rising sun. The mist was beginning to lift, but the chill in the air remained, creeping into his bones like the memories of past cases that haunted him. Each one felt like a weight pressing down, each victim a reminder of the lives they hadn't been able to save.

He clenched his jaw, frustration boiling just beneath the surface. His heart raced as he replayed the images in his mind,the broken body, the blood, the sickening poem that felt like a personal affront. It was as if the killer was calling him out, daring him to catch up, to understand the twisted logic behind the violence.

He stepped closer to the edge of the dock, the wood creaking under his weight. The water was deceptively calm, but he knew better. There was darkness beneath the surface, just as there was in the heart of the person who had committed this crime.

As he stood there, the wind picked up, rustling the leaves of nearby trees and sending a shiver down his spine. He thought of the victim,the man whose life had ended here, whose last moments had been filled with terror and pain. William felt a familiar tightness in his throat. This wasn't just a case; it was a human tragedy, a life extinguished too soon.

His thoughts drifted back to the words on the Polaroid, the chilling poem that had sent a jolt of anger through him. "The lake will claim its due." What did that even mean? Was this killer using the water as a metaphor for justice? Or was it simply a twisted fantasy?

THE MASK AND THE MAN

Tyler lay awake, staring at the ceiling as soft morning light filtered through the blinds. His arm rested protectively around Emily, who was still asleep beside him. The quiet rhythm of her breathing filled the room, a reminder of the fragile peace between them. The aftermath of the previous night was scattered across the room: clothes thrown haphazardly on the floor, empty wine glasses, and the faint, lingering scent of alcohol.

He hadn't slept well, not that it showed. Tyler had perfected the art of appearing composed, even when his mind was in turmoil.

"I play this part so well," he thought, his eyes drifting to the ceiling. "The loving boyfriend, the aspiring author. But it's all an act. Every smile, every gentle touch,it's a mask." His gaze shifted down to Emily, her face soft with sleep, a peaceful smile on her lips. "She has no idea who I really am. What I'm capable of."

Emily stirred, stretching beside him. Her eyes fluttered open, hazy with sleep, as she looked up at him with that same affectionate smile she always wore in the mornings.

"Morning," she murmured, her voice a soft whisper. "Did we really stay out that late?" Tyler turned to face her, forcing a smile as if everything was normal. "Yeah. You were the life of the party."

She chuckled softly, pushing herself up on one elbow. "Well, someone had to be. And look at you,up early, cooking breakfast?" He laughed lightly, slipping out of bed and stretching his arms. "Just trying to be a functional adult."

"Mm, I could get used to this." Emily sat up, rubbing her eyes. "What's on the agenda today?"

Tyler moved to the kitchen, already mentally going through the motions of making breakfast. His hands were steady, cracking eggs into the pan as he spoke. "I've got that interview with the local journalist this afternoon. Some piece about my book."

"Oh, that's right." Emily smiled, watching him from the counter. "Exciting! What's the journalist like?"

Tyler's expression darkened for a split second before he quickly masked it with another smile. "Just a guy from the local newspaper. Nothing too serious."

"A local journalist," he thought. "Someone who could get too curious. I'll have to keep my guard up. Can't let anyone dig too deep."

Emily didn't seem to notice the shift in his tone. She was already moving on to another topic. "And don't forget,dinner with Kate and William tonight."

Tyler flipped the eggs in the pan, his attention shifting back to her. "Right. And after that, we're hitting the club?"

"Yeah," she said, grinning. "Another night with the usual crowd. It'll be fun,some good drinks, dancing, catching up with friends." He laughed again, more genuine this time. "Two nights in a row? What kind of bad influence are you?"

Emily giggled. "Oh, you love it. Don't pretend you don't."

"I do love it," he thought, staring at her across the counter. "The normalcy. The laughter. The facade I wear so well." His eyes darkened again, his thoughts drifting. "But it's exhausting, hiding the other part of me. The part she can never see."

As they sat down to breakfast, Emily continued chatting, oblivious to the storm brewing inside him. Tyler ate mechanically, nodding at the appropriate moments but lost in thought.

He recalled something he overheard last night, a brief mention of a name that caught his attention: Perry Maxwell. A familiar chill settled in his bones.

"Perry Maxwell," Tyler mused silently, stabbing his fork into a piece of bacon. "Drug dealer. Human trafficker. A predator, hidden behind a respectable facade." His eyes glinted darkly as his mind spun through the possibilities. "Someone who deserves what's coming to him. The thrill of the hunt... irresistible."

Tyler clenched his jaw, refocusing as Emily spoke again. She had no idea of the darkness that loomed just below the surface of his thoughts.

"So, we'll meet Kate and William for dinner," Emily said, smiling as she sipped her coffee, "and then the club, like we planned. It'll be fun."

Tyler smiled faintly, nodding. "Yeah, it'll be good to unwind."

"And maybe later tonight," he thought, his mind returning to Perry Maxwell, "I'll finally get to focus on what really matters." The hunt.

"Speaking of the book," Emily asked, pulling him back to the present, "how's it going? You never let me read the new stuff."

"It's coming together," Tyler said, smiling. "The protagonist is a demi-god struggling with his own darkness. He's powerful, but it's like he's constantly torn between two worlds. One foot in each, but neither really accepting him."

Emily tilted her head, intrigued. "It sounds intense. Darker than your last book."

"Darkness suits me," Tyler replied, his smile faint. "It's shaping up to be something special."

He paused, watching her across the table, her eyes filled with admiration. "I love her," he thought, the weight of the realization pressing down on him. "I want to marry her. Have a family. But how can I share my life with her when so much of it is... this?"

Emily reached for his hand, giving it a gentle squeeze. "You're brilliant, you know that?"

Tyler smiled, though it didn't reach his eyes. "Yeah," he said softly, "but don't tell anyone. It'll ruin my reputation."

She laughed, not seeing the struggle beneath his smile. He watched her, conflicted. "She deserves better than this. She deserves a normal life." He clenched his jaw, the darkness inside him stirring. "But can I ever stop? Can I ever let this other life go?"

They ate in comfortable silence, but Tyler's mind was already elsewhere, planning his next move. Later tonight, when the world was once again shrouded in darkness, he would focus on what really mattered.

The hunt.

DANCING AROUND THE EDGE

Tyler sat across from Jerry in the bustling coffee shop, his fingers curling around the warm mug of coffee in front of him. The steady hum of conversation filled the air, blending with the clinking of cups and the soft hiss of the espresso machine. Jerry's eyes were on him, probing, as if searching for cracks in the façade Tyler wore so well.

"Your new book... it's darker than the last," Jerry said, his tone casual, but there was something behind his words, something more pointed. "What inspired you to go that route?"

Tyler leaned back slightly, keeping his expression neutral. He'd been expecting this. "Writers evolve," he replied, his voice calm. "The stories I write... they just follow where the character takes me. Sometimes, that path is darker."

Jerry nodded, jotting something down in his notebook. "Interesting. But with this one, it feels personal, like you're drawing from something deeper. Especially with the way you delve into the mind of a killer."

Tyler smirked, taking a slow sip of his coffee. "Every writer brings a little bit of themselves to the table. But it's all fiction at the end of the day." He let the words hang in the air, watching Jerry for a reaction.

Jerry tapped his pen thoughtfully against the notebook. "Of course, but the detail in the violence, the way your protagonist teeters on the edge of morality, it's striking. Makes you wonder if you've ever been close to that edge yourself." His eyes gleamed as he leaned forward slightly, as though trying to peer into Tyler's mind.

"Why is he pushing so hard?" Tyler thought, keeping his outward composure. "He's too interested in the darkness."

Tyler chuckled, shaking his head slightly as he looked away. "Personal? I mean, sure, you can't write without putting some part of yourself into it. But I don't have any skeletons in my closet." He glanced back at Jerry, adding with a smirk, "If that's what you're asking."

"Yet," Tyler thought, his smile never faltering.

Jerry's smile widened slightly, his fingers still tapping lightly on the notebook. "No skeletons, huh? Well, it's just fiction, right?"

Tyler's eyes flicked toward the notebook, where Jerry had been scribbling away. He didn't need to see the words to know what kind of questions were being formed in the journalist's mind. "But," Tyler thought, "he's trying to dig deeper. He wants more."

"Of course," Tyler said, his tone breezy. "It's all just fiction. Nothing to lose sleep over."

But Jerry wasn't done. He leaned back, studying Tyler as if trying to see beyond the mask. "As someone who spends so much time in the minds of killers... have you ever wondered how close you could get to that edge? If you were one of your characters, I mean."

"There it is," Tyler thought, feeling the familiar pulse of control rising in his chest. "He's trying to get under my skin. But I won't let him."

Tyler's grin widened, though his eyes remained sharp. "We all have our limits. I just know how to imagine crossing them without actually doing it."

Jerry's gaze lingered on Tyler, his smile thinning as he took in the response. "Right. Well, I suppose that's what makes you so successful. You can walk up to that edge without ever falling over."

"You have no idea," Tyler thought, his grip tightening on the mug.

Jerry remained silent for a moment, his pen resting idly on the edge of the notebook. Tyler could feel the weight of his scrutiny, the way Jerry was watching for even the smallest crack. But Tyler wasn't going to give him that satisfaction. "Thanks for the compliment," Tyler said, his tone light as he finished the last of his coffee. "It's always fun talking about the creative process."

Tyler stood, offering his hand. "I've got another meeting soon, though. Can't spend all day in the shadows."

Jerry took his hand, the smile never fully reaching his eyes. "Of course. I'll be looking forward to seeing how your next book plays out. Something tells me there's more to it than meets the eye."

"He knows," Tyler thought, his pulse quickening. "Or at least... he suspects."

"You'll just have to wait and see," Tyler said, his voice calm as ever, before turning to walk away.

As Tyler made his way out of the coffee shop, he could feel Jerry's eyes on his back, watching him. "He's too curious," Tyler thought. "I need to end this soon before he starts seeing more than just the storylines."

Behind him, Jerry sat back in his chair, the friendly demeanor slipping as his gaze darkened. The camera zoomed in on Jerry's notebook as he scribbled a final note: "Tyler Grayson. More than a writer?"

Tyler stepped into the sunlight, the heat warming his skin, though it did nothing to dispel the cold knot tightening in his chest. "He's getting too close," Tyler thought, his mind already racing ahead. "I'll have to deal with him soon."

For now, though, Tyler let the tension ease from his shoulders. He put on his sunglasses, his lips curving into a small smile as he walked away from the café. "Jerry doesn't know who he's playing with," Tyler thought. "Not yet, anyway."

THE PLOT THICKENS

Tyler glanced over at Emily, the warmth of her laugh filling the room, pulling him momentarily away from his darker thoughts. She was tugging at his hand playfully, coaxing him toward the door. Her carefree nature was such a contrast to the storm that brewed in his mind. A storm only he could control.

"You're making that face again," Emily teased, her voice full of affection.

Tyler chuckled, shaking his head. "What face?"

"The one where you're plotting something," she said, giggling, her eyes bright with warmth.

"You have no idea," Tyler thought, the words echoing in his mind. Out loud, he teased, "I was just thinking about how I'm gonna survive another night of your crazy friends at the club."

Emily laughed, pulling him closer as she opened the door. "You'll be fine. I'll be right there with you. Besides, you might actually have fun this time."

"Fun? Fun will be getting Perry out of the way. Fun will be seeing his blood mix with the lake water," Tyler's inner voice whispered, but he forced a smile. "For now, I'll smile. I'll laugh. I'll be the loving boyfriend, while the rest of my mind focuses on the kill."

"Fine. But if I fall asleep in the middle of the dance floor, it's on you," Tyler said, smirking as he grabbed his jacket and followed her out.

"You're such a drama queen," Emily rolled her eyes playfully.

"Drama, sure," Tyler thought. "But there'll be no drama when I get Perry alone."

The night loomed ahead of him. Two parts of his world were about to collide,the loving boyfriend on one side, the predator on the other. As they stepped into the night, Tyler felt the familiar surge of adrenaline. Tonight, he'd play both roles perfectly. No one would ever know. Not even Emily.

And Perry Maxwell wouldn't see it coming.

A NICE NIGHT OUT

The restaurant was softly lit, with cozy booths tucked into quiet corners, creating an inviting atmosphere. Tyler and Emily sat across from William and Kate, their table cluttered with drinks and appetizers. Laughter and the clinking of glasses filled the air, wrapping them in a warm, relaxed ambiance.

William raised his glass, a genuine smile lighting up his face. "To my family. It's nice to finally be out with all of you, away from the station."

Kate grinned, her teasing nature coming to the forefront. "Well, if I didn't see it myself, I wouldn't believe it. William Grayson, out of the office for more than five minutes."

Emily laughed lightly, her eyes sparkling with affection. "It is pretty rare. But we're glad you could make it."

Tyler smirked, his playful tone adding to the lightheartedness. "It's good to know you remember what life outside the precinct looks like, Dad."

William chuckled, shaking his head in mock exasperation. "Alright, alright. I get it. I've been busy." He turned serious, glancing at

Emily and Tyler. "But I'm trying to make more time for what really matters."

Emily seized the moment, her teasing tone returning. "About time."

"It's a good thing he's focusing on family tonight. That'll keep him distracted while I handle what I need to later. Perry Maxwell won't be a problem by the time this night is over."

William shifted the subject. "So, what's new with you two?"

Emily's excitement bubbled over. "Tyler's been working on his new book. It's a dark fantasy. It's so good!"

Tyler took her hand, a smirk playing on his lips. "She might be a little biased." He paused thoughtfully, then continued, "But yeah, I've been working hard on it. Trying to finish it up soon. I've also been thinking a lot about... the future." He looked at Emily with warmth. "Marriage. Family. The next steps."

William leaned forward, a proud smile spreading across his face. "That's great to hear, son. You're planning for the future. It's important to think ahead."

"I want that. I want it all with her. Marriage, a family... something real. But how do I balance that with the darkness inside me? The side of me she can never know about?"

Kate chimed in, her grin broadening. "Maybe you'll dedicate this one to Emily, or your future kids?"

Tyler laughed lightly, feeling the warmth of their support. "Yeah, maybe."

"Dedicate it to Emily? Sure. But the truth is, it's the darkness that fuels me. The part of me that lives in the shadows, away from them."

Suddenly, William's phone vibrated on the table, cutting through the conversation. He glanced at the screen, his brow furrowing with concern.

"Sorry, one second," he said, sighing as he picked up the phone. He answered, his expression shifting to one of focus.
Kate and Emily exchanged a glance, while Tyler casually sipped his drink, the chatter around them fading.

"What is it?" William's voice turned serious, his face tightening as he listened. "James Holt, you said?"

"James Holt? So they've finally identified the body. I wondered when they'd piece that together." Tyler thought, keeping his outward calm.

William paused, processing the information. "Alright, thanks for the update. We'll go over everything in the morning." He hung up, turning back to the table.

Emily leaned forward, concern etched on her face. "Is everything okay?"

William shrugged it off, attempting to mask his worry. "They've identified the guy from the lake. His name was James Holt." He leaned back in his seat, trying to regain the relaxed atmosphere. "But I'm off the clock tonight. They'll handle it until tomorrow."

"James Holt. A rapist, a killer. He deserved what he got, but now William knows his name. Not that it matters. There's nothing that can connect me to him."

"Still, I can't get sloppy. Perry Maxwell's up next, and this needs to be perfect. Kill him fast, dump the body, get back to Emily. No time for mistakes tonight."

Kate nodded approvingly at William. "Good call. We're off duty. This is family time."

"Exactly. Tonight's for us," William said, relaxing again. "I'll deal with the case later."

Tyler smirked, trying to lighten the mood. "Good to see you're not letting it ruin your night."

"Good. Stay off the case, Dad. Focus on your family. Stay away from Perry tonight, and everything will go smoothly."

Kate shifted gears again. "Tyler, tell us more about the new book. I'm curious, dark fantasy, right?"

Tyler nodded, taking a moment to gather his thoughts. "Yeah. It's about a demi-god who's trying to find balance between his powers and the darkness inside him. He's got all this potential, but he's constantly pulled toward something darker, something more dangerous." He paused, weighing his words. "The story's about his struggle to reconcile the two sides of himself."

"It's about me. About trying to live in both worlds, the normal life with Emily, the future I want... and the killer that I am. The darkness is always there, no matter how much I want to hide it."

William nodded, genuinely interested. "Sounds like you've got something special there. You've always had talent, Tyler."

Emily leaned in, her eyes sparkling with pride. "I'm so proud of him. He's putting so much of himself into this book."

"If only she knew just how much of me is in it. The darker parts, the pieces I keep hidden from her."

"I want to marry her, have kids with her. But can I really live both lives? Or will one always come at the expense of the other?"

As they continued talking, William seemed more engaged with his family than usual, laughing and joking along with Kate and Emily. For a moment, the heavy cloud of the case seemed to lift, a fleeting moment of normalcy.

But Tyler sat there, smiling outwardly while his thoughts raced. He was already planning the next step of his night, the urgency of his secret mission pushing against the warmth of the moment.

THE HUNT

Tyler sat in the club, though the throbbing music barely registered in his mind. Neon lights washed over the sea of dancing bodies, illuminating moments of sweat, joy, and chaos. Emily laughed beside him, nursing a drink, her hand brushing his knee as she spoke animatedly to William and Kate. But Tyler's mind was elsewhere.

His eyes locked onto Perry Maxwell, who was seated just a few tables away. He was laughing, too. Enjoying his drink, utterly oblivious to the monster sitting just a few feet from him.

"Perry Maxwell," Tyler thought, his fingers tapping lightly against the glass of whiskey in his hand. "Right fucking there. A thief, a drug dealer, a lowlife who thinks he's untouchable. But tonight, you'll know what it's like to meet someone who can't be escaped."

The thought gave him a thrill, a low hum of anticipation vibrating through him. His gaze flicked back to the group for a moment, just long enough to nod along with William's joke. Tyler forced a smile. He was good at that. After all, wearing masks was second nature to him now.

William, raising his glass, grinned. "You kids have more energy than me these days. Dinner, and now a club? I don't know how you keep up."

Emily grinned, nudging Tyler playfully. "You're not old yet! You can still hang, right babe?"

Tyler barely heard her. His mind was already at the table across the room. But still, he smiled, his mask firmly in place.

"Yeah," he said, the word feeling like a formality. "I can hang."

His eyes slid back to Perry, who was taking a long drag from a cigarette, laughing at something one of his buddies said. The image of Perry's carefree face burned itself into Tyler's brain, fanning the flames inside him.

"I just need him to step outside." His thoughts turned darker, the familiar rush of anticipation quickening his pulse. "That's all it takes. I'll make it quick. Emily won't suspect a thing. I'll be back before anyone even notices I'm gone."

Emily leaned into him again, her voice soft but teasing. "Are you having fun? You seem distracted."

Tyler turned to her, summoning that soft smile he knew she loved. His hand slipped over hers. "Of course I am. It's been a great night." But even as he said the words, his eyes caught sight of Perry rising from his seat. The lowlife stubbed out his cigarette, pushing his chair back, making his way toward the exit.

Tyler's heart quickened. "Perfect."

He leaned in, planting a quick kiss on Emily's cheek. "I think I just saw an old friend from school. I'm gonna say hi real quick. I'll be back."

Emily smiled, nodding. "Alright, don't be long."

William, overhearing, chuckled. "Go on, say hi. Just don't leave us too long with Kate's taste in music."
Kate threw her Coworker a playful glare. "Hey, my taste in music is great."

But Tyler was already sliding out of the booth, his path set. He moved through the thrumming crowd with ease, slipping between the swaying bodies like a shadow, his focus entirely on Perry's retreating form

The moment Tyler stepped outside, the club's noise fell away. The night was cool, the air still thick with the faint scent of alcohol and sweat from inside. Perry Maxwell stood just ahead of him, oblivious to the danger creeping up behind him. The idiot was lighting another cigarette, completely unaware.

"Perry Maxwell," Tyler thought, the familiar weight of the chloroform rag in his jacket pocket. "A man who's hurt people. Women. Kids. The law never touched you, but I will."

Tyler's movements were smooth, practiced. He had done this before, after all. Many times. He moved closer, each step silent against the cracked pavement.

"Just a few more steps." His breath was steady, controlled. "Don't turn around. Don't realize what's coming."

Perry, lost in his own world, leaned against the brick wall, exhaling a cloud of smoke into the night air. Tyler was inches away now, the chemical smell of chloroform tickling his nose. His fingers curled around the rag, and in one swift, deliberate motion, he lunged. The rag clamped over Perry's mouth before the bastard could even react. Tyler yanked him backward, pulling him deeper into the shadows, away from the glow of the club's back door. Perry's eyes widened in panic, his body thrashing wildly as he tried to scream. The cigarette dropped from his fingers, forgotten as his hands flew up to claw at the rag.

Tyler held firm, his grip unrelenting. He leaned close, his voice a low whisper in Perry's ear. "Shhh. It'll be over soon."

The fight drained out of Perry's body within seconds. His arms dropped, his legs buckling beneath him. He slumped against Tyler, unconscious.

Tyler let out a slow breath, his heart still steady. He scanned the alley. Empty. Good. He crouched down beside Perry's limp body, pulling the familiar weight of the scalpel from his bag. The silver blade glinted under the faint light, its edge razor-sharp. Tyler smiled,a cold, empty smile,as he ran his thumb over the blade.

"Always start with the eyes." The thought slid through his mind, as natural as breathing. "They're the windows to the soul, and Perry doesn't deserve to see anymore."

With precise, deliberate movements, Tyler pressed the tip of the scalpel against Perry's right eyelid. The skin split easily, blood welling up as he carefully carved around the eye socket. The blade slid in, cutting the optic nerve, and with a soft, sickening pop, the eye came free.

Tyler held the eye between his fingers for a moment, admiring the work. Then he dropped it into a small plastic bag.

"One down."

He turned his attention to the left eye, repeating the process with the same meticulous care. Perry didn't move. His body remained slumped against the wall, his face slack, mouth slightly open. It didn't matter. He wouldn't be needing his eyes where he was going.
The second eye joined the first in the bag.

Next came the tongue.

Tyler pried Perry's mouth open, his fingers wrapping around the slick, limp muscle. It wasn't the first time he'd done this, and it wouldn't be the last. His scalpel slid easily under the base of the tongue, severing it with a quick, clean slice. Blood pooled in Perry's mouth, dribbling down his chin as Tyler tossed the tongue into the bag with the eyes.

"You won't speak again," Tyler thought, wiping the scalpel clean against Perry's shirt. "Not ever."

Satisfied with the preparatory work, Tyler set the scalpel aside and pulled out his real tool,a battery-powered chainsaw. The quiet hum of the motor sent a thrill through him. He always loved this part.

"This will be quick. Efficient." He pressed the button, and the chain whirred to life.

Tyler stepped back, adjusting his stance as he positioned the chainsaw over Perry's left shoulder. Blood sprayed as the blade tore through flesh and bone, the sound of the saw drowning out the wet crunch of cartilage being obliterated. Tyler's face was spattered with warm blood, but he didn't flinch.

His movements were methodical, practiced. He guided the saw down, cutting through Perry's arm with the precision of a surgeon. Blood sprayed across the alley in rhythmic arcs, painting the walls and pooling on the ground beneath him.

One arm severed.

He moved to the right side, repeating the process. The chainsaw's whirring was almost soothing, drowning out the world around him. Tyler didn't rush. He never rushed. This was art. He needed to savor it.

By the time Perry's torso was reduced to a bloodied, dismembered mess, Tyler felt a deep sense of satisfaction settle into his bones. He pulled off his blood-splattered gloves, tossing them into the black trash bag he'd prepared. His hands were steady as he reached into his bag one last time.

The Polaroid camera felt heavy in his grip, familiar. He snapped a picture of Perry's mangled corpse, watching as the image slowly developed, the grotesque scene coming into focus. Tyler flipped the photo over, grabbing a pen from his jacket pocket.

He wrote carefully, the ink flowing smoothly across the back of the Polaroid.

"In shadows deep, where silence dwells, A chainsaw roars, justice compels. Eyes removed, innocence reclaimed, Vengeance served. A heart untamed."

Tyler dropped the Polaroid into the pool of blood beside Perry's remains, watching it soak in. It was his calling card. A message. A warning.

He worked quickly now, stuffing Perry's dismembered limbs into black trash bags, tying them up tight. He hauled the bags toward his car.

Tyler worked with calm efficiency, making sure every piece of Perry Maxwell's dismembered body was packed away, sealed tight in thick black trash bags. The smell of blood hung in the air, metallic and raw, but it didn't faze him. It never did. His focus was absolute, his movements swift and deliberate. As he loaded the final bag into the trunk of his car, he glanced around the dark alley one last time. Empty. Quiet.

"Thirty minutes," he reminded himself. "Plenty of time to get it done. Emily will never know. She'll be inside, thinking I'm just catching up with an old friend."

Tyler slammed the trunk shut, the noise echoing through the empty alley. His blood-soaked clothes clung to him, heavy with the scent of death. He peeled off his jacket and shirt, tossing them into a separate bag he'd stashed earlier, then pulled on a clean set of clothes he'd hidden in the club bathroom before the night began. Always prepared. Always two steps ahead.

He felt a sense of calm wash over him as he pulled the hood of his jacket up, shrouding his face in shadow. The job was done. Clean. Efficient. No one would ever trace Perry

Maxwell's disappearance back to him. Perry was just another name on the long list of forgotten men who had crossed Tyler's path. Another soul ripped apart by Tyler's sense of justice, by his need for control.

But as he finished pulling his new clothes into place, something caught his attention. A sound. The faint squeal of tires from the alley's entrance. Tyler froze, his body tense. Slowly, he turned, his heart hammering in his chest as he peeked around the corner toward the source of the noise.

An SUV had pulled up, headlights dimmed but unmistakable. For a moment, Tyler's breath caught in his throat as he watched the driver's side door open, and out stepped a man Tyler hadn't expected to see again so soon.

Jerry West.

"What the hell is he doing here?"

Tyler's jaw clenched as he watched Jerry step out of the vehicle, his eyes scanning the alley like a predator surveying its territory. Jerry's face was expressionless, but there was a sharpness in his gaze that sent a chill down Tyler's spine. This wasn't a coincidence. Jerry West, the journalist who had interviewed him just days before, had followed him. He had been watching, waiting for something. And now he was here, standing far too close to Tyler's car,and the bags of human remains sitting in the trunk.

Jerry lingered by the vehicle for a moment, his eyes narrowing as he took in the scene. Then, as if he knew exactly where to look, his gaze shifted toward the trunk of Tyler's car.

"He knows." Tyler's mind raced. "Or he thinks he knows. But why follow me?"

Tyler ducked back into the shadows, his thoughts spinning. He couldn't act now, not with Jerry so close, but this was a problem that couldn't be ignored. He'd underestimated the journalist. He hadn't accounted for someone like Jerry,a man who could smell a story brewing from a mile away. A man who wouldn't stop digging until he uncovered the truth.

"Damn it." Tyler clenched his fists, his body coiled with tension. "I'll have to deal with him. But not tonight."

Jerry finally turned away from the car, his expression unreadable. He lingered for a moment longer, then got back into the SUV, driving off into the night without looking back.

Tyler exhaled slowly, his heart still pounding in his chest. Jerry had come too close. Far too close.

Tyler stood in the dark alley for a few moments, forcing his breathing to steady. He would deal with Jerry. In time. But right now, he had to focus on the task at hand. He couldn't afford any mistakes. Not now. Not when he was this close to getting away with it.

After making sure the coast was clear, Tyler retrieved the last of his things, careful to leave no trace of his presence. The alley was silent again, as if nothing had ever happened. Just another forgotten corner of the city, another night lost to the shadows.

Once everything was packed up and Perry's remains were securely in the trunk, Tyler pulled out his phone. He glanced at the time. Twenty-eight minutes. Just enough. He typed out a quick text to Emily, telling her he'd be back in a few minutes, then slid the phone back into his pocket.

The club was still packed, the heavy bass reverberating through the walls as Tyler stepped back inside. The neon lights and the sound of laughter washed over him, but it all felt distant, muffled, as if he were walking through a haze.

His mind was still in that alley, with Perry's dismembered body stuffed into trash bags in the trunk of his car.

Emily spotted him immediately, waving him over with a bright smile. Tyler returned the smile, though it didn't quite reach his eyes. He slid back into the booth beside her, wrapping an arm around her waist. She leaned into him, her warmth pressing against him, but he felt cold. Detached.

"Did you find your friend?" she asked, her voice light and teasing.

Tyler nodded, taking a sip of his drink. "Yeah. Just a quick chat."
William raised an eyebrow. "You were gone for a while. That must've been some chat."

Tyler smiled again, the mask slipping back into place. "Old friend. Lots to catch up on."

Kate rolled her eyes. "You're so mysterious sometimes, Tyler."

He just chuckled, leaning back into the booth as the others continued to talk and laugh around him. But his mind was elsewhere, his thoughts circling around Jerry West like vultures.

"He knows." The thought pulsed through him, relentless. "He's not stupid. He'll come back. He'll keep digging."
But that was fine. Tyler would be ready.

Just like he'd been ready for Perry.

Just like he'd always be ready.

Tyler slid back into the booth, letting the familiar chaos of the club wash over him. The neon lights strobed in sync with the pulsing bass, casting splashes of pink, purple, and blue across the sea of bodies swaying on the dance floor. He could feel the vibration of the music in his chest, a steady rhythm that seemed to match the calm, controlled beat of his heart. The booth was the same. The people around him,Emily, William, Kate,were the same. But inside, Tyler was a different man.

He had just cut a rapist apart.

A murderer. A child molester. A monster. And yet, Tyler thought, "I'm the one who just dismembered him in an alley behind this very club."

Emily leaned into his side, her body warm against his, oblivious to the blood that had spattered across his hands minutes earlier. She smiled up at him, her eyes dancing with happiness, like everything in her world was perfect.

Tyler smiled back, softly brushing her hair from her face. But in his mind, that smile cracked apart. "How easy it is," he thought, "to pretend."

Emily pulled him closer, her lips near his ear. "Dance with me," she whispered, her breath warm against his skin.

Tyler nodded, standing up and taking her hand as they made their way to the crowded dance floor. The neon lights flashed across their faces, casting them in a dreamlike glow. Bodies moved all around them, lost in the beat, lost in the moment. But for Tyler, it wasn't just a dance. It was something else entirely.

"I just killed a man," he thought, watching the lights flicker and shift. "I sliced his body apart, pulled his eyes out of his skull, cut out his tongue... and now, here I am, holding Emily, smiling like nothing ever happened. How can I do this? How can I switch between these lives so easily?"

The music pounded louder, and Tyler spun Emily gently, watching her laugh as she moved. Her happiness was real, genuine. She had no idea that the man she loved had just slaughtered another human being minutes ago.

"What would she think if she knew?" Tyler wondered, his inner voice calm, detached. "Could she ever look at me the same way? Or would she run, horrified by the darkness that lives inside me?"

Emily's hands were soft in his, her movements graceful as they moved together with the rhythm. The beat of the club music drowned out everything else, every thought, every scream that had echoed in the alley moments earlier.

"I live in two worlds," Tyler thought, his smile never faltering. "One with Emily, where I'm the man she loves, the man who's thinking about marriage and kids... and the other, where I'm a killer, cutting down men like Perry Maxwell without a second thought."

He could feel the sweat on his skin, the heat from the dance floor mixing with the adrenaline still coursing through his veins. The blood had been washed away in the club bathroom, but the memory of Perry's screams, his struggles, were still fresh in Tyler's mind.

"Am I a monster too?" Tyler wondered, his thoughts slipping deeper. "Or am I just balancing the scales? Perry was evil. He deserved what he got. But how long before the line between justice and my own darkness disappears completely?"

Emily looked up at him, her eyes full of trust and affection. "I love you," she whispered, resting her head on his chest as they swayed together.

Tyler's chest tightened. "I love you too," he said softly, but in his mind, the words sounded hollow. "I love her... but she can never know. She can never see the darkness inside me."

The song changed, and the crowd surged around them, pressing in closer. Tyler's mind swirled with thoughts of Perry, his hands shaking as he tried to fight back, the feel of the scalpel slicing through skin, the blood splattering across his face,and now here he was, lost in the crowd, the club lights flickering like nothing had happened.

"I live two lives," Tyler thought, pulling Emily closer as they moved in sync with the beat. "But one day... one of these lives is going to destroy the other."

Justice

The neon lights of the club blurred in the rearview mirror as Tyler pulled onto the main road, the engine humming softly beneath them. The weight of the night pressed down on him, heavier than the body stashed in the trunk of the car. His hands tightened around the steering wheel, knuckles white as he forced himself to breathe, to calm the storm brewing inside his head.

Emily sat beside him, her head resting against the passenger window, humming the remnants of the last song they'd danced to. She was drunk, but not too drunk. Just enough to make her oblivious to the nightmare lurking only a few feet behind them. Just enough to make her unaware of the blood he had scrubbed from his skin minutes before they left the club.

She smiled, her eyes closed, her body loose and relaxed. "That was fun," she murmured. "It's been a while since we've gone out like that."

Tyler forced a smile, glancing over at her, his heart pounding harder with every mile that took them closer to home. "Yeah," he said, his voice tight. "It was... good to get out."

"Why are you so tense?" Emily opened her eyes, looking over at him with a soft, tipsy smile. "You seem... I don't know... distant."

Tyler's mind was already elsewhere, plotting, calculating. "How am I going to get her inside without raising suspicion? How do I explain if she wants me to stay with her, not let me out of her sight until morning? I need time, space, to dump Perry Maxwell's body before anyone notices something's wrong."

He cleared his throat, trying to keep his voice steady. "I'm just tired, that's all. It's been a long night."

Emily reached over, resting her hand on his arm. "I had a great time tonight, though. I really needed this."

Tyler nodded, barely listening, his thoughts racing. "How can I get her inside? If I don't move soon, the smell's going to start leaking from the trunk. I have to act fast." He pulled onto their street, the familiar houses lining either side, their home just a few blocks away. The clock on the dashboard glowed in the darkness, each minute slipping away faster than the last.

As they neared the driveway, Tyler's pulse quickened. "I'll put her to bed first," he decided. "Let her fall asleep. Then I'll sneak out. Dump the body. Get rid of any evidence. Come back before she even notices I'm gone."

"Home sweet home," Emily murmured, her voice dreamy as they pulled into the driveway. Tyler killed the engine, listening to the silence that followed, his heart beating loud in his ears.

He unbuckled his seatbelt, turning to her with a soft smile. "Let's get you inside," he said, trying to sound casual. Emily nodded, yawning as she fumbled with her own seatbelt, her fingers clumsy from the alcohol. Tyler quickly moved around to her side, opening the door and helping her out.

"Thanks, babe," she said, leaning into him as they made their way up the front steps. "I'm so tired... I think I'm going to crash as soon as my head hits the pillow."

Tyler's stomach twisted at her words. "Perfect. If she's out cold, she won't even hear me leave." They stepped inside the house, the warmth and familiarity of their home wrapping around them. Tyler guided her to the bedroom, his mind already two steps ahead. "How can I justify killing people so easily?" he wondered, his thoughts dark as he helped Emily out of her shoes. "Is it truly justifiable to kill someone if it means someone else won't die? Is an eye for an eye actually still okay in modern times?"

Emily collapsed onto the bed, her body sinking into the mattress with a contented sigh. "Come to bed," she mumbled, her eyes already closing.

"I will," Tyler said softly, brushing a strand of hair from her face. "Just let me lock up first."

She nodded, too tired to question him, too drunk to notice the tightness in his voice. Within minutes, her breathing slowed, her body relaxed completely. She was asleep.

Tyler stood over her, watching her for a moment, a pang of guilt stabbing at him. "I love her. I do. But what would she think if she knew?" He swallowed hard, his mind spinning. "I truly don't know. But what I do know is that I have to keep killing. For myself."

He slipped out of the bedroom, careful not to make any noise. His footsteps were light as he moved through the house, locking the front door and double-checking that Emily was still asleep before heading back out to the car.

The cool night air hit him as he stepped outside, his breath visible in the cold. He opened the trunk, the faint smell of death hitting him immediately. Perry Maxwell's dismembered body was stuffed into black trash bags, tied tightly to contain the mess. Tyler glanced around the quiet neighborhood. No one was watching. No one would see him leave.

He lifted the bags into the trunk of his other car, the one he kept for nights like this,an old beater that no one would recognize or question if seen near the docks.

"Time to get this over with," he thought, sliding into the driver's seat and pulling away from the house.

The drive to the docks was short, his mind racing the entire way. "Is it wrong to do what I do?" he asked himself. "Perry was a rapist, a murderer, a child molester. He deserved to die. But does that make me any different from him? Am I just another killer hiding behind a justification?"

The docks loomed ahead, dark and deserted at this hour. Tyler pulled the car to a stop, glancing around to make sure no one was watching. The night was still, the water lapping softly against the pier.

He worked quickly, dragging the bags from the trunk and carrying them to the edge of the dock. The black water stretched out before him, cold and unforgiving. Tyler felt a strange calm wash over him as he hefted the first bag over the side, watching it disappear into the darkness.

"One less monster in the world," he thought, moving to the next bag. "But how many more are there? And how many more will I have to kill to feel like I'm making a difference?"

With the last of the bags gone, Tyler stood at the edge of the dock, staring out at the water. "Is it enough? Will it ever be enough?"

He turned, wiping his hands on his jacket as he made his way back to the car. The drive home was quiet, the adrenaline slowly fading as he pulled into the driveway. He parked the car, careful to leave no trace of the night's work, and slipped back into the house.

Emily was still asleep, her body curled under the blankets, peaceful and unaware. Tyler undressed quietly, slipping into bed beside her, his mind still buzzing with the questions that wouldn't go away.

"I don't know if what I'm doing is right," he thought, closing his eyes. "But I know I have to keep going. For Emily. For myself. For the darkness that lives inside me."

As sleep finally pulled him under, Tyler reached for Emily, pulling her close, as if her warmth could somehow keep the darkness at bay.

But deep down, he knew,there would always be more bodies, more blood, more nights like this. And as long as there were men like Perry Maxwell in the world, Tyler would keep killing.

Because in the end, that was all he knew how to do.

GHOSTS OF THE PAST

William leaned back in his chair, the worn leather cracking beneath him as he stared at the white board on the wall. His eyes traced the details of the crime scene, but his mind was somewhere else, floating somewhere between the horrors of the scene and the weight of the present. He rubbed his hands against his temples, trying to push away the throbbing sensation that drilled into his head since the morning.

"Where were we?" William's voice came out more hoarse than he intended, his exhaustion seeping into every word he spoke.

Kate cleared her throat and motioned a marker towards the white board, circling the blurry outline of the shoe print that sat on the board. "The shoe print," she said, her tone careful. She had been watching William closely for the past hour, sensing the storm growing inside him. "We need to cross-reference it with past suspects."

William nodded, but the gesture was hollow. His thoughts were disconnected, flickering between the case and his family like a broken reel, images of his wife, Mariah, flashed through his mind, her laugh, her smile, and then the cold empty silence of her lifeless body after she was taken from him. He swallowed hard, trying to hide the wave of emotions threatening to rise to his surface.

Kate must have noticed his distraction because she took charge, her voice firm yet angelic. "I'll handle the print," she said, not waiting for him to respond. "Why don't you go get some fresh air, take the rest of the day off? Maybe check in on Tyler's book signing tomorrow? It could do you some good."

William shot her a grateful look, but his lips moved as if to say something, but the words never came. Before he could muster the courage to responde, one of the detectives on the far end of the table spoke up, his voice slicing through the tension in the air.

"We did get a hit on the victim's identity, I called you last night to explain, but you were with family." The detective's tone was flat, almost emotionless. "James Holt. we ran the blood from the crime scene through our database, and he has quite the rap sheet."

The name hit William in the chest like a brick, his entire body tensing at the sound of it. His back straightened as he looked up, eyes wide with anger and recognition. It couldn't be. Not him. Not that man,

"James Holt?" William's voice was barely above a whisper, but it carried the weight of unsolved pain and grief. His stomach twisted inside of itself, as the name rolled off his tongue, a name nobody had spoken in years but it had never truly been forgotten.

Kate raised an eyebrow, sensing the shift in William's demeanor. She watched him closely, her gaze sharp and curious, but she didn't say anything. Not yet

Without thinking, William spun his chair around, facing his computer, his fingers flying across the keys of the keyboard with a speed that even surprised him. He was on autopilot now, driven by instinct and the need to remember. He pulled up the police database, his heart pumping in his chest as the file loaded onto the screen.

There it was, "James Holt." Multiple charges, Drug trafficking. Assault. But it was the next line that made William's breath catch in his throat, his hands froze over the keyboard.

"Murder of Mariah Grayson."

For a moment, everything around him faded into nothingness. The sounds of the room hummed in the background, the low hum of conversation, even the faint buzzing of the fluorescent lights, all of it was drowned out by the roaring thoughts inside his head. He blinked, trying to focus, but all he could see was Mariah's face, her wide trusting eyes staring back at him through the fog of memories.

"No," William muttered, shaking his head as if the motion alone could hide the truth inside of him. "It can't be."

Kate had moved closer, her breath shallow as she peered over his shoulder at the screen. When she saw the name, her hand flew to her mouth, a quiet gasp escaping her lips. "William... is that...?"

"Yeah," William said, his voice low and strained, barely holding back the fury building inside him. "That's him. Holt... he was the one who killed Mariah."

Silence fell over the room, thick and oppressive. Every eye was on William, but no one dared speak. They all knew the story,everyone in the precinct did. William Grayson, the detective who had lost his wife to a brutal gang killing, the case that had haunted him for years. And now, it had come back to him in the form of a mutilated body on the docks.

"He got off," William continued, his voice trembling with barely-contained rage. "Mistrial. One of his gang members killed the judge, and Holt walked free. Just like that."

Kate's face tightened, the weight of the revelation settling over her like a shroud. She knew what this meant to William. She had seen the way Mariah's death had changed him, the way it had hardened him into the man he was today. But seeing Holt's name again, tied to yet another murder,it was like reopening a wound that had never truly healed.

"William," she said softly, placing a hand on his shoulder, "I'm so sorry."

He shook his head, his eyes never leaving the screen. "Sorry doesn't change anything, Kate," he said, his voice rough with emotion. "He's dead now, but it's not enough. It's never going to be enough."

His phone buzzed again, vibrating against the table like an unwelcome reminder of the outside world. William gritted his teeth, the frustration boiling over as he grabbed the phone. "What now?" he muttered, his voice edged with irritation.

Kate stepped back, giving him space. She could see the strain in his face, the way his hands trembled slightly as he looked at the screen. She wanted to help, to ease the burden he carried, but she knew there was little she could do. This case,it was too personal, too painful.

"Maybe we should take a break," she suggested, her voice soft but firm. "Go to Tyler's signing tomorrow. It'll be good for you to step away from this for a minute."

William hesitated, the words sinking in. His mind was still racing, torn between the revelation about Holt and the need to keep pushing forward, to keep investigating. But Kate was right. He couldn't keep going like this, not without breaking.

"Yeah," he finally said, his voice barely above a whisper. "Yeah, maybe you're right."

Kate gave him a small, sad smile, her hand resting lightly on his arm. "We'll figure this out, William. One step at a time."

He nodded, but the tension in his body didn't ease. The weight of the case, of Mariah's memory, was still there, pressing down on him with relentless force. As they gathered their things to leave, William cast one last glance at the screen, his eyes locking on the name "Mariah Grayson."

It was a name he would never forget, a ghost that would haunt him for the rest of his life.

Kate noticed the way his gaze lingered, the way his hands clenched into fists at his sides. She didn't say anything, but she felt the same weight settle over her. The case wasn't just another murder investigation,it was a part of William's past, a wound that had never healed.

As they walked out of the room, the silence between them was heavy, filled with unspoken words and shared pain. The world outside felt colder, the night air biting at their skin as they stepped onto the street. But the real coldness, the real chill, was inside William, deep in the pit of his chest where the memory of Mariah still lived.

As they reached the car, Kate glanced at him, her expression soft but filled with concern. "We'll get through this, William," she said quietly, her voice barely audible over the hum of the city around them.

William didn't respond. He couldn't.

THE GAME BEGINS

Tyler lay still in the soft, dim light of the morning, the faint glow of the morning light creeping through the blinds in his and Emily's bedroom. The gentle rise and fall of Emily's breathing filled the quiet room, a peaceful contrast to the sheer chaos building inside him. Tyler's eyes were fixed on the ceiling, but his mind was elsewhere, far beyond the walls or ceiling of their shared apartment. Today was the day. Tyler was finally going to kill the man who could destroy his work. He had been planning this for weeks, after stealing a file from his fathers desk. It was finally going to be set in motion, and there was no turning back.

Yet, despite the familiar hum of adrenaline coursing through his veins, he turned his head to watch Emily sleep. Emily, Peaceful, innocent, oblivious. Her face was relaxed, her hair splayed across her pillow. She looked so calm, so untouched by the world Tyler had built for himself. The world of blood, lies, vulgarity, and shadows. Tyler's chest anchored at the thought.

"I could watch her like this forever," he thought, feeling a deep cram of emotion. "I love her more than anything in this world. One day, I'll marry her. We'll have kids. Maybe we'll even run far away from this shitty city, from the chaos I built. Build a life of calm, peaceful sights, where the darkness can't touch us."

But that thought was just a fantasy, A fleeting beautiful lie he taught himself, to entertain himself from the quiet moments where he didn't have a victim on his plate. Bloodied by a knife, cut to pieces, A lie where reality hadn't crashed back into his head. The truth of the matter was cold and brutal: Emily could never know the real him. And he knew that. She wouldn't understand that side of him. Hell he hardly understood that side of him. But what he did know was that it was there, it was just as much a part of him as the loving nurturing side of him. And that is exactly why he had to keep it hidden, locked away, like the many bloody secrets he carried.

Carefully, Tyler slipped out of bed, moving with the precision of a man who was used to creeping around in the shadows. Emily stirred, her hand twitched toward his side of the bed, but she didn't wake. Tyler exhaled softly, standing overtop of her, watching her sleep peacefully for a moment longer before turning away. He needed to focus now. Focus on what was important.

He dressed quickly, dark jeans, a hoodie, and sneakers. Simple, practical, hidden, Anonymous. This morning required subtlety, precision. Everything had to go according to his plan. He turned his shoulder, glancing down at Emily one last time before leaving. Her peaceful form is a stark contrast from the storm just below Tyler's surface. His heart twisted and turned painfully, knowing he could never be the man she thought he was. No matter how much he wanted to be.

"What if what Emily deserves is a nice house and a good husband, a life where she can live peacefully knowing that the love of her life will come home every day at the same time, without the risk of being caught doing what I do," He thought to himself his emotions finally breaking the ice. "What if what she got instead was me, a cold blooded killer, a killer who keeps pictures of his victims in notebooks hidden away in the back of his desk, a monster."

In the kitchen, he grabbed a piece of paper and his favorite pen, scribbling down a quick note. The words came easily, loving, reassuring. A smokescreen.

"Emily, I went out for a bit to clear my head. Needed to catch my breath after that long night of partying, but I left a box of your favorite donuts on the counter. I'll be back before you know it. I love you more than anything."

He set the note on the kitchen table, next to a box of powdered sugar topped, lemon filling filled donuts, Emily's favorite. He picked them up the night before, right after dumping the body of the child molester, Perry Maxwell. It was perfect. When she woke up, she would read the note, smile, and think everything was hunky dory. Just another day, For a little while, at least, he could keep the facade alive

Tyler grabbed his keys and silently slipped out the door, the cool morning breeze hitting his face as he stepped out onto the empty street. He pulled his hoodie up over his head and began walking, his footsteps soft on the pavement below him. Blending in with the quiet stillness of the neighborhood.

The city was still asleep. Streetlights buzzed faintly, casting long shadows on the empty sidewalks. Tyler moved quickly, his mind sharp, focused. Three Blocks. That's all he needed to cover. Just three blocks between him and the place Victor Muracr's car was parked. Everything was already in place. Today, Tyler's game would truly start.

"Victor Murcar," Tyler thought, his mind conjuring the man's image, an elite soldier turned hired gunman. "He's killed more people than anyone could think of, just like me. His kills are all under the radar. He's too close with the police. And too good at staying hidden. He is the reason They're tearing up the lake searching for bodies, My bodies, like James Holt's."

James Holt. The name triggered something dark in Tyler's chest. Holt had been a victim, but not of the system. A man like Holt only played a bigger, greater part in the scheme of things. No, Victor was the real problem. Victor was the cleaner, the one who made sure those connected to the rich and powerful never faced consequences for their sins and crimes.

"But today," Tyler thought, the edges of his mouth curling into a faint smile, "he's going to make his final mistake. Today, Victor Murcar becomes my next victim."

Tyler walked with purpose, keeping his head down, his hands tucked into his pockets. Just another guy taking an early morning stroll. Nothing to notice. He rounded the final corner, and there it was, Victor's car. A sleek, black SUV, parked in front of a brownstone. Nondescript, blending into the neighborhood. But Tyler knew better. It was always there, always the same spot, like clockwork.

He approached the SUV casually, bending down to tie his shoelace as he neared the vehicle. His fingers worked quickly, pulling a small black device from his pocket, a tracker, no bigger than a quarter. Undetectable. Invisible unless you knew exactly where to look. In a single smooth motion, Tyler attached the device to the underside of the driver's side mirror.

"Perfect," Tyler thought, straightening up. "Now I'll know every move he makes, everywhere he goes. He won't even realize he is being watched."

Just as he finished, the SUV's lights flashed, and a soft beep signaled the car unlocking. Tyler's heart skipped a beat, but he didn't panic. He kept moving, walking casually away as if nothing had happened. As if his pulse wasn't racing in his throat.

Behind him, the front door of the brownstone creaked open, Tyler glanced over his shoulder, just in time to see Victor Murcar step outside. The man was tall, broad-shouldered, his face hard and calculating. The kind of man who commanded attention without saying a word. Tyler quickly turned the corner, out of sight, his heart pounding in his chest.

"I've got to move faster," Tyler thought, forcing his breathing to slow. "If he spotted me, it's over. But no... focus. He didn't see you. He's just going about his day. He has no idea he's being hunted."

Tyler picked up his pace, his pulse still quick but controlled. He wouldn't let the fear take over. Not now. This was just the beginning of the game, the first move on the board. Victor didn't even know he was playing yet. But soon, very soon, he would.

Three blocks away, Tyler slowed down, his heartbeat finally steadying. He allowed himself a small smile.

"It's almost too easy," he thought. "The tracker will lead me straight to him, wherever he goes. And when the time is right..." His smile darkened. "Victor won't see it coming."

By the time Tyler reached his apartment, the city was beginning to wake. He slipped back inside, the quiet stillness of the morning greeting him once more. Emily was still asleep, completely unaware of the deadly game unfolding just outside her world.

Tyler leaned against the door for a moment, letting the tension in his body ease. Everything was going according to plan. Victor Murcar was just a piece on the board,a dangerous piece, sure,but nothing Tyler couldn't handle. Soon, the game would end, and Tyler would be the one standing on top.He walked into the kitchen, glancing at the note he'd left for Emily, the box of donuts still sitting on the counter. A faint smile crossed his lips. He could play the part of the loving boyfriend for a little while longer. But soon... very soon... the real him would emerge again.

For now, he waited, the calm before the storm.

SHADOWS IN THE LIGHT

Tyler pressed his back against the front door, letting the weight of the midday heat roll over his skin. The house stood before him, a fortress disguised as a home, casting long, severe shadows across the street. He adjusted his black hoodie, wiping the sweat from his eyebrows. But his eyes never left the door. This was it. The moment he had been preparing for. Every detail, every action had to be flawless, failure was not an option.

Tyler knelt down, the lockpicking tools slipping effortlessly into his hand like an extension of his own body. Tyler's fingers moved quickly, the metal picks dancing inside the lock with a quiet precision honed through years of experience. His movements were calm, methodical, each click of the tumblers inside the lock falling into place brought him one step closer. He listened intently, his breathy steady, his pulse normal, until finally, the last pin slid into place

Click.

The door gave a soft creak as it inched open, and Tyler slipped inside, closing the door quietly behind him. The air inside was cool, almost too cool. As though the place had been stripped from the warmth of humanity. Murcar's presence lingered in every corner, every shadow. The smell of bleach and disinfectants, faint but distinct, Clung in the air, mixing with the metallic scent of gun oil and something that tastes like iron. Something stale, almost like dried blood.

The house was immaculate. Way too clean, too organized. As if the place had not seen a habitant in ages. It was sterile, with every piece of furniture in its place, every surface glowing under the faint silver sunlight coming through the blinds. A soldier's touch, Tyler thought as his eyes swept over the living room. Every inch of it was a reflection of the owner, cold, calculated, a machine trained and built for efficiency and death.

"This place feels like a cemetery,"tyler thought, crouching low to scan the area for any signs of security systems or traps. "Controlled. Cold. Murcar's not your average killer. He's a professional… Like me, highly dangerous."

His senses were on high alert as he continued deeper into the house. His footsteps silent against the polished hardwood floors. The walls were lined with military medals and plaques. Each one was a testament to Murcar's service. There was no warmth in them, no pride, only a sense of duty fulfilled with ruthless precision. Tyler's eyes flicked to the small photos placed on the shelfs, snapshots of Murcar in his uniform, shaking hands with high ranking officers, standing in warzones, always the same cold expression on his face. He was not just a soldier. He was a lion in a field of gazelles. He traded one battle for another.

"A shame such an honorable man is going to die like a coward," Tyler thought. "Hopefully I don't share the same fate."

Tyler reached for a set of drawers and paused before opening them, listening intently for any sounds beyond the house's oppressive silence, and stillness. The faint hum of the refrigerator in the kitchen was the only noise. Confident he was alone, Tyler carefully opened the top drawer, revealing a chilling sight. Rows of handguns, each one precisely cleaned and ready for use, were lined up like soldiers awaiting orders. Beneath the weapons lay neatly stacked boxes of ammunition and tactical gear, including a live grenade, all arranged with a voice that spoke volume of Murcar's aggressive nature.

"Fully loaded, as if he really has something to hide," Tyler thought as he moved his hands covered with leather gloves across the gun's surface. "He's ready for a fight, and with him, I don't want to pick one."

He closed the drawer quietly, his fingers brushing over the smooth wood, careful not to leave any prints. Every movement was a deliberate and careful movement. Measured and cautious. There was no room for a mistake, that could be the death of Tyler. Murcar wasn't your run of the mill thug, he was a machine built for war, he was calculated, efficient and deadly. If Tyler was not careful, it could be his final mistake.

Tyler moved to a large wooden cabinet, crouching in front of it, The lock was larger, more heavy than the one on the front door, but that didn't matter. Tyler's fingers worked quickly, the lockpicking tools sliding into place with practiced precision. His heartbeat remained steady, his breathing still controlled. Each click of the tumblers was a grave reminder of the weight pressing down on him.

With a final, almost imperceptible click, the lock gave way, and Tyler swung the cabinet door open slowly, to not make a noise. His breath caught in his throat like an ice cube.

Inside was a small wooden box, old and worn, its surface marred with scratches and what look like dried blood. The box looked out of place here, like an artifact from another life, one far more brutal and unfeeling. Tyler hesitated for a moment before lifting the lid.

What he saw made his blood run cold.

A wedding ring, caked in dried blood, lay nestled at the top of the box. But it was not alone. Beneath it were dozens more, each one similarly stained, the blood long since dried and darkened. The sight of them, symbols of love, twisted and defiled, sent a chill down Tyler's spine. He stared down at the rings, his jaw tightening as his mind pieced together the grotesque truth.

"These aren't just memento's, they're trophies," Tyler thought. "Just like the pictures I keep of my victims, a memory of the brutality they caused." his fingers brushed against one of the rings. "He's a butcher. These belonged to people he's slaughtered. People ripped from their lives, their families. I can't even comprehend that pain."

Each ring told a story, each one a testament to the people Murcar had taken, husbands, wives, their lives torn apart and reduced to these bloodstained tokens. Tyler's hand hovered over the rings, his stomach turning with a mix of disgust and rage. He had known Murcar was a killer, but this… this was something far darker. The rings weren't just trophies, they were symbols of power, of domination over the lives he had destroyed.

Tyler closed the box carefully, his heart pounding in his chest as he placed it back in the cabinet. His hands trembled slightly, but his mind remained sharp, focused. He couldn't let the horror of it all distract him. He needed to finish what he'd come for.

He moved deeper into the house, his eyes scanning for anything that might give him more insight into Murcar's twisted mind. In a nearby drawer, he found a small stack of pictures, each one more horrifying than the last. The images were grainy but clear enough to make Tyler's stomach drop, mutilated bodies, fingers missing, eyes carved out, each corpse arranged in cult-like positions. These were Murcar's victims, men and women he had tortured and killed over the years.

"The bastard is a fucking copy cat." Tyler's blood boiled, his hands trembled as he flipped through the photos. "How the hell has nobody pieced this together. He doesn't just kill, he tortures them, just like me. He leaves behind symbols of their love, soaked in their blood."

Tyler felt a surge of anger welling up inside him, his pulse quickening as the full extent of Murcar's copycat atrocities settled icer him like his Abyssal Passenger. But before he could process any further, his phone vibrated in his pocket, the sudden noise cutting through the loud silence. Tyler's eyes snapped to the screen. The tracker on Victor's car had signaled again.

Victor was on the move.

"Time to go," Tyler thought, his body tensing as the urgency of the situation set in. "This isn't over. He's a fucking copy cat killer, except his crimes are way worse than mine, I have to stay ahead of him, this tracker is the only way I can get to him."

Tyler moved quickly, slipping his phone back into his pocket as he closed the drawer and cabinet. wiping down every surface he'd touched with careful precision. He couldn't afford to leave a single trace behind. He had been inside long enough, and every second he lingered increased the risk of being discovered.

As he approached the front door, his senses were on high alert. He pressed his ear to the door, listening for any sounds from outside. Nothing. With one last glance around the room, he slipped out of the house, pulling the door shut softly behind him.

The midday sun hit him like a wave, harsh and blinding after the cool darkness inside Murcar's house. He stood for a moment, letting the heat seep into his skin, his mind racing. He had what he needed. The rings, the photographs,they were all proof of the monster Murcar truly was. But more importantly, Tyler had the upper hand. The tracker would lead him straight to Victor, and when the time was right, Tyler would end it.

He walked quickly down the street, blending into the city's noise and bustle, the house shrinking behind him. But even as he put distance between himself and Murcar's fortress, the weight of what he had discovered clung to him. How many more lives had Murcar destroyed? How many more rings were out there, sitting in bloodstained boxes, waiting to be found?

"Soon," Tyler thought, his jaw clenched as he disappeared into the crowd. "Very soon, the real me will emerge again."

With that, he left Murcar's world of blood and death behind, his mind already calculating his next move.

HUNTING GROUND

"I'll follow him. See where he leads me. The more I know, the easier it'll be to take him down. But not yet. He's too dangerous to rush."

His internal monologue was cold and methodical, his mind already leaping to the next steps. Blending seamlessly into the crowd of pedestrians, Tyler moved down the street, his thoughts fixed on Victor. Every detail he had gathered, every scrap of information, was carefully cataloged in his mind. He knew Victor wouldn't stay in one place for long. The man was too smart for that,too used to staying ahead of the law, of anyone hunting him. But Tyler wasn't like the others who might have tried. He wasn't rushing in, guns blazing, hoping for a clean shot.

He was waiting. Watching.Victor's apartment complex loomed ahead, an eyesore against the city's skyline as dusk settled into night. The building was a relic of a forgotten past, neglected and falling apart. Mold clung to the cracked walls like a sickness, and the dim lighting flickered sporadically, casting eerie shadows that twisted along the corridors. It was the kind of place where the city's lost and broken ended up, and no one cared. No one asked questions.

Victor Murcar walked through the dim hallways with the confidence of a man who knew he owned this space, even if it was in ruins. His footsteps were heavy, echoing off the cracked walls as he made his way to the basement. In his hand, he clutched a ring of keys, their jingling the only other sound in the decaying building. His expression was unreadable, but his body language screamed control, he was a predator returning to his den.

At the end of the corridor, he unlocked a door with a loud creak, pushing it open to reveal the horror within. The basement was dimly lit, the walls stained with grime and decay. Dirty mattresses were scattered along the floor, but it wasn't the filth that made the air thick. It was despair. The room reeked of sweat, fear, and the metallic tang of dried blood.

Victor stepped inside, his shadow stretching long across the bound figures lying along the walls. The women, shackled and gagged, barely moved. Some were bruised, their bodies weakened from abuse. Others were so far gone, they barely seemed conscious. Their eyes, however, told the story their bodies couldn't, the raw, primal fear of prey staring up at a predator.

Victor's hand reached out, rough fingers tracing the bruised cheek of one of the women. She flinched at the contact, but her bonds held her in place. His touch lingered, sending shivers of dread down her spine. He leaned in close, his voice a low rasp.

"Another long night, ladies. We'll make it count, won't we?"

His words hung in the air like a death sentence. He turned his attention to another woman, grabbing her roughly by the throat. Her gagged cry was muffled, barely audible as he yanked her toward the center of the room. Her eyes bulged, terror and pain swimming in them as she struggled for breath. Victor's grip didn't loosen. He stared into her face with cold detachment, the act as casual as checking the time. The door behind him closed with a resounding thud, sealing off any hope of escape.The city streets were bathed in the glow of neon lights as Tyler drove, his hands gripping the steering wheel tightly. The red blip on his phone's tracker moved steadily across the screen, leading him directly to Victor's apartment complex. Tyler's jaw clenched, his eyes fixed on the road as the tension inside him built.

"Where is he going? This isn't just a safe house. This is something else. Something darker. It's no ordinary drop-off point... it's a hunting ground. I can feel it."

The city blurred past in streaks of light and shadow, but Tyler was focused. His mind raced, turning over every possibility, every scenario that could unfold. He couldn't afford to make a mistake. Not with someone like Victor. The man was cunning, dangerous, and Tyler knew that whatever was waiting for him inside that building, it wasn't going to be simple.

The GPS showed him closing in, only a few blocks away now.

"I need to get close enough. But I can't rush in blindly. I don't know what's waiting for me. What kind of sick world this guy has built for himself. The cleaner I move, the better."

He pulled the car to the side of the road, shutting off the headlights before parking in the shadow of a narrow alleyway. The street was quiet, dark, with no one in sight. Tyler moved quickly, slipping out of the car and blending into the night, his black hoodie pulled low over his head. His lockpicks were ready in hand as he moved toward the apartment complex.Victor worked with a calm precision, tightening a leather belt around the wrists of the woman he had selected. She trembled, her breaths coming in short gasps as he tied her to the chair in the center of the room. The other women, their eyes wide with terror, watched in silence, their cries muffled by the gags. The air was thick with their fear, but Victor seemed to revel in it. He pulled a small, rusted knife from his pocket, running his fingers along the dull edge.

"Let's start slow tonight. Let's make sure we savor this."

He watched the building. From where he stood, it looked completely abandoned,no lights in the windows, no movement at all. It could have easily been mistaken for just another derelict building, forgotten by the city. But Tyler knew better.

"What the hell…"

Tyler crouched across the street from Victor's apartment complex, his gaze sharp as he watched the building. From where he stood, it looked completely abandoned,no lights in the windows, no movement at all. It could have easily been mistaken for just another derelict building, forgotten by the city. But Tyler knew better.

His phone buzzed, the tracker's signal strong. It was inside the building.

"He's in there. What are you hiding, Murcar? What kind of monster are you when no one's watching?"

Tyler moved quickly, crossing the street with the silence and stealth of a shadow. He kept his hood low, blending into the darkness as he approached the building's back entrance. His fingers worked the lock with ease, and within seconds, the door clicked open. Tyler slipped inside, immediately assaulted by the stench of rot and decay.

The stairwell was narrow and reeked of mold. The paint peeled from the walls in chunks, and the lights flickered overhead, casting ghostly shadows that danced along the cracked tiles. Every step Tyler took was measured, his movements careful as he made his way down the hallway, his senses heightened.

"This place is a tomb. No one comes here by choice. It's a graveyard for the living. Where the lost come to die."

The basement was his destination. The tracker led him there, and Tyler trusted it. He moved with purpose, descending the rickety stairs, his footfalls light but deliberate.

Tyler's heart beat heavily in his chest as he descended into the depths of Victor Murcar's world. The deeper he went, the colder the air became, the rot in the walls mixing with the unmistakable stench of fear and decay. His mind sharpened, every sound amplified,the distant buzz of a dying light, the creaking floorboards, and the rhythmic dripping of unseen water.

The door at the end of the hall came into view, old and worn, looking as though it hadn't been opened in years. But Tyler knew better. Murcar was here. He paused, pressing his ear against the door. Silence. No voices, no movement. He reached into his pocket and pulled out his lockpicks. The mechanism was old, giving way with a quiet click. Tyler gently pushed the door open and slipped inside, taking in the room.

It was worse than he imagined.

Old tools hung from rusted hooks, some splattered with dried blood. Dirty tarps were spread across the concrete floor, covering stains that had long soaked into the ground. Against the far wall, a large metal cabinet caught his attention. Its imposing size and industrial locks made it clear this wasn't for ordinary storage.

"What are you keeping in here, Murcar? Guns? Evidence? Or something worse?"

Tyler's fingers worked swiftly, the lock yielding under his practiced touch. As the doors swung open, his breath hitched. Inside the cabinet were trophies,rings, wallets, and IDs, each one smeared with dried blood, stacked in neat rows. Photos were pinned to the back of the cabinet, images of women, many of whom Tyler recognized from missing person reports. The reality of what Victor Murcar had done to these women, what he had been doing for years, twisted Tyler's stomach.

"He's been doing this for years. No one's caught him. No one even knows. But now I do."

A faint sound interrupted his thoughts,the soft creak of the floor above him. Footsteps. Tyler's body tensed as he pocketed the last of the evidence, his mind racing. Victor was moving again, probably heading toward the basement. There wasn't much time. He had to act now.

Victor Murcar stepped into the hallway, his eyes scanning the space as he took a slow drag from his cigarette. His body language was relaxed, but his eyes held a sharpness, as if he sensed something was off. He exhaled, the smoke curling around him like a dark cloud as he moved toward the basement stairs. He had unfinished business downstairs.

Tyler pressed his ear against the door, hearing the distant echo of Victor's heavy boots coming closer. His pulse quickened, adrenaline surging as he crouched behind a stack of crates. The basement air was thick with the smell of stale blood and sweat, a chilling reminder of the horrors that had taken place there. Tyler's gaze darted to the unconscious women scattered across the room,helpless, beaten, and unaware of the fight about to unfold.

Victor's footsteps grew louder as he descended the stairs, each creak of the old wood reverberating through Tyler's bones. He couldn't afford to make a mistake. Not now.

"Whatever he's hiding, it's down there. But I have to be careful. I can't rush this. One wrong move, and he'll catch on."

The basement door swung open, the room bathed in an eerie glow from the single dim bulb hanging from the ceiling. Tyler crouched lower, his breath slow and steady as he watched Victor enter. He was massive,broad shoulders, towering height, a hulking figure that dominated the space. Tyler could see the tension in his muscles, the way his hands flexed around the cigarette he held. This was a man used to violence, a man who relished in it.

Victor moved toward the center of the room, his eyes scanning the walls and floors for any sign of disturbance. The women's muffled sobs filled the space, but Victor seemed unfazed. To him, this was routine.

Tyler waited, every muscle coiled, eyes locked on the monster before him.

Victor crossed to the nearest woman, who was bound to a rusted metal chair. She was shaking, her breath ragged and uneven as she tried to shrink away from his looming presence. He placed a hand on her head, his fingers weaving through her matted hair as he whispered something Tyler couldn't hear. Then, without warning, he yanked her head back, his grip tight and possessive, his voice low and threatening.

"You were good tonight. You know that? Might've been the best I've had in a while."

The woman whimpered, her body trembling violently in the chair. Victor's fingers tightened in her hair, and she winced in pain, unable to do anything but endure it.

Tyler's eyes darkened, his fists clenching at his sides as he watched. His breath came faster, the primal instinct to intervene warring with the careful plan he had made. He couldn't let Murcar keep doing this. Not tonight. Not ever again.

Victor turned, pacing toward the other women scattered across the mattresses on the floor. He raised his voice, taunting them as he revved up a power saw. The blade whined, its mechanical hum growing louder and more menacing with every second.

Tyler couldn't wait any longer. It was now or never.

With a fluid motion, Tyler lunged from the shadows, catching Victor off guard. In one swift move, he pressed a chloroform-soaked rag over Victor's face, wrapping his arm tightly around the man's neck. Victor's body jerked violently as he thrashed, his free hand swinging a wild punch that grazed Tyler's side. Tyler held his ground, his grip iron-tight as Victor struggled to pull the rag away.

"Go down. Go down, you sick bastard."

The two men staggered backward, Victor's hulking frame almost pulling Tyler down with him. He was strong, far stronger than Tyler anticipated, but the chloroform worked quickly. Victor's movements became sluggish, his resistance fading as his strength ebbed away.

With one last heavy breath, Victor's body went limp. He crumpled to the ground with a dull thud, the saw slipping from his grip and clattering to the floor.

Tyler stood over him, his breath coming in sharp, ragged bursts. His entire body buzzed with adrenaline, but his mind was clear. Victor was down, but it wasn't over yet. Tyler's eyes flicked to the bound women, their wide, terrified eyes locked on him. He knew what they were thinking,he could see the desperation in their gaze. They wanted to be saved.

But this wasn't about saving them.

This was about ending Victor Murcar.

Tyler stepped over the unconscious body, the woman's silent cries fading into the background as he moved toward the door. His hands were steady, his mind laser-focused. This was only the beginning.

"It's not over yet. But it will be soon."

Tyler disappeared into the shadows, leaving Victor Murcar in a heap on the cold basement floor, his reign of terror finally facing its end.

COPYCAT

Tyler stands over Victor Murcar's limp body, the soldier's face twisted unnaturally, frozen in the shock of unconsciousness. The stench of sweat and stale air thickens around him, but Tyler doesn't flinch. He kneels, wiping the slick sweat from his brow, his breaths controlled and even. The heat of the basement wraps around him like a suffocating blanket, but he maintains his focus.

"Heavy bastard." Tyler's inner voice hums with calculated annoyance as he reaches for Victor's collar. "How do I make someone like you disappear?"

Victor's body is massive, far bulkier than the usual prey Tyler hunts, but it doesn't matter. Tyler is methodical in his approach, every movement slow and deliberate. He clenches his jaw as he drags Victor's dead weight toward the stairs, inch by inch. His muscles strain, but his mind remains sharp, always calculating, always thinking two steps ahead.

"A guy like you? A goddamn war hero." Tyler's thoughts simmer beneath his calm exterior. "Someone this high-profile? Police, media... William. They'll all be watching. No mistakes. No slip-ups. You vanish tonight, Victor. Into thin air."

He reaches the basement door, pausing just before stepping through. His eyes drift back to the women bound and gagged in the shadows, their eyes pleading, wide with terror. They had witnessed everything. Victor's screams. The brutality of the night. His gut tightens for a moment, a flicker of something that feels like remorse. Disgust at the sight of them. But he quickly swallows it, locking it away. Now is not the time for weakness.

"Not about them. This isn't about them. Stick to the plan." He inhales sharply, shoving the basement door shut behind him, sealing the women inside their prison once more.

The air cools slightly as he emerges into the apartment, and the rush of adrenaline spikes through his veins as he pulls Victor's lifeless form across the cold floor. He pauses near the kitchen window, his eyes narrowing as he peers outside, scanning the empty street. No movement. No witnesses.

"The lake would've been simpler," Tyler muses as he glances down at Victor's limp body. "But I need something bigger. This has to be perfect. No one will come looking in a place like this. Not immediately, anyway."

With a grunt, he opens the back door and steps into the night, the chill biting at his skin. The car waits in the shadows, its trunk open like a waiting mouth. Tyler maneuvers Victor's body inside, muscles trembling under the weight, but determination steels his movements. He slams the trunk shut with a firm thud and climbs into the driver's seat. The roar of the engine pierces the silence as the car rumbles to life. His eyes narrow on the road ahead, his mind already shifting into the next phase.

The lights of the city blur past the windshield, glowing like distant fireflies in the night. Tyler's knuckles whiten as his grip tightens on the steering wheel, his focus locked on the mission ahead. The interior of the car feels smaller with each passing second, like the walls are closing in, but he keeps his breathing steady.

"Victor Murcar," Tyler's inner voice speaks in a slow, calculated cadence. "An elite soldier. A celebrity. A murderer. You're not like the others. Everyone will come looking for you."

His foot presses harder on the gas as the car weaves through the near-empty streets, skirting the fringes of the city. Tyler's mind is alive with strategies, contingency plans, and what-ifs. Every detail matters. Every second.

"I could dump you in the lake," he thinks, his eyes darting toward the rearview mirror, "but I need to send a message. I need to make this look... perfect."

Ahead, the towering silhouette of the abandoned skyscraper cuts into the sky, rising like a forgotten monument. It looms over the city like a gravestone, dark and foreboding. A place no one dares to visit anymore. No prying eyes. No cameras.

Perfect.

Tyler pulls the car into an alley beside the structure, parking in the shadows. He steps out, his eyes sweeping across the quiet street before making his way to the trunk. With a low grunt, he pulls Victor's body from the car, draping the man's massive form over his shoulder like a sack of cement. His muscles scream in protest, but Tyler is relentless. He drags Victor toward the entrance of the abandoned building, the weight of the task pulling at him, but not enough to break his resolve.

"This place is a tomb," Tyler muses, pushing through the decaying door, stepping into the hollow, dust-filled space. "No one comes here. Not anymore."

The air inside is thick with dust, the faint smell of mildew and rot hanging in the darkness. Tyler's footsteps echo down the deserted hallways as he carries Victor's body deeper into the building. The floor creaks beneath him with each step, but the sound is muffled, swallowed by the oppressive quiet.

"Victor Murcar, the war hero," Tyler's thoughts hum darkly as he makes his way to the stairwell. "But you're no soldier anymore. You're just another killer. A copycat, at that."

Reaching the stairwell, Tyler shifts Victor's weight on his shoulder, taking the stairs one at a time. His breath comes in shallow bursts, his body struggling under the weight, but his mind is sharp.

The climb is slow, deliberate. Each floor is darker than the last, the walls crumbling with neglect. But Tyler isn't here to admire the decay. He's here for one reason.

At the top of the stairwell, Tyler pauses, pressing his hand to the door. The rooftop is just beyond.

He pushes it open, stepping into the open air.The wind whips around him, tugging at his clothes as he emerges onto the rooftop. The city sprawls out below, glittering like a sea of lights. For a moment, Tyler stands at the edge, gazing out over the horizon, feeling the weight of the moment settle over him.

Victor's body slumps onto the cold concrete as Tyler lays him down, his mind already racing to the next step.

"He's not just a target. He's a message. One that has to be loud enough to make them notice but quiet enough to keep them guessing."

Tyler crouches beside the unconscious figure, pulling a small vial from his pocket. Smelling salts.

He waves them under Victor's nose, watching as the man's body jerks awake with a gasp. Victor's eyes snap open, wide with confusion and fear. He glances around wildly, taking in his surroundings,the ropes binding his wrists and ankles, the darkened sky above, the city lights below.

The rooftop was silent except for the faint hum of the city below. Tyler stood motionless, his eyes locked on Victor Murcar, who was bound and gagged, hanging precariously from the edge of the building. A thick noose was tied around Victor's neck, the rope taut as Tyler held the other end, keeping him from falling to his death,at least for now.

Victor's eyes darted frantically, his breath coming in ragged gasps as he struggled against the bindings. His feet dangled inches from the edge, and every slight movement sent jolts of panic through him as the rope around his neck tightened.

Tyler remained calm, his voice low and menacing. "You wanted to play in my world, Victor. You thought you understood me. But you don't. You never did."

Victor's muffled cries for help were useless. There was no one around to hear him, and even if there were, it wouldn't matter. Tyler's grip on the rope tightened slightly, causing Victor to jerk forward, choking as the noose dug deeper into his neck.

"I kill because I am death," Tyler said coldly. "You? You kill because you're pathetic. A copycat. A pretender."

Victor's muffled protests grew more desperate as his body squirmed, but Tyler ignored them. He crouched down next to Victor's trembling form, his voice soft but filled with icy malice.

"William is still looking for me," Tyler said. "You're going to tell him to stop. Right now."

He reached into Victor's coat pocket and pulled out his phone, then calmly removed the gag from Victor's mouth. Victor gasped for air, his voice raspy and strained from the pressure on his neck. Tyler raised an eyebrow, waiting.

Victor's voice was hoarse, broken by fear. "Please… please, I'll do anything. I'll tell him. I'll make the call. Just… don't kill me."

Tyler's expression remained impassive. He handed the phone to Victor and dialed William's number, keeping his hand wrapped around the rope, ensuring Victor wouldn't forget how precarious his situation was.

The phone rang, and after a tense moment, William answered. "Victor? Where the hell are you? I've been trying to reach you all night."

Victor's voice trembled as he spoke, the terror unmistakable in every word. "William…

it's me. I need you to call off the search. There's… there's nothing left to find. I'm leaving town."

William hesitated. "What are you talking about? Victor, you've been acting strange. What's going on?"

Victor glanced at Tyler, his body shaking as he felt the noose tightening slightly with each second that passed. "I'm serious, William. Call off the search. It's over. I've… I've made a mistake. There's nothing else to look for."

William's tone softened, as if trying to make sense of what he was hearing. "Victor, are you in trouble? What's going on? You can talk to me."

Victor's breath hitched. "Just trust me. Stop the search. Please."

There was a long silence on the other end of the line. Finally, William sighed. "Alright, Victor. If you're sure. I'll stop the search. But you owe me an explanation when you get back."

Relief washed over Victor, his body going limp in the noose as he let out a shaky breath. "Thank you… thank you, William."

William paused, then added, "Just get out of there, Victor. We'll talk when you're safe."

Victor ended the call, his trembling fingers barely able to hold the phone. He looked up at Tyler, hope flickering in his eyes. "I did what you asked. I called him. He's stopping the search."

Tyler's eyes remained cold and emotionless. "I heard."

Victor nodded frantically. "So… I can go now, right? You said if I made the call, you'd let me live."

Tyler tilted his head slightly, as if considering the words. Then, without a hint of emotion, he said, "Did I?"

The color drained from Victor's face. His mouth opened, but no sound came out as the realization hit him. "You… you said…"

Tyler crouched down beside him again, his voice calm, almost gentle. "I said you'd live if you called him. But I never said for how long."

Victor's eyes widened in horror. "Please… no… please! I did everything you asked!"

Tyler stood up slowly, his hand still gripping the rope. "You did," he acknowledged, as if it were nothing more than a passing observation.

Victor's breathing became rapid and panicked as he struggled to form words. "You promised… you said,"

"I said I'd let you live long enough to call him," Tyler corrected, his voice cold. "But you're not walking away from this."
Without another word, Tyler stepped back and released his hold on the rope. The tension in the noose snapped instantly, and Victor plummeted over the edge of the building, the rope around his neck snapping taut as his body jerked violently. The sickening sound of bone snapping echoed through the night air. Victor's body hung limply, swinging in the breeze as Tyler stood above, watching in silence. The city lights blinked far below, indifferent to the life that had just ended.
 "I kill because I am death. And death shows no mercy."
Tyler turned away, his steps deliberate and unhurried as he moved away from the edge. There was no need to look back. Victor had played his part, and now, like all the others, he

was nothing more than a forgotten piece in the game.

He pocketed Victor's phone and melted into the shadows, his work unfinished, but never rushed. Tomorrow, the city would wake to another headline, another mystery. But by then, Tyler would be long gone, moving toward his next target.

The world below carried on as it always had, unaware that death had visited its rooftops tonight.

A FRACTURED PIECE

Tyler quietly unlocked the front door, stepping inside the dimly lit house. The soft glow of the TV filled the living room, flickering across the walls like shadows cast by ghosts. Emily was curled up on the couch, the remote loosely held in her hand as the late-night movie played in the background. Her hair was slightly tousled, and her eyes were half-closed with sleepiness, but she was awake, just barely.

Seeing her there, peaceful, tugged at something deep inside Tyler. For a moment, the horrors of the night melted away, swallowed by the comforting sight of Emily in the quiet safety of their home.

"She has no idea. No clue about what I just did. And she never will," Tyler thought as he closed the door behind him, the quiet click barely registering in the silence of the room. He slipped off his shoes and walked toward her, his muscles still taut with adrenaline, though his face remained calm, composed, as if he had spent the last few hours working on his book rather than disposing of a body.

"Hey, babe," Tyler said softly, his voice breaking the stillness. "You're still up?"

Emily glanced over at him, her sleepy eyes brightening as a warm smile spread across her face. "I couldn't sleep," she murmured, stretching her arms above her head. "Thought I'd wait up for you."

He leaned down to kiss her forehead, his lips brushing against her skin. Even as he sat beside her, pulling her closer, his mind raced with images of Victor, of the dismembered body, of the lake swallowing the evidence. But he shoved it all down, focusing instead on the warmth of Emily beside him.

"I went for a walk to clear my head," he lied smoothly, the words slipping out as easily as breathing. "Got caught up thinking about some ideas for the book."

Emily rested her head against his shoulder, her fingers tracing light patterns on his arm. "Yeah? Any breakthroughs?" she asked, her voice drowsy but curious.

Tyler smiled, as if the ideas crowding his head were about plotlines and character arcs, not blood and murder. "Actually, yeah. I was walking around, and it just hit me. I couldn't shake it, so I stopped by a café to write it out before I forgot. Lost track of time, but I think the book's ending just got a whole lot better."

Emily lifted her head to look at him, her eyes sparkling with admiration. She had always loved how passionate he was about his work, how deeply he dived into his stories. "Sounds like a stroke of genius," she said, her smile widening. "I can't wait to read it when you're done."

He brushed a strand of hair behind her ear, his touch gentle, though his thoughts were anything but. "She deserves more. More than the lies, more than the double life. But I can't stop. I won't stop."

Tyler pulled her closer, savoring the feel of her in his arms. Despite everything,the darkness that clung to him like a second skin,there was a genuine love for Emily buried beneath it all. A love that, in another life, could have been simple and pure. But in this life, it was tainted, corrupted by secrets and blood.

"I was thinking…" Tyler's voice trailed off, hesitating for just a second. He looked down at her, the perfect picture of innocence curled up against him. "After the book signing tomorrow morning, maybe we could get out of town for a bit. Just the two of us. Go to some museums, have a nice day together."

Emily's eyes lit up at the suggestion. She sat up a little, her excitement bubbling to the surface. "That sounds amazing! We haven't had a day like that in forever. I'd love it."

Tyler grinned, glad to see her so happy. He leaned in, brushing his lips against hers, their kiss lingering longer than usual. There was something deeper in it tonight,a shared passion,but for Tyler, it was also a reminder of what kept him tethered to this life. Emily was his anchor to normality, the thing that stopped him from slipping completely into the darkness.

The kiss deepened, and for a brief moment, all the noise in Tyler's head faded away,the murders, the lies, the blood,it all dissipated in the warmth of Emily's embrace. He lost himself in the feel of her lips against his, the way her hands gently cupped his face, how her body molded to his as she leaned into him. For that fleeting moment, Tyler was just a man in love.

"I could stop," he thought, his heart pounding in his chest. "Right now. I could just… let go of the other side. Be with her. Make a life."

But as the kiss ended and they pulled back slightly, Tyler's eyes flickered with the truth he refused to acknowledge. He couldn't stop. Not now. Not ever.

Emily rested her head against his chest, her breathing even and steady. Tyler wrapped his arms around her, holding her close as they sank further into the couch. The TV droned on in the background, but neither of them paid it any attention.

"We'll make a day of it tomorrow," Tyler murmured, his voice soft as his hand absently stroked her hair. "After the signing, it'll just be us."

Emily smiled against his chest, her voice barely a whisper as sleep pulled her under. "Just us… I like the sound of that."

Tyler stared up at the ceiling, his fingers continuing their gentle rhythm through her hair. "Maybe this is enough. Maybe I don't need to be both. But… what if I do?"

He glanced down at her, a small smile tugging at the corner of his lips as her breathing slowed, steady and soft.

Tomorrow, he would be the loving boyfriend. The successful author. The perfect son. But

tonight… tonight, he was something else entirely.

As Emily drifted off to sleep, Tyler's mind buzzed with the weight of his double life, the lies he wove, and the darkness that lurked just beneath the surface. For now, though, he allowed himself this fleeting moment of peace, knowing it wouldn't last.

Emily shifted slightly, her body adjusting in his arms, her voice soft but clear. "Tyler?" she whispered, her words slurred with sleep. "Yeah?" he answered, his voice low.

"Where did you really go tonight?" she asked, her tone gentle, but there was a subtle edge to the question, a hint of suspicion lurking beneath the surface.

Tyler's heart skipped a beat, but he didn't flinch. He kept his voice even, calm. "I told you. Just went for a walk. Needed some air."

Emily didn't respond right away, and for a moment, Tyler thought she'd fallen back asleep. But then she whispered, "I believe you."

But her words didn't quite match the way she shifted in his arms, a slight tension in her body that hadn't been there before. Tyler's jaw clenched, but he said nothing, holding her close as she finally let sleep take her.

"She knows. She's starting to see through it," he thought, the peaceful moment dissolving into something sharper, more fragile.

Tyler closed his eyes, letting the quiet of the house settle around them, but he knew it wouldn't last.

THE CALM BEFORE

Morning sunlight filtered through the curtains, casting a soft, golden glow over the kitchen. Emily moved with ease at the stove, her humming barely audible over the sizzle of pancakes. The air was filled with the comforting scents of breakfast,fresh coffee, scrambled eggs, and the sweetness of syrup. The aroma wrapped the room in a sense of warmth, creating a stark contrast to the thoughts brewing inside Tyler's head.

He sat at the kitchen table, one hand cradling his coffee mug, the other scrolling absently through his phone. His eyes would lift every few moments, catching glimpses of Emily, her back to him, hair tied up in a loose bun, the kind of effortless look she pulled off so naturally. She was glowing in the morning light, and for a second, Tyler let himself focus on her,just her.

Emily turned around, carrying two plates piled high with pancakes, fruit, and eggs. She grinned as she set the plates down, sliding one toward Tyler.

"Breakfast is served," she said, a playful smile tugging at the corners of her lips.

"Figured you needed a good start before your big day."

Tyler returned the smile, though it didn't quite reach his eyes. "You're spoiling me. Thanks, Em." He looked down at the pancakes, the perfect golden brown that reminded him of quieter mornings,mornings where the weight of what he did in the dark wasn't looming over him.

Emily sat across from him, taking a bite of her food before glancing up, curiosity dancing in her eyes. "So, book signing first, then what? You've got something up your sleeve. I can tell."

He nodded, swallowing the coffee that suddenly felt too hot, too bitter. "Yeah, I've got something planned." His smile widened, though inside, the lie settled like a stone in his stomach. "Thought we'd check out that science museum after."

Her face lit up with excitement, the kind of childlike joy that made him almost forget what the day really held. "You're serious? I've been dying to go! This is perfect."

Tyler nodded again, trying to mirror her enthusiasm. "Yeah, figured it'd be a fun way to spend the day together. We haven't had a chance to do something like this in a while."

Emily reached across the table, squeezing his hand. "You're amazing, you know that?" She smiled, her eyes full of warmth. "This is exactly what we need."

Tyler squeezed back, feeling the guilt and conflict stir inside him. Anything for you, Em, he thought but couldn't bring himself to say out loud. He couldn't tarnish this moment with the truth.

His thoughts darkened. The museum isn't just a date spot today. She works there,my next target. A quiet drug dealer, lacing fentanyl behind the scenes. By day, she's a respected museum curator, but at night… Today isn't just about us. It's about justice.

"Tyler?" Emily's voice pulled him from the downward spiral of his mind.

"Hm?" He blinked, offering her a reassuring smile. "Sorry, just got caught up thinking."

Emily shook her head, a soft chuckle escaping her. "Always lost in your own world. Must be another plot twist you're cooking up." Her eyes sparkled with admiration, the same way they always did when she talked about his writing.

"Something like that," he said, offering a smirk. More like cleaning up someone's plot. He forced the thought away, taking a bite of pancake, letting the sweetness dissolve on his tongue.

She tilted her head, watching him closely. "You're sure everything's okay? You've been a little… off lately."

Tyler's grip tightened slightly around his fork, but he kept his expression even. "I'm fine," he lied smoothly. "Just a lot on my mind with the book and the signing."

Emily smiled, clearly satisfied with his answer. "I get it. You've been juggling a lot." She paused for a moment before her smile softened into something gentler, something deeper. "But, after today, we can just relax, right? Just us."

Tyler met her gaze, feeling a pang in his chest. He wanted to tell her everything. He wanted to believe in the simplicity she spoke of. But there was no just them. Not anymore.

"Yeah," he said, his voice quieter, more thoughtful. "Just us."

Emily turned her attention back to her food, but Tyler's mind continued to spin, the gears in his head grinding against each other. He could picture the museum, the narrow corridors, the closed-off rooms where his target worked. He imagined slipping in unnoticed, blending into the crowd of tourists and families, just another visitor. It would be clean. It would be fast.

Emily sighed contentedly, bringing his attention back to the table. "You know," she started, her voice teasing but soft, "I think this is the first time you've actually planned a day like this without me pushing for it."

He chuckled, feigning amusement. "What can I say? I'm full of surprises."

Her eyes twinkled. "I'll believe it when I see it. But seriously, Tyler, I'm glad you're taking a break. You've been… distant."

Tyler paused, his fork halfway to his mouth. "Distant?"

She shrugged, reaching for her coffee. "Not in a bad way, just… preoccupied. You're always so focused. I guess I'm just happy you're letting go for a day."

He felt his chest tighten. She wasn't wrong. He had been distant,trapped between two worlds, two versions of himself. The writer she loved and the man he became when the darkness called.

"I've just been stressed about the book, that's all," Tyler replied, his voice steady, though his thoughts were anything but. He could feel her studying him, her eyes searching for something beneath the surface.

"I know," Emily said quietly, sipping her coffee. "I just hope that once this book is out, you'll be able to relax."
Tyler gave a noncommittal nod. "Yeah, me too."

The kitchen fell into a comfortable silence, but beneath it, there was tension,unspoken and lingering. Tyler could feel it, the way her questions danced around the edges of suspicion. She wasn't entirely convinced, and maybe, just maybe, she was starting to notice the cracks.

But she wouldn't push. Not yet.

Tyler glanced up from his plate, watching Emily as she continued to eat, her mind seemingly at ease. She has no idea what I've done. What I will do. And she can't ever know.

For now, though, he allowed himself to exist in this moment. The quiet domesticity, the warmth of the sun spilling over them, the smell of pancakes and coffee. A day like any other,at least to Emily.

But for Tyler, this was just the beginning of the end.

THE MASK OF A AUTHOR

The bookstore was packed with excited fans, their faces lit with anticipation as they clutched copies of Tyler Grayson's latest book. The sign at the entrance proudly announced, "Tyler Grayson Book Signing Event Today!" A few posters of Tyler's brooding author portrait lined the walls. His dark hair, carefully tousled for the shoot, and the confident smile he wore looked effortlessly charming, an image that had undoubtedly helped sell thousands of books.

Inside, Tyler sat behind a long table, a sharp contrast to the chaos around him. His professional grin stayed in place, the role of the charming author now second nature. Beside him, Emily beamed with quiet pride. Her warm hazel eyes followed every fan interaction, and she radiated a quiet joy, glad to be a part of Tyler's success.

Tyler's fingers worked swiftly, signing book after book, offering short personal messages to his fans as they stepped up. The line was long, snaking through the aisles, but

Tyler had developed a rhythm, each encounter a brief dance of small talk and autographs.

"Thanks so much for coming out today," he said to a fan, smiling as he handed over the signed book. "I hope you enjoy the story." The fan, a young woman with bright red lipstick and an overly enthusiastic smile, giggled as she accepted the book.

"I'm sure I will! I just love everything you write," she gushed, leaning in just a bit too close.

Tyler kept his smile polite, the words flowing easily despite the woman's clear flirtation. "Glad to hear it. Thanks for the support."

As the fan sauntered away, her hips swaying in an exaggerated manner, Emily's eyes narrowed ever so slightly, her smile faltering for just a second before she composed herself. She leaned over, nudging Tyler playfully, masking her discomfort with humor.

"You're really in your element, aren't you?" she said, her voice light but with an underlying tension Tyler didn't miss.

He turned to her, his smile softening into something more genuine. "You know me. I could do this all day," he said, squeezing her hand briefly. Then he added, "But maybe later we'll swap the writing for something more relaxing. Like a dinosaur skeleton at the science museum."

Emily chuckled, though there was still a glimmer of something more behind her laugh. "You're still stuck on that museum trip, aren't you?"

"I want to show you the coolest parts of the city," Tyler said, winking at her. "Plus, I get to hang out with my favorite person."

Emily's tension melted away at that, her smile growing more sincere. She gave his arm a gentle squeeze, her warmth returning.

As they shared the moment, a stunning blonde approached the table, her designer dress hugging her curves perfectly. She was wearing a shade of lipstick that seemed to pop against her flawless skin, and her eyes sparkled as she leaned in.

"Mr. Grayson, I'm such a huge fan," she purred, pushing a book toward him. "You're even more handsome in person."

Tyler chuckled awkwardly, signing her book. "Thanks. Glad you could make it," he said, handing the book back with practiced ease.

The blonde lingered, her eyes raking over Tyler, and for a second, she glanced at Emily with a subtle air of superiority. "I can't wait to read your next one," she added, her voice dripping with suggestion.

Emily's smile was tight, her posture stiffening beside Tyler. "He's been working really hard on it," she chimed in, her tone friendly but edged with something sharper. Tyler could feel the tension, though he did his best to smooth over the moment.

"Thanks for coming," he said again, dismissing the blonde with a final smile as she sauntered away, her hips swaying in a way that Tyler knew hadn't escaped Emily's notice.

As the line continued to move, Emily's eyes occasionally flicked toward each woman that came up to Tyler, especially the ones who seemed a bit too interested in more than just his writing. Though Emily tried to remain composed, the subtle tension was building. She reached for her cup of coffee, taking small sips between signing books, her face a careful mask of calm.

Tyler leaned toward her during a lull, his voice low. "You okay?"

Emily looked at him, her smile faint. "Of course. Why wouldn't I be?"

Tyler recognized the deflection, but before he could press further, another fan stepped forward. A statuesque brunette with long legs and a dangerously low-cut top slid her book across the table.

"I've read everything you've ever written," she breathed, her fingers brushing lightly against Tyler's as he signed her book. "You're an inspiration."

Tyler could feel Emily stiffen next to him, though she kept her expression neutral. The brunette flashed Emily a cursory glance before turning all of her attention back to Tyler.

"I'm sure this one will be just as brilliant," the woman said, leaning in just enough for Tyler to notice the faint scent of her perfume.

"Thanks," Tyler replied, his smile automatic as he quickly handed the book back. The brunette lingered for a moment longer, her gaze smoldering before she finally walked away.

Emily didn't say anything, but Tyler could feel the tension radiating from her. He shifted uncomfortably in his seat, his mind spinning as he tried to juggle the various emotions swirling around him—the professional demands of the signing, the creeping guilt of his secret life, and the subtle jealousy that was beginning to simmer between them.

He turned to Emily, placing a hand on her leg under the table. "You sure you're okay?" he asked, his voice low.

Emily gave him a tight smile. "I'm fine. Just... a lot of attention today."

Tyler could see she wasn't entirely fine, but he let it go for now, focusing back on the line of fans. They were nearing the end of the event, the crowd thinning out as the last few people approached the table. Tyler signed books mechanically, his thoughts elsewhere.

Just as the event was winding down, William Grayson and Kate Miller entered the bookstore. Tyler hadn't expected them to show up, and his eyes widened in surprise when he spotted his father among the remaining crowd.

"Dad! Kate!" Tyler stood up, flashing a boyish grin.

William approached with an easy smile. "Well, look at you. All grown up and famous."

Tyler couldn't help but laugh, stepping forward to embrace his father. It was a rare, relaxed moment between them. William, usually so stern and focused on work, seemed genuinely at ease for once.

"You actually made it," Tyler said, shaking his head in disbelief.

"Of course we did," Kate chimed in. "We wouldn't miss your big event."

Emily stood up and smiled warmly at the pair, her previous tension momentarily forgotten. "It's great to see you both."

William glanced at the line of fans, his eyes twinkling with pride. "You've done well for yourself, son."

Tyler smiled, feeling a mixture of pride and guilt at his father's praise. The life William thought he saw—the successful author, the loving boyfriend—was only half the story. The other half, the darker half, was hidden beneath the surface, lurking like a shadow.

As William and Kate prepared to leave, William gave Tyler a rare, affectionate pat on the back. "We're proud of you, Tyler. Keep it up."

Tyler nodded, swallowing the lump of emotion that rose in his throat. "Thanks, Dad."

Kate gave Emily a hug, her smile warm. "You two have fun at the museum. It sounds like a great day."

Emily beamed, clearly excited for their upcoming plans. "We will. Thanks for coming."

As William and Kate walked away, Tyler watched them go, his thoughts swirling with conflicting emotions. He couldn't help but think about how different his life might have been if he had followed a different path. If he hadn't embraced the darkness inside him.

But the moment passed, and he turned back to Emily, his smile back in place.

"Ready to head out?" he asked, his voice light.

Emily nodded, her excitement for the day ahead returning. "I'm ready."

Tyler packed up the remaining books and cash, carefully stowing everything in his bag. As they walked out of the bookstore hand in hand, Tyler felt a brief moment of peace. But lurking just beneath the surface was the truth he couldn't ignore—the museum trip wasn't just for Emily. He had other plans.

As they approached the car, Tyler's eyes flicked toward a sleek black sports car parked down the street. Inside, Jerry West, the journalist, sat watching them, his gaze sharp and predatory. Tyler's jaw tightened. Jerry had been poking around too much lately, getting too close.

But that was a problem for later. For now, Tyler had a date with Emily—and a target to eliminate.

"Let's pack for our adventure," Tyler said, his voice smooth and confident as he opened the car door for her.

Emily beamed at him, completely unaware of the storm brewing just beneath the surface.

"I can't wait," she said, her voice full of excitement.

Tyler smiled, his dark thoughts hidden behind a charming façade. "One more target," he thought, "and then I'll give Emily the day she deserves."

As they drove away, Jerry West watched them from the distance, his curiosity piqued. "Let's see where this leads, Grayson," he muttered to himself, shifting in his seat as he scribbled more notes. The hunt was on

SHADOWS OF SECRETS

Tyler stood at the edge of the bed, folding a sweater with ease, his expression blank, almost detached. On the other side of the bed, Emily hummed softly, the melody carrying a sense of calm that contrasted the sharp tension building in the pit of Tyler's stomach. Her smile was effortless, and her movements were relaxed and unhurried as she packed her bag, the excitement evident in the bounce of her steps.

"I'm really excited about this," she said, breaking the silence that settled between them. She held up a pair of neatly folded jeans and placed them into her suitcase, glancing over at Tyler with a smile that reached deep into her hazel eyes. "You know, just getting out of the city, away from everything."

Tyler looked back up from putting the sweater in his bag, catching her gaze for a moment before he turned his attention back to his bag. He offered her a half-smile, one that didn't quite reach his eyes, and shrugged. "Yeah, it'll be good. Relaxing, just us…. And we might even get to meet up with Tony."

Emily's hands stilled, and the room seemed to grow a fraction quieter as she turned to face him fully, a curious arch forming in her eyebrows. Her voice carried a hint of skepticism as she asked, "Tony? You mean the Tony that throws crazy parties?"

Tyler chuckled, but there was an unnoticeable edge in the sound, something guarded that lingered beneath the surface, his Abyssal Passenger. "Yeah, Tony! He said he might have something going on this weekend, I figured we're in town, mine as well go."

Emily let out a short laugh, but there was an undertone of concern that didn't quite match her amusement. "Last time we went to one of his parties, you ended up beating the living hell out of a guy."

A shadow passed over Tyler's face, darkening his features as his expression hardened. The memory flickered through his mind, his fist slamming into the guy's jaw, the crack of bone, the blood, the satisfying rush of power surging through him as he made his point clear. "I mean, he was asking for it," He replied, his voice taking on a cold, protective edge. "No one touches my beautiful girl like that."

Emily relaxed, moving toward him with a gentle sway, her hand finding its place over his head. She looked up into his eyes, her voice dropping to a whisper. "I know. And honestly… I liked it, seeing you protect what you love. But still you spent the night in the slammer."

She tried to lighten the mood, flashing him a light hearted smile, but the worry didn't leave her eyes entirely. "We shouldn't make a habit out of asking your dad to bail your ass out of jail."

Tyler grinned, His Abyssal Passenger gazing out on the world for a moment as he wrapped his arm around her waist, pulling her closer. Yeah, I guess. But I'd do it again if I had to."

His tone carried weight beneath the words, a promise that went beyond his calm surface. Emily heard it, but she didn't fully understand it, and she brushed off the edge that crept into the back of her mind with a lighthearted shake of her head. "Just try to keep it chill this time, okay? I don't want to have to pick you up from the police station again."

Tyler's expression chilled as he looked down at her, his arm tightening slightly around her as if he was anchoring himself to the moment. He nodded, forcing a smile that was meant to reassure her. "I promise. This weekend is about us, No drama, just good times."

Emily's smile glistened, and she leaned into him, resting her head against his chest for a brief moment. His heart beat calmly under her ear, its rhythm betraying nothing of the thoughts swirling in his mind. They stood like that for a few seconds longer, a fragile facade of normalcy holding them in place before they finally returned to the task at hand.

As they packed in comfortable silence, Tyler's thoughts drifted to the plans he laid out in secret, the things he'd do under the cover of the night, the justice he would deliver with his own two hands. "Tony's party might be wild." he thought, "but I have bigger plans for this weekend. Plans that no one, not even Emily can know about."

Tyler glanced toward the window as a shiver of unease ran through him, but he shrugged it off, brushing off the feeling as just pre-trip jitters. He finished packing, zipping up his bag with a decisive motion.

Outside, a sleek black SUV parked a short distance down the road, hardly visible through the shade of the large oak tree in front of Tyler's apartment. Jerry West sat inside, his posture relaxed yet alert as he scribbled in a leather-bound notebook, his eyes fixed on the house in front of him. He could see the faint movement of Tyler and Emily through the second floor window, their silhouettes casting shadows against the drawn curtains.

`   Jerry's gaze sharpened, his mind racing through the pieces he had been gathering, trying to fit them together into a coherent story. He watched as Tyler moved through the house, his every step calculated, his demeanor casual. But Jerry knew better than to trust his appearance, "What the hell are you hiding, Tyler?" he muttered to himself, his voice barely more than a whisper

Jerry's notebook filled with hasty notes, and observations of Tyler's recent behavior, the strange disappearances of criminals around town, the subtle cracks in the carefully crafted persona of the city's best author. Jerry had a hunch that whatever story Tyler was living in, it wasn't the one who sold to the public.

Emily aggressively zipped up her bag, giving Tyler a playful shove that broke the tension between them. She looked at him, the excitement bubbling back to her surface.

"Alright then hot stuff, let's get this show on the road."

Tyler returned her smile, though the edges of it didn't quite match the pull the Abyssal Passenger had on his mind. He grabbed his bag from the bed and followed her out of the room, his footsteps lighter than they had been seconds ago. But his thoughts remain anchored in the darkness, even as he tries to push them aside. "It's just a weekend," he reminded himself. "Just a few day's to love my girlfriend."

As they headed out of the room, the last rays of the afternoon sunlight spilled through the window, casting a long shadow across the wall. The air felt heavy with unspoken truths, with secrets that pressed against the fabric of their lives, threatening to unravel at any moment.

Tyler took a deep breath as they stepped out into the hallway, ease settling into his posture. Emily's laughter echoes down the corridor, bright and carefree, while Tyler's thoughts remained hidden beneath the surface. "If only she knew the truth," he mused. Glancing at her from the corner of his eye as they walked down the stairs. "I'd give anything to be the man she thinks I am."

But that version of himself was a ghost, a meer mirage he could only maintain for so long before his Abyssal Passenger crept back in.

Jerry's pen stilled as he caught the sight of Tyler and Emily walking out from the front door, their bags in hand. He watched as Tyler locked up the house, his movements smooth, almost too practiced. There was something off about the way Tyler glanced around his neighborhood, a fleeting look of suspicion that vanished as quickly as it had appeared.

Jerry's grip tightened around his pen. His curiosity turned into something sharper. "Let's see where this leads, Grayson," he muttered, settling deeper into the shadows of the car.

Tyler opened the passenger door for Emily, a small smile playing at his lips as she settled into her seat. He looked back at the house before sliding into the driver's seat beside her. As the engine rumbled to life, a sense of finality settled over the scene, like the closing of a book that had only just begun to reveal its darkest chapters.

The car pulled away from the curb, merging into the flow of traffic, and Jerry watched them disappear down the street, his expression thoughtful. His notebook lay open on the dashboard, filled with the beginnings of a story yet to reach its conclusion. Whatever Tyler was hiding, Jerry was determined to uncover it, no matter how deep the ink stains ran.

Inside the car, Tyler glanced at Emily as she settled back into her seat, her eyes closing as she let the wind whip through her hair. He forced a smile, one that barely touched the edges of his corrupt thoughts. The tension between the carefully crafted life and the darkness lurking within him simmered beneath the surface, unseen by Emily but very much alive in his mind.

He reached over, taking Emily's hand as they drove, his grip firm, and possessive. "One , more weekend, one more game," he thought to himself, the words ringing in his dark, corrupt mind. "Then maybe I'll find a way to have it all… or lose everything."

And as the car rolled on, vanishing into the distance, the shows followed close behind, promising secrets yet to be revealed.

HIDDEN CURRENTS

The sun streamed through the windshield casting long beams of light across the dashboard as Tyler maneuvered the car along the highway. He kept his focus on the road, his hands gripping the steering wheel with a tension he could not quite shake. Beside him, Emily shifted in her seat, fiddling with the radio until she found a station playing a heavy melody that filled the car with a sense of excitement. She rested one hand on Tyler's knee, offering him a reassuring squeeze, her other hand tapping aggressively to the drum line of the music.

"You know, I've been thinking about names again," she said, as she turned down the music from the radio. She shot him a sidelong glance, a playful smile dancing on her lips. "For the baby, you know... whenever we decide to get to that part."

Tyler forced a chuckle, trying to match her lighthearted tone. "Oh yeah? And what's the latest contender?"

Emily's eyes glinted with mischief, and she rolled her eyes. "No, no, you first. I want to know what name you've been holding out on me."

Tyler's smile tightened, and he shifted in his seat, the leather creaking beneath him. He was all too aware of the black car trailing a few lengths behind them, its dark exterior blending into the shadows cast by the trees lining the highway. He knew it was Jerry. He recognized the make and model—just like the one that had been parked down the street outside their house that morning. Forcing himself to focus on Emily, he pushed the tension down. "Alright, alright. I've got one—if it's a boy... how about Dexter?"

Emily paused, her hands stilling on the radio as she turned fully toward him. Her face lit up with a smile, her eyes wide with delight. "Dexter? Oh my God, Ty, I love it. Dexter Grayson—it sounds so... strong."

Tyler risked a longer glance at her, his heart softening for a moment at her genuine excitement. Her warmth was like a balm against the darkness that lurked within him. "You think so? I thought it might be a little... dark."

Emily shook her head adamantly, strands of her hair brushing against the car seat. "No way. It's perfect. Besides, who wouldn't want a badass name like Dexter?"

Tyler let out a laugh, but his eyes flicked back to the rearview mirror, his smile fading as he caught sight of Jerry's car still keeping pace behind them. His blood began to simmer, a low burn of anger bubbling up inside him. What the hell is Jerry doing? How long is he planning to follow them?

Emily's voice cut through his thoughts. "And if it's a girl... well, you already know my choice."

Tyler feigned a thoughtful expression, raising an eyebrow as if trying to remember. "Hmm, remind me..."

"Aislinn!" Emily said, her voice bubbling with enthusiasm. "After my favorite character in that book I told you about."

Tyler nodded, the name rolling around in his mind. "Right, right. Aislinn Grayson. I gotta say, it's got a nice ring to it."

Emily's excitement was contagious, and for a moment, Tyler let himself relax, letting the thought of a future—one that wasn't marred by secrets—take shape in his mind. But as much as he tried to focus on the present, the nagging presence of Jerry's car loomed large in the back of his mind, a shadow that refused to let go.

Emily beamed at him, leaning back in her seat with a contented sigh. "I'm so excited for today. Can you believe it's been two years since we first went to the science museum?"

Tyler blinked, Emily's words pulling him back into the conversation. He glanced at her, seeing the genuine joy in her face, and nodded. "Yeah, I remember that."

Emily's laughter filled the car, a sound full of nostalgia. "That was such a crazy day. I still can't believe Kate introduced us right after that... crime scene. What were the odds?"

Tyler felt a flicker of memory surface—Kate, her voice tired after a long day, introducing him to Emily at the scene of a crime that had left a mark on all of them. He swallowed hard, forcing himself to nod, keeping his expression neutral even as the memories rushed back. That was when he first started killing.

Emily's expression sobered, and she glanced out the window, the lightheartedness slipping from her face. "I mean, that crime scene was horrible. That poor kid..."

She shook her head, as if trying to banish the memory, but Tyler could see the haunted look in her eyes. He gripped the steering wheel tighter, his knuckles turning white. He remembered it too—every gruesome detail. He remembered the chaos, the look in the kid's eyes, the helplessness that had clawed at him. He remembered the overwhelming need to take justice into his own hands.

"Yeah, it was awful. But... at least they caught him," he said, his voice strained. He could hear the tension in his own words, and he knew Emily heard it too. Her hand slipped from his knee, moving to curl around his, offering a gentle squeeze.

"I know. But hey, let's not let that spoil our day, okay?" she said, her voice brightening, though a shadow lingered in her eyes. "We've got a book signing, a trip down memory lane, and... maybe, just maybe, some cotton candy if we're lucky."

Tyler forced a chuckle, glancing at her. Her optimism was relentless, her warmth a stark contrast to the darkness he carried within. It was part of what he loved about her—how she could always find the light, even when he couldn't.

Emily changed the subject with a smile. "Speaking of your books... your new one, it's so different from the others. I mean, a romance? You surprised me with that."

Tyler offered a half-shrug, his gaze fixed on the road ahead. "I thought I'd... switch it up a bit. And I guess... a lot of it was inspired by us."

Emily's eyes widened, and a blush crept up her cheeks, a smile slowly spreading across her face. "Really? You never said that."

Tyler shrugged again, keeping his tone casual, though the lie tasted bitter on his tongue. "I guess I wanted it to be a surprise."

Emily's smile grew, and she leaned back in her seat, her gaze lingering on him with a tenderness that made something inside him ache. "You know, you're full of surprises, Tyler Grayson."

Tyler's smile tightened as he glanced again into the rearview mirror, seeing Jerry's car still trailing them, its presence like a dark cloud on the horizon. His inner monologue took on a harsher edge, thoughts swirling with barely concealed anger. "What do you want, Jerry? You think you can just follow me? Watch me? You're making a mistake. A big one."

He forced his expression to soften as he turned back to Emily, his voice dropping to a softer, more intimate tone. "Yeah, and today's just getting started."

Emily didn't notice the tension in his voice, the way his eyes kept darting to the mirror. She simply smiled, looking forward, her hand resting lightly on his knee again. Her expression was open, trusting, oblivious to the storm brewing inside him.

The road stretched out before them, the science museum looming closer in the distance, its glass dome reflecting the afternoon sun. Tyler's heart quickened as they neared their destination, but his mind remained tethered to the black car behind them. He knew Jerry was there, watching, waiting. And Tyler knew that it was only a matter of time before he'd have to deal with this threat.

As they turned off the highway, merging onto a quieter road lined with trees, Tyler's eyes flicked back to the mirror one last time. Jerry's car remained in view, keeping a cautious distance, like a predator stalking its prey.

Tyler forced a breath, glancing sideways at Emily, who was oblivious to the dark thoughts coursing through his mind. "Just focus on her," he told himself. "Make today count."

He put on a smile for her, but the shadows lingered beneath the surface, curling around his thoughts like smoke. Today might be about memories and smiles, but the darkness was never far behind.

And as the car continued down the road, carrying them toward their destination, Tyler couldn't help but feel the weight of the secrets pressing down on him, pulling him deeper into the shadows that he knew he had.

THE MUSEUM OF NIGHTMARES

Tyler and Emily weave their way through the crowd in the insanely busy science center, their hands held tight together so they don't get lost in the crowd. Families, kids, and tourists surround them, each eager to explore the exhibits. Emily's face lights up as they pass through the lobby, her excitement glowing on her face.

Tyler allows himself to be led, scanning the room with a quick sweep of his eyes. He catches sight of a black sports car parked outside, and his gut tightens. His Abyssal Passenger grows cold knowing that Jerry is close by, watching.

In the main exhibit hall, the towering skeleton of a tyrannosaurus rex commands Emily's attention. She gazes up at it, wide-eyed and starstruck. "Ty, look at this! It's huge! I mean just look at those teeth," she exclaims, pretending to shudder in fear.

Tyler smirks, playing along with Em's fear. "Yeah, I'd really hate to be on the wrong side of that thing."

But his focus quickly drifts, catching a figure leaning casually against a railing in the distance it was Jerry. The man's camera is up, its lens pointed directly at Tyler. Tyler feels his blood simmer as he forces a smile for Emily

"He's tailing me like it's some kind of sick fucking game," Tyler thinks. "One day, he'll regret sticking his nose where it doesn't belong."

Emily, oblivious to Tyler's Abyssal Passenger, tugs on his arm with a wide grin. "Come on loser, where's your sense of adventure? Let's go see the space stuff next!"

Tyler follows, though his gaze lingers on Jerry, whose smirk grows as he adjusts the camera lens yet again. A dark thought fits through Tyler's mind before he turns his attention back to his girlfriend, still allowing her to drag him away.

They step into the dimly lit space exhibit, where the stars are thrown all across the ceiling, and tiny models of planets spin around overhead. Emily's eyes sparkle like a child with a large rock candy sucker as she looks up. "I remember coming here on our first date, it feels as if it was just yesterday doesn't it?"

"It does," Tyler replies with a small smile. "I remember how you thought the Mars rover was the cutest thing you had ever seen."

Emily laughs, nudging him playfully. "It is! I mean look at the thing! It's like a little space puppy!"

Tylers sight drifts for a moment, catching sight of a woman slipping toward the far end of the room. His pulse quickens. It's Hannah Demarcus, the reason why Tyler took Emily to the science center. "Hannah Demarcus. You seriously think you are untouchable don't you? Peddling that poison ruining lives, today will be your final day, you will live your last moments working a shitty job."

Emily's voice pulled him back. "Ty? You okay?"

He blinks, turning to her with a forced smile. "Yeah, yeah. Just lost in my thoughts."

She squeezes his arm. "No getting lost today mister heart stealer. I need my museum buddy at full capacity."

Tyler chuckles, letting her pull him toward the next section. But his mind stays on Hannah. She's moving toward the restrooms. Away from the crowds He glances back at Emily, who's smiling at an exhibit on ancient astronomy, completely unaware. "Keep looking at the stars, Em. Just for a moment longer."

Out of the corner of his eye, Tyler catches another sight of Jerry, lurking near the exhibit entrance. His finger hovers over the camera's button, snapping pictures of every move that The Inked Reaper makes. Tyler's thoughts turn from his normal average life to his Abyssal Passenger. "Jerry, you really don't know when the fuck to quit do you?"

Emily is too caught up in a display to notice Tyler's anger growing. He edges closer to the family restroom, where Hannah has disappeared. HE looks back at Emily one last time, seeing her smile and excitement. He softens for a moment. "Stay safe, Em. I'll be back before you know it."

He calls out to her, keeping his tone calm and light. "Hey, I'm just gonna hit the restroom real quick. You go on ahead, I'll meet you back at the medical section."

Emily glances back, her smile bright. "Okay but don't take too long. There's this really cool exhibit on historical medicine I want us to see together."

Tyler nods. "Of course my dear."

She turns back to the displays completely unaware of what is brewing deep inside him. As she disappears into the next room, Tyler's expression hardens, his eyes narrowing with murderous intent. He heads toward the restroom, his heartbeat quickening. "This is it. Hannah. Your time is up."

His thoughts are a mix of anticipation and darkness as he closes the distance to the restroom, every step bringing him closer to his abyssal passenger/ He knows Jerry is behind him, that Emily is somewhere just beyond, and he knows today, his code will be broken.

THE ASHES OF DELUSION

Tyler entered the family restroom, the door clicking shut softly behind him. Hannah stood at the sink, washing her hands, utterly oblivious to the monster that loomed behind her.

"Locks were made for a reason," he muttered under his breath, his voice laced with dark amusement.

She barely had time to turn before Tyler lunged, clamping a cloth soaked in chloroform over her face. Hannah's muffled cries came out in short panicked bursts as she struggled against him, but it was a useless effort. Her thrashing slowed, her knees buckling beneath her, and finally, her body slumped, her eyes finally fluttering closed.

"Shh, just go to sleep," Tyler whispered softly, his voice almost tender as her consciousness faded.

He dragged her limp form out of the restroom, moving with purpose down a deserted service hallway. His grip on her wrist was firm but careful, ensuring no one would see the unconscious woman trailing behind him.

"This is why I chose the least busy day," Tyler though his inner voice calm cool and collected. "No one's going to witness this, no cameras either. Perfect."

At the end of the hall, a door marked "Employees Only" creaked open as he pulled Hannah inside, the sound echoing in the near-empty space. The room smelled of dust and neglect, cluttered with old crates and unused equipment.

Tyler dragged Hannah to the center of the room and strapped her to an old metal table with heavy ratchet straps, securing her wrists and ankles with the precision of a true killer. As the chloroform wore off, her eyelids began to flicker. Panic set in the moment she realized she could not move.

"Mmmph! Mmmph!" Her muffled screams filled the space, her eyes wide with terror as she tugged helplessly against the straps. Tyler leaned in close, his face inches from hers, His expression was cold and devoid of any trace of humanity. "What's that? I have no fucking clue what you are trying to say."

With a swift, aggressive motion, he ripped the cloth from her mouth, allowing her to gasp for air.

Please! Don't hurt me! Hannah's voice was hoarse, ragged with fear. "I swear I'll do anything!"

Tyler's lips curled into a genuine smile. "Oh, I'm not here to cause any trouble, Hannah. I just need to have a little chat."

He began pacing in front of her, savoring the fear radiating off her in waves. Her breath came in shallow, panicked gasps, and her eyes followed his every move.

"What do you want from me?" she begged, her voice trembling. "Just let me go!"

"You're a real piece of work, you know that?" His tone was mocking, dripping with disdain. "Selling drugs to little kids, and you think you are some sort of fucking savior. Honestly it's almost adorable."

Tears streamed down her face as she sobbed, the desperation in her voice growing. "I do it to stop them from getting hooked on the harder stuff! My son got in trouble, and I didn't want that to happen to anyone else!"

Tyler shook his head slowly, his eyes gleaming with dark arousal. "Oh, how noble, selling laced pills is your way of saving the world? You really are living in a fantasy, aren't you?"

"I swear!" she wailed, her body shaking violently against the restraints, shaking the table. "I was trying to help them! I never wanted to hurt anyone!"

Tyler leaned in closer, his face contorted into a mockery of sympathy. "But you did hurt them Hannah. You just couldn't see it through your veil of delusion."

He straightened up, pulling out a power drill from behind a nearby crate. The glint of the steel bit under the dim lights was menacing, a promise of agony. He held it up, with the white of the drill filling the room with a horrific hum.

"You are just as guilty as the others, maybe even worse because you actually believe your fucking lies," he said, his voice low and dangerous.

Hannah's screams pierced the air. "No! Please! You don't have to do this! I swear, I'll stop!"

But Tyler's expression remained cold, detached. "Oh, I know you think that. You want to paint yourself as the victim here, but deep down you know what you did. You have hurt countless lives. And now, it's time for you to pay."

Her sobs intensified, her pleas becoming frantic. "Please I swear to god! I'm not a bad person! I was just trying to survive!"

Tyler's gaze darkened, his lips curling into a smirk. "Survive? You seriously think that justifies what you have done?"

With a cruel laugh, he pressed the drill bit against her skull. The sound of metal grinding against her flesh and into her bone was nauseating, the pressure required to pierce the surface was tough and intense. Hannah's creams reached a new pitch of horror as the bit dug deeper into her head, her body convulsing violently against the restraints. The sound was unbearable, a wet crush as the drill bit broke through the bone and the layers a flesh beneath.

Tyler grunted with effort. His arm steady despite the resistance. Blood spurted from the wound, spraying across his gloves and face. But he did not flinch.

Hannah's screams grew weaker, her voice raw and destroyed. Her eyes rolled back into her head, her body still twitching as the drill burrowed deeper. Tyler's hands grew firm and unrelenting, even as her body began to go limp.

"Not my typical kill this time," he muttered to himself, his voice almost contemplative. "I can't leave behind evidence, or it would be too suspicious."

Hannah was still alive, barely clinging to the last threads of consciousness, when he finally pulled the drill away. Blood pooled on the table beneath her, her breathing shallow and ragged.

"Looks like you didn't think this one through did you?" Tyler said softly, licking the blood from the drill bit.

With mechanical efficiency, he dragged her half-conscious body to the incinerator on the other side of the room. The flames roared to life as he opened the thick metal door, the heat scorching his skin even from a distance.

Hannah's eyes fluttered open just as he shoved her into the flames, her body jerking violently as the fire engulfed her. Her screams echoed off the walls. Louder, shriller than anything before. The sound of her flesh sizzlin filled the room, the smell of her burning hair and skin filling Tyler's nostrils with bliss.

She thrashed inside the incinerator, her skin blistering and peeling away in the inferno. Her voice became a guttural wail, the agony of being burned alive overwhelming every ounce of strength she had left. The fire consumed her slowly, deliberately, and Tyler watched cackling with excitement and joy as she was reduced to nothing but ash and charred bones.

"Sorry, Hannah," he whispered almost mockingly. "No easy way out for you."

Her final screams died with the crackling of the flames, leaving nothing but the deafening roar of the incinerator in its wake. Tyler turned and walked away, his heart still pounding, the thrill of the kill a bitter, dark satisfaction that coursed through his entire being.

A DANCE IN THE ABYSS

Tyler stared out the window as the rhythmic thump of music rattled through the car. Tony's house was alive, the colorful strobe lights flickering across the front yard, casting brief flashes of vibrant reds and blues. It was almost hypnotic, and for a moment, Tyler forgot the events of the day. He glanced over at Emily, her soft smile a beacon of warmth against the chaos of life.

"Let's do this," Tyler grinned, reaching for the door handle.

Emily laughed, giving him a playful nudge. "You ready to show off those dance moves you keep bragging about?"

"Oh you know it," Tyler replied, his voice lighter than it had been in days. He stepped out of the car, shaking off the lingering tension."But no promises on how good they'll actually be."

They approached Tony's house, hand in hand, the thudding bass vibrating through the pavement. The door swung open before they could knock, and Tony greeted them with his usual over the top enthusiasm.

"TYLERRR!" Tony shouted, pulling Tyler into a hug so forceful it almost knocked him off balance. "And you brought the lovely lady too!" He winked at Emily, stepping aside to let them in

The house was packed, bodies swaying in sync with the pulsating music. Red and blue lights flickered overhead, the room spinning in an intoxicating blur of color. Tyler followed Tony to the makeshift bar, the smell of alcohol already thick in the air

"First round's on me!" Tony grinned, pouring tequila into shot glasses. Tyler and Emily grabbed theirs, clinking the glasses together.

Emily smirked at him. "Are you going to be able to keep up?"

Tyler laughed, the alcohol loosening him up, making the edges of reality blur. "Fucking try me!"

Hours passed, and Tyler's grip on reality began to slip. At first, it was small things, the flicker of lights seeming too bright, the laughter around him too loud, the static buzzing in his ears. But as the night wore on it got worse. The faces around him distorted in the flashing lights, like grotesque masks stretched too thin.

Tyler found himself in the middle of the living room, his body moving to the beat with reckless abandon. He was too far gone to care about how he looked, his movements jerky and wild. The crowd cheered him on, laughing at his exaggerated dance moves, but their laughter sounded off, hollow to be exact, like distant echoes. He couldn't tell if they were laughing with him or at him. Did it really matter?

"Look at this guy!" someone shouted. "Where have you been hiding those moves?"

"They are classified my friendo," Tyler responded with a sloppy grin. "Top secret."

But even as he said it, his mind raced, slipping in and out of coherent thought. Emily watched him from the sidelines, a mixture of amusement and concern in her eyes. She laughed, but it didn't reach her eyes. Something was wrong. Tyler could feel it

He stumbled back toward her, grabbing another drink from Tony. "You keep going like that, you're going to pass out on my couch," Tony joked, his voice distant and muffled.

"Maybe that's the plan," Tyler slurred, though the words felt heavy on his tongue. He downed the shot, the room spinning around him as he draped an arm over Emily's shoulders.

"Dance with me, Em. Let's show these amateurs how it's fuckin done!"

Emily laughed, but there was a nervous edge to it. "You've had enough, honey," she said, but Tyler wasn't listening. He pulled her into the center of the room, swaying to the beat with exaggerated enthusiasm. The room blurred into a whirl of color and noise, and for a moment, it felt like the world was slipping away, like he was teetering on the edge of his Abyssal Passenger.

The front door burst open again, but this time, it wasn't a rowdy partygoer stepping inside. It was Jerry

He stood in the doorway, scanning the crowd with cold calculated eyes. His face was expressionless, but the tension in his jaw betrayed the simmering anger beneath the surface. He wasn't there to dance or drink. He was here for something else, something darker

Tony who had been near the bar, noticed immediately and rushed over, a nervous grin plastered on his face

"Sir?" He greeted lowering his voice as he stepped in close. "What the hell are you doing here, man?"

Without a word, Jerry pulled out his badge, flashing it briefly before sliding it back into his jacket. "Just here on business," he said, his voice flat. His fingers lingered on the handle of the gun holstered beneath his coat, a silent message that Tony didn't miss.

Tony's face paled slightly, his eyes flicking toward the crowd before settling back on Jerry. "Business, huh?" he muttered under his breath. "At my party? This isn't…"

"Don't worry boy, I won't make any trouble," Jerry cut in his tone sharpening. "I'm just here to watch. You keep your mouth shut, and no one has to know I was here. Got it?"

Tony swallowed, nodding reluctantly. "Yeah, yeah I got it. Just… keep it cool alright? Don't go flashing that gun around."

Jerry offered a tight, humorless smile. "Relax. I'm just here to enjoy the freak show."

Jerry watched from the corner, his fingers brushing the grip of his gun as he took in the scene. Tyler was unraveling, falling apart piece by piece right in front of him. He scribbled another note in his pad, his gaze never leaving the young man.

"Look at this arrogant little prick," Jerry muttered under his breath, his voice dripping with disdain. "Dancing like nothing in the world fucking matters. Just you wait."

He took a swig from the flask he had tucked in a pocket inside his coat, the alcohol burning down his throat. His eyes narrowed as Tyler pulled Emily closer, his movements more erratic, more desperate.

The music thumped louder, but Emily wasn't smiling anymore. She glanced over at Tony, who was nervously eyeing Jerry from across the room. "Maybe you should get him out of here before something happens," Tony whispered to her, his voice scared and tight.

Emily nodded, her face serious now. She reached for Tyler's arm, gently tugging him toward the door. "Alright babe. Time to call it a night," she said softly.

Tyler swayed, his grin fading into a look of confusion. "But I was… I was having fun," he slurred.

"I know, but you need sleep, honey," Emily coaxed, guiding him away from the crowd. "We both do."

She managed to pull him toward the door, his body leaning heavily on hers as they navigated through the mass of dancing bodies.

Jerry watched them go, his jaw clenched, his eyes narrowed.

"Run along, kid," Jerry muttered under his breath, scribbling one last note. "Enjoy your fun while you still can."

Outside, the cool night air hit them like a wall. Emily helped Tyler into the car, his head rolling back against the seat. She sighed, brushing a stay lock of hair away from his forehead.

"You really went all out tonight, didn't you?" she said softly, her voice filled with a mixture of amusement and concern.

Tyler grinned lazily, his eyes half closed. "Anything for you, Em," he mumbled his words slurred and distant.

Emily smiled faintly, shaking her head as she started the car. They drove off, the music from the party only fading into the background as they vanished into the night.

But Jerry's shadow still lingered inside, watching from the darkness, waiting.

THE DESCENT

The museum stood silent against the night, a fortress of forgotten history. Its grand exterior was deceptive, masking the darker secrets buried within. Jerry approached the side entrance. His jaw clenched, his eyes scanning the quiet street before slipping inside. The dim glow of emergency lights flickered weakly along the walls, casting long shadows that crept toward him like fingers reaching in from the past.

He didn't care. Not about the shadows. Not about history. His mind was singular, consumed by one thought: Tyler Grayson

Tyler motherfucking Grayson.

Every beat of his heart, every breath he took was a reminder of his failure, of how close he was to ending it, how close he had come to catching the smug little bastard. But Tyler always slipped through his fingers, just like every time before.

Not Tonight.

The storage room was a claustrophobic maze of forgotten artifacts and crates that hadn't seen daylight in years. The air was stale, thick with dust that clung to his throat as he move carefully, the wooden floorboards creaking under his feet. His flashlight flickered to life, a sharp beam slicing through the darkness. It landed on shelves filled with relics of the past, shattered vases, old scrolls, and history that had no place in the world Jerry knew.

He didn't give a damn about history. The only thing that mattered to him was the present, and the trail that had led him there, to this almost forgotten room in the depths of the museum.

Jerry's hands shook slightly as the light caught something on the floor, a dark, wet, stain spreading across the wooden boards. His heart thudded in his chest as he crouched down, his fingers brushing over the liquid. It was tacky to the touch, fresh enough to still hold its shape.

He lifted his fingers into the beam of the flashlight, staring at the blood smeared across his skin. His lips curled into a grin, his teeth bared like a predator scenting his prey.

"This is it," he whispered, barely able to contain the glee in his voice. "This is fucking it."

Jerry stood, his blood soaked fingers trembling as he scanned the room. The Inked Reaper had been here. Tyler had been here.

There was no doubt in his mind. The blood was proof, the only confirmation he needed. His mind raced as he envisioned Tyler standing here, methodically hiding his tracks, concealing the body with the same cold, calculated precision that kept him free for so long.

The thought that Tyler, his smug, untouchable face, sent a wave of rage surging through Jerry's body. He kicked over a nearby box, sending it crashing to the floor, but the noise barely registered in his ears. He was focused. His eyes darted around the room, searching for any signs of a body, any trace of a victim Tyler hadn't erased.

But there was nothing

Nothing. Just blood. Just another fucking dead end.

"Where the fuck is it?" Jerry's voice rose, trembling with frustration as he flung another box off the shelf. The papers inside scattered across the floor, some landing in the blood, staining the fragile pages red.

His hands balled into fists. He could feel his control slipping, the thin veneer of his professional life crumbling under the weight of his anger. How many times had Tyler slipped through his fingers? How many bodies had he actually left behind, with no way to prove it was him?

Jerry had always known Tyler was guilty. He could feel it, deep in his bones.it wasn't just Intuition, it was years of tracking Tyler, of watching him, waiting for him to make a mistake. But Tyler never did. He was careful, methodical, always two steps ahead.
And every time Jerry thought he had him, every time he felt that rush of victory, Tyler found a way to tear it all down.

"Where the fuck is the goddamn body?!" Jerry roared, his voice echoing off the walls as he flung another stack of papers into the air. His breathing was ragged, his vision blurred by the raw hatred burning inside him.

He hated Tyler. Hated the way he played everyone around him, the way he fooled them into thinking he was just some golden boy with a genius mind. They couldn't see past the charm, the lies. But Jerry did. He'd always seen it, the darkness lurking beneath Tyler's perfect façade.

No one else believed him. Not even Kate. She would listen, nod, but there was always doubt in her eyes. She didn't understand, not the way Jerry did. She hadn't lived in Tyler's shadow for as long as he had.

Jerry kicked a crate, the sharp sound cutting through the silence. "It's all fucking circumstantial!" he hissed through gritted teeth. "Nothing's gonna fucking stick."

He wanted to punch something, to tear the whole damn place apart. But it wouldn't change anything. Tyler had been here, he could feel it in his bones, but he'd cleaned up. Hidden whatever trace of the body there might've been. Just like always. Just like the others.

Jerry clenched his fists until his knuckles turned white. He was so goddamn close. He could feel the weight of it pressing down on him, the weight of failure gnawing at his insides. He'd never hated anyone as much as he hated Tyler Grayson. No one had ever gotten under his skin like that kid had.

"Goddammit," he muttered, kicking another crate for good measure.

Outside, the cool night air hit Jerry like a slap in the face as he stormed into the parking lot. He ripped open the door of his car and dropped heavily into the driver's seat, gripping the steering wheel so tight his knuckles turned white. His entire body was vibrating with the rage he barely managed to contain.

Tyler Grayson.

His fucking name was like poison in Jerry's mouth. He'd spent years chasing after the kid, unraveling every thread, following every lead. But Tyler always slipped away. He was untouchable, like a ghost who only left blood and chaos in his wake.

Jerry's phone buzzed in his pocket, the screen lighting up with a message from Kate. He didn't want to look at it, didn't want to hear her tell him to be careful. He didn't need careful. He needed results. But he looked anyway, the cold light from the screen illuminating his face as he read the text.

"Is it him?"

Jerry clenched his jaw, his teeth grinding together as he typed a response.

"It has to be," he muttered under his breath, his fingers tapping rapidly across the screen. No other motherfucker fits.

He sent the message, his hand trembling with barely suppressed rage. How many times had they come this close? How many times had he been on the verge of catching Tyler, only for it to slip away?

His phone buzzed again. Another message from Kate.

Be careful, Jerry.

Jerry scoffed, his lip curling in disdain as he tossed the phone onto the passenger seat. "Careful, my ass," he muttered, glaring out the windshield at the museum looming darkly in the background. "I'm not letting that piece of shit get away with this. Not again."

He took a deep breath, forcing himself to calm down, but the rage wouldn't go away. It simmered just beneath the surface, always there, always ready to explode. He could see Tyler's face in his mind, that smug, arrogant smile, like he knew he'd won. Like he knew he'd always get away with it.

Not this time.

Jerry's hand twitched toward his gun, his fingers brushing the cool metal of the grip. He didn't care about the rules anymore. Didn't care about playing nice, about following the law. Tyler had crossed the line too many times. He'd killed too many people, ruined too many lives. Jerry had watched as body after body piled up, with no way to pin it on Tyler.

But Jerry wasn't going to wait for justice anymore.

"I'll fucking nail you, Tyler," he whispered, his voice low and dangerous. "One way or another."

He started the car, the engine growling to life as he sped out of the parking lot, his mind set on one thing, catching the Inked Reaper. Across town, in the soft glow of her apartment bedroom, Kate lay under the covers, her phone still in her hand. She stared at the screen, her eyes distant as she read Jerry's last message.

"It has to be him."

Her heart sank. She didn't want to believe it. Didn't want to believe that the boy William had trusted, the one who had been part of their lives, could be capable of something so monstrous.

Next to her, William stirred, turning over in his sleep. His face, usually so hard and lined with worry, was softened in sleep, unguarded in a way Kate rarely saw. She glanced down at her phone one last time before locking the screen and setting it aside.

William shifted closer, his arm slipping around her waist as he brushed a strand of hair away from her face. His touch was tender, a reminder of everything they weren't supposed to be.

"What are you thinking about?" he asked, his voice soft, still heavy with sleep.

Kate sighed, her fingers resting lightly on his arm. "Just… how complicated this is."

William nodded, his eyes opening slowly as he looked at her, but he didn't pull away. Instead, he reached for her hand, entwining his fingers with hers. "I know. We shouldn't have… but I can't bring myself to feel sorry for it."

Kate looked at him, her expression caught between regret and contentment. "I know what you mean. I feel the same way. But what now Will?" Her voice was barely a whisper, a soft confession in the quiet dark.

William's hand tightened around hers. He didn't look away, his gaze holding hers with an intensity she felt down to her bones. "I don't know," he admitted, his tone serious yet gentle. "But right now, I just want to be here with you. No overthinking. No regrets. Just… this."

Kate's eyes softened, a faint, almost defeated smile touching her lips as she leaned into him, letting herself savor the warmth of his embrace. She wanted to freeze this moment, to hold on to the feeling of safety, of closeness. But she knew that, come morning, They'd have to face the truth, that they were walking on a line that could destroy everything.

She closed her eyes, pressing her forehead against his. "Just for tonight, then," she whispered, a fragile surrender.

William's arms tightened around her, his lips brushing her temple in a soft, silent promise. "Just tonight."

They stayed like that, wrapped in each other's arms, clinging to a fleeting escape from the weight of their lives. In the quiet dark, the world outside seemed to melt away. The cases, the questions, the mounting suspicion surrounding Tyler, all of it felt distant, like echoes from another life.

But reality had a way of creeping back, as relentless as the dawn.

Kate's thoughts drifted to Jerry's text, his certainty that Tyler was guilty. The evidence was mounting, each new discovery tying Tyler to the Inked Reaper. But the thought of it was unbearable. She could still remember Tyler as a brilliant young man with a bright future, a friend to William's family. She didn't want to believe he was a heartless killer, that he was capable of such brutality.

And yet, she could feel the doubt growing at her. Jerry wasn't one to jump to conclusions. If he was convinced Tyler was the Reaper, then maybe… just maybe… he was right.

But then there was William, loyal, principled, and so determined to believe in people's goodness. She could see how much it would pain him to question Tyler, his own flesh and blood, to even entertain the thought that his own son could be so monstrous. And if Tyler really was the Inked Reaper… if they were wrong about him…

The weight of it all threatened to suffocate her.

William's steady breathing grounded her. Anchoring her in the present moment. She clung to the warmth of his embrace, letting herself believe that just for tonight, things could be more simple. That she could be here, with him, without the shadows of doubt or duty pulling them apart

In the quiet, she felt a pang of guilt, guilt for what they had. For the secrets they were keeping. She knew they were breaking every rule, that they were venturing into dangerous territory. But right now all she could feel was the warmth of his hand in hers, the gentle rise and fall of his chest.

"Will," she whispered, her voice barely a breath.

"Hmm?" His response was soft, almost lost in the dark.

"I don't want to lose this… lose you."

He opened his eyes, his gaze meeting hers with a steady intensity. "You won't. No matter what happens, Kate, I'll be here." His voice was firm, resolute, as if he were making a promise he intended to keep.

But they both knew the truth. Morning would come, and with it, the weight of the Inked Reaper case. The lines that would be redrawn, the barriers between them restored. And Tyler's shadow would loom over them, a reminder of what a fragile world they inhabited.

For now, however, they held each other close, letting the silence of the night wash over them, a sanctuary from the storm gathering outside. It was a brief reprieve, a moment of peace in a world unraveling.

SHADOWS IN THE REARVIEW

The hotel room was a tangle of Tyler's clothes and crumpled blankets, dimly lit by the soft morning glow creeping through the half-drawn curtains. Tyler lay sprawled across the bed, yesterday's hoodie bunched up around his shoulders, its hood half obscuring his face. The remnants of the previous night clung to his face. The remnants of the previous night clung to him, the stale scent of alcohol, the echo of loud music in his ears, and the bone deep exhaustion he couldn't shake off.

Emily leaned over him, her face gentle as she nudged his shoulder, her voice lifting with a mix of sweetness and teasing.

"Wake up, part animal. Time to get up."

Tyler groaned, the sound low and rough as he pulled the hood down further, trying to shield himself from the world. His head throbbed, a dull, relentless pulse pounding through his temples. He sat up slowly each movement sharp and uncomfortable

"Feels like I was stabbed in the head with a broken broom," he muttered, pressing a hand to his forehead.

Emily chuckled, a soft sound that seemed far too cheerful for his current state. "Well that's what tequila and no restraint will do to you. Come on, pancakes downstairs. Grease and carbs will help."

With a groan, Tyler forced himself upright, managing a half-smile that was more of a grimace than a grin. He stumbled his way to the bathroom, splashing cold water on his face in a futile attempt to shake off the heaviness clinging to him. He stared at his reflection, seeing shadows under his eyes and a tension that even the night of reckless drinking couldn't wash away. He pulled on an oversized hoodie and sunglasses, hoping the layers would disguise his rough edges as much as possible.

Down in the lobby, they found a quiet two seat table tucked away in the breakfast area. Tyler sat slouched over a plate of pancakes, his fingers wrapped tightly around a mug of coffee, which he sipped with half lidded eyes. His gaze swept around the room now and then, taking in the bustling atmosphere but never lingering long enough to be noticed.

Emily sat across from him, a smile tugging at her lips as she nudged his arm. "Looked like you had a good time last night," she teased. "You actually danced! And not just awkwardly, I mean you really went for it."

Tyler offered a faint smile, the memory of the previous night hazy at best. "Guess I just needed to blow off some steam," he replied, before catching her gaze. "But you had fun, Right?"

Her smile softened, eyes warm as she looked at him. "I had a blast. I love seeing you… relaxed. It's like I get to see a whole other side of you."

Tyler's smile faded, and he looked down at his fingers tracing patterns on the table. Another side. She had no idea how much of him she was missing. But he pushed the thought away, forcing a light laugh. "Yeah, maybe I do need to loosen up a little bit more often."

They ate in comfortable silence for a few moments, the clinking silverware and murmur of others filling the space. But Tyler's hand started to tap rhythmically against the table, his eyes flickering between his food and the hotel lobby. He couldn't shake a creeping unease, his instincts buzzing at the edge of his awareness.

Emily noticed the shift, her gaze lingering on him as she took a sip of her coffee. "You okay? You seem… jittery."

"Yeah just… tired. Too much excitement." He forced a chuckle, trying to brush it off. "And the coffee hasn't kicked in yet."

She smiled, but her eyes lingered on him, a trace of worry there. He shifted uncomfortably under her gaze, trying to keep his expression casual. When he finally glanced back up at her, he leaned forward, attempting to steer the conversation somewhere safer.

"We should probably head out," he suggested, trying to keep his tone light. "Need some fresh air. Clear my head."

Emily didn't hesitate, standing up and throwing away their plates. They stepped out into the morning chill, the crisp air biting against Tyler's skin and cutting through the fog lingering in his mind. He tugged his hood up shielding himself from the world as they made their way to her car. Sinking low into the passenger seat, he closed his eyes, willing the quiet to steady his nerves.

As Emily drove through the city's quieter streets, Tyler's gaze stayed locked on the side view mirror, his expression tense and unreadable. His eyes were sharp behind the dark lenses, scanning every car, every turn, every fleeting shadow. An odd comfort came from the steady rhythm of the road, yet his mind remained far from peaceful.

Emily glanced at him with a small smile, breaking the silence. "Still feeling the aftermath?"

Tyler chuckled, giving her a half-hearted nod. "Yeah… though the hoodie and sunglasses look kinda helps."

She laughed, the sound light and genuine. "Well, at least we got a chance to just enjoy ourselves. You don't get to do that often enough."

Her comment hit harder than she'd intended. For a split second, Tyler's guard slipped, and his face softened, a hint of gratitude in his eyes. "Yeah…" He paused, his gaze drooping to the floor mat. "Thanks for looking out for me."

They drove in silence for a bit, the cityscape shifting around them as the morning sun grew higher. Emily reached over, placing a comforting hand on his, her touch grounding him.

The quiet between them grew heavier until Tyler spoke again, his voice low, almost hesitant. "You know… I think I need to call my dad later. Get some more… research material for the book. You know, case files and stuff."

Emily raised an eyebrow, intrigued, "More case files? You're really diving deep into this one, huh?"

"Yeah I want this story to feel real, you know? Like… authentic." He hesitated carefully choosing his words. "I need some first hand info on past criminals, the kind of people that slip through the cracks."

Emily watched him with a curious smile, "Only you would be researching case files for 'authenticity.' But… it sounds fascinating, actually."

Her words brought him back to the present grounding him in a way he hadn't expected. He gave her a small, grateful smile, though his gaze flickered back to the mirror, ever watchful

As they drove on, the car with Jerry grew smaller in the distance, but Tyler knew that he couldn't keep running forever. Jerry was relentless, and he'd stop at nothing to catch The Inked Reaper.

But Tyler was equally determined. He would not go down without a fight. Not until he finished what he started.

And as the city streets opened up before them, he tightened his fists, his mind steeling itself for the battle ahead.

CONVERSATIONS IN THE DARK

The office was quiet, filled with the familiar scent of worn leather and faint traces of spilled ink. Tyler dropped into his favorite writing chair waiting for him at his desk. The faint morning light slipped through the half open curtains, casting soft shadows across the room.A hoodie hooded low over his head, Tyler leaned back, letting out a long sigh. The night felt like it clung to him, thick and unyielding.

Just then, the door cracked open, and Emily entered, her smile warm as she watched him unwind.

"Alright," she said, leaning over to press a gentle kiss to his forehead. "I'm off to work."

Tyler smiled, reaching up to give her hand a quick squeeze. "I'll try not to get lost in my head too much."

She chuckled, glancing around the organized chaos of his office. "Make sure you actually try. I'll see you tonight."

He watched her go, the door clicking softly behind her, leaving the room with only him and his thoughts. "She's too good to me," he thought, feeling the usual pang of guilt for the secrets he kept from her. But he buried it, focusing on what he had to do next.

Tyler glanced at his phone, scrolling through his contacts until he landed on "Dad." He hit dial and waited, setting the phone to speaker as he leaned back in his chair, his fingers drumming against the armrest.

After a few rings, William answered, sounding a little groggy, as though he'd just woken up. "Hey kid, good morning. How's it going?"

Tyler managed a slight grin. "Morning, Dad. Just… recovering from a little too much fun last night. Figured I'd call and check in."

A chuckled crackled through the line, tinged with a trace of hesitation. "Glad to hear you're living it up. What kind of trouble were you up to?"

"Oh, you know," Tyler shrugged, his voice light. "Nothing too crazy… although I might need to lay off the tequila for a while."

"Good to see you're finding a balance," William said, a shadow slipping into his tone. Tyler's brow furrowed, catching the strange infliction in his father's voice.

"Everything alright? You sound… off."

There was a brief pause, and then a heavy sight. "Oh, yeah… late night. A lot on my mind."

Tyler leaned forward, curiosity sparking. "Anything you want to talk about?"

"No, it's nothing for you to worry about. Just… one of those weeks." William's voice held a slight edge of frustration, a weight that Tyler could feel even through the distance. It wasn't like his father to be distracted. The Inked Reaper case was clearly wearing on him more than he'd let on.

Tyler decided to shift the subject. "Well, listen… I was actually calling about my new book. Thought I might get your help with some… source material."

There was a soft chuckle. "More research, huh? Haven't I given you every nasty case file under the sun by now?"

Tyler allowed himself a sly grin. "Almost. But this one is different. I want it to feel raw, real, something only you could get."

A pause followed, William considering, almost as though he could see Tyler's intentions beneath the surface.

"Alright," William said finally, a guarded chuckle in his voice. "But only if you promise me this book's going to be worth it. I'm risking boundaries here, son."

"You know I will." Tyler leaned back, a hint of that familiar hunger glinting in his eyes. "This one's going to be my best yet."

There was a grunt of approval, but William still sounded distanced, as though his mind was still tangled in something else.

"Just… be careful, Tyler. Inspiration's one thing, but don't get too close to the darkness. It has a way of swallowing people whole."

Tyler's lips curled into a faint smirk. "Don't worry, Dad. I can handle it."

UNSETTLING INQUIRES

The morning air was crisp, cutting into Jerry's skin as he stepped out of his car, tugging his jacket tighter Against The chill. The doctor's office loomed in front of him, Modest yet ugly imposing, and he could feel a hint of adrenaline surged through him as he stared at the unassuming brick facade."Just another layer to peel back," he thought, a faint smirk pulling at the corners of his mouth

As he made his way to the entrance, Jerry took a steadying breath. His footsteps echoed in the silence as he crossed the parking lot, The Sounds underscoring his anticipation. He had long been suspicious of Tyler Grayson, a young writer whose reputation seemed too carefully crafted. "Nobody's that squeaky clean," he thought. "People love him because they think he is harmless. But everyone has their darkness." And Jerry was going to be the one to drag Tyler's into the light.

The waiting room was nearly empty. A single patient sat in one corner, flipping through a magazine, while the receptionist sat behind a polished counter, her eyes glued to the computer screen. She barely registered Jerry's presence as he walked up, her attention absorbed by whatever was on the monitor

Jerry cleared his throat, and she looked up, momentarily startled before adopting the usual professional mask.

"Excuse me," he said, his voice low but firm. "I'm looking for Emily Taylors. Is she around?"

The receptionist's eyes narrowed ever so slightly, evaluating him with quiet suspicion. Her gaze flickering over his outfit, taking in the sharp lines of his jacket, the notebook in his hand, and the press badge clipped to his belt. After a moment of hesitation, she pointed him down the hallway.

"She's on break," the receptionist said, her voice edged with mild annoyance. "You can find her in the break room, down the hall, and the last door on the right."

Jerry gave a curt nod. "Thank you." He offered her a forced smile before turning away, already focused on the task ahead. As he walked down the corridor, the fluorescent lights above cast a sterile glow, heightening the clinical silence around him. The atmosphere felt stifling, and he felt a familiar rush of nerves morph into the excitement of the hunt. Emily Taylors wasn't just a footnote in his investigation; she was someone close enough to Tyler to potentially give him a glimpse into the shadows behind Tyler's image.

Emily was sitting at a small table, her back slightly hunched as she sipped from a disposable coffee cup, scrolling absentmindedly on her phone. Her face softened in a small, relaxed smile as she scrolled through her messages. She was so engrossed that she didn't notice Jerry enter until the door clicked shut behind him.

Startled, Emily looked up, her eyes widening as Jerry crossed the room with measured steps and sat down across from her. He didn't waste any time, setting his notepad on the table, his eyes sharp and focused.

"Miss Taylors, right? Thanks for making time," he said, sounding as though he were addressing a colleague rather than a stranger. "I'm Jerry." He leaned forward, his pen poised. "I'm working on a piece about Tyler Grayson's career, his life behind the scenes."

Emily's surprise was quickly replaced by a polite smile. She glanced down at her coffee, swirling it absently before replying, "Oh! Well,

Tyler's a pretty private guy, but… I'd be happy to help however I can."

Jerry's smile was thin, almost predatory as he studied her response. "I appreciate it," he said, flipping open his notepad to a blank page. "Let's start with something simple. How does Tyler unwind? Outside of writing, what does he do for fun?"

Emily's face relaxed a little, a genuine smile crossing her lips. "He loves reading and researching, honestly. He's such a bookworm." She chuckled softly."Sometimes we go hiking, or we'll binge watch old mystery shows together. It's kind of a little tradition we have."

Jerry tapped his pen against his notepad, jotting down a few notes as if deeply interested. "Mystery shows, huh?" he said. "And does he ever mention his own… inspirations? Maybe authors who influenced him?"

"Of course," she replied, seemingly oblivious to his intentions. "He loves anything suspenseful, Poe, Doyle, Christie, he's fascinated by people who explore the darker side of humanity."

Jerry's pen slowed, his gaze sharpening. "Interesting," he said, his tone deceptively light. "Speaking of the darker side… has Tyler ever told you about any… personal struggles? Maybe things that trouble him? Urges, or… temptations?"

Emily's smile faltered slightly, her fingers tightening around her coffee cup. "Temptations?" She laughed, but the sound was strained. "No, nothing like that. Tyler's sweet. He just gets into character for his writing, that's all. Nothing… strange."

Jerry held her gaze, his expression unyielding. "Sure," he said, his tone as neutral as Switzerland. "But, hypothetically… have you ever worried he might be keeping secrets? Maybe something deeper than just his book plots?"

A flicker of discomfort crossed Emily's face, but she forced a smile, trying to maintain her composure. "Well… I trust him," she said slowly. "I mean he's creative, but he's not hiding anything sinister, if that is what you're asking."

He nodded, though his skepticism was barely hidden. "Right. Just curious. And one more thing: would you say Tyler has certain… patterns? Like, specific times he goes on walks, or goes for a drive, behaviors he repeats often?"

Emily shifted uncomfortably, clearly becoming wary of his line of questioning. She shrugged, attempting to brush it off. "Not really… He's not always predictable, but that's just him being a writer. His routines can be all over the place."

Jerry watched her intently, his eyes never leaving her face. For a moment, he was silent, as though contemplating her words, then finally he closed the notepad, a smug expression settling on his face.

"Very helpful. Thanks, Emily. Appreciate it."

Emily nodded, her polite smile returning, though there was an undeniable awkwardness in her posture. "So… when will this be published?" She asked, trying to sound casual but clearly anxious.

Jerry's smile didn't reach his eyes. "You'll see soon enough," he replied, his tone thick with implication.

Emily's eyes flickered with a hint of apprehension, but she forced a laugh, brushing it off. "Alright, well… I'm glad I could help. Tyler doesn't really like attention, but if it's a good piece, I'm sure he will be alright with it."

"Good piece?" Jerry thought, almost amused. "This isn't just a piece, sweetheart. It's an expose."

Jerry walked back out into the parking lot, the cold air hitting him as he exhaled, relishing the thrill that hummed under his skin. Emily's evasiveness had only reinforced his suspicions. She might trust Tyler blindly, but her discomfort spoke volumes. Her loyalty was admirable, he supposed, but loyalty was also dangerous. He couldn't help but feel that with one more conversation, one more layer peeled back, he'd be staring Tyler's secrets in the face.

As he unlocked his car he muttered to himself, a dark smile creeping across his face. "Got you now, mother fucker."

THE ABYSSAL BECKONS

Tyler sat alone in his dimly lit home office, the soft hum of his computer filling the silence. The screen cast a pale glow across his face, illuminating his features with a cold light. He clicked open a newly received email from his father, William. Attached was a folder, bulging with scanned files from past and recent cases, the very cases William had been fighting to keep under control. Tyler smirked, anticipation building within him. His father had no idea these files were being shared with a killer, the very killer he was unknowingly hunting.

"Let's see what you've got for me, Dad," Tyler muttered under his breath, clicking open the first file in the folder.

As he scrolled, familiar names and faces flickered past, their charges and crimes laid bare in a sterile police jargon. Petty thieves, fraudsters, a few low level traffickers. Nothing particularly motivating. Until he reached the fifth file.

Eric Perbary

The name caught his eye immediately, his Abyssal Passenger awaking inside as he clicked expand on the folder. A titles flashed across the screen:

ERIC PERBARY ALIAS: "THE JANITOR KILLER"

The images that followed were stark, brutal. A series of crime scene photos showed the aftermath of Eric's final attack, his wife's battered body lifeless on the floor, surrounded by chaos. Tyler's fingers gripped the edge of his desk, his knuckles turning white as he scrolled each file. His Abyssal Passenger stirred, whispering it's quiet but familiar urges, intensifying the thrill unfurling in his veins

"Strangled her with an electrical cord. Dismembered her after death," Tyler read aloud, his voice low, almost reverent. The text was clinical, but his mind was already painting the scene in vivid color, an unfiltered replay of Eric's depravity filling his imagination. "Cleansed his home, sanitizing it from evil…"

A dark smile tugged at the corner of Tyler's lips. "Fitting for someone like you."

His gaze sharpened, tracing over the details of Eric's trial. His eyes narrowed as they met the next line:

FOUND NOT GUILTY BY REASON OF INSANITY. RECENTLY DISCHARGED WITH MANDATORY CHECK-INS.

As he continued to read, an unmistakable hunger stirred within him, clawing upward, dark and insatiable. The need to balance the scales felt visceral. His hands itched, tingling with excitement as he absorbed each fragment of Eric's life, each line of the file layering more fuel onto the fire growing within his chest. He wanted to kill this man, to feel the precise moment Eric's body grew limp beneath his hands. To hear that last gasp of air.

Another line caught his attention, dragging him deeper into the abyss:

OCCUPATION: JANITOR STATUS: LIVES ALONE. NO KNOWN FAMILY, DISCHARGED CONDITIONALLY, WITH PSYCHIATRIC FOLLOW UP.

A nearly inaudible chuckle slipped past Tyler's lips. He could almost taste Eric's inevitable fear, almost feel the life leaving his body. "You won't be 'cleansed' this time," he whispered.

And then he saw it, tucked in the list of occupational history, an entry that made his blood run cold, then boil in the span of a heartbeat.

WORKS PRIMARILY WITH CHILDREN

His mind went silent, each word resonating in his thoughts. Children. He clenched his fist, feeling the rage simmer just below the surface. How many of them had Eric tainted with his filth, slipping through the cracks, hiding his sins under a thin mask of 'recovery'? The abyss within him urged him onwards, whispering the same call it always did when he found a target deserving of his wrath. But tonight, the voice was louder, nearly deafening.

"Eric Perbary." he whispered to himself, each syllable laced with venom. "You've been marked."

Tyler leaned back in his chair, his mind already working, connecting the dots like a hunter stalking his prey. He began sketching out a mental map, tracing Eric's known habits, his routines, his movements. The file gave him pieces of Eric's life, just enough to sketch a roadmap leading directly to him.

A new idea formed in Tyler's mind, a secluded spot, nearly forgotten. He knew of an old lumber mill just outside of town, a place that had been forgotten, now little more than a ghost of industry past. He imagined its dusty halls and broken windows, the perfect stage for the justice Eric deserved.

"A quiet place," he murmured, his fingers trailing over the table's edge as if feeling the cool steel of a blade. "Somewhere hidden. Only we'll know."

The abyss within him began to shift, wrapping itself around his mind, urging him forward, whispering in a voice he couldn't ignore. He felt it settle over him like a shadow, darker, thicker, and more consuming than ever before. The voice spoke of justice, of violence, of cleansing. It called on him to enact a punishment as brutal as the crimes themselves.

His eyes turned to the crime scene photos, to the horror Eric had wrought without consequence. As he studied the details, he could almost feel his heart rate slow, a strange sense of calm washing over him. "An eye for an eye," he thought, as the shadow within him tightened its grip, as comforting as it was terrifying

His Abyssal Passenger was his, a gift as much as a curse. And tonight, it will feed.

OLD WOUNDS AND UNFINISHED BUSINESS

Kate settled into the quiet corner booth of the coffee shop, the ambient murmur of voices and clinking coffee mugs drifting around her. She wrapped her hands around the warm cup in front of her, eyes sharp and observant, tracing the faces and movements of those around her. The need to stay alert had long ago become second nature, a habit born from years of hunting shadows and chasing truths others were too afraid to see.

The chime of the door opening snapped her out of her thoughts. Jerry walked in, his figure briefly outlined against the evening light spilling through the door. He scanned the room with a frustrated grimace before his gaze landed on her. For a split second, his expression softened, a glint of the man he'd once been peeking through, but it was quickly replaced by the familiar mask of resentment. He strode over, his movement tense, almost angry.

Without a word, he slid into the booth across from her, the air between them thick with unsaid words and unhealed wounds.

"Well," Jerry muttered, folding his arms and leaning back, "Here we are, I'd say it's nice to see you but…" He shrugged, letting the words hang.

Kate lifted her coffee to her lips, unbothered. "No need for pleasantries. We both know why we are here."

A tense silence settled over them, both waiting for the other to speak first. It was a battle of wills, a silent reminder of who they once were to each other. Finally, Jerry's frustration bubbled over, breaking the stalemate.

"I've got him, Kate." His voice low, a mix of triumph and bitterness. "Tyler Grayson. I know he's the Inked Reaper."

Kate's eyes flickered, caught between interest and skepticism. "Tyler Grayson? Really?" Her voice held a hint of doubt, as if daring him to convince her.

Jerry's jaw tightened, his fists clenching on the table. "You think I'd waste your time if I wasn't sure?" His voice cracked slightly, a thread of desperation weaving through his words. "I've been watching him carefully. The patterns are all there. Every time he disappears, every strange excuse he gives. Emilly filled in the blanks without even realizing it."

Kate's eyebrows lifted slightly, her expression unimpressed. "Emily?" she asked, feigning casual interest while studying him. "You really went there? I thought you were done harassing her."

Jerry scoffed, his face twisting with disdain. "It's not harassment if she's blind to the truth," he hissed "Tyler's slipping up, Kate. He thinks he's clever, but he's just like the rest of them. No killer can stay hidden forever."

There was something raw in Jerry's voice, a desperate conviction that bordered on obsession. It reminded her of the man she once loved, the man who had seen monsters in the shadows long before she could. But now, she wasn't so sure he could tell the difference between shadows and reality.

"And yet," Kate countered, voice calm, "here we are, sitting in a coffee shop instead of a courtroom. If it were that clear-cut, you'd have already handed him over. So what's the holdup?"

Jerry's face darkened, his expression hardening with barely contained anger. He leaned back, rubbing his temples with a frustrated groan. "My other job is starting to sniff around. They're getting suspicious, asking why I keep disappearing, wanting answers I can't give. I know if they catch wind of this, of what I've been doing on my own, my career is done." His eyes, though filled with resentment, held a flicker of fear. "And so is my chance to catch him."

Kate leaned back, watching him carefully. "Since when did protocol ever stop you, Jerry?" She arched an eyebrow. "You've never been one to let rules get in the way of personal vendettas. Or have you forgotten how that works?"

Jerry's jaw tightened, the familiar flare of resentment in his eyes. "Don't lecture me, Kate," he muttered, his voice barely more than a growl. "Not after you left. We were engaged, remember?" His voice wavered with bitterness. "But you threw it all away… for him. For the fucking Inked Reaper."

Kate closed her eyes briefly, memories she'd buried surfacing against her will. She took a deep breath, willing herself to stay composed. "You think I wanted that?" Her voice was laced with frustration. "You think I wanted to choose between the life we could have had and the chance to stop a killer?"

Jerry's silence was his only answer, his fists clenched so tight his knuckles were white.

She looked away, forcing herself to stay calm. "I couldn't sit by and pretend it wasn't fucking happening jerry. You wanted to ignore the whole damn thing. You wanted to believe we could just fucking… walk away from all of this shit." Her voice softened, though her gaze remained steely. "But I just couldn't do it… I fucking tried."

Jerry's face contorted, anger blazing in his eyes. His fists trembled slightly, and for a moment, he looked as though he might explode. But he simply took a shaky breath, his expression hollow. "You chose him, Kate," he said quietly, the hurt evident beneath his anger. "And it fucking destroyed us."

Kate looked away, her expression hardening. "I didn't choose him, Jerry," she whispered. "I chose the case. The fucking truth. You were too damn stubborn to see it for what it was."

He slammed a fist down on the table, making their mugs rattle. Several patrons glanced over, but he didn't seem to notice. His hands were shaking, his face flushed with barely restrained fury. "It doesn't matter now," he said through gritted teeth. "I don't have much time. If I can't get something fucking solid on Tyler soon, They're going to catch me, and he'll slip through our fingers. I can't let that happen."

Kate regarded him with a skeptical expression, clearly unconvinced. "So, you're really sure?" She studied him, searching for any hint of the old Jerry, the man who once understood the difference between obsession and truth. "You're not just seeing what you want to see?"

Jerry's eyes flashed with determination. A dangerous gleam in his gaze. "Trust me, Kate. Tyler Grayson is the god damned Inked fucking Reaper. I'd stake my life on it." He leaned in, his voice barely above a whisper, his words filled with a conviction that bordered on madness. "But I can't do this alone. They are closing in on me. If you still care about justice or whatever it was that drove you to leave me, I need your help."

Kate's face remained unreadable, her eyes flickering with a mixture of frustration and lingering regret. Her voice softened, though it held an edge of warning. "All right, Jerry. But if you're wrong—if this is just another one of your obsessions…" She let her words trail off, the implication clear.

Jerry's face hardened, his expression defiant. "I know what I'm doing, Kate. You think I'd drag you into this if I didn't?"

For a long moment, they held each other's gaze, their shared past lingering in the air between them. The hurt, the betrayal, the bitterness—all of it lay unspoken, buried beneath layers of anger and regret. Yet, in that moment, they found a fragile truce, a shared purpose reigniting between them.

"For both our sakes," Jerry said, his voice barely more than a whisper, "let's hope I'm not wrong. We don't get a second chance at this."

Kate nodded slowly, her expression resolute but tinged with sadness. "We'll catch him, Jerry. And this time, I'm not walking away."

He gave her a curt nod, his face shadowed by a grim determination. But as he leaned back, a faint crack in his composure betrayed a flicker of doubt, an unease that suggested he was beginning to unravel, his obsession blinding him to the cost. His hands still shook slightly, his face flushed with the anger he was barely holding in check.

Kate's gaze softened for just a moment as she watched him, a pang of sadness tightening in her chest. She could already see the faint glimmers of a downfall he refused to acknowledge—a fire that would burn through everything, consuming him from the inside out.

They parted without another word, each lost in their own thoughts, bound by a past neither could escape and a hunt that would either bring them closure… or destruction.

THE MILL OF SINS

The city was drenched in shadows, its streets narrowing into silent, sinuous veins of concrete that wound through the darkened landscape. Tyler's car moved like a shadow itself, gliding through the gloom as he trailed the worn out silhouette of Eric Perbary;s battered pick up truck. He kept his distance, his gaze unblinking, his grip tight on the wheel as he felt the familiar thrill rising in his chest.This was no ordinary night.

With his phone to his ear, he softened his voice, a careful mask slipping into place.

"Hey, babe. Just wanted to let you know, I'm heading out with Tony for a couple of drinks. Won't be too late. I'll be back after you get home," he murmured, the faintest hint of a smirk slipping into place

Emily's voice soft and slightly disappointed came through, "Alright, just don't stay out too late. You know I worry.

Tyler's smirk deepened as he watched the truck ahead take a sharp turn onto an unmarked dirt path leading away from the main road, veering further into the night. "You know me, a couple of hours, tops. Just… trying to get some inspiration," he replied, his words a darkly amused whisper.

Her faint laugh tickled his ear, but he was already slipping the phone into his pocket, his focus locked on Eric's tail lights as they lurched forward and then stilled, fading into a darkened patch beside a decaying, half collapsed structure in the distance. Tyler took a deep breath, feeling the familiar heaviness of the Abyssal Passenger, the nameless, clawing darkness within him, stirring to life, like some ancient thing waking.

Eric's truck sat like a corpse in the night, haphazardly slumped against the ghostly skeleton of the lumber mill. Tyler killed his engine, every muscle in his body primed with deadly precision as he slipped out of the car, moving like a predator through the dark. Gravel crunched under his feet, and the fetid stench hit him like a punch to the gut, rotting flesh, mingling with the metallic bite of blood and rust.

The sounds from inside were unmistakable, the low hum of a lumber saw, its blades biting into something solid, sending wet pulpy sounds out into the night. Tyler's lips curled with a mixture of disgust and anticipation, his pulse thrumming as he edged toward the half-opened door.

"Let's see what you're really made of," he breathed, his voice barely a whisper.

He slipped through the doorway, stepping silently across the filthy floor, feeling the sludge of decaying matter squelch beneath his boots. The rancid air was thick, pressing against him, swallowing every breath. He advanced toward the dim, sickly yellow light spilling from a room ahead.

Inside the room, the gruesome tableau stopped him cold. Eric Perbary was hunched over a makeshift table, a twisted grin stretched across his face as he worked with grim efficiency. Before him lay a body of an unrecognizable man, limbs sprawled at unnatural angles, skin peeled back in uneven strips, slabs of hacked flesh separated in meaty chunks. Blood had pooled around Eric's feet, soaking into the grimy floorboards and dripping in slow, viscous streams into a line of crusted metal buckets.

Tyler's nose wrinkled, the scent of spoiled meat and iron thick enough to coat his throat. The Abyssal Passenger writhed inside him, clawing at the walls of his chest, equal parts repulsed and exhilarated. Every nerve felt sharpened, every sense tingling with hyperawareness.

Eric must have sensed the shift in the room, because he turned suddenly, his bloodshot eyes locking onto Tyler's with a feral almost hungry grin.

"Look what the cat dragged in. Thought you could just peek, did ya?" Eric's voice was a guttural rasp, his grin stretching into a sneer.

Without warning, he lunged, wielding the humming saw like a savage weapon. Tyler, sluggish from the remnants of a hangover, barely managed to dodge. The blade's teeth grazed his upper arm, biting into his flesh and spraying blood across the walls in a dark crimson arc. Tyler screamed in agony, clutching the wound, feeling the hot, wet stickiness as blood streamed through his fingers.

"You call this a 'craft?' Pathetic," he sneered, stepping back to assess.

But Eric was relentless, coming at him again with the saw buzzing viciously. Tyler's gaze darted to a broom leaning against the wall. In one swift motion, he grabbed it. Snapping the handle over his knee. Now armed with a jagged spear of wood, he sidestepped Eric's wild swing and swung hard.

The stick connected with the saw, knocking it out of Eric's grip. It clattered to the floor, still humming angrily as it spun in lazy circles. Eric's snarl turned feral as he lunged again, teeth bared. Tyler twisted, driving the broken broomstick into Eric's thigh with brutal force. Eric screamed, his voice raw, a strangled sound that echoes off the blood streaked walls.

"You little piece of…" Eric choked, but Tyler's voice cut him off, mocking and cold.

"Oh, what psychopaths have become today… all bark, no brains."

Eric staggered, his leg a mess of blood and torn muscle, but he still managed to clutch a nearby hook, using it to pull himself upright. Tyler the twisted satisfaction in his chest like a hot, pulsing thing, feeling the darkness guide his every move.

With a quick, precise thrust, Tyler drove the sharp end of the broomstick into Eric's jaw, forcing it upward with a sickening crunch. The jagged wood pierced through bone and flesh, emerging in a grotesque spray from the back of his neck. Blood and saliva poured down Eric's chin, his mouth working soundlessly as his eyes widened, panic and agony twisting his expression.

Eric's hands flailed weakly, clawing at the broom handle as if he could pry it out. His eyes locked with Tyler's, wide and glassy, filled with the dawning horror of his own demise. Tyler watched, unflinching, as Eric's body slumped forward, his weight bearing down on the impalement, the wood sinking deeper, skewering him like some monstrous, blood-soaked effigy.

Tyler stood over Eric's twisted, blood-drenched corpse, the rank stench of death thick enough to leave an oily film in his mouth. He pulled out his phone, his expression cold as he snapped a photo of the carnage, capturing every sickening detail.

He flipped the photo, scribbling an ominous verse on the back with methodical precision.

"Blood-soaked sins in silent halls,
A killer's end where darkness falls."

The verse flowed from him with ease, an unsettling calm settling over him as he surveyed the wreckage. Moving with detached efficiency, he grabbed a roll of trash bags from his car, taping them together into makeshift body bags, a strange calm overtaking him as he worked.

The Abyssal Passenger was quiet now, momentarily sated by the brutal justice dealt. Tyler wiped his hands on a stained rag, smearing the red further across his skin before he finally stood, taking in the nightmarish scene one last time.

He dragged the bulging bag to his trunk, his face and clothes smeared with dried, sticky blood. Tossing them in without a second glance, he took a deep breath, feeling the raw rush of adrenaline settle as he closed the trunk with a solid, final thud.

Slipping into the driver's seat, he glanced back at the darkened mill, now silent and heavy with death. Tyler's lips twisted into a smirk, muttering to himself, "One more monster… taken out with the trash."

The engine purred as he drove off, his car vanishing into the darkness, leaving the blood-soaked mill and its horrors behind.

SILENT REQUIEM

The moon hangs low and heavy, casting an eerie, silvery glow across the water. The dock creaks softly under Tyler's boots as he steps out of his car, the silence settling around him like a shroud. His boat rocks gently against the dock, bobbing in time with the subtle pull of the waves, a small, sturdy vessel that seems ready to take on any burden he might heap upon it tonight.

Tyler stands on the deck, rolling out thick plastic sheets with meticulous precision. He works methodically, each movement deliberate, each fold pressed tight along the edges of the boat to ensure not a single drop of blood will escape. Tonight, he's not just covering his tracks, he's transforming the boat into a contained slaughterhouse, a place for the darkest parts of himself to emerge without consequence.

The cold air bites against his skin, but it's not enough to keep him grounded. He feels the Abyssal Passenger looming within him, a silent, insistent force pressing down on his chest, urging him onward. Its voice is like a pulse in his ears, urging him to unleash himself fully, to leave no piece of Eric Perbary unscarred.

Tyler opens the trunk of his car, reaching for the plastic-wrapped corpse slumped inside. Even through the layers of plastic, the body is unwieldy, the dead weight a reminder of what he's come to finish. He hoists it onto his shoulder with a grunt, feeling every ounce of its heft, and carries it onto the boat, his eyes dark with purpose. His gloved hands grip tight, the material stretched taut around his fingers, already stained from his earlier work.

With a final, steadying breath, he throws Eric's body onto the boat with a dull thud that echoes in the stillness of the night.

Inside the boat's cramped cabin, Tyler lines up his tools with ruthless precision. Bone saw, heavy duty knife, hammer, bolt cutters. Each tool has a specific role to play, and he takes a moment to test the weight of each one, feeling the cold steel settle into his grip.

The body lies sprawled out on the table, encased in layers of thick plastic that rustle as he begins to unwrap it. He tears the plastic away slowly, each layer revealing more of the twisted, limp corpse beneath. The stench hits him full-force, thick, pungent, the kind of rot that clings to the back of his throat. He barely reacts, his face impassive, his mind already disconnected, sliding into the space where horror becomes routine.

"Pathetic," he murmurs to himself as he examines Eric's bloated, pale skin, mottled with the first signs of decay. "All that bravado… and now look at you."

Tyler's fingers curl around the bone saw, and he presses the teeth of the blade against Eric's upper arm, just below the shoulder. He steadies himself, leaning into the first cut with brutal force. The saw's jagged edge catches on the skin, and he grits his teeth, pressing harder. A gritty, nauseating crunch fills the cabin as the blade sinks into flesh, scraping against bone.

Blood begins to well from the wound, thick and dark, spreading across the plastic-wrapped surface in a slow, viscous pool. The saw bites deeper, grinding through muscle, tearing fibers apart with each brutal stroke. The smell intensifies, a rank mix of copper and spoiled meat that fills the small cabin.

Tyler's hands grow sticky with blood, his gloves slick as he works, the saw jerking with every twist and pull. Eric's arm finally detaches with a wet pop, tendons snapping like overstretched rubber bands. The limb flops heavily against the table, a grotesque, lifeless thing that only minutes ago had been part of a living, breathing monster.

"Nothing but pieces now," Tyler mutters, more to himself than to the corpse.

He drops the arm into a heavy-duty trash bag, sealing it with a strip of duct tape. He repeats the process with the other arm, working with a detached focus, each movement efficient, each cut precise. Blood splatters against his face, mingling with the sweat beading on his forehead. He doesn't flinch.

Moving to Eric's legs, Tyler grips the ankle and positions the saw just above the knee. The blade grinds against the kneecap, splintering bone with a sickening crunch that reverberates through the cabin. His muscles strain as he saws through the dense bone, feeling each jolt travel up his arm, each brutal pull of the blade echoing through his body.

"You hid in the dark, thought you were untouchable," he growls, his voice low, almost guttural.

The leg detaches with a final, gruesome twist, the limb flopping onto the plastic with a sickening splat. Tyler pauses, wiping his forehead with his forearm, smearing a streak of blood across his skin. The air is thick with the stench of death, the taste of it lingering on his tongue like rusted metal.

He works his way up to the torso, his hands now coated in a slick layer of blood, his gloves sticking with each movement. He reaches for the heavy-duty knife, pressing the blade between Eric's ribs, twisting it to break through the fragile cage of bones that once protected his organs. The sound of cracking bones fills the air, each pop and snap a visceral reminder of the brutality of his work.

With a steady hand, Tyler carves through the torso, sectioning it piece by piece. His movements are almost mechanical, each cut precise, each incision deliberate. Intestines spill out onto the table, coiled like grotesque ropes, glistening under the dim light. Blood oozes from every cut, pooling beneath the body in thick, dark rivulets that flow over the plastic in slow, glistening streams.

He stuffs each section into black trash bags, sealing them with duct tape, ensuring that no blood will seep through. The weight of the bags is heavy, each one a testament to the grim work he's completed, each one a piece of the monster he's taken apart.

Tyler stands on the edge of the boat, his arms covered in blood stained plastic gloves, his face streaked with a mixture of sweat and dried blood. He hefts the bags overboard one by one, listening to each one hit the water with a heavy, final splash. The sound is satisfying, a dark lullaby that soothes the Abyssal Passenger within him, silencing the relentless urge that has driven him to this moment.

As the last bag vanishes beneath the surface, Tyler leans against the boat's railing, his breath coming in slow, even gulps. The satisfaction of his work settles over him like a dark cloak, the Abyssal Passenger purring with approval as it recedes into the depths of his mind.

"No more monsters," he whispers to himself, his voice barely audible over the gentle lapping of the waves. "Just silence."

The water ripples, the remnants of Eric Perbary sinking into oblivion, swallowed by the inky depths. Tyler watches as the final bubbles rise to the surface and vanish, leaving the dock silent once more.

THE INKED LOVE

The room is warm with a soft, golden glow from the bedside lamp, casting gentle shadows across the walls. William and Kate lie together on the bed, their breaths still a little heavy, the silence between them thick with the unspoken words of everything they've been through. Kate reaches up, her fingers trailing slowly along the line of William's jaw, a softness in her eyes that reveals just how far her guard has dropped.

William catches her hand, his thumb brushing over her knuckles, savoring the moment. They've been here before, but somehow, this feels different, gentler, yet weighted with the knowledge that nothing about them has ever been simple.

"Seems we keep ending up like this," she whispers, a touch of humor mixed with something more vulnerable.
His gaze holds hers, the corner of his mouth lifting in a slight smile. "Maybe because we're not done yet."

Kate's lips pull into a small, conflicted smile. She wants to protest, to remind him of all the reasons this shouldn't work, but instead, she leans closer, letting herself be pulled in by the quiet understanding they share. Their hands intertwine, fingers lacing together as if to anchor them in the present, just for a little longer.

They stay like that, the intensity building between them as they study each other's faces. Neither wants to break the silence, but finally, it's Kate who speaks, her voice barely above a whisper.

"What are we doing, Will?"

He sighs, his gaze drifting briefly to the ceiling before coming back to her. "I don't know," he admits, running his thumb gently across her hand. "Maybe just trying to make sense of... all of this. Of us."

Kate's expression softens as she props herself up on one elbow, taking a long look at him as if she's seeing him for the first time. "If this were anyone else, we'd have a clear line," she murmurs, searching his eyes. "But with you... I can never seem to draw one."

William reaches up, his fingers tucking a loose strand of her hair behind her ear, his touch lingering against her cheek. "It's never been easy for us, Kate."

She leans into his touch, closing her eyes for a moment, breathing in his familiar scent. Then, resting her forehead against his, she takes a deep breath, allowing herself to be present with him in a way that feels rare and raw.

For a while, they simply hold each other in the silence, words unnecessary, their quiet understanding enough to fill the room.

FILMMAKER'S WET DREAM

Tyler sat hunched over a mess of papers on his desk, surrounded by open notebooks, loose documents, and a file labeled "James 'Jim' Lauer." He skimmed through each page, his eyes sharp and focused, taking in every detail. The man in the clipped photograph seemed average, even innocent, but Tyler's gaze betrayed a cold calculation. He read through police reports, crime scene photos, and witness statements with an almost clinical detachment, his mind already beginning to trace a pattern in the information.

But then he felt a familiar warmth behind him—Emily's arms slid around his shoulders, her gentle touch breaking through his intense focus. Tyler allowed himself a small smile, feeling her press against him, her presence easing the tension that had built over hours of study.

"Well, good morning," he murmured, without looking up.

"Good morning to you, too," she replied, her voice soft, her cheek resting on the top of his head. "How long have you been up?"

He shrugged, flipping to another page in the file. "A couple of hours. Couldn't sleep."

She glanced down, her gaze landing on the file. The name James 'Jim' Lauer stood out, but she didn't say anything, her face softening as she stayed close to him.

"Working on your new book?" she asked, her voice light, though he could sense a flicker of curiosity beneath it.

Tyler nodded, glancing down at his notes. "Something like that. The usual dark stuff. You'd probably think I'm morbid if you knew the half of it."

Emily chuckled softly, her embrace tightening slightly. "Well, I like you exactly as you are—even if you do live in this world of mystery and murder," she teased, her tone brightening. "Speaking of which... we do have plans today, you know."

Tyler finally turned, meeting her eyes. "Do we?"

"Yes," she said, flashing him a warm smile. "You, me, and Tony are going to the film festival this afternoon. They're showing a short on the Inked Reaper."

At the mention of the Inked Reaper, Tyler's expression remained neutral, though his mind sharpened. He kept his voice casual. "Who wrote it?"

She stretched, running a hand through her tousled hair. "Some local filmmaker named Jim Lauer. Ring any bells?"

Tyler kept his face impassive, but his grip on the pen in his hand tightened just slightly. He glanced back down at the file to see Jim Lauer's driver's license photo, a grainy image of the man smiling awkwardly for the camera. A small, detached smirk crossed his lips.

"Sounds like an interesting guy," he said dryly.

Emily rolled her eyes, nudging him playfully. "Come on. It'll be fun. You could use a break from... all this," she said, gesturing at the cluttered desk and the file still open in front of him.

Tyler sighed, closing the folder and setting it aside. "Yeah, yeah. You're right," he said, reaching up to pat her hand resting on his shoulder. "Thanks for the reminder, Em."

Emily leaned down, pressing a quick kiss on his cheek. "Anytime. Now, go shower. We're leaving in an hour," she said, her tone light as she disappeared into the kitchen.

Tyler watched her go, his smile fading slightly as soon as she was out of sight. He opened the file again, his gaze returning to Jim Lauer's photograph. The Abyssal Passenger stirred within him, that familiar dark pull that reminded him why he did this, why he needed to. His fingers absently traced the edge of Lauer's photo, the corners of his mouth lifting in a faint, twisted smirk.

"Soon, Jim. Real soon," he whispered to himself, barely audible.

A SILENT JUDGE

Tyler leaned by the window, his gaze tracing the sleepy, quiet street below. His apartment was mostly still, except for the faint hum of the city filtering through the glass. He stayed perfectly still, arms crossed, lost in a calm yet intense focus.

The sharp click of the front door broke his concentration, and Tyler turned just as Tony came striding in with his usual air of nonchalance, bringing an almost tangible energy with him. Tony's grin was infectious, a burst of carefree confidence that filled the room, clashing slightly with the solemn quiet of Tyler's space.

"Hey, man. Got enough caffeine in you yet?" Tony's voice echoed, casual and lively, a tone that always seemed to break through Tyler's often-serious demeanor.

Tyler allowed himself a smirk, though his expression held a distance. "Working on it." He paused, crossing his arms with a measured glance at Tony. "Got here early, didn't you?"

Tony shrugged, brushing it off with an easygoing laugh. "Couldn't wait. It's not every day we get to watch a movie about a mystery that's still unfolding, right?"

Tyler's eyebrow arched ever so slightly, his expression showing a brief flicker of distaste. He almost looked at Tony as though he were seeing him from a new perspective, or perhaps studying him with the kind of scrutiny he reserved for his writing research.

"A movie about a killer who hasn't even been caught yet..." Tyler's voice was dry, holding a tinge of something darker. "Kind of premature, isn't it?"

Tony chuckled, unbothered, and wandered further into the room, reaching for a book on Tyler's coffee table, one that Tyler knew was filled with accounts of serial killers and psychological profiles.

"Maybe. But people don't care about 'closure,' Ty. They're fascinated by the kills, the thrill." Tony flipped through the pages casually. "The fact that he's out there, somewhere... it's like catnip to them."

Tyler's face remained impassive, but there was a subtle tightening of his jaw, an intensity lurking beneath his cool exterior. He took a deliberate step closer to Tony, his gaze fixed on him in that unsettling way he had when he was really paying attention.

"So, it's more about the spectacle?" he asked, his voice calm yet probing. "The blood, the fear, all that? Not about the person behind it?"

"Exactly!" Tony said, glancing up, his expression brightening as if he'd hit on something profound. "That's the appeal. It's like... this killer, the Inked Reaper, he's a ghost story in real life. People love the mystery, but they love the... the drama of it even more."

Tyler's eyes narrowed, his gaze sharp, almost piercing. "And you? What's your take on it?"

Tony blinked, taken aback, but his laugh was lighthearted. "Oh, come on, Ty. You know I'm all in for the thrill. It's dark and twisted, but... it's fascinating. You know what I mean."

A heavy silence stretched between them, a beat too long, as Tyler held Tony's gaze, studying him as if searching for something deeper, or perhaps waiting for him to falter. Tony's smile faded, and he shifted uncomfortably under the intensity of Tyler's stare.

Tony frowned, glancing at Tyler with a hint of wariness. "What? What's that look?"

Tyler's tone was calm, almost cold. "Just... making sure I understand your fascination."

The air seemed to thicken, tension building as Tyler's gaze held Tony's for a beat longer than necessary. Tony's discomfort grew, but he chuckled awkwardly, brushing it off with a laugh that held an edge.

"Jeez, Ty. You're acting like I'm a fanboy for a serial killer or something," Tony said, trying to keep his tone light, though it came off defensive. "It's just... morbid curiosity, okay? Same reason people read all these murder books you write."

Tyler's lips twitched, a hint of something unreadable flashing in his eyes before his expression hardened. "I wonder if it's the same, though. Reading about it... and admiring it. There's a fine line."

A frown settled on Tony's face, irritation seeping into his tone. "Hold on. Are you... are you seriously judging me?" Tony's voice dropped, his gaze sharpening in return. "Look, just because I find it interesting doesn't mean I admire it. You of all people should get that. You write about killers, Ty. Hell, you are fascinated by them."

Tyler's eyes darkened, and he took a small, deliberate step closer, his voice dropping to a low murmur. "Maybe. But I don't romanticize them."

Tony scoffed, waving off the statement with a dismissive hand. "Oh, come on. No one's 'romanticizing' anything. It's a story, Ty. Just like the ones you create."

They stared each other down, both refusing to look away, and the silence that followed was thick, almost tangible. Finally, Tony looked away, scratching the back of his neck, his laugh strained.

"You know... if it bothers you that much, maybe you shouldn't go today."

Tyler's expression flickered, something unreadable in his gaze, but he quickly tamped it down, his voice forcibly calm. "Don't be dramatic. I'm going because you wanted to see it. I just... don't get why people are so obsessed with a maniac running around killing people. Doesn't make sense."

Tony muttered under his breath, a note of irritation in his voice. "Says the guy who's written, what, three novels on serial killers?"

Tyler's jaw tightened, his patience clearly waning, but he kept his arms crossed, his gaze steady and unwavering. "That's different. I write for a purpose."

Tony rolled his eyes, a humorless laugh escaping him. "And Jim Lauer, the guy who made this film, he doesn't have a purpose?" Tony's voice grew firm, his tone sharpening. "Everyone's got a purpose, Ty. Not everything's as black and white as you want it to be."

Tyler's mouth twisted into a smirk, his voice laced with sarcasm. "Right. So, we're just all morbid thrill-seekers, is that it?"

Tony sighed, visibly frustrated, shaking his head as he turned away slightly, his fingers tapping restlessly against the edge of the coffee table. "Look, man. I'm not gonna apologize for finding this stuff interesting. And if you think it's weird or twisted... then maybe you need to take a look at what you're doing. Because at least I'm not the one obsessing over files of real people."

The words hung in the air, biting, heavy with unspoken implications. Tyler's eyes darkened, his gaze hardening as he forced a cold, hollow laugh. "You're right. I should look in the mirror sometime."

They stared each other down, both tense, unwilling to back down. The silence between them grew, weighted with mutual irritation and something far darker, a recognition of the shadows they both kept hidden from each other.

Finally, Tony let out a sigh, dropping his gaze, the frustration in his face easing just slightly. "Look, Ty..." His voice softened, his tone almost apologetic. "I get it, okay? Maybe I crossed a line. But... people handle things differently. This is just my way of coping, of understanding, I guess."

Tyler's expression softened, though the darkness in his eyes remained, a slight smile tugging at the corners of his mouth. "Yeah... I get it."

For a brief moment, an understanding seemed to pass between them, the tension loosening just enough for Tony to glance around, breaking the heavy mood with a small, forced laugh.

"So... still want to go?" he asked, his tone lighter, as if eager to move past the conversation.

Tyler hesitated, his gaze lingering on Tony for a beat before he nodded, a ghost of a smirk appearing on his lips. "Yeah, let's go. Maybe I'll learn a thing or two."

Tony chuckled, relieved, clapping Tyler on the shoulder with a familiar ease. "There's the Tyler I know. Come on, man. It'll be... interesting."

They shared a slightly forced laugh, though an underlying tension remained in the air, a silent acknowledgment that both were holding back darker thoughts. As they prepared to leave, Tyler glanced once more toward the table where the file lay, his mind already calculating, his gaze dark and contemplative as he followed Tony out the door.

HUMAN FILTH

The bustling lobby of the theater hummed with anticipation, an electric mix of excited murmurs and nervous laughter. Eager filmgoers clustered together, sipping on overpriced sodas and cradling tubs of popcorn, sharing hushed predictions and theories about the Inked Reaper movie they were all there to see.

Tyler's lip curled slightly as he scanned the crowd, his eyes flitting from one face to another, lingering on the avid expressions of people who seemed almost intoxicated by the thrill of impending horror. He could see it in their eyes, a ravenous curiosity that sickened him.

"This is why I hate humans," he thought, crossing his arms tightly. "They flock to blood and misery like flies. Always so quick to turn someone's nightmare into their entertainment."

Tony nudged him playfully, oblivious to the darker thoughts simmering in Tyler's head. "Hey, you alright, man?" Tony chuckled, sensing his friend's tension but mistaking it for pre-movie jitters. "You look like you'd rather be anywhere but here."

Tyler cast him a sidelong glance, shrugging in a way that seemed casual enough, though there was a flicker of something much colder in his eyes. "Just don't get the appeal. They're celebrating a monster."

Tony laughed, his voice bright and carefree, a stark contrast to the seething contempt Tyler was struggling to contain. "Nah, it's not that deep. People are just intrigued by the kills, not the killer himself. It's like some twisted art form to them."

Before Tyler could retort, someone new stepped forward, cutting through the crowd with an air of smugness that made Tyler's stomach twist with annoyance. Jerry—the name alone irritated Tyler—moved with a cocky self-assurance as he approached them, his hand already outstretched as though they were old friends.

"Tyler Grayson, right?" Jerry's voice oozed with self-satisfaction as he extended his hand toward Tyler, though his gaze lingered curiously. "And Tony," he added, with a nod at Tony, who accepted the handshake a little too eagerly for Tyler's taste.

Tyler didn't move. He stared at Jerry, his expression darkening as he assessed the man in front of him. Jerry's slicked-back hair, his overly confident grin, the smug glint in his eyes—it all rubbed Tyler the wrong way. It wasn't just Jerry's appearance that grated on him; it was the way he carried himself, like he had a claim on everyone's attention.

"Didn't expect to see you here, Jerry," Tyler said, his tone flat, almost daring. "But I guess this is the kind of thing you'd enjoy."

Jerry laughed, apparently unfazed by Tyler's coldness. He waved a dismissive hand, the picture of unearned confidence. "What's that supposed to mean? A little harmless intrigue never hurt anyone, right? Besides, it's not every day we get to see a movie about a killer still out there."

Tyler's jaw tightened. The comment struck a nerve, and he struggled to keep the disgust off his face. "Harmless? Making a spectacle out of someone's death? Real tasteful."

Just as the tension between them started to thicken, a familiar voice cut through the charged atmosphere. Kate and William, Tyler's father, had joined them, likely drawn by the strained exchange. Kate gave a polite nod in greeting, her gaze flicking between Tyler and Jerry with a hint of concern.

"Hey, Tyler. Tony." Kate's voice was light, but Tyler could sense her alertness, the way her eyes scanned the scene, picking up on the unspoken tension. "You all ready for the… show?"

Tyler turned to her, his expression softening just a fraction. "I wouldn't call it that."

William nodded, crossing his arms as he gave Jerry a disapproving look. "Yeah, I'm with Tyler. Exploiting someone's death for a few cheap thrills… seems a bit twisted."

Jerry didn't even flinch. He merely shrugged, flashing his confident grin as he redirected his attention toward Kate, an air of smug amusement about him. "Come on, Kate. Isn't this why people are here? To confront the darkness? Understand what they can't control?"

The words made Tyler's skin crawl. His fingers twitched at his side, and he forced himself to breathe slowly, fighting the urge to snap back. Jerry's words were like an itch he couldn't scratch, an irritation that dug under his skin, threatening to drag him deeper into a resentment he had to keep buried.

"Confronting darkness?" Tyler interrupted, his voice sharper than he'd intended. "Or indulging it?"

"Maybe it's just curiosity, you know?" Tony interjected, glancing between them with a nervous smile, as if hoping to smooth things over. "Some people just find these stories… interesting. It's not always malicious."

Tyler shot Tony a sharp look, his eyes flashing with a silent accusation. The betrayal stung, even if it was minor. Tyler had never liked people making excuses for others, especially people like Jerry.

"Interesting?" Tyler's tone was a razor's edge, slicing through the noise around them. "Or exploitative?"

Kate's hand found his shoulder, her touch grounding him slightly. She gave him a soft look, her voice soothing. "It's just a film, Tyler. Just… keep that in mind."

Jerry took advantage of the silence, that infuriating smirk never leaving his face. "Exactly. Just a film." His tone was thick with condescension, his smile a mocking challenge. "Besides, if you're all so against it, why are you here?"

Tyler met his gaze with a smirk of his own, a cold, calculated expression that didn't reach his eyes. "To make sure it's as garbage as it sounds."

An uneasy silence settled over the group. For the first time, Jerry's confidence faltered, a flicker of something like doubt crossing his face. He chuckled awkwardly, brushing off Tyler's icy words with a shrug, but Tyler could see it—the slight shift in his posture, the way his eyes avoided Tyler's gaze.

"You know, Jerry," Tyler said, his voice deceptively light, though his eyes held an unsettling intensity. "It must take a special kind of person to feel so at home with someone else's misery. Really… takes something special."

Jerry cleared his throat, his gaze flicking to Tony, as if seeking backup. "Come on, Ty. It's not like that. People are just… curious. There's nothing wrong with that."

Tyler leaned in slightly, his voice dropping to a near-whisper, though the menace was unmistakable. "Curious, huh? Or maybe you just like the thrill. Maybe, somewhere deep down, you actually… enjoy it."

Tony shifted uncomfortably beside him, casting a nervous glance between Tyler and Jerry. "Hey, guys, let's just… chill, yeah?"

"Tyler's right, though," William said, his voice steady, a frown etched into his features. "Turning death into entertainment… there's something inherently wrong with that."

Jerry's laugh was forced, strained now, and Tyler couldn't help but enjoy the discomfort that finally showed on his face. "Guess I didn't know you all were so… sensitive about it."

Tyler took a step closer, his gaze never wavering from Jerry's face, relishing the way Jerry's confidence seemed to shrink under his stare. "It's not about sensitivity, Jerry. It's about respect. Some of us don't need to feed off tragedy to get a thrill."

For a split second, there was a flicker of something dark and fearful in Jerry's eyes. He looked at Tyler, truly looked at him, and there was an edge of uncertainty there, as if he were seeing him in a new, unsettling light.

Kate cleared her throat, breaking the tension, her hand pressing more firmly on Tyler's shoulder. "Alright, enough, everyone. Let's just… enjoy the film, okay?"

Tyler finally tore his gaze away from Jerry, though his expression remained stony. He took a deep breath, trying to shake off the lingering anger that simmered in his veins.

"Yeah," he said softly, his voice laced with a hint of dark sarcasm. "Let's enjoy the… art."

As the doors opened, ushering the crowd into the theater, Tyler shot one last look at Jerry, a cold, calculating smile playing on his lips. Jerry met his gaze, but there was a new wariness there, a hesitation that betrayed his earlier confidence. It was a small victory, but to Tyler, it was enough.

He fell into step beside Tony as they entered the theater, a disturbing satisfaction simmering beneath his composed exterior. For the rest of the evening, Tyler's thoughts would replay this encounter in his mind, savoring the subtle fear he'd managed to implant in Jerry's head, a fear that Tyler knew would linger long after the lights dimmed and the screen came to life.

BIRDS OF A FEATHER

The café was alive with noise—a disorienting blend of excited chatter, clinking glasses, and the constant hum of machinery as coffee and espresso drinks were churned out to meet the demands of the festival-goers. People were packed closely together, their laughter cutting through the room in bursts, their voices rising and falling in animated waves.

Tyler felt suffocated. He didn't know if it was the overheated room or just the press of bodies, but everything felt claustrophobic. Every voice around him grated on his nerves, every laugh seemed mocking, as if the crowd was conspiring to pull him under their insatiable fascination with death and tragedy. His jaw tightened, and he did his best to keep his breathing steady, though he could feel his patience wearing thin.

Emily walked alongside him, her hand brushing against his arm as they maneuvered through the crowd. She glanced up, noticing the subtle tension in his face. Her brow furrowed with concern, and she gave him a gentle nudge, trying to bring him back down from the seething frustration she knew was building inside him.

"Hey… you okay?" Emily's voice was soft, laced with the familiar warmth that usually helped ease his discomfort. She had a way of grounding him that no one else did, but today, the crowd seemed too much to ignore.

Tyler forced a smile, but he knew it wasn't convincing. His eyes darted around the room, his gaze lingering on people laughing as they hovered by the food counters. "I'm fine," he replied, though his tone was tense. "I just… you know I hate big crowds."

Emily chuckled softly, slipping her arm around his back in a comforting gesture. She gave him a light squeeze as they reached the front of the line, trying to distract him. "Yeah, I know." She paused, studying his face as if searching for the real source of his irritation. "They just… get under your skin, don't they?"

Tyler scoffed under his breath as they moved through the line, picking up a couple of sandwiches and drinks. He muttered lowly, his words laced with bitterness, "More like bugs swarming a carcass. It's like they don't even realize this whole festival is glorifying death. The way they hover, chatter… it's disgusting."

He cast a disdainful glance at a group of people nearby, who seemed to be deep in conversation about the Inked Reaper movie. The fascination on their faces, the way their eyes lit up as they speculated about the crimes, turned his stomach.

Emily sighed, guiding him to a quieter table in the far corner of the café, away from the majority of the crowd. She understood his need for distance, and she followed his gaze, her face reflecting a hint of sympathy as she took in the scene. "I get it," she said as they sat down. "People can be… oblivious. But, hey, it's just a film festival. Maybe they're here because they're fascinated with the mystery, not the death itself."

Tyler shook his head, scoffing at her suggestion. "Fascinated?" he repeated, his tone dark. "They're here because they enjoy it, whether they admit it or not." His voice dropped lower, his eyes narrowing as he continued, almost to himself. "They get some kind of thrill out of knowing someone suffered. It's disgusting."

Emily watched him closely, her brows knitting together with concern as she tried to gauge his emotions. She reached across the table, placing her hand over his. "Hey, you're an author. You're used to smaller crowds. Maybe that's all this is—just an adjustment."

Tyler gave her a tight smile, appreciating her attempt to soothe him, though he could feel his frustration still simmering under the surface. "Maybe," he replied, though he wasn't convinced. He searched for the right words, glancing around the room as he tried to put his thoughts into perspective. "But it's like… I just see them differently. They're drawn to tragedy like flies. Can't get enough of it."

Emily leaned in, her gaze steady as she met his eyes. She spoke softly, her tone full of understanding. "I understand, but don't let them ruin your day. They don't know the first thing about you. And… I don't want you getting all worked up over people you'll never even talk to."

Tyler took a deep breath, her words working to ease his tension, even if just a little. She was right—he shouldn't let them get under his skin like this. "Thanks," he said, his shoulders visibly relaxing as he took a sip of his drink. "I… I don't mean to get so… intense. It just…" His gaze drifted around the room, landing on a group nearby who were laughing and gesturing animatedly. "It's like they're parasites. Here for cheap thrills, not respect."

Emily chuckled, a playful smile crossing her lips as she leaned closer, trying to lighten the mood. "Don't start calling everyone bugs," she teased. "Or they'll kick you out of here." She leaned even closer, her voice dropping to a whisper. "Besides, I kind of like having you all to myself back here."

For the first time that day, Tyler felt his frustration ease a bit. He smirked, his gaze softening as he looked at her. But then, out of the corner of his eye, he noticed something that made his smile vanish. Two tables down, a man was sitting alone, hunched over a notebook, scribbling intently as he glanced up every so often. It was Jerry.

Tyler's expression darkened, his eyes narrowing as he watched Jerry, who seemed completely oblivious to their attention, focused entirely on his writing. Tyler muttered under his breath, his voice laced with irritation, "Looks like someone's taking notes on my life." He leaned in closer to Emily, his gaze never leaving Jerry. "That guy gives me a bad feeling."

Emily followed his gaze, her expression curious as she took in Jerry's intense scribbling. She shrugged, her voice gentle as she tried to soothe him. "Maybe he's just… you know, a fan. People love authors, Tyler. They want to know what makes you tick."

Tyler scoffed, still glaring at Jerry. "Maybe, but he's been following me around like he's writing a profile. Something about him doesn't sit right."

Emily gave his hand a reassuring squeeze, her voice soft. "You're not here for him. Just ignore it." She offered him a gentle smile. "I'm here. I've got you."

Tyler's gaze softened as he looked back at her, but he couldn't shake the unease gnawing at him. He half-joked, "If he's really writing something about me, he better at least get my good side."

Emily laughed, nudging him playfully. "There's a good side? You've been brooding since we walked in here."

They both laughed, and for a moment, Tyler felt himself relax, the noise of the café fading into the background as he focused on

Emily. But his eyes flicked back to Jerry, who was still scribbling in his notebook, oblivious to their laughter.

Emily noticed his gaze and rolled her eyes with a sigh. "Alright, tough guy," she said, giving his hand a playful squeeze. "Ignore him. Focus on the here and now." She smiled, her eyes meeting his with a warm, steady gaze. "Focus on me."

Tyler finally turned his attention fully to her, his shoulders relaxing as he allowed himself to be drawn into her calming presence. "You're right," he murmured, his voice soft. "I'm here for you." He leaned in close, his eyes locked on hers. "Thanks for always bringing me back down."

Emily smiled, leaning her head on his shoulder as the two of them settled into a comfortable silence. The noise of the crowd faded away, replaced by a quiet calm that only she seemed able to bring him. For a moment, everything felt okay—until Tyler's gaze drifted back to Jerry, who glanced up and caught his eye briefly before looking away.

Tyler's expression hardened, and though he quickly shifted his focus back to Emily, he couldn't shake the unsettling feeling that had lodged itself in his chest.

A FANFEST FEEDING

The lobby buzzed with the low hum of conversations and laughter. Tyler stood near the entrance, scanning the crowd, his gaze sharp and assessing. People milled around him, their faces glowing with excitement, unaware of his scrutiny. The sound of their chatter gnawed at him.

"Humans," he thought, his mouth curving into a faint sneer. "Always looking for thrills in the worst places. They eat this up like candy—every gruesome detail, every hint of blood."

Emily, standing beside him, gave him a sidelong glance, sensing his tension. She kept her voice light as she leaned in closer.

"Relax, it's just a film, Tyler," she murmured, nudging him playfully. "Maybe it won't be so bad?"

Tyler forced a half-smile, his attention shifting past her. Amid the bustling crowd, his gaze landed on a tall, wiry man with a wiry, intense look in his eyes. The man met Tyler's stare and broke into a grin, making his way over.

"Tyler Grayson!" The man extended his hand, his smile broad. "The writer himself. I was hoping we'd cross paths tonight."

Tyler took the hand, his grip firm but cool. "James, right? You're the one behind this Inked Reaper film."

"Guilty as charged," James replied with a smirk. "I can't lie—your books were a big inspiration. The way you capture those dark details...it's like you understand what goes on in a killer's mind."

Tyler arched an eyebrow, studying him with a mixture of intrigue and caution. "Is that so? And what exactly is it you think I 'understand'?"

James chuckled, leaning in conspiratorially. "The thrill," he said quietly. "The way fear seeps into the bones of everyone who hears about a killer on the loose. Especially one who's... untouchable."

Tyler's expression remained unreadable, but there was a flicker of disdain in his eyes. "So you admire the idea of a killer who never gets caught?"

"Oh, more than admire. I'm fascinated," James said, his voice lowering. "The Inked

Reaper...he's the ultimate artist, in my opinion. Every kill is like a masterpiece, left for someone else to discover."

Tyler's jaw tightened, his gaze sharpening as he looked at James, a trace of a sneer tugging at the corner of his mouth. "Or a twisted obsession."

James laughed, undeterred. "Twisted? Maybe. But, come on—don't we all have a little darkness inside? Some of us just...act on it."

Across the lobby, Jerry West sat alone, watching the interaction from a distance, his eyes narrowing with suspicion. Kate Miller leaned over from a nearby seat, whispering close to him.

"Looks like Tyler's making friends," she murmured, her tone carrying a hint of amusement.

"With the wrong people, as usual," Jerry muttered, his jaw clenching as he glared at James.

Noticing Jerry's stare, James raised a hand and gave a cheeky wave. "Ah, Jerry West. I assume you're here to soak up a few insights about the Reaper?"

Jerry's eyes narrowed, his forced smile barely masking his irritation. "Just here to see how much fiction you've churned up, Lauer. Don't go getting any ideas."

James only smirked, turning back to Tyler, his expression alight with a mix of intrigue and mischief. "See? That's why I love this character. The Reaper pushes people's buttons—especially those who think the law is the answer to everything."

Tyler's gaze chilled as he looked at James. "And you're proud of that?"

"Absolutely," James said, grinning. "The Reaper's more than just a character. He's a legend. People want to know him, understand him. Imagine being someone so feared, so...unknown."

Tyler's eyes darkened, his voice low. "It's easy to admire from a distance. When you're the one dealing with death every day, it's not as glamorous."

James shrugged, unfazed. "Maybe that's why you write so well. But hey, I wouldn't be surprised if the Reaper himself was sitting in this very room tonight."

For a brief moment, something cold flashed in Tyler's eyes, but he quickly masked it with an indifferent look. "Let's hope he's enjoying the show."

Emily, sensing the tension building between them, touched Tyler's arm gently. "Why don't we head inside? The movie's about to start."

Tyler nodded, his gaze lingering on James a moment longer. "Sure. Let's get this over with."

As they walked away, James called after them, his voice carrying a hint of smugness. "Looking forward to hearing your thoughts, Tyler. It's not every day you get to watch a killer's legacy unfold!"

Emily held onto Tyler's arm as they made their way toward the theater entrance, glancing at him with a trace of concern.

THE DARK MIRROR

The theater darkened as the opening credits rolled, casting an ominous glow across the screen. Tyler shifted in his seat, his gaze fixed forward, unblinking. The excitement around him faded into a murmur of anticipation, but to him, it was a cloying reminder of the morbid fascination people held for things they didn't understand.

Beside him, Emily fidgeted, glancing at him occasionally. Her hand brushed his, fingers curling in a tentative hold. Tyler's hand remained still, cool in her warm grasp. She could sense something unsettled in him, but she said nothing, only offering that gentle, grounding touch.

The screen flickered, cutting to a grainy shot of a rain-soaked alleyway. Shadows crept along the walls, bleeding into the dampness of the pavement. A figure emerged, a towering shape cloaked in black, dragging a lifeless body across the ground. Limbs twisted at unnatural angles, bones protruding under pale, lifeless skin as the figure heaved the corpse into view. The camera zoomed in, capturing every detail, every grotesque inch of death.

Emily's grip on Tyler's hand tightened as her eyes widened. She leaned toward him, whispering, "Pretty intense, huh? Didn't think they'd go for such a...graphic start."

Tyler's expression barely changed, but his jaw tightened ever so slightly. "They're aiming for shock value," he muttered. "The more blood, the more they think people will pay attention."

Emily chuckled nervously, trying to lighten the mood. "Maybe it's just their way of...staying true to the subject? I mean, you've written some intense stuff too."

Tyler's eyes hardened. "There's a difference between portraying horror and reveling in it."

Silence hung between them as they turned back to the screen. On it, the figure in black crouched over the body, pulling out a jagged blade, glinting under the streetlamp's cold light. Slowly, with a methodical precision, the killer began carving into the flesh—a mark Tyler knew too well.

This wasn't just a film; this was mockery. Every cut, every brutal stroke of the blade, felt like a taunt. Tyler's hands clenched in his lap, his nails digging into his palms as he forced himself to stay composed.

Inside, though, his mind churned with contempt. "This isn't admiration," he thought, watching the scene unfold. "It's mockery. They're turning him into a sideshow attraction, some cheap thrill for a crowd that'll forget by morning."

Emily shifted beside him, her discomfort growing as the scene continued. The screen cut to the killer's lair, a dimly lit room cluttered with tools of his trade. A metal table stood in the center, gleaming under harsh lights, and beside it, a wall covered in photographs—a morbid gallery of his victims.

She leaned close again, her voice soft and tentative. "Do you think the real Reaper is watching this somewhere? Maybe…taking notes?"

Tyler glanced at her, the faintest smirk playing on his lips. "If he's watching, he's probably just as unimpressed."

Emily laughed, but it was a nervous sound, filled with tension she couldn't shake. Tyler's attention snapped back to the screen as the killer moved, stalking his next victim down a deserted street. Every step was silent, calculated. Tyler's eyes narrowed, studying the movement, the predatory grace that was almost too close to reality.

It was disturbingly accurate, and a cold unease settled in his stomach. "They don't know a damn thing," he thought, anger bubbling beneath his calm exterior. "They're making him into some cartoonish villain. It's nothing like...nothing like the real thing."

Emily must have sensed the shift in his mood, for she leaned in again, her voice barely above a whisper. "Hey, are you okay? You seem...tense."

Tyler forced himself to relax, unclenching his fists and resting his hands on the armrest. "It's nothing," he said, his voice neutral. "Just...don't care for the glorification of it all."

Emily nodded, returning her attention to the screen, though her gaze drifted to him now and then, a shadow of concern in her eyes. She could tell this was affecting him more deeply than he let on, and it left her uneasy.

The film dragged on, each scene more brutal, more grotesque than the last. The killer's methods were detailed, almost lovingly captured. Every wound, every drop of blood, was shown in explicit detail, as if the director reveled in the violence. Tyler leaned forward, his focus sharpening, analyzing each frame with a growing sense of dread.

"This is more than just a film to him," he thought, his mind racing. "He's documenting, cataloging...it's like he's paying homage. But to what?"

The climax of the film unfolded with the killer in his lair, walls covered in photographs and diagrams, detailed plans for each kill. Tyler's eyes flickered over the images, his heart pounding as he recognized one—a woman, her body positioned in a way that mirrored a scene from his own memories. It was too close, too exact.

A quiet rage simmered within him, and he whispered under his breath, "No... That can't be..."

Emily looked at him, alarmed by the intensity in his voice. "Tyler, are you okay? You look...angry."

He forced a smile, a hollow gesture that didn't reach his eyes. "Just...appalled, that's all. This whole thing feels like an insult."

"Maybe that's the point?" she offered, trying to reassure him. "To show how horrible it is? I mean, people should feel disgusted, right?"

He shook his head, his voice a low murmur. "There's a line between horror and glorification. This crosses it. It's not about understanding; it's about indulging."

Emily stared at him, sensing there was more beneath his words, something he wasn't saying. She wanted to ask, to pry, but the expression in his eyes held her back. So, she turned back to the screen, though her gaze drifted to him occasionally, worry etched in her features.

On screen, the killer's final scene played out in grotesque detail. He stood over his latest victim, a camera in hand, snapping photos in rapid succession. The flash illuminated the blood-streaked room, casting eerie shadows across the walls.

Tyler's jaw tightened as he watched, feeling the weight of each image, each calculated movement. He glanced over his shoulder, catching sight of James Lauer seated several rows back, a smug smile on his face as he watched his creation unfold.

"This isn't art," Tyler thought, his anger seething just beneath the surface. "This isn't even horror. This is a cheap attempt to glorify something he doesn't understand. And I'll make sure he realizes that."

The film finally faded to black, and the lights came up, casting an unsettling brightness over the room. The audience stirred, some clapping, others looking disturbed, but Tyler remained still, his gaze fixed on the blank screen.

Emily touched his arm, offering a soft, comforting smile. "It's over, Tyler. Let's get out of here."

He nodded, but his eyes lingered on the screen for a moment longer before drifting back to James, who was already looking at him, a smug smile plastered across his face.

Tyler stood, pulling Emily along as they made their way to the exit. His gaze remained forward, his mind simmering with quiet resolve.

PIT OF SHADOWS

Emily was asleep, her face soft, relaxed—peaceful in a way Tyler knew he'd never fully understand. He watched her for a moment, the rise and fall of her breathing, before slipping out of bed as silently as he could. The cold night air bit through his clothes as he dressed, his gaze drifting back to her just once more before he disappeared into the shadows.

The construction site loomed in the darkness, a steel skeleton against the night sky. Wet cement pooled in the pits around him, and the air held a damp, metallic scent that clung to his skin. Tyler moved through the maze of beams and half-constructed walls, every nerve tingling with anticipation. The stench of raw earth and machinery coated his lungs, and he let it fuel his focus. He wasn't here for the view. He was here to find James.

A duffel bag landed with a sickening splat in one of the pits, sinking slowly into the thick, gray sludge. Tyler watched it settle, his face impassive, yet his eyes held a lethal focus.

He could feel James nearby, watching. The familiar prickling sensation on the back of his neck confirmed it.

A figure emerged from the shadows, tall, rough-looking, his face split by a knowing smirk.

"Didn't think I'd get an audience tonight," James said, his voice dripping with mockery. He held Tyler's gaze, the amusement in his eyes deepening as he studied him.

Tyler didn't flinch, didn't react. "Guess I wasn't in the mood to let you have the last word."

James chuckled, a low, throaty sound that echoed through the empty lot. He glanced down at the duffel bag, the smirk spreading across his face. "Figured you'd get my invitation," he sneered. "Not bad, huh?"

"It's pathetic," Tyler replied, his voice cold, calculated. "You're trying too hard, James. All this—" he gestured around the site, at the bag sinking into the cement—"it's cheap. A lousy performance for someone who thinks he's got it all figured out."

James's eyes narrowed. "You're the Inked Reaper, right?" he spat. "That makes us the same."

Tyler's jaw tightened. "No. You kill for sport. I kill because people like you don't deserve to walk free." His voice held a deadly edge, but his expression was still unreadable, controlled.

James shrugged, unbothered. "We both get a thrill from it, don't we? Don't pretend you're any different, Tyler. You've got the same darkness inside you. Why else would you be here?"

Tyler's grip on the knife in his pocket tightened, the tension between them like a live wire. "I'm nothing like you, James. What I do has purpose. You… you're just a parasite." He took a step forward, his gaze cold and unyielding.

James laughed, his smile widening. "Oh, I'm the parasite? Coming from the kid who hides behind daddy's badge, playing judge, jury, and executioner. Tell me, Tyler, does he even suspect? Does your precious Emily have any idea who she's dating?"

Tyler's vision blurred red for a moment, but he reined it in, his voice barely above a whisper. "You don't get to talk about her."

"Oh, I'll talk about her all I want," James taunted, his voice laced with venom. "Bet she wouldn't be so smitten if she knew her boyfriend's hobbies." He cocked his head, watching Tyler's reaction. "Face it, Tyler, you're just as twisted as I am. Just as addicted to the kill."

A scream cut through the tension—a young girl's voice, filled with terror, slicing through the silence like a blade. Tyler's head snapped toward the sound, his pulse quickening.

James's smile turned cruel. "Think you can save her?" He leaned back, arms crossed, watching Tyler with a twisted amusement. "It's a trap, Reaper."

The door slammed shut behind Tyler as he took a step forward, locking him into a narrow pathway of rusted metal beams and concrete barriers. Red lights blinked from high above—a security camera, its lens focused directly on him.

Tyler's hand clenched around the handle of his knife, his heart hammering. "You really went all out for this, didn't you, James?" he muttered to himself.

A soft, eerie whisper echoed through the maze.

"Are you lost, Reaper?"

Tyler ignored it, stepping further into the twisting metal labyrinth, each footstep echoing against the concrete floor. Strobe lights flickered from overhead, casting jarring shadows that shifted and moved with each step. His pulse thrummed in his ears, senses heightened as he rounded each corner, eyes scanning for any sign of James.

At the end of the path, he saw him—camouflaged in shadows, holding a young girl by the neck, her eyes wide with terror. Her cheeks were streaked with tears, her breath coming in panicked gasps.

"Let her go," Tyler commanded, his voice calm but steely.

James's grin grew wider. "She's just a loose end. Like the others." Without hesitation, he brought the blade to her throat and slit it in one swift, brutal motion. The girl's scream choked off, her body crumpling as he shoved her forward, watching as she disappeared into the pit below.

Tyler stood frozen, staring down at the pit, the thick cement swallowing her up. Fury boiled inside him, a rage so intense it felt like it would consume him whole.

James's mocking laughter rang out. "What's the matter? Not the ending you wanted?"

Tyler turned, his face a mask of controlled rage. He picked up a sledgehammer from a nearby pile, gripping it tightly as he advanced on James, his voice low and filled with barely restrained violence.

"I'm going to kill you, James," he said, each word heavy with promise.

James's smirk faltered, a flicker of fear crossing his face as he took a step back. "W-wait… you don't have to do this. I was just… just having some fun."

"Fun?" Tyler's voice was a deadly whisper. "The Inked Reaper doesn't give forgiveness." Without another word, he swung the sledgehammer, the force of the blow shattering James's shoulder with a sickening crunch.

James screamed, stumbling back, clutching at his ruined arm. "No! Please… please!"

But Tyler's face was cold, unrelenting. He swung again, the sledgehammer connecting with James's ribs, the bone shattering beneath the impact. James crumpled to the ground, gasping, blood bubbling from his lips.

"Please," James whimpered, his voice hoarse, his body twisted and broken. "Stop…"

Tyler looked down at him, his gaze as sharp as a blade. "You wanted to see the Reaper?" he said softly, a mocking edge to his tone. "Take a good look." He pulled out his phone, snapping a photo of the blood-slicked scene, the twisted agony on James's face captured in stark detail.

James, barely conscious, tried to speak, choking on his own blood. Tyler knelt down beside him, his voice low and mocking. "What was that? You were saying something?"

With a final, brutal swing, Tyler brought the sledgehammer down, crushing James's skull. The blood splattered across the concrete, warm and thick, seeping into the cracks, leaving a trail of red that spread like veins.

Tyler took a deep breath, the world returning to silence. Slowly, he pushed James's lifeless body over the edge, watching as it sank into the wet concrete, the dark water swallowing him whole, erasing all traces.

ECHOES IN THE DARK

Tyler Grayson kept his eyes on the empty highway ahead, his knuckles turning white as he clenched the steering wheel. The car's engine purred quietly in the solitude of the night, but beneath that hum, another sound filled the space: soft, elegant notes from a piano concerto. The classical music drifted through the car, weaving a strange harmony with the violence and adrenaline that still pulsed under his skin. The haunting melody seemed to echo the turmoil inside him—a contrast of beauty and brutality. Each note, each lingering vibration of the piano strings, was like a reminder, pulling him deeper into reflection.

The road stretched endlessly before him, flanked by shadows of trees swaying in the breeze. The white lines marking the asphalt slipped beneath his car in a rhythmic pattern, hypnotic in their steadiness. Tyler's eyes stayed trained on the road, but his mind was elsewhere, replaying every detail of the night—the look in James's eyes, the final, desperate gasp, the sinking feeling in his gut as he finished the act. The memory twisted in his thoughts, vivid and raw, and he could still feel the sledgehammer's weight in his hands.

A part of him tried to reconcile what he had done, but he knew there was no easy way to justify it. He wasn't sure he wanted to. The Inked Reaper was who he had to be, who he had chosen to become, yet sometimes, in these quiet, solitary moments, he felt as though it was the Inked Reaper who would one day consume him entirely.

He tightened his grip on the steering wheel, the leather creaking under the pressure. Tyler hadn't anticipated the emptiness that would follow the act. All the anger he'd poured into every swing of the hammer, every step, every breath—it had dissipated like smoke, leaving him hollow, a vessel filled only with memories he couldn't erase. He had wanted this to feel like justice, like a necessary evil, but it felt like something else entirely. Something darker. Something that was starting to feel as endless as the highway that lay before him.

Finally, the familiar outline of his house came into view. His heart began to beat with a different rhythm, faster, as if the walls within held more than just his secrets. Emily was inside, asleep, peaceful and unknowing. Tyler slowed the car, pulling into the driveway with the headlights casting a brief, soft glow over the front porch. It felt strange, this act of coming home after what he had done. But this was his life—split in half, one part darkness and one part normalcy. Or as close to normalcy as he could manage.

Tyler killed the engine, and the silence that followed was deafening. He sat there for a moment, fingers still gripping the wheel, his mind flickering through all he had left behind on that concrete site. James's face, frozen in terror; the lifeless bodies sinking into the pit; his own hands covered in blood. His breathing quickened, and for a second, he felt the weight of it all pressing down on him, squeezing every last drop of air from his lungs.

But then, he shook his head, exhaling slowly. Now wasn't the time to let the memories linger. He pushed open the car door, the cool night air filling his lungs as he stepped out, steadying himself. The house loomed before him, dark and quiet, as if it too was holding its breath. Tyler locked the car, pocketing the keys, and made his way to the front door. He twisted the knob gently, slipping inside with a practiced silence.

The faint ticking of the clock in the hallway was the only sound in the stillness. He took off his shoes, careful not to make a sound, and padded through the house with soft steps. His muscles ached, a dull reminder of the night's events, but he forced himself to ignore it. His mind was already slipping into the role he had perfected—Tyler, the boyfriend, the son. Not the Inked Reaper, not tonight.

As he reached the bedroom, he paused at the doorway, taking in the sight of Emily curled up under the blankets, her chest rising and falling with each peaceful breath. She looked so serene, her face softened by sleep, her hair spread across the pillow like a halo. For a moment, Tyler felt an ache in his chest, a pang of something he couldn't quite name. Guilt? Regret? Or maybe just the cold, aching distance between them—the secret he kept that would forever keep her just out of reach.

He moved quietly, slipping out of his clothes and into a t-shirt and sweatpants. Every movement felt like it required careful thought, as though any small noise might shatter the fragile peace of the night. He slid under the covers beside Emily, the mattress dipping slightly under his weight. She stirred, a soft sigh escaping her lips as she shifted closer, her hand brushing against his. Tyler tensed at the touch, his heart beating a little faster.

Her hand found his, fingers curling around his in her sleep. She was seeking him out, even now, unconsciously reaching for the connection that he was keeping from her. Tyler swallowed, staring up at the ceiling, his mind still a battlefield of memories and dark thoughts.

As he lay there, he tried to silence the voices in his head, to block out the echoes of James's last words, the sickening crunch of bones, the feel of blood slick on his skin. But the memories played on a loop, refusing to let him forget. He squeezed Emily's hand, grounding himself in the warmth of her touch, the reminder of something real, something good, something untouched by the darkness he'd welcomed into his life.

Emily murmured something in her sleep, her hand tightening around his, as if sensing the turmoil within him even as she dreamed. Tyler closed his eyes, drawing in a deep, steadying breath. He let the rhythm of her breathing calm him, pulling him back from the edge. She was his anchor, the one thing that kept him tethered to the world he was trying to protect—even if it was from himself.

As he finally began to drift off, the memories started to blur, losing their edge, softened by the warmth of Emily beside him. But even as sleep pulled him under, a whisper of doubt remained, lingering at the back of his mind. He wondered how much longer he could keep this up—this delicate balance between light and shadow, between love and violence.

The last thought that flitted through his mind before he succumbed to sleep was as heavy as it was inevitable: How much longer before it all came crashing down?

PIECES OF THE GAME

The fluorescent lights buzz faintly in the quiet office, casting a dim glow over the scattered papers and photographs on Detective Kate Miller's desk. The room smells faintly of stale coffee, a testament to the long hours she and her partner, Detective William Grayson, have spent poring over the Inked Reaper case. A heavy, oppressive silence hangs in the air, broken only by the rustling of paper as Kate shifts through the stack of crime scene photos, her fingers trembling slightly.

Across from her, William stands, arms folded tightly, his gaze fixed on one photo in particular—a fresh snapshot of the Janitor Killer, his body sprawled on a cold concrete floor, eyes vacant, a wooden broom handle grotesquely piercing through his skull, skewered like a macabre art display. The janitor's bloody face is twisted in a final, silent scream, the broom handle protruding from the back of his head at a harsh angle, anchored deep in the floor.

Kate notices William's clenched jaw, the faint muscle twitching as he stares at the horrific image, a mixture of frustration and rage darkening his features.

Beside the photo, a small white card catches her eye. Its pristine surface seems almost out of place against the violent image beneath it. She picks it up, feeling the weight of the Inked Reaper's message in her hands. Turning it over, her stomach tightens as she reads the words scrawled across it in bold, elegant handwriting:

"A janitor keeps the dirt at bay,
But in filth, he lived another way.
Now he lies cleansed by his own broom;
A servant sentenced to his tomb."

The words are chilling, almost taunting. Kate's mind races, dissecting every line, every curve of ink, searching for clues. Beneath the poem, a signature in dark, bold letters: "TIR." She can almost feel the mocking sneer behind each stroke, as though the Inked Reaper himself were watching her reaction with grim satisfaction.

She flips the card over again and notices a strange design on the back—black ink smudged in a series of lines that, at first glance, seem random. But as she examines it more closely, she realizes the marks aren't random at all. It's a piece of a larger image, like a jigsaw puzzle waiting to be assembled.

"William." She holds up the card, her voice barely above a whisper, an edge of awe and horror mingling in her tone. "This... it's part of something bigger. The back of this card—it's part of an image. He's left us pieces."

William steps closer, his eyes narrowing as he examines the card in her hand. He remains silent, his mind whirring as he processes this new piece of the Inked Reaper's twisted game.

"This isn't just about leaving a message," he says through gritted teeth. "He's showing us something. He's marking his territory, mocking us with every single card. And now... he's leaving us a goddamn picture."

Kate tilts her head, her eyes flickering with understanding. "It's not just a message for the victims," she says quietly, almost reverently. "This... this is for us. To show he's watching. And he's daring us to keep up."

A heavy silence settles over the room. William paces, his steps methodical yet edged with fury. His mind flashes back to each crime scene, each card left behind—pieces of a larger image that he hadn't noticed until now.

Kate takes a deep breath, feeling the weight of realization settle in. She arranges the cards they have so far on the desk, their backs facing up. The black lines and shapes begin to form the vague outline of something, though it's incomplete. She realizes the Inked Reaper must have planned this from the very beginning, taunting them with each new piece, slowly revealing his masterpiece, one crime at a time.

"He thinks he's untouchable," William mutters, more to himself than anyone else. "Leaving us breadcrumbs... turning this entire investigation into his personal chess game."

Kate meets his eyes, a determined glint shining in her gaze. "He may think he's untouchable, but that just means he's bound to slip up. Arrogance always leaves room for error. We just need to figure out where."

William's fists clench, and he nods, his jaw set in grim determination. The photo of the Janitor Killer, the broom handle gruesomely protruding from his skull, seems to taunt him with its stillness.

THREADS OF SUSPICION

Jerry's apartment is cramped, an overwhelming blend of obsessive organization and utter chaos. The glow from a single dim lamp illuminates the tiny space, casting long shadows across walls plastered with papers, notes, and photos. From the doorway, it's impossible to miss the overwhelming amount of work spread out across every surface—a mind caught in the grip of unrelenting determination.

The pinboards are the heart of it all. They stand tall against opposite walls, each representing a distinct purpose, split like Jerry's own focus. On the left, the faces of friends, family members, and acquaintances linked to Tyler Grayson. Printed images show candid moments, smiles, gatherings, and even quiet interactions. Next to each image, Jerry has placed handwritten notes detailing connections, timelines, and potential alibis, marking each name with a red cross—the mark of innocence. Beneath some of these faces are more personal details: birthdays, addresses, interests. Jerry has crossed out each of these, too, coldly organized to ensure he's left no stone unturned. This side of the room emanates an air of calculation, a ruthless insistence on narrowing down everyone in Tyler's orbit, ruthlessly eliminating all but one.

Across the room, the second pinboard is entirely different. It's a darker shrine, almost reverent in the way the images are displayed. This board holds photographs of every one of Tyler's victims, each picture framed in sickly yellowed light as if aging with the memory of the crime. Beneath each victim's photo is a meticulously printed copy of the poem left at the scene—haunting, vivid words set in harsh contrast against the grisly photos. Jerry has typed each one, centering the font and printing them on thick, weighty paper. There are thin red threads connecting certain poems to specific events or names, each detail contributing to Jerry's perception of Tyler as the Inked Reaper. The symbolism is unmistakable, and with each new detail, Jerry's obsession grows.

On his cluttered desk, open case files compete for space with notebooks, highlighters, and markers in every color. Scattered among these are stacks of post-it notes bearing scribbled phrases and questions, each one as haunting as the last: "What connects them?" "Father's influence?" "Patterns in poetry?"

A buzzing sound pulls Jerry from his concentration. His phone lies face up, casting a small beam of light into the room as "Edward" flashes across the screen. Jerry's fingers hover before finally pressing 'accept.'

"Edward," Jerry greets, his voice calm but curious.

The voice on the other end is a stark contrast—panicked, frayed. "It's... it's bad, Jerry," Edward sputters, his words coming in quick, erratic bursts. "They're starting to dig deeper into the missing kids' cases. If they find anything..."

Jerry's face remains unmoved. He leans back into his worn leather chair, crossing his legs casually. "Calm down," he says, keeping his voice deliberately slow, almost bored. "What exactly are they looking into?"

There's a long pause on Edward's end before he finally says, "They're re-interviewing people, going over old files. I don't know how close they are to anything, but it's more than before." His voice breaks, his desperation evident. "I mean, what if they actually—"

Jerry cuts him off smoothly. "They're covering old ground. Nothing's tying us, remember?"

Edward breathes heavily on the other end, the sound harsh in Jerry's ear. "That's what you said last time," he replies, voice cracking with doubt. "But I'm not— Look, I don't have your... patience for this. If they catch a thread—"

Jerry's eyes narrow as he stares at his pinboard. His grip on the phone tightens. "They won't find a thing," he replies, his voice like steel. "Keep your head on straight. Got it?"

There's a reluctant mumble of agreement before the line goes silent. Jerry places his phone on the desk, not even sparing it a glance as he refocuses on his pinboards. His gaze sharpens as he considers each detail on his "Tyler" board. Here, small glimpses into Tyler's world are arranged almost reverently, as though he's studying every part of the young man's life.

Pinned beside a photograph of Tyler's high school yearbook photo are smaller snapshots of his life—moments with Emily, his girlfriend; a shot of him at the marina, with a vague outline of his father in the background; even a newspaper clipping announcing the release of Tyler's debut novel. Jerry lingers over the book's image, tracing his finger along the title, lips pulling into a faint, knowing smile.

He glances back to the other board, where his gaze falls on a chilling scene from the "Janitor Killer" crime. The victim's lifeless body, contorted in horror, lies slumped with a broom handle jammed grotesquely through the skull. Above it, pinned with care, is a poem left at the scene, scrawled with unsettling clarity and signed with three letters: "TIR."

Jerry's eyes narrow, tracing the letters. He murmurs to himself, "Not Tyler's initials, but something else. The Inked Reaper... his mark." His gaze drops to a note attached beneath the photo, a small card he's recently pinned there. The back of it is marked with intricate lines and shading. When he tilts his head, he notices a small, almost invisible corner of a larger picture—a shape only revealed when more pieces are added.

He turns to another victim's photo, lifting the attached poem card to its reverse side. A similar pattern appears, faint but undeniable, as though the cards were pieces of a grand design.

"Each card... part of something bigger," he whispers, realization dawning. "This isn't just a taunt. He's constructing a message... an image."

As he steps back, the breadth of the Inked Reaper's game becomes more chillingly clear. One victim's card reveals a dark corner; another, a splash of ink that could be blood. Each one is incomplete alone, but together, they paint a vision of terror—a macabre calling card. The vision that Jerry sees forming is no coincidence; it's intentional, part of the Reaper's twisted artistry.

Breathing deeply, Jerry shifts back to the cluster of photos linked to Tyler's life. A flash of light from the streetlamp outside casts a faint shadow over Tyler's image, as though mocking Jerry with the answer he's missing. Tyler's father, William Grayson, appears in one photo, his badge pinned proudly on his chest. A dark parallel forms in Jerry's mind, tying father and son, law and crime. His fingers tap rhythmically against the edge of the desk, his mind racing.

"Maybe… maybe he's leaving these clues for more than just the thrill. Maybe it's a message to the police—to his father."

A realization seeps into Jerry's mind, dark and undeniable. He knows he's onto something real, something potent, and he savors the power of the knowledge, feeling closer to Tyler than ever before.

UNSEEN THREADS

The early morning light drifts softly through the curtains, casting a gentle glow over the quiet room. It's a serene scene, nearly untouched by the worries Tyler Grayson carries in the darker parts of his mind. He stirs beneath the sheets, stretching slowly, his gaze settling on Emily, her dark hair splayed out over the pillow, her breathing steady and peaceful. For a fleeting moment, he lets himself sink into the calmness of her presence, feeling almost human in the embrace of morning.

Tyler's gaze is intense as he watches her, a mixture of admiration and something else—a possessive, protective shadow that lingers beneath the surface. He knows, deep down, that Emily represents the last part of his life untouched by the darker urges that consume him. The last piece he hasn't tainted. He reaches out, tucking a stray strand of hair behind her ear, lingering as if the contact might absorb some of her innocence.

But reality intrudes, a reminder pulling him back to the present. His jaw tightens slightly as he mutters, "Tony. Right. Can't keep him waiting all day."

Tyler slips carefully out of bed, making a mental checklist of everything that awaits him beyond the safe cocoon of Emily's warmth. He stretches, feeling the tension build again in his shoulders as he does, almost an armor of stress and calculation settling over him.

He returns to Emily's side, bending down to plant a gentle kiss on her forehead, his lips barely brushing her skin. She stirs slightly, shifting under the covers but doesn't wake. Tyler feels an odd sense of relief that she remains oblivious to his world. As he pulls away, a faint, almost wistful smile crosses his lips—a brief farewell to the innocent life he's crafted with her. Then, he straightens, the soft smile fading into something colder, sharper, as he grabs his jacket and heads out the door.

The car door shuts with a dull thud as Tyler slides into the driver's seat, the familiar leather creaking under his weight. He adjusts his rearview mirror and pauses, catching sight of a car parked further down the street—a figure behind the wheel, almost blending into the early morning shadows. But Tyler recognizes the vehicle instantly: Jerry's car.

The sight of it stirs something deep and volatile in him. His jaw tightens, and a dangerous gleam sharpens in his eyes. This isn't the first time he's spotted Jerry lurking nearby, always too close, watching in a way that ignites Tyler's fury. He's been tolerant so far, allowing Jerry's obsession with the case to go unchecked, but each appearance chips away at Tyler's patience. He can feel his control slipping, a thin thread pulling tighter with each encounter.

With a final glarc in the mirror, he reaches for his phone, dialing Tony. The line rings twice before Tony's voice fills the car.

"Hey, Tony, it's me," Tyler says, his voice calm but his eyes fixed on Jerry's car in the rearview. "Gonna be a bit late to our coffee run, but I'll be there soon."

Tony's response is easygoing, oblivious. "No worries, man. Just don't leave me sitting too long, you know?"

Tyler forces a chuckle, the sound brittle. "I'll be there eventually."

He hangs up, his mind working, and glances again at the shadowy outline of Jerry's car. For a moment, his fingers tap restlessly against the steering wheel, the gesture betraying his simmering frustration. Then, as if a switch flips, he picks up his phone again, tapping into his security camera app.

On the screen, a grainy but live feed of the marina flickers to life. Tyler zooms in, his gaze narrowing as he spots Kate Miller in conversation with the security guard. The man is a rough-looking figure—mid-fifties, overweight, his uniform rumpled and untidy. Tyler's jaw clenches as he observes the exchange, reading the security guard's discomfort even from a distance.

"Great," he mutters, his voice low and taut. "So, they're looking into the marina now…"

He pinches the screen, zooming in on the security guard's face, noting every detail—dark circles under the man's eyes, a nervous glance over his shoulder, the way his hands fidget as he talks to Kate. It's clear that she's pushing, probing into a place that Tyler has carefully crafted to be overlooked. His boat, sitting in its slip, represents a lifeline to his darker impulses, a vessel for the release of every urge he's buried under the façade of a normal life. He knows that if Kate keeps investigating, she'll start asking questions that lead directly to him.

His fingers grip the steering wheel, the knuckles whitening with each thought of Kate's interference. A flicker of dark calculation crosses his face as he whispers to himself, "If they keep digging, they'll see the boat's been out every other night. That'll raise questions…"

He clenches his jaw, the words barely audible as they pass through gritted teeth. "And that guy… he's still working there, isn't he? A security guard with a record that dirty…"

The realization settles in, and Tyler scoffs, shaking his head slightly, disgusted by the sheer incompetence of the marina's management. They've allowed a man with a tainted past to guard their grounds, a loose thread in Tyler's otherwise meticulous cover. If he's honest with himself, he feels almost insulted that this man stands as an obstacle in his path. He's sloppy, careless—a liability in every sense of the word.

His thoughts turn, shifting like the clicking of a lock as a plan begins to form. He can feel the pieces falling into place, the cold logic wrapping around his anger, directing it with precision. It's a thought that comes naturally, as if his mind were already prepared for this eventuality.

"If Kate keeps pushing," he mutters, his voice low and deadly, "that guy's going to become a liability. And I can't have them piecing things together."

The implications hang in the air, a silent promise. He taps his fingers on the wheel, his mind calculating, considering the easiest way to remove this obstacle without drawing suspicion.

The anger that's been simmering within him grows darker, more potent. Tyler's smirk returns, cruel and satisfied, as he whispers to himself, "Guess I'll have to get rid of him before it's too late. One less loose end."

With a smooth, almost predatory movement, he shifts the car into gear, glancing once more at the rearview mirror where Jerry's car sits ominously, an ever-present thorn in his side. But Jerry is a problem for another day. Right now, Tyler's focus is sharp, pinpointed on one thing: neutralizing the security guard before his world unravels any further.

Tyler pulls out into the street, his mind already calculating each step, each move he'll make to eliminate this threat. His anger fuels him, a dark energy that sharpens his every thought, every intention. He feels the thrill of control, the satisfaction of a plan well-constructed, and a cold certainty settles over him.

As he drives away, he allows himself a final, fleeting thought: a warning for those who continue to cross his path. They may think they're closing in, that they're getting closer to discovering his secrets. But Tyler knows better. He's always one step ahead, and anyone who dares to challenge him will learn just how far he's willing to go to protect his carefully built world.

WHISPERS IN THE CAFÉ

Tyler's car pulls smoothly away from the curb, leaving the quiet street and its suburban calm in his rearview mirror. As he drives, his face is an impassive mask, but there's a flicker in his eyes, a glint of something darker, as if each turn of the wheel is winding up the tension inside him. His mind works methodically, planning, calculating his next move, the world around him slipping into background noise.

The café is alive with a steady hum, the sound of espresso machines steaming milk and the constant murmur of conversations mingling with the occasional clink of coffee cups. The air smells of roasted beans, vanilla, and faintly of cinnamon, creating an inviting warmth that Tyler barely acknowledges as he steps through the door.

He pauses near the counter, letting his gaze drift across the room as he takes in the details around him. To his left, a middle-aged couple is deep in a hushed argument over a phone bill, their voices clipped and tense. To his right, two students are poring over thick textbooks, highlighters flashing in and out of their hands. But it's a booth tucked in the back corner that catches his attention—a hooded teenager and a girl hunched over a laptop, engrossed in whatever's on the screen.

The boy, Ethan, has a hood drawn up over his head, shadowing his face as he types quickly, the speed of his fingers suggesting familiarity with what he's doing. His friend, Kaleigh, leans close, her brow furrowed in concentration. Every few moments, she casts a furtive glance around the café, as if to make sure they're not being watched. Her gaze sweeps right past Tyler, who smirks, amused by her paranoia.

As he observes them, Tyler catches glimpses of the screen—a detailed digital map, coordinates flashing, rows of data in tiny font. He has no idea what they're up to, but the way they huddle together, their heads close, sharing whispered words, hints at something they'd rather keep hidden.

He lets his smirk fade as he turns away, taking his coffee from the barista with a nod before heading toward the back. There, at a table near the window, Tony waits for him, stirring his coffee absentmindedly. Tyler can sense the tension in his friend even before he sits down, the faint lines of worry etched in Tony's face as he stares into his cup.

Tyler slides into the seat across from Tony, setting his coffee on the table and leaning back, his eyes once again flicking to the corner where Ethan and Kaleigh are still absorbed in their covert project. He takes a sip, his gaze thoughtful as he mutters, "Looks like we've got ourselves a conspiracy club in here today."

Tony follows his line of sight, snorting softly. "Gotta love it. Everyone's got a secret theory these days. Maybe even us."

Tyler chuckles, the sound low and mirthless. "Guess we're not the only ones with something to hide."

The two share a smirk, the tension between them easing momentarily. Tyler shifts, crossing one leg over the other and regarding Tony with an unreadable expression. They've been friends long enough that Tony should know Tyler better than anyone, but lately, even he seems to be questioning that familiarity. Tyler picks up on it in the way Tony's eyes occasionally flicker with doubt, the way his responses sometimes come a beat too late, as if he's processing something he doesn't want to admit.

"So," Tyler says casually, tracing his finger along the rim of his cup, "that party… I couldn't help but notice you looked a little on edge. Something happen?"

Tony's expression shifts, caught off guard. He stirs his coffee absently, his gaze dropping to the swirling liquid. "Well… not exactly. It was a good time, but… there was that one random reporter."

Tyler's eyes darken slightly, his face hardening. "Jerry?"

Tony nods. "Yeah. He was asking questions, you know? Nothing direct, but you could tell he was fishing for something. I don't know, man… it just felt off."

Tyler waves a hand dismissively, leaning back with a casual smirk. "Don't worry about him. He's just trying to stir up a story. Guy thinks he's gonna write the next big exposé or something."

Tony doesn't look convinced. He lifts his coffee to his lips, taking a slow, thoughtful sip before setting it down and meeting Tyler's gaze. "Funny how you just attract that kind of attention. It's like they're convinced you've got some dark secret."

Tyler chuckles, but the laugh is edged with something sharper, something darker. "Maybe I do. Wouldn't that just make it all the more interesting?"

The joke lands, but there's a strange intensity behind it that makes Tony shift in his seat, uneasy. He studies Tyler, searching his friend's face as if hoping to find a crack, a sign that the words were just that—a joke. But Tyler's expression is as smooth and controlled as ever, his gaze unreadable.

After a moment, Tony sighs, running a hand through his hair. "Just… don't get too deep into anything you can't get out of, alright? Friends are supposed to keep each other out of trouble, not drag them into it."

Tyler's face softens, just slightly, as he leans forward, resting his elbows on the table. "You're a good friend, Tony. Don't worry about me. I'm the same guy I've always been. If anything, the one thing I'm good at is staying out of trouble."

The words are meant to reassure, but Tony's faint smile doesn't reach his eyes. There's a shadow there, a lingering doubt that

Tyler can feel pressing down on them, thickening the air between them. He watches Tony carefully, assessing his friend's reactions, the way his fingers tap rhythmically against the side of his cup, the subtle furrow in his brow.

A MILLION MILES AWAY

A faint glow slips between the blinds, spreading over Emily's bed and casting a soft, golden light across the room. She stirs, her hand instinctively reaching out to the side where Tyler would usually be, her fingers brushing against cool, empty sheets. Emily's brow furrows, a sleepy confusion clouding her face as her hand glides over the undisturbed space.

She blinks her eyes open, adjusting to the morning light, and glances at her phone on the nightstand. The clock reads 7:30 AM, but the screen is blank—no messages, no missed calls. She frowns, a crease forming between her brows. Tyler usually sends a good morning text if he's not staying over.

With a slight shake of her head, she dismisses the thought and rises slowly from bed, stretching. A hint of unease remains, but she pushes it aside as she pads softly toward the bathroom.

Emily leans over the sink, splashing water on her face and patting it dry with a towel. She lingers, meeting her own reflection in the mirror. There's a hint of worry in her eyes, something she doesn't quite understand yet. Reaching for her toothbrush, she glances at her phone again, almost expecting to see Tyler's name flash across the screen. But there's nothing.

"Weird… you always text," she murmurs, almost as if to the reflection staring back at her.

Emily pushes a breath through her nose, brushing off the nagging feeling, and finishes her routine. She takes a moment to look around the apartment—a quaint but tidy space with a cozy, lived-in feel. Her favorite blanket is draped over the couch, and a small stack of novels rests on the coffee table. It's her own little sanctuary. But today, something feels off, a little emptier than usual. She shakes off the thought, grabbing her keys before heading out.

The clinic lobby is bright and welcoming, with colorful posters on the walls and toys scattered across a play area. Children's laughter and chatter fill the space as parents shuffle in and out, juggling bags and strollers. Emily walks in, her face composed but distant. She offers a distracted smile to a few familiar faces before heading toward her coworker, Lisa, who's setting out a new stack of pamphlets at the front desk.

Lisa looks up as Emily approaches, catching the hint of tension in her friend's eyes. "Morning, Em," she says, her voice laced with a hint of concern. "Everything alright?"

Emily manages a smile, though it doesn't quite reach her eyes. "Yeah… just didn't sleep well, I guess." She shifts her gaze toward the coffee machine in the corner, the comforting aroma tempting her.

Lisa studies her for a beat longer, noting the faint worry lines at the corners of Emily's eyes. "Well, there's fresh coffee in the lounge if you need a little pick-me-up," she offers, giving Emily's shoulder a gentle squeeze.

Emily nods, her smile softening as she murmurs, "Thanks, Lisa."

As she heads toward the lounge, Emily pulls out her phone once more, glancing at the screen. Still nothing from Tyler. Her fingers hover over the screen, debating for a moment before finally tapping his number.

Tyler's phone buzzes on a cluttered table, surrounded by notebooks, pens, and various scattered pages of handwritten poetry. The apartment itself is sparse and meticulously organized, a contrast to the chaos of his creative space. The only sign of life is a mug on the counter, half-empty, steam still faintly rising from it.

Tyler walks into the room, his face stony and focused, a subtle tension etched into his features as he glances at the buzzing phone. Seeing Emily's name on the screen, he pauses, his jaw clenching slightly before he swipes to answer.

"Hey," he says, his tone warm but controlled.

Emily's voice is soft on the other end, but there's an undercurrent of unease. "Hey… didn't hear from you this morning. Everything okay?"

Tyler glances around his apartment, a place that feels more like a fortress than a home. "Yeah, sorry about that. Got caught up in some work early. You know how it is."

Emily's voice is laced with a faint hint of skepticism. "Right. Figured you might be working." She pauses, and Tyler senses the slight hesitation. "It's just… you usually send a message. I thought maybe you'd… forgotten?"

He chuckles, but it's a hollow sound, almost rehearsed. "Guess I did. My bad, Em. Just got lost in it."

She doesn't reply immediately, a soft sigh filtering through the line. Tyler shifts his weight, leaning against the counter, and waits, sensing that there's more she wants to say.

"Well, don't get too lost, alright?" she says, trying to sound lighthearted but unable to mask the vulnerability in her tone. "Sometimes it feels like you're a million miles away."

The words hit Tyler harder than he expects, a flicker of something—guilt? Frustration?—crossing his face. He forces a smirk, even though she can't see it. "That's part of the creative process. But I'm here… and I'm all yours once this is over."

Emily chuckles softly, though he can sense the lingering concern in her laugh. "Alright. I'll hold you to that. I just… I miss you sometimes, Tyler. Even when we're together."

The words hang heavy between them, pressing into a silence that Tyler struggles to fill. There's something raw in her voice, something that gnaws at him even though he'd rather ignore it.

"I miss you too, Em," he says finally, his voice low. "More than you know."

For a moment, he lets the truth of it seep into the silence, allowing himself to feel it. But even as he says it, a darker thought flickers in his mind, reminding him of the secrets he holds, the life she has no idea he leads.

Emily breaks the silence, her tone forced into a brightness he knows is for his sake. "So… lunch later? We could grab something quick if you're free?"

Tyler's response comes a beat too late. "Yeah, sure… maybe. I'll let you know."

On her end, he can almost hear the frustration seeping into her voice as she sighs softly. "You're a tough guy to pin down, you know that?"

He laughs, masking the tension he feels. "Occupational hazard."

Emily can't help but laugh along, though a trace of tension lingers in her voice. "Well, don't work yourself into a spiral," she murmurs. "I know how you get."

Tyler's eyes darken for a brief moment as he stares out the window, the city stretching out before him like a maze of opportunities and obstacles. "You and me both."

Another silence falls between them, both of them acutely aware of the distance growing, a chasm widening with each word unspoken. Emily's voice is soft, almost pleading, as she sighs again, "Okay… I'll let you get back to it. Just… take care of yourself, alright?"

"Always," Tyler says, his voice calm but distant, a cool detachment slipping back into place as he ends the call.

As the line goes dead, Emily stares at her phone, the unsettled feeling growing into a gnawing ache. She sits in the clinic lounge, surrounded by the warmth and cheer of her familiar workplace, yet feeling inexplicably alone.

Emily sat alone in the clinic lounge, cradling a warm coffee cup between her hands. The muted pastel colors of the room and the motivational posters on the walls usually felt comforting, but today, they seemed to blur and fade into the background. Conversations from the hallway floated in and out of earshot, and laughter occasionally echoed from the reception desk. She tried to focus on her coffee, swirling it slowly, watching as ripples formed and disappeared, her thumb tracing the rim absently.

"Hey," a familiar voice said gently. "Everything alright? You look like you've seen a ghost."

Emily looked up, blinking as if pulling herself out of a trance. Lisa, her coworker and close friend, stood there, holding a cup of tea and a clipboard, her expression a blend of concern and warmth. She set her things aside and sat down beside Emily.

Forcing a small smile, Emily shook her head. "I'm okay. Really," she murmured. "It's just... Tyler."

Lisa raised an eyebrow, giving her a knowing look. Tyler. Emily's boyfriend—the one with the intense focus on his work, the artist who seemed to live half in his own world.

"Ah," Lisa said, her tone light but empathetic. "The artist's life, huh? You know how they get with their 'creative process,' right? Like they're the only ones on the planet."

Emily managed a faint chuckle. But the smile quickly faded, replaced by a flicker of worry. She lowered her gaze, staring into her coffee as though it held answers she couldn't quite grasp.

"But this feels different, Lisa. It's not just him being buried in his work. Lately, it's like… there's a part of him I can't reach. Like he's slipping away, bit by bit." Her voice softened, edged with an almost reluctant vulnerability. "I feel like he's hiding something from me."

Lisa's face softened. She reached over, resting a hand on Emily's shoulder. "Have you tried talking to him about it?"

Emily nodded. "I have, but every time I bring it up, he just brushes it off. Says it's part of the process." She paused, fingers tightening around the coffee cup. "But I don't know… it's like he's not really there, even when he's sitting right next to me."

Lisa nodded, her expression thoughtful. "Maybe he just needs some time. You know guys like Tyler—they get lost in their heads sometimes. He'll come around."

Emily's lips curved into a small, wistful smile, appreciating Lisa's comforting words, though a trace of worry lingered in her eyes. She took a deep breath, trying to push away the gnawing uncertainty in her chest.

"Yeah," she murmured softly, more to herself than to Lisa. "I hope so."

THE URGE

Tyler eased his car into the gravel-strewn parking lot of the marina, his gaze immediately darting to the rearview mirror. He scanned his surroundings with a habitual, predatory caution, his jaw tightening as his eyes fell on a familiar sedan parked a short distance away. It was Jerry's car—no mistaking the slightly crumpled fender on the driver's side and the telltale badge on the dashboard. Tyler's fingers curled around the steering wheel, grip tightening until his knuckles turned white, an unwelcome heat prickling beneath his skin. Jerry had become an inescapable shadow, his presence clinging like a persistent fog, always lurking in the periphery.

"Can't shake him…" Tyler muttered, his tone edged with frustration.

He paused, taking a deep, controlled breath as he calmed the surge of irritation. His mind, always so sharp, processed quickly, and he forced himself to loosen his grip. The mask he wore every day—the calm, collected exterior—had to remain in place. Composure was essential. He reached for the car door, hesitated, then exited, his movements calculated as he strolled across the lot.

At the edge of the dock, he noticed the marina guard—a burly man with a perpetually bored expression—standing a few feet from his boat. The guard's gaze was fixed on it, his eyes narrowing slightly as he peered over the bow. Tyler's mind buzzed with questions. Was he genuinely curious, or had he been tipped off? Either way, the scrutiny was unwelcome. With each passing second, Tyler's irritation grew, his calm unraveling thread by thread.

Tyler approached slowly, suppressing the urge to let his anger show. Instead, he wore a polite smile as he closed the distance between them, calling out to the man with a casual nod.

"Need a hand with something?" he asked, voice smooth as silk, hiding the simmering tension beneath.

The guard straightened up immediately, his demeanor shifting from casual to guarded in an instant. Tyler could almost smell the man's discomfort, his wariness like a faint, acrid scent in the air.

The guard forced a shrug, attempting to brush it off. "Nah, just making rounds. Routine check." His words were clipped, rehearsed, and

Tyler's eyes narrowed slightly, picking up on the man's unease like a predator sensing weakness.

"Right." Tyler's tone was light, laced with friendly curiosity. "I noticed you were checking out my boat. Do you get a lot of people wandering around down here?" He added a hint of concern to his voice, as if he, too, was invested in the security of his belongings.

The guard's eyes flickered, a hint of something uncertain passing over his face. His gaze darted momentarily toward Jerry's car across the lot, though he quickly covered it up. "Sometimes," he replied, trying to sound nonchalant. "Just doing my job."

Tyler didn't break his gaze, his eyes holding the guard's with a quiet intensity. He took a step closer, lowering his voice just enough to add a note of confidentiality. "Ran into anyone interesting lately? Maybe a woman… someone who looked like she might be a detective?"

The guard shifted, caught off-guard by the question. There it was—a brief flicker of recognition. His face gave it away before he could mask it. He quickly adopted a neutral expression, nodding. "Just asking about boat rentals," he replied, his voice tight. "Nothing unusual."

A tight smile spread across Tyler's face, his eyes hardening almost imperceptibly. He knew when someone was lying; it was an instinct he'd honed over years of carefully studying people, dissecting their weaknesses. This guard was hiding something, and Tyler's patience was wearing thin. He took a step back, feigning acceptance as he tucked his hands into his pockets.

"Just a friendly chat about boat rentals, huh?" His tone was light, almost mocking, his eyes glinting with a barely concealed menace.

The guard took a step back, trying to create space, but Tyler smoothly stepped forward, blocking his path. The guard swallowed, his confidence wavering as he met Tyler's gaze.

"You're sure that's all?" Tyler's voice dropped to a cold murmur, his irritation surfacing in each carefully controlled syllable. "No other questions? No… nosing around?"

The guard's nervousness was palpable now, his face twitching slightly as he averted his eyes, unable to meet the intensity of Tyler's stare. "I told you, just asking about rentals," he mumbled, the words rushing out. "Nothing else."

Tyler held the silence for a long moment, letting the weight of his gaze sink in, a silent warning. Then he took a step back, offering a tight, humorless smile. "Alright," he said, voice deceptively calm. "You take care, then."

The guard nodded, his face flushed as he hurried down the dock, casting one last, wary glance over his shoulder. Tyler watched him go, his blue eyes cold, calculating. It wasn't the first time someone had gotten too close to his secrets, and he knew it wouldn't be the last. But this interference—it was becoming a thorn too deeply embedded to ignore.

Across the lot, Jerry watched the scene unfold, his eyes narrowing as he noted the subtle shift in Tyler's posture, the barely-there tension in his shoulders. He jotted down a quick note, adding it to a growing list of observations he'd been compiling over the past few weeks. Something was off about Tyler, something Jerry couldn't yet put into words but felt in his gut.

Tyler turned, his gaze flicking briefly toward Jerry's car, his face betraying no emotion. But in that fleeting glance, Jerry sensed something—a warning, a threat lurking just beneath the surface.

Later, on the Open Water

Tyler leaned back in his seat, gripping the wheel of the boat as it sliced through the open water. The breeze whipped around him, carrying with it the faint, metallic tang of salt. For a moment, he closed his eyes, letting the rhythmic sounds of the lake calm him, the gentle sway of the boat lulling him into a dangerous sense of peace. Out here, he could breathe. He could be himself—whatever that meant.

But the peace was fleeting. Jerry's presence at the marina lingered in his mind, a stubborn reminder of the scrutiny closing in around him. He could almost feel Jerry's eyes, prying, digging, searching for cracks in the carefully constructed façade Tyler had built.

"Can't shake him… always watching," he muttered, barely audible over the hum of the engine. "Like a parasite, digging into things he doesn't understand."

A dark chuckle escaped him, humorless and cold. The shadows in his mind stirred, shifting like creatures lurking beneath a still surface, waiting for the right moment to rise. Tyler gripped the wheel tighter, his mind a twisted labyrinth of anger, frustration, and the slow, creeping hunger for retribution.

As the boat drifted further from the shore, Tyler's thoughts grew darker, his mind slipping into a place he rarely allowed himself to visit. He leaned forward, peering into the water, watching as the waves distorted his reflection. There was something unsettling about the image staring back at him—something almost… other.

He exhaled slowly, a shiver running down his spine. "The abyssal passenger… it's been there all along," he murmured, his voice barely a whisper. "But now… now it's clawing to the surface."

The words tasted bitter on his tongue, foreign yet familiar, like an echo from the depths of his mind. He knew what it meant. The rage he'd buried, the darkness he'd tried to keep hidden—it was seeping through the cracks, demanding release.

"Jerry…" he muttered, a smirk tugging at his lips. "He wants to push me… force my hand."

He could see it clearly now, the path stretching before him like a dark, twisted road. If Jerry wanted darkness, Tyler would give it to him. He'd let the abyss swallow him whole, drag him into the depths where even the brightest light couldn't reach.

With a final, chilling smile, Tyler straightened, his resolve hardening. He turned the boat back toward the shore, his mind set, his course clear.

UNSHAKEN WATERS

The parking lot at the marina was nearly empty, the quiet air broken only by the occasional rustle of leaves or the distant hum of a motorboat on the lake. Jerry sat alone in his car, parked near the boat dock, staring out at the tranquil water in front of him. Though the water was calm, reflecting the last light of the day in a wash of orange and pink, Jerry felt anything but peaceful. His fingers drummed against the steering wheel in a restless, uneven beat as he checked his phone for the fourth time in ten minutes. No messages. No call. Nothing but the dim glow of the lake outside, as if mocking his anxiety.

"Come on, Kate," he muttered under his breath. He felt the knot in his stomach tightening. Every instinct told him they were close—too close to turn back now.

His phone buzzed suddenly, and the word "KATE" lit up the screen. Relief flooded him, only to morph into tension as he saw the time. She was late—almost an hour. He answered on the first ring, his voice a mixture of hope and urgency.

"Kate. Finally. I was starting to think you wouldn't call." He tried to keep his voice light, but the strain slipped through.

There was a pause, one that stretched a beat too long, and in that silence, something unsettled him. Kate's breath, shallow and hesitant, lingered on the other end. The calm before a storm, he thought, his fingers tightening around the phone.

"Jerry…" Her voice wavered, and Jerry felt a chill run down his spine. "I don't think I can do this."

The words hit him like a punch to the gut. Jerry gripped the steering wheel with one hand, taking in a deep, deliberate breath. He forced himself to respond evenly, despite the swirl of frustration simmering beneath the surface.

"What do you mean, 'can't do this'? We're so close, Kate. You're the only one willing to go this far with me."

The line was quiet. He could almost hear her debating, weighing everything in her head. Her voice came back, tentative but edged with fear.

"I know, Jerry. I know what I said. But…" She let out a shaky sigh. "I've been thinking about it. If William finds out—if he even gets a hint of what we're doing… I could lose everything. My job, my career, my credibility—it's all on the line here."

For a moment, Jerry couldn't speak. He swallowed, his gaze hardening as he stared out at the water. It was too late to back down, and he wouldn't let her slip away now. Not with so much at stake.

"Kate, we've talked about this. William won't know." His tone was steady, as if sheer logic would persuade her. "You're too smart to get caught, and besides, you're doing the right thing. We're exposing something big here. Think of the impact, the justice—this could be what finally takes Tyler down."

She didn't answer right away, and he could almost feel her shrinking back. "But at what cost?" Her voice was small, almost defeated. "Jerry, this isn't just about you or Tyler anymore. This is about William, too. If he finds out I've been working behind his back… it'll destroy him. It'll ruin everything he stands for."

The words made Jerry's teeth clench. William Grayson, always the pillar of virtue, the unwavering "good cop." But Kate's hesitation, her reluctance—it made his blood boil. "And what about what Tyler has destroyed, Kate?" His voice was sharper now, anger slipping through. "He's hurt people—good people. You know what he's capable of. Are you really going to turn your back on that because of William's pride?"

"It's not just pride, Jerry!" Her voice rose, tinged with a desperation that cut through his anger. "William… he believes in the law, in the system. If he finds out I've been undermining that, it'll break him. He's dedicated his life to upholding justice." She took a shuddering breath, as if steadying herself. "And what if he turns on me? Or worse, what if he… goes after you?"

Jerry's jaw tightened, his free hand forming a fist against the steering wheel. Her fear—the way it clouded her, kept her from seeing clearly—made him want to scream. He forced his voice to remain level. "This is bigger than William's beliefs, bigger than his career or yours. This is about stopping a killer. You know what Tyler is. You've seen the evidence. Don't tell me you're willing to walk away because of some career risk."

Kate's hesitation filled the line. "I know he's dangerous, Jerry," she whispered. "But you're asking me to risk my life, my future, my family's legacy—all of it." She let out a bitter laugh, the sound fractured. "And for what? To satisfy our curiosity?"

A surge of frustration flared in Jerry's chest. "Curiosity? This isn't some damn game, Kate. This is about justice. About making sure people like him don't keep slipping through the cracks. You're not just risking your career; you're risking lives by backing out."

He could hear her breathing on the other end, fast and shallow. "I can't, Jerry," she said, her voice almost inaudible. "I can't lose everything I've worked for."

He took a deep breath, trying to steady himself. "You're the only one helping me, Kate. The only one who sees what's really going on. Without you… I don't stand a chance."

"I'm sorry, Jerry." Her voice was a whisper now, raw and broken. "But I have to protect myself. I can't risk everything for something that might destroy me."

There was silence again—a heavy, aching silence. And then, quietly, she added, "I'm out."

The line went dead.

For a moment, Jerry just stared at his phone, the empty silence ringing in his ears. He could feel his chest tightening, a hollow ache spreading through him as the enormity of her betrayal sank in. Kate, his one ally, had abandoned him. Left him alone to face the storm.

The frustration twisted inside him, sharp and relentless. Without thinking, he slammed his fists against the steering wheel, his body shaking with a raw, desperate rage. He pounded it again and again, a guttural scream tearing from his throat.

"Damn it, Kate!" he roared, his voice cracking as he slammed the wheel once more. "You're leaving me to fight this alone!"

He gasped for breath, his chest heaving as he struggled to regain control. His fingers trembled, curled into fists, his body taut with tension. Slowly, he sank back into the seat, the anger fading to a bitter resolve.

His hand reached out, and he turned off the phone, as if severing that last connection would somehow make the pain easier to bear. But it didn't. The loneliness settled over him, heavy and inescapable, pressing down on him like a weight he could never shake.

For a long time, he sat there in the dim light, staring at his own reflection in the rearview mirror. His face was drawn, eyes shadowed with exhaustion. He could feel the sweat cooling on his skin, damp and sticky from the intensity of the moment. Reaching over, he grabbed an old towel from the passenger seat, wiping his face and neck, trying to regain his composure.

As he patted his face dry, he forced himself to breathe slowly, deeply, letting the calm settle over him. This wasn't the end. He wouldn't let it be. Kate's betrayal stung, but it only steeled his resolve. If he had to face Tyler alone, then so be it. He'd find a way.

With a final, steadying breath, Jerry tossed the towel aside, his gaze sharpening as he looked out at the water. The sun had disappeared behind the horizon, leaving the lake in shadow, but his path was clear. He wouldn't let Tyler slip away, no matter who stood in his way.

In the fading light, Jerry's eyes hardened, his jaw set in grim determination.

PIECES OF THE PUZZLE

The world around Tyler is dark, the night thick and impenetrable as his boat glides quietly back into the marina. The lake stretches out into an eerie stillness, the water reflecting shadows that seem to creep toward him, drawn by something in his aura. The usual tranquility of the night doesn't touch Tyler tonight. His mind is consumed, his thoughts a twisted knot of frustration and rage that's simmered all evening, building like a storm.

As his boat drifts into the slip, he catches sight of a figure near the marina house. A slight, nervous man in a faded security uniform stands just beyond the edge of the dock, hands in his pockets, eyes trained on the ground. It's the guard, and he can barely meet Tyler's gaze. Tyler's lip curls in disdain. There's something about the guard's presence here, at this hour, that pricks at his instincts, a sharp needle of suspicion. He observes the man for a long moment, noting the way his hands fidget, the occasional sidelong glances, the way his breath hitches as he sees Tyler step off the boat. A hint of anger flashes through Tyler, but he buries it, allowing only a calm, calculated expression to settle over his features.

The marina house is dim, shadows pooling around corners as Tyler steps inside, the guard moving a few steps ahead, clearly hoping to avoid him. But Tyler isn't in the mood to be ignored.

The guard tries to disappear into the shadows, head ducked as if hoping Tyler will lose interest. But Tyler's footsteps follow him like a hunter stalking prey. Each step deliberate, each sound reverberating with a quiet authority that fills the space between them. The guard stiffens, glancing back as he realizes Tyler isn't letting him go that easily.

Tyler's eyes are cold, an abyss stretching into something darker, something predatory, as he finally speaks.

"Think I didn't notice you snooping around my boat?" His voice is low, controlled, but with an edge sharp enough to cut through steel.

The guard stammers, his hands trembling as he raises them in a defensive gesture. "I-I wasn't snooping," he chokes out, voice quivering. "I swear… I don't know anything."

Tyler's gaze narrows, his jaw clenching as he steps forward, closing the distance between them. There's a heaviness in his movements, a power simmering beneath the surface that makes the guard stumble back.

"Oh? Then why were you here, lurking around?" Tyler's hand shoots out, gripping the man's throat with a practiced strength. His fingers press into the guard's skin, not enough to cut off his air entirely but enough to send a message—a warning of what's to come if he doesn't get answers.

The guard gasps, his fingers clawing helplessly at Tyler's hand. "Please," he wheezes, panic blooming in his eyes. "I'm… I'm a changed man. I've done my time! I don't want any trouble. I didn't say anything!" Tyler tilts his head, studying the guard's face with a cruel curiosity, as though he were examining something foul. He tightens his grip, the pressure intensifying just enough to make the man struggle, to remind him of his vulnerability.

"'Changed man,' huh?" Tyler's tone is dripping with disdain, each word a cold slap. "That's convenient. You 'changed' people always think forgiveness is automatic. That because you've done your time, you get to walk away clean." His grip tightens, his fingers biting into the man's skin.

The guard squirms, his breathing ragged as he tries to twist away, panic flooding his face as he realizes Tyler has no intention of letting go. Desperation fills his voice as he stammers, "Please… I didn't mean any harm. I swear!"

Tyler's lips curl into a humorless smirk, his eyes darkening. "Harm, huh? You think you know what harm is?" He releases the guard's throat just long enough for him to gasp in a breath, then slams him back, pinning him against the cold metal railing at the edge of the dock.

In a smooth motion, Tyler pulls him forward, dragging him toward the water, ignoring the guard's frantic pleas. The guard's shoes scrape against the dock, his breaths coming faster and faster, each one more desperate than the last. Tyler can smell the fear radiating off him, can feel the pulse of terror beating in the man's neck.

"You think this is a game?" Tyler hisses, his voice laced with a dark satisfaction. "Because I'm not playing."

They reach the edge of the dock, and Tyler forces the guard to his knees, gripping his shoulders with merciless strength. The man is trembling, tears slipping down his cheeks as he stares up at Tyler, pleading silently for mercy he's not going to receive.

Tyler leans down, his face inches from the guard's, his breath hot against the man's cheek. "You said you're a changed man," he murmurs, his tone eerily soft. "But tell me… what about people like me?"

The guard's eyes widen in horror as Tyler shoves his head forward, pushing him down toward the edge of the dock. The murky water laps against the wood, cool and dark, waiting.

In one swift motion, Tyler shoves the guard's head beneath the surface, holding him down with unyielding strength. The man thrashes, bubbles rising to the surface as he struggles, his muffled screams lost beneath the water's surface. Tyler's grip is steady, his muscles coiled with lethal intent as he watches the water churn around his victim.

Inside him, something stirs—a shadow, a dark passenger that feeds off the terror in the man's eyes, the feeling of power as he holds life and death in his hands. Tyler feels its presence, a subtle, dark force that seems to whisper, urging him on, stoking his rage with every passing second.

Tyler pulls the guard's head up just enough for him to gasp in a breath, water streaming from his face as he coughs and sputters, his body shaking violently. "Information," Tyler snaps, his tone cold and demanding. "Kate wanted information. What did you tell her?"

The guard blinks, dazed, his mind struggling to process the question through the haze of terror and lack of oxygen. He coughs, shuddering as he tries to find his voice. "She… she wanted footage," he chokes out. "Of the dock. She asked me… to pull every camera recording… of you coming and going."

Tyler's expression hardens, a flicker of fury crossing his face as he realizes just how close someone came to uncovering his secrets. He gives the guard a sharp, cruel smile, a promise of the pain yet to come.

"Why would she need that footage?" he demands, his voice like ice.
The guard's eyes widen in renewed terror, his body trembling as he stammers, "I-I don't

know… she just… said it was important. I didn't ask questions. I swear!"

Tyler's patience wears thin, his fingers digging into the man's shoulders as he shoves him back under the water. This time, he holds him down longer, watching the bubbles rise as the guard thrashes, his body flailing wildly. Tyler's jaw clenches, the dark voice inside him growing louder, urging him on, feeding off the fear and the power.

"Changed man," Tyler mutters under his breath, his lips curling in disgust as he watches the guard struggle. "Changed… but still willing to sell me out.

The guard's thrashing grows weaker as Tyler holds him down, his fingers locked in an unyielding grip, pressing with merciless force. He can feel the man's resistance fading, the frenzied kicks slowing, becoming more desperate, each movement a silent plea for mercy. But Tyler has none to give.

He finally yanks the guard's head back up, watching as the man sputters, water cascading from his mouth and nose. His eyes are wide and unfocused, as if he's been dragged to the edge of death and back, gasping for air, his chest heaving as he stares up at Tyler in pure terror.

Tyler leans in close, his voice a venomous whisper. "Is that all, then? Just some footage?" His eyes are sharp, probing, seeking any sign of deceit. "If you're lying to me, you'd better say it now."

The guard's lips tremble, his voice a broken whimper. "I swear… I swear it's all she wanted. I don't know why—she just said… she needed to watch your movements." His face crumples, tears streaming down his cheeks as he stares at Tyler, barely able to form words. "Please… I have a family. I don't want any trouble."

Tyler's expression shifts, a dark mockery of sympathy crossing his face. "A family?" he repeats, his tone dripping with scorn. "And what? You think that means you're worth something? That having a family makes you untouchable?"

The guard's hands grasp at Tyler's shirt, clutching weakly, desperation twisting his features. "I… I'm different now," he pleads, voice cracking. "I swear… I'm not who I was. I'm trying… to be good."

Tyler chuckles, a low, humorless sound that fills the silence around them. "Different," he says, the word sharp and bitter. "Everyone's different when they think they're about to die."

He tightens his grip on the guard, pulling him close enough for their faces to nearly touch. "But you think I believe that? You think I'll let you crawl back to your pathetic little life because you're a 'changed man'?" Tyler's voice is quiet, but there's a lethal edge in it, a promise of what he's willing to do. "People like you… you don't get to walk away."

The guard's eyes dart around wildly, his breath hitching as he realizes the weight of Tyler's words. His body is shaking, a fresh wave of panic surging through him as Tyler drags him roughly across the dock, his grip unrelenting. Each step is heavy, deliberate, as he forces the man toward the water's edge, ignoring his pleas and the choked sobs spilling from his lips.

"Please," the guard begs, his voice a broken whisper. "I didn't mean… I didn't want any of this. Just… let me go. I'll disappear. I'll never come back."

Tyler's lips twist in a sneer. "Oh, you'll disappear, all right."

He shoves the guard down to his knees, his expression cold, calculating, as he watches the man's shoulders slump, the realization settling in his eyes that no amount of begging will change his fate. Tyler steps forward, his voice dropping to a dark, chilling tone that leaves no room for doubt.

"Tell me everything Kate asked," Tyler says, his tone merciless. "And I mean everything."

The guard's voice trembles as he speaks, each word a frantic attempt to save himself. "She… she only asked for footage. Said she needed every recording of you coming and going. I don't know why. I thought maybe…" He trails off, his face twisted in fear as he glances up at Tyler, uncertain if he should continue.

"Maybe what?" Tyler demands, his grip tightening.

The guard swallows hard, his voice barely a whisper. "Maybe… maybe she knows. Or suspects… something."

A flicker of something dangerous flashes in Tyler's eyes, and he shoves the guard's head back under the water, holding him down, feeling the man's body convulse in a desperate, silent scream. Tyler's breathing quickens, a dark satisfaction filling him as he watches the guard struggle, his limbs flailing uselessly against Tyler's strength.

The seconds stretch on, each one dragging out the guard's suffering, his life slipping away with every heartbeat that pulses against Tyler's hand. Tyler feels a twisted satisfaction in it, a dark thrill that stirs in his chest, whispering that this is where he belongs, in the shadows, holding power over those who think they're safe.

Finally, Tyler yanks the guard's head up, letting him gasp in a ragged breath, his body shuddering violently as he clings to consciousness. The guard's face is pale, his lips blue from the cold water, his body weak and trembling as he stares up at Tyler, his eyes hollow, resigned to the fate he can no longer escape.

Tyler leans down, his voice barely a whisper, a dark smile twisting his lips. "No one asked you to be here," he murmurs. "No one asked you to get involved. But now… you're part of the mess. And you can't undo that."

The guard's mouth opens, but no sound comes out, his voice lost, his mind fractured under the weight of what Tyler has shown him.

Tyler takes a step back, watching as the man collapses forward, his body slumping against the dock as he shivers, broken and defeated. But Tyler isn't done. Not yet. He reaches down, lifting the guard by the collar, dragging him toward the edge, where the water laps quietly, waiting, an indifferent witness to what's about to unfold.

"Maybe you were 'changed' once," Tyler says, his voice soft but laced with malice. "But in the end, you're just another piece of the past. And I don't leave loose ends."
With one final, brutal motion, he forces the guard's head beneath the surface, holding him down as the man's struggles weaken, his body thrashing one last time before going still. Tyler releases his grip, watching as the man's lifeless body sinks into the darkness below, swallowed by the lake, leaving nothing behind but a ripple on the water's surface.

For a moment, Tyler stands there, his breath steady, his mind calm, the night settling back into an eerie silence around him. He feels the darkness within him settle, satisfied for now, as he stares out over the water, his thoughts turning to what comes next.

Tyler stands motionless for a moment, staring down at the guard's body sprawled across the deck. The rhythmic slosh of the lake is the only sound around him, muffled by the weight of the night. Shadows cling to every corner, thickening the air with an oppressive stillness that Tyler finds oddly serene. He rolls his shoulders, feeling the anticipation settle into a strange calmness. He's done this before, but tonight feels different—charged with the tension and defiance he sensed earlier, as though it's an act of personal reclamation.

In one smooth motion, Tyler pulls out a weathered roll of tools from a hidden compartment near the boat's helm. He lays them out meticulously beside the body, each instrument glinting faintly under the dim moonlight. His gloved hands are sure and steady as he unwraps them, each blade freshly sharpened, gleaming and ready. A collection designed not for speed but for control. For precision.

He crouches beside the guard, whose lifeless face is twisted in a grotesque mask of terror, eyes still wide open, mouth parted as if in a final, unheard plea. Tyler studies the expression briefly, a slight smile curling his lips as he reflects on the irony—how many times had this man stared down others in a position of weakness, taken pleasure in his authority? Now he is powerless, his empty eyes as hollow as his promises of being a "changed man."

Taking a firm hold of the guard's shoulder, Tyler rolls him slightly onto his side, positioning the arm away from the torso with practiced ease. His fingers press against the muscle, feeling the familiar resistance beneath the surface. With a faint exhale, he raises the bone saw, feeling the weight of it settle into his palm. It's a small, precise tool with fine teeth, suited to meticulous work—he can feel each ridge of the blade under his fingertips, its edge biting into his glove as he tests its readiness.

In one controlled motion, he lowers the saw, pressing it against the guard's shoulder just above the socket. The fabric of the shirt gives way with barely a sound, tearing as the blade punctures the flesh below, digging into the muscle. Tyler begins to saw, each stroke deliberate, the resistance from flesh and tendon offering a grim satisfaction. The serrated teeth catch slightly at first, then bite deeper, a faint wet squelching mingling with the sound of metal against bone.

Tyler's gaze doesn't waver as he works. He watches intently as each layer separates, the muscles peeling back to reveal the pearly sheen of tendons stretching, straining against the relentless pressure of the blade. The grinding of the saw against bone sends faint tremors up his arm, reverberating in his shoulders as he pushes through, a small bead of sweat forming at his temple. He feels the sickening slip as the bone gives way, allowing the arm to loosen with a final, slick tear.

He pauses for a moment, holding the severed limb in his gloved hand. Blood seeps from the open socket, pooling on the deck in thick, sticky streams, each drop dark as ink in the pale moonlight. Tyler feels a strange satisfaction bloom within him, a cold pride in his work. He lets the limb dangle briefly, watching as the muscles slacken and the fingers curl slightly, as though the guard were reaching for something that would never come.

With a flick of his wrist, Tyler drops the arm over the side of the boat, watching it disappear into the inky depths below. It makes barely a ripple, swallowed by the dark water without a trace.

He turns back to the body, feeling a renewed focus, his mind sharpening as he moves to the guard's opposite arm. He positions himself, angling the saw against the shoulder joint, and begins again. This time, he applies even more pressure, the rhythm of the blade slicing through the sinew and tissue sending a visceral thrill down his spine. The wet sound of tearing flesh, the faint grinding against bone—it all feels ritualistic, as though each movement solidifies his control, an art form in its own right.

The guard's limp body jerks slightly under the force of his cuts, the dead weight pulling against him as he works. Blood pools beneath the severed joint, dripping down in thick rivulets that glisten as they cascade over the edge of the boat. Tyler barely notices, his focus honed on the task as he wrenches the second arm free with a final, wrenching snap.

One by one, he discards the parts into the lake, watching with a clinical detachment as each piece sinks below the surface. They vanish into the lake's dark recesses, the water quickly washing away any trace of blood.

Turning back to the torso, Tyler wipes a splatter of blood from his cheek, leaving a faint streak on his glove as he reaches for a smaller, serrated knife. His eyes harden as he angles the blade toward the man's legs, aligning it just above the knee. He presses down, the blade slicing through skin and muscle, each sawed stroke exposing more of the crimson-soaked tissue below.

Tyler steadied himself over the guard's lifeless form, taking a moment to breathe in the eerie quiet that now surrounded him. The guard's drenched body lay sprawled across the deck, water pooling beneath, dripping from his soaked clothes and limp hands. The air around them grew thick with the scent of lake water mingling with the man's fear—something primal and unsettling that seemed to hang in the cold night breeze.

Slowly, Tyler knelt down beside him, his hand steady as he reached for a concealed, razor-sharp blade he kept beneath the deck compartment—a tool he'd cleaned and sharpened with ritualistic precision. Tyler's mind was void of any hesitation, focused only on the methodical, gruesome work before him. In his chest, a pulse quickened, a rhythm that matched the dark intent in his mind, something ancient and consuming.

"Actions have consequences," he muttered, voice low and detached, as if he were simply discussing a mundane task. "And you—you should've known better."

With precise, controlled movements, he began his work. His first cut was deep and unhurried, starting at the shoulder, blade slicing through flesh and sinew. He could feel the resistance as his blade hit bone, a grinding sensation that seemed to vibrate up his arm. Tyler didn't flinch; instead, his grip tightened, his focus intensifying as he worked the blade, sawing slowly, letting the splintered fibers and gritty textures connect with his mind in vivid, morbid clarity. The guard's body resisted him even in death, muscle and tendon pulling against the blade's advance, each press digging through the stubborn mass.

Tyler's breathing became measured, controlled, each exhale hissing through clenched teeth. He could feel a strange satisfaction with each severed joint, each limb that detached with a final, silent surrender. The world around him had shrunk, reduced to nothing but the wet, nauseating sounds that filled the boat—a symphony of flesh meeting steel.

The night grew darker, the lake enveloping his actions like a silent accomplice. In the murky water, each discarded piece created ripples that quickly disappeared, swallowed by the lake's depths.

Back on the dock, Tyler's steps echoed softly against the wooden planks. He moved with practiced precision, every action intentional and devoid of hesitation. He could still feel the damp residue on his hands, the faint reminder of his task lingering in the grooves of his fingers, but he felt no urge to rush the cleanup. If anything, the steady pace brought him a strange sense of calm, like a ritual he had perfected over time.

In the dim marina lights, Tyler took stock of his surroundings, ensuring he left no trace, no detail overlooked. He had planned every step meticulously, leaving no room for error. As he knelt by his boat, he noticed a single droplet on the edge of the deck—a minuscule mark, nearly invisible to the untrained eye, but glaring in his. With a steady hand, he wiped it away, restoring the pristine surface.

Stepping inside the marina house, Tyler's gaze scanned the room, noting any area that might hint at his presence. Satisfied, he grabbed a rag and doused it with a sharp-smelling cleaning agent, scrubbing down every surface he might have brushed against, his hands moving methodically, rhythmically. His mind, however, had already drifted back to the next step—the perfect alibi, the careful cultivation of his ordinary life.

As he finished, he washed his hands under the cold tap, watching the faint remnants of the lake water slide off his skin, the temperature biting but strangely grounding. He observed his reflection in the cracked mirror, noting the calm, impassive eyes staring back at him, the face of someone who, to anyone else, might appear ordinary—unremarkable even. It was a face he knew well, one that betrayed nothing of the darkness lurking beneath.

After drying his hands, he took one last glance around, ensuring every trace had been eradicated. Stepping out onto the dock, he inhaled the night air deeply, allowing it to fill his lungs, feeling the weight of the night lift as he mentally shed the intensity of the evening's events. The lake was as it always had been, calm and silent, as if it had already forgotten its new secrets.

Walking away, Tyler didn't look back. He moved with ease, a slight smirk pulling at the corners of his mouth.

CANDLELIT CONFESSIONS

Tyler adjusted the stem of a single crimson rose in its vase, his fingers steady despite the whirlwind of thoughts swirling in his mind. The table was set meticulously: a crisp white tablecloth, two porcelain plates framed by polished silver cutlery, and wine glasses gleaming under the warm candlelight. Every detail was deliberate, meant to create an illusion of simplicity and elegance, yet laden with intent.

The soft strains of classical music wafted through the room, a gentle counterpoint to the flickering candle flames. Tyler stepped back to survey his work, nodding faintly. The scene was perfect. It had to be.

A gentle knock broke the stillness, and Tyler's lips twitched into a faint smile. He strode to the door and opened it to reveal Emily, standing there with an expression of quiet surprise. She wore a simple yet elegant dress, its soft blue hue complementing her luminous skin. Her hair fell in loose waves around her shoulders, framing the warm smile spreading across her face.

"Tyler," she breathed, stepping inside and taking in the setup. "This is beautiful. I didn't expect…" She trailed off, her eyes catching the glow of the candles, the carefully plated dishes, and the faintly shimmering rose.

Tyler chuckled softly, moving to pull out her chair. "I wanted tonight to be special. Just the two of us."

She slid into the chair, her hands brushing lightly against his. "You didn't have to do all this." Her voice was touched with awe. "I mean, you already do so much."

"It's not about what I have to do," Tyler said, his tone quiet but firm. He poured wine into her glass, the rich red liquid catching the light. "It's about what I want to do."
Their eyes met for a moment, and Tyler felt the familiar pull, a gravity that seemed to exist solely between the two of them. He handed her the glass, their fingers brushing briefly, and a small spark of warmth flared between them.

"So," Emily said, setting her glass down and cutting into her meal. "You have to tell me. Did you actually cook all of this yourself, or did you bribe someone to help?"

Tyler laughed, a sound that felt surprisingly natural. "I promise, it's all me. I might've watched a few YouTube videos to get it right, but I think I managed okay."

She took a bite, her eyes lighting up as the flavors hit her palate. "Okay? Tyler, this is amazing! I'm officially impressed."
Tyler smiled, leaning back slightly as he watched her enjoy the meal. "Good. That was the goal."

"You're setting the bar way too high," Emily teased, pointing her fork at him. "Now I'm going to have to come up with something to top this."

"You don't have to top anything," Tyler said, his voice dropping into a more serious tone. "Just being here with you… that's enough."

Emily's playful smile softened into something more earnest. She reached across the table and rested her hand on his. "You're too hard on yourself, you know that? You deserve to be happy, Tyler. More than anyone I know."

Tyler's jaw tightened for a fraction of a second, a flicker of something unreadable crossing his face. "Sometimes I'm not so sure," he murmured, almost to himself.

Emily squeezed his hand, her voice firm. "Well, I'm sure. You're a good person, Tyler. Even if you can't see it right now, I do. I always have."

The candles burned low by the time they moved to the couch, sitting close enough that their knees brushed. Emily curled up slightly, resting her head against the back of the couch, her face tilted toward Tyler.

"You really went all out tonight," she said, her voice soft. "It's like you wanted to spoil me."

"Maybe I did," Tyler replied, a small smile tugging at his lips. "Or maybe I just wanted to remind myself how lucky I am." Emily blushed faintly, her fingers tracing idle patterns on the couch's fabric. "You don't have to do all this to remind me. I already know how much you care."

Tyler turned toward her fully, his expression growing more serious. "It's not just that, Emily. Sometimes I feel like I don't… deserve any of this. Or you."

Her brows knit together, and she reached out to cup his cheek, forcing him to meet her gaze. "Don't say that. You're kind, thoughtful, and stronger than you realize. Whatever you've been through… it doesn't change who you are now."

Tyler's throat tightened. Her words cut through him, striking a part of him he thought he had buried long ago. "What if you don't know everything about me?" he asked quietly. "What if there are parts of me you wouldn't like?"

Emily tilted her head, her expression unwavering. "Then show me. Whatever you're afraid of, I want to see it. That's what love is, Tyler. It's about accepting the whole person, not just the parts that are easy."

For a moment, Tyler couldn't speak. The intensity of her words, her unwavering belief in him, was almost too much. He leaned forward and kissed her softly, as if trying to absorb her faith into himself.

The bedroom was bathed in a warm, ambient glow, the curtains drawn just enough to let a sliver of moonlight in. Tyler and Emily moved together slowly, their touches deliberate and tender. Every kiss lingered, every movement filled with quiet intensity.

Emily ran her fingers through his hair, her eyes locking onto his. "I've never felt this close to anyone," she whispered, her voice filled with wonder.

Tyler brushed a strand of hair from her face, his fingers trembling slightly. "I don't deserve you," he murmured, his voice rough with emotion. "But I want to. I want to be someone worthy of you."

"You already are," Emily replied, her voice firm. "You're everything I've ever wanted."

Their connection deepencd as the night stretched on, every moment shared between them feeling weightier than the last. Tyler held her close, his hands firm but gentle, as if afraid she might slip away.

Later, as they lay entwined, Emily rested her head on Tyler's chest, her breath soft and steady against his skin. Tyler's fingers traced absent patterns along her back, his mind drifting despite the warmth of her presence.

"What are you thinking about?" Emily asked softly, her finger trailing along his collarbone.

Tyler hesitated, then exhaled. "I was thinking… I wish I could freeze this moment. Just stay here, like this. Everything feels so… right."

Emily tilted her head up to look at him, her eyes shining. "Then let's keep making moments like this. We don't have to think about anything else right now."

Tyler nodded, but his gaze flicked to the ceiling, his thoughts already pushing against the boundaries of their shared peace. He knew the darkness would creep back eventually, but for now, he let her warmth anchor him.

As sleep overtook them, Tyler tightened his arms around Emily, silently vowing to protect her from everything—even himself.

MORNING SHADOWS

The soft morning light streams through the blinds, casting golden stripes across the countertops. The air is warm, filled with the comforting aroma of sizzling pancakes and freshly brewed coffee. Tyler stands at the stove, his movements precise and fluid as he flips a pancake in the skillet. The quiet crackle of batter meeting heat punctuates the peaceful silence.

Emily sits at the kitchen counter, wearing one of Tyler's oversized T-shirts, her legs crossed as she leans her elbows on the polished surface. A faint smile plays on her lips as she watches him work.

"You know," she says, tilting her head, "I didn't realize you could cook. You're full of surprises, aren't you?"
Tyler glances over his shoulder, his lips curving into a soft smile. "Only for you," he replies, his voice carrying a teasing warmth.

He slides the final pancake onto a plate and sets it in front of her, the stack perfectly golden. Beside it, he places a small dish of butter and a bottle of maple syrup. Without missing a beat, he pulls up a stool beside her, joining her at the counter.

Emily picks up her fork, inspecting the pancakes with playful skepticism. "They look good, but the real question is… are they edible?"

Tyler chuckles, pouring syrup over his own plate. "I guess you'll have to be brave and find out."

She takes a tentative bite, her eyes widening in exaggerated delight. "Oh my God. You're actually good at this. Where did you learn to cook like this?"

"Lots of trial and error," Tyler replies, his tone light. "The key is not setting the kitchen on fire. Once you've got that down, everything else just falls into place."

Emily laughs, shaking her head. "Well, I'm impressed. You're officially my personal chef now."

"Happy to take the job," Tyler says, his voice warm. But as they settle into eating, a shift occurs in his demeanor. His smile softens, and his gaze becomes distant, as though he's carefully weighing his next words.

Emily notices, her fork pausing midair. "What's on your mind?" she asks, her voice laced with curiosity.

Tyler sets his utensils down, his hands resting on the counter. "There's actually something I wanted to talk to you about," he begins, his tone casual yet deliberate. "This… guy. Jerry. He's been a bit of a nuisance lately."

Emily's brow furrows slightly, her concern immediate. "Jerry? Who's that? Is he bothering you?"

Tyler nods, leaning back on his stool, his expression thoughtful. "In a way. He's always hanging around, like he's got nothing better to do. It's unsettling—almost like he's trying to keep tabs on me."

Emily frowns, setting her fork down. "That sounds frustrating. Have you tried talking to him? Maybe he doesn't realize how he's coming across."

Tyler's lips twitch into a faint smile, though there's an edge to it—a subtle flicker of something darker. "You think I should just… talk to him?"

"Yeah," Emily says, leaning forward, her voice earnest. "Sometimes people act weird because they don't know how to communicate.

Maybe he's just awkward and doesn't mean any harm."

Tyler tilts his head, pretending to mull it over. "You're probably right. A conversation might be exactly what he needs."

Emily smiles, her face lighting up with encouragement. "See? Just clear the air. And if he keeps being weird, you can always tell him to back off. Or," she adds, smirking, "I can come scare him off for you."

Tyler chuckles, reaching across the counter to take her hand in his. Her fingers are warm, soft against his own, and he strokes her knuckles absently as he gazes into her eyes. "You're always looking out for me," he says softly. "I don't know what I'd do without you."

Emily squeezes his hand, her smile turning gentle. "You won't ever have to. I'll always be here for you."

The words linger in the air, their intimacy wrapping around them like a warm blanket. Tyler's expression softens, and for a moment, his calculating mind quiets, replaced by the faintest hint of longing.

As they return to their meal, the conversation lightens. They exchange playful banter, laughing about their favorite childhood meals and debating the superiority of waffles versus pancakes. But beneath Tyler's calm exterior, his mind churns. Jerry's name echoes in his thoughts, accompanied by the image of Emily's trusting smile.

The plates are empty now, crumbs scattered across them as Tyler gathers them up and carries them to the sink. Emily leans against the counter, sipping her coffee and watching him with quiet appreciation.

"You know," she says, her voice soft, "you really didn't have to go all out like this. Just being here with you is enough for me."

Tyler glances over his shoulder, his hands submerged in soapy water. "I wanted to," he says simply. "You deserve to be treated like this. Like you're special."

Emily sets her coffee down, crossing the room to wrap her arms around him from behind. She rests her cheek against his back, her voice muffled but tender. "You make me feel special. Every single day."

Tyler pauses, his hands still in the sink. For a fleeting moment, a pang of guilt flares in his chest—a rare and unwelcome intrusion. He swallows hard, pushing it down, and forces a smile as he turns to face her.

"You bring out the best in me," he says, cupping her face in his hands. "Even when I don't deserve it."

Emily frowns slightly, her hands resting on his chest. "Why do you keep saying that? You deserve everything good, Tyler. You're an amazing person. You just have to believe it." He kisses her forehead, his lips lingering there as he murmurs, "Maybe someday I will."

Later, as they lie together in bed, Emily's head resting on his chest, Tyler stares at the ceiling. Her breathing is slow and even, a sign that she's drifted into sleep. His fingers absentmindedly trace patterns on her back, but his mind is far from restful.

Jerry's name surfaces again, accompanied by the weight of Emily's earlier words. You're an amazing person. You just have to believe it.

Tyler's jaw tightens. He knows she believes in him, sees him as something he can never truly be. And as much as he wants to preserve her perception, he knows the darkness within him is not something that can be tamed.

His lips press into a thin line as he shifts slightly, careful not to wake her. His mind is already planning his next move, the resolve hardening in his chest. For Emily's sake, he would keep his secrets buried. But for Jerry? There would be no mercy.

WHEN THE HUNTER BECOMES THE HUNTED

Jerry, sensing Tyler's approach, straightens in his seat. His lips twist into a smug grin as he rolls down the window. The sunlight reflects off the car's windshield, casting harsh glares across both men's faces.

"Well, well, Mr. Grayson," Jerry says, his tone dripping with mock politeness. "What a surprise."

Tyler stops just short of the car door, his face expressionless, yet his eyes bore into Jerry with an intensity that borders on dangerous. "You know, I don't usually like company," he says, voice as cold as steel. "But you're making yourself comfortable here, aren't you, Jerry?"

Jerry raises an eyebrow, clearly unfazed. He leans forward, resting an elbow on the window frame with a casual confidence that borders on arrogance. "It's a public street, Tyler," he replies, his tone light but laced with a challenge. "I'm just doing my job, after all."

Jerry gestures around him, as if to remind Tyler of the ordinary, bustling world outside this tense bubble between them. "And this..." he says, with a self-satisfied smirk, "is going to be the pinnacle of my career. Exposing someone like you? It'll make my name unforgettable."

Tyler's lips curl into a smirk, though there's no humor in it. "You think you know something about me, don't you?"

Jerry's grin widens, his eyes gleaming with a thrill that borders on sick enjoyment. "Oh, I know more than you'd like," he replies, voice dripping with satisfaction. He leans closer, relishing every word. "How's that for unsettling? I know you're more than just that charming writer you like to pretend to be. And I think the world would like to know about that, too."

Tyler clenches his jaw, his face an unreadable mask. Yet, there's a glint of danger in his eyes as he takes a step closer, towering over Jerry as his voice drops to a menacing whisper. "You've got no idea what you're inviting on yourself," he says, his tone colder than ice. "Keep playing with fire, and you're gonna get burned. Badly."

Jerry laughs, the sound sharp and taunting. He leans back, looking up at Tyler with an expression that borders on cocky. "Oh,

please," he says, waving a hand dismissively. "Don't play coy with me, Tyler. I'm dying to meet the monster you try so hard to keep in a cage. Maybe that's the real story. So why don't you show me a little taste of it?"
For a long, tense moment, they stare each other down, neither man willing to look away. Tyler's hand twitches slightly at his side, his fingers curling into a fist. The fury simmering beneath his calm exterior finally bubbles over, and in one swift movement, his hand shoots out, grabbing Jerry by the throat and pulling him halfway through the car window.

Jerry's grin falters, his eyes widening in shock as Tyler's grip tightens, his fingers like iron around Jerry's neck. "Be careful, Jerry," Tyler says, his voice barely more than a growl. "Monsters don't play by your rules. You keep poking around, you might just see a side of me that'll haunt you forever."

Jerry struggles slightly, his breath coming in short gasps, yet the defiance in his eyes doesn't waver. "Please, Tyler," he chokes out, his voice strained but still mocking. "I've seen monsters. You're nothing but a sad kid trying to scare someone. I want more than threats—I want the truth."

Tyler's fingers tighten around Jerry's throat, his face inches from Jerry's, his expression chillingly calm. "You want the truth?" he says, his voice a deadly whisper. A slow, dark chuckle escapes his lips. "Careful what you wish for. Sometimes the truth isn't a story you live to write."

Blood rushes to Jerry's face as he gasps for breath, but even in his weakened state, he manages a mocking grin. "I'm not scared of you, Tyler," he rasps, his words punctuated by the faintest hint of laughter. "You're just a kid with an attitude. So go on—show me what you got."

For a split second, something wild and feral flickers in Tyler's eyes. His muscles tense, his jaw clenched so tight that his teeth ache, as every ounce of restraint he's built over the years begins to slip. He pulls Jerry closer, his voice a low, menacing growl that cuts through the air. "I'm going to give you one chance, Jerry. Walk away now… or I'll make you regret every breath you take from here on out."

Jerry's grin only widens, his arrogance undeterred. "Then do it, Tyler," he taunts, his voice hoarse but defiant. "Make me regret it. I'm waiting."

Without another word, Tyler's fist rears back and crashes into Jerry's face with a sickening crunch. The sound of breaking bone echoes in the silence as Jerry's head snaps back, blood immediately pouring from his shattered nose. Jerry gasps, his hand flying to his face, his eyes widening with a mixture of shock and pain.

But even as blood seeps between his fingers, Jerry's expression remains defiant. He laughs, the sound weaker but no less mocking. "Is… that it?" he chokes out, blood dripping onto his shirt. "You're… pathetic."

Tyler's face remains a mask of pure, simmering rage as he leans in closer, his voice low and dangerous. "This is your only warning, Jerry," he says, his tone colder than ice. "Cross me again, and I'll make sure you won't walk away next time."

Jerry coughs, his laughter faint but filled with twisted satisfaction. "See, that's what I wanted to see," he breathes, his voice dripping with smug satisfaction. "Maybe you've got a little more monster in you than I thought."

Tyler's fingers tighten around Jerry's throat for one final, dangerous moment. His face is inches from Jerry's, his eyes dark and unrelenting as he whispers, "You have no idea who you're dealing with, Jerry. Keep pushing, and I'll show you a side of me you'll wish you'd never uncovered."

He releases Jerry with a sudden, forceful shove, watching as he stumbles back into his seat, clutching his face with blood-stained fingers. Jerry meets Tyler's gaze one last time, his voice hoarse but laced with defiance. "Oh, I'll keep pushing, Tyler," he says, his tone dark and triumphant. "And soon, the world's gonna know the real you."

Tyler stands there, watching in silence as Jerry starts the car and speeds off, the tires screeching against the asphalt. He doesn't move, his fists clenched at his sides, his expression dark and unwavering.

For a long moment, Tyler stands alone in the empty street, his mind a storm of rage and bitter satisfaction. He watches the spot where Jerry's car disappeared, his jaw clenched tight as he allows himself a single, dark thought. "He won't live long enough to tell my story."

THE MONSTER IN THE BASEMENT

The front door clicked shut behind him with a faint thud, the sound muffled by the plush carpet. Tyler's eyes adjusted quickly to the dim interior, his gaze darting over the meticulously kept foyer. Family photos adorned the walls, smiling faces frozen in time, and a faint smell of lemon cleaner lingered in the air.

"Perfect little life," Tyler muttered, shaking his head as he stepped further in. "It's always the ones with the spotless floors and the fake smiles."

His gloved hand drifted to the drawer of a side table, pulling it open. The soft creak of the wood barely broke the silence. Inside, nestled between a stack of old receipts and a set of keys, lay a loaded handgun. Tyler picked it up, inspecting it with quiet amusement.

"A gun? Really?" he murmured, slipping the safety on before setting it back down. "You shouldn't have this, Carson. Not someone like you."

He left the drawer open as he moved deeper into the house, his steps deliberate and silent. Every corner he turned revealed more evidence of Carson's carefully crafted facade—an award plaque on the wall for "Outstanding Community Service," a set of pristine golf clubs in the corner, a family portrait that seemed to radiate warmth. Tyler stopped in front of the portrait, studying Carson's face.

"You probably fooled everyone," he said, his voice low, almost conversational. "Everyone but me."

As he continued, his sharp eyes caught a hairline crack in the wall, barely visible under the soft lighting. It was a thin, vertical line that disrupted the otherwise perfect surface of the paint. Tyler's head tilted as he approached it, pressing his fingertips against the edge.

"Well, well," he whispered, a grin spreading across his face. "What are you hiding, Carson?"

The crack gave way under his touch, revealing a hidden door that creaked open to expose a dark staircase leading downward. The air that wafted up was damp and metallic, carrying a faint, unmistakable scent of old blood. Tyler's grin faltered, his expression hardening as he stepped inside.

The wooden stairs groaned faintly under his weight, and the further Tyler descended, the heavier the air became. The metallic tang grew stronger, mingling with the musty scent of neglect. He reached the bottom and paused, taking in the scene before him.

The basement was dimly lit by a single, flickering bulb swinging gently from the ceiling. Against one wall stood a large metal cage, its bars rusted and stained. Nearby, a heavy table bore an array of tools—scissors, knives, and a hacksaw—all encrusted with dried blood. The floor beneath the table was marked with dark stains, their shapes irregular but unmistakably sinister.

Tyler's breath hitched, his jaw tightening. He took a slow step forward, his boots crunching against something brittle. He looked down—a shard of bone, splintered and yellowed with age.

"You really outdid yourself, didn't you?" he said softly, his voice thick with disgust. "How many lives ended down here, Carson? How many screams did these walls absorb?"

His hand hovered over the table, brushing lightly against a bloodstained scalpel. For a moment, his reflection stared back at him in the polished blade, his own eyes dark with fury. He set it down carefully, his gloved fingers trembling slightly.

"This isn't justice," he muttered. "This is chaos. This is evil."

A sound broke his thoughts—a faint click from above. Tyler's head snapped up just as the door at the top of the stairs slammed shut. The echo reverberated through the basement, the finality of it ringing in his ears. He bolted up the stairs, grabbing the handle and shaking it violently.

"Damn it!" he hissed, slamming his fist against the door. "Carson!"

His breathing quickened as he backed down the stairs, pacing in tight circles. The basement seemed to close in on him, the walls pressing tighter as his calm facade began to crack.

"Think," he muttered, raking a hand through his hair. "Think, damn it. There's always a way out."

He scanned the room with fresh determination, his sharp eyes analyzing every detail. The cage, the tools, the walls—each held potential, each could be a weapon or a clue. He approached the cage, gripping the rusted bars. The metal groaned under his touch.

"This is where you kept them, isn't it?" he said, his voice low and dangerous. "Locked them up like animals. Stole their freedom, their lives... and you thought no one would find out."

A bitter laugh escaped him as he turned back to the table, grabbing a crowbar that lay among the tools. He tested its weight in his hands, a grim smile tugging at the corners of his mouth.

"You thought you could trap me?" he said, his voice rising. "You think this changes anything? You don't know who you're dealing with."

Tyler swung the crowbar against the cage with a resounding clang, the noise reverberating through the basement. Again and again, he struck, the force of each blow fueled by a mixture of rage and determination. The rusted bars finally gave way, one snapping loose and clattering to the floor.

"That's one problem solved," Tyler muttered, his breath coming in sharp bursts. "Now for the real one."

He turned his attention to the door, inspecting the hinges. One looked worn, the screws barely holding it in place. Tyler gripped the crowbar tighter, wedging it under the hinge and pulling with all his strength. The metal creaked and groaned before snapping free.

"Almost there," he whispered, a flicker of triumph in his voice.

The final hinge gave way, and the door creaked open. Tyler stepped back, his chest heaving as he stared into the darkness beyond. He adjusted his gloves, a dark, predatory smile spreading across his face.

"You thought you could trap me, Carson?" he said, his voice cold and steady. "Big mistake. I'm coming for you, and there's no cage in the world that can keep me out."

With one last glance at the bloodstained basement, Tyler disappeared into the night, his mind focused on one thing: making Carson pay.

FRACTURED LINES

The warm hum of the café filled the silence, muffled conversations and the faint hiss of an espresso machine offering a comforting background to the tension lingering between William and Kate. The booth they occupied was tucked in a corner, a perfect bubble of privacy amidst the busyness. But for the two of them, the world beyond the small table felt far away, lost in the tangled web of emotions neither could fully unravel.

William cupped his coffee mug, staring down into the dark liquid as if it might offer answers. His jaw tightened, his thoughts a maelstrom of conflict. Across from him, Kate traced a finger along the rim of her cup, her eyes darting between him and the table. She finally broke the silence.

"We can't just leave it hanging in the air, William," she said, her voice steady but tinged with vulnerability. "Not after last night."
He looked up, meeting her gaze. The usual sharpness in his eyes was dulled, softened by uncertainty. He nodded slightly, though his grip on the mug remained firm.

"You're right," he admitted. "We need to talk about it."

Kate leaned forward, her elbows resting on the table, but her fingers fidgeted—a subtle giveaway of the emotions she tried to suppress. "What does it mean, William? For us, I mean." William leaned back, releasing the mug and running a hand through his hair. The gesture made him look older, more tired than she was used to seeing. His sigh was heavy, laced with weariness.

"I don't know," he said finally. "It felt... different. But different doesn't mean it's not complicated."

Kate frowned, her brows knitting together. "It's only complicated because we're making it complicated," she countered. "We work well together, William. We always have. So why should this—why should we—be any different?"

He let out a bitter chuckle, shaking his head. "Kate, you know it's not that simple. The department... they have rules, expectations. Relationships like this—"

"Relationships like this?" Kate interrupted, a teasing smile tugging at her lips. "Are we calling it that now?"

William faltered, momentarily caught off guard by her lighthearted jab. "I didn't mean—"

She leaned back, crossing her arms, her smile fading. "I know what you meant. But I also know that we can't let what other people might think stop us. We've been through too much together to let this... thing between us be dismissed as a problem."

"It's not a problem," he said quickly. "It's just... complicated."

"You keep saying that," Kate shot back, frustration creeping into her tone. "But what are you so afraid of, William? Are you scared of what people will say, or are you scared of what this could actually mean for us?"

Her words hit him harder than he wanted to admit. He looked away, his gaze drifting to the window beside them. Outside, the city moved on, oblivious to the turmoil playing out in their little corner of the world. He sighed again, quieter this time.

"I don't want to ruin what we have," he said finally. "Professionally, we're solid. We trust each other in ways most partners never could. If we... if this goes wrong, it doesn't just affect us. It affects the work, the cases, everything."

Kate softened, though her frustration didn't entirely fade. She reached across the table, her hand resting on his. The touch was light, tentative, but it held a steadying force.

"William, the work is always going to be there," she said gently. "But if we keep putting everything else aside for it, what's left for us at the end of the day? We can't keep pretending there's nothing between us. It's exhausting."

He looked down at her hand over his, then back up at her face. Her eyes held a mixture of determination and something deeper—something he wasn't sure he deserved. He wanted to believe her, wanted to take the leap she seemed so ready for, but the weight of his doubts held him back.

"And what about the Reaper case?" he asked, his voice quieter. "It's consuming me, Kate. Every lead we chase, every clue we uncover... it's like we're still miles away from understanding him. And the closer we get, the more dangerous it feels."

Kate's expression darkened slightly at the mention of the case. She pulled her hand back, resting it in her lap as she straightened. "The case is always going to be dangerous,

William. But you can't let it control every part of your life. You can't let him control you."

"It's not just him," William admitted, his voice dropping to a near whisper. "It's Jerry too."

Her gaze sharpened, and she tilted her head. "What about Jerry?"

He hesitated, clearly weighing how much to reveal. Finally, he leaned in, lowering his voice further. "I don't trust him, Kate. I think he knows more than he's letting on. And if he does, if he's figured out something about the Reaper... or about us..."

Kate's jaw tightened, and a flicker of something unspoken passed over her face. "If he knows something, then we deal with it," she said firmly. "But you can't let him dictate your life, William. You're giving him too much power."

William nodded slowly, but his shoulders remained tense. "It's not just power he has, Kate. It's leverage. And I can't shake the feeling that he's waiting for the right moment to use it."

A silence settled between them, heavy and charged. Kate broke it, her tone softer now. "We're stronger together, William. Whatever's coming, we'll face it. But we can't do that if you keep pushing me away."

He met her gaze, his own conflicted but softening. Slowly, he reached for her hand again, his touch firmer this time.

"You're right," he said quietly. "We are stronger together. But if we do this—if we're really going to be together—we have to be careful. We can't let anyone, not even Jerry, know what's between us."

Kate nodded, relief flickering in her eyes, though her expression remained serious. "Then we move forward," she said simply. "Together."

William squeezed her hand gently, a small smile breaking through the tension. For a moment, the weight of the world seemed lighter. But somewhere in the back of both their minds, they knew the reprieve was only temporary.

As they left the café, the city seemed colder, the shadows darker. The Reaper was still out there, and so was Jerry. But for the first time in a long time, William felt a spark of hope—a reminder that, even in the darkest of times, he wasn't alone.

HE'S BROKEN

The evidence room felt colder than usual, though the temperature hadn't changed. Fluorescent lights flickered sporadically, casting a sterile glow over rows of files, sealed bags, and crime scene photos. The faint hum of a vending machine filled the silence, a hollow sound that did little to mask the tension.

Detective William Grayson stood motionless before the large corkboard dominating one wall, its surface covered in photos, diagrams, and notes pinned with precision. Red string wove a chaotic web between victims, locations, and dates, each thread a physical manifestation of a two-year nightmare. At the center of it all was a new addition: a collage of photos depicting the Inked Reaper's most recent victim.

The image haunted him. A young man, mid-twenties, lay sprawled on the floor of a dingy motel room. Tattoos had been carved into his skin with horrifying precision, spelling out Justice is blind in grotesque detail. Blood had pooled beneath the body, seeping into the threadbare carpet like a scar on the room itself.

William's jaw clenched as he traced the lines of the photo with his eyes. There was something deliberate about this one. Too deliberate. He had seen patterns before, but this was different. Personal.

"Will?"

The soft voice pulled him from his thoughts. Kate Miller stood nearby, flipping through the accompanying file. She glanced at him, concern etched on her face. Kate always had a way of maintaining her composure, but even she couldn't hide the unease radiating from this case.

William didn't respond immediately. Instead, he reached out and gently touched the photo at the center of the board. His fingers lingered on one particular detail—a faint design carved into the victim's arm.
The shape was unmistakable.

A ring.

Not just any ring.

His wife's ring.

"Will, what is it?" Kate asked, stepping closer.

His voice came out quiet, almost trembling, as though he didn't want to give the thought life. "This ring... my wife wore one just like it."

Kate frowned, moving to examine the photo more closely. "William, it's just a detail. It doesn't mean—"

"Don't," he interrupted, his tone sharper than intended. He turned to face her, his eyes blazing with a mixture of grief and fury. "Don't tell me it's nothing, Kate. This bastard knows. He's sending a message."

"Sending a message?" Kate echoed, trying to keep her voice steady.

William gestured to the collage, his hand trembling. "This isn't just about the victims anymore. It's about me. He's dragging her into it—dragging my past into this."

Before Kate could respond, William ripped the photo from the board, crumpling it in his fist. He slammed it onto the table, his frustration spilling over. "This son of a bitch isn't just targeting criminals. He's taunting me. Using their pain to get inside my head."

Kate stepped forward, reaching out to touch his arm. "Will, stop. You're letting him win. That's exactly what he wants."

"How can I not?" William barked, pulling away from her. His pacing quickened, the small room suddenly feeling suffocating. "Every move he makes, every detail he leaves behind—it's like he knows me. Like he's two steps ahead, always watching. And now this? He's mocking me. Mocking her."

Kate's patience snapped. "William!" Her voice echoed through the room, cutting through his tirade.

He froze, startled by the sharpness of her tone.

Kate closed the distance between them, her voice firm but calm. "You need to stop. Right now. Focus on what's in front of you—the evidence, the facts. If you start thinking like him, you're going to lose. And if you lose, he wins."

William's chest heaved, his anger battling with a growing sense of despair. "I don't care anymore," he muttered, his voice cracking. "I don't care what it takes. I don't care who I have to become. This has to end."

Kate stared at him, her expression unreadable. Then, in one swift motion, she grabbed his face with both hands and kissed him.

The kiss was firm, almost forceful, not born of passion but desperation—a jarring attempt to snap him out of his spiraling thoughts.

William stood frozen, too stunned to react. When she pulled back, her hands still on his face, her eyes locked onto his with an intensity that matched his own.

"You listen to me," Kate said, her voice low and steady. "You are a damn good detective. The best I've ever worked with. But if you let this bastard get under your skin, he's going to win. And I'm not going to let that happen. Do you hear me?"

William blinked, her words cutting through the fog of his rage. He lowered his head, his shoulders slumping slightly. "I'm sorry," he whispered. "It's just... I can't stand the thought of him knowing about her. It feels like he's..."

"Violating something sacred," Kate finished for him.

He nodded, his hands balling into fists at his sides.

Kate stepped back, her expression softening. "We're going to catch him, Will. Together. And when we do, he'll rot for the rest of his miserable life."

William took a deep breath, forcing himself to focus. "Together," he echoed.

Kate gave him a small, encouraging smile before turning back to the board. She picked up the crumpled photo and pinned it back in place. "Now, let's figure out how he knows so much about you. Because if he's been watching you, he's slipped up somewhere. And we're going to find it."

William nodded, his resolve hardening. "He slipped up," he said, more to himself than to her. "And when we find it, we'll bring him down."

The two of them fell into a determined silence, their earlier emotions set aside as they focused on the task at hand.

SHADOWS IN THE LIMELIGHT

The faint hum of the air conditioner blended with the methodical rhythm of Tyler's fingers on the keyboard, creating an almost meditative harmony. Words filled the screen of his laptop, flowing with the effortless precision that had earned him accolades as a literary prodigy. A steaming cup of black coffee sat within reach, wisps of vapor curling into the air.

Behind him, the soft clink of utensils broke the silence. Emily, wrapped in an oversized sweater and pajama shorts, moved about the kitchen with an ease that spoke of routine. She hummed softly—a tune Tyler couldn't quite place but found oddly comforting. She worked on breakfast, her bare feet making light, padding sounds on the hardwood floor.

Tyler paused mid-sentence, glancing over his shoulder. The sunlight streaming through the blinds caught the golden highlights in her messy ponytail.

"Smells good," Tyler said, the corners of his lips lifting.

Emily glanced back, grinning. "You're biased. It's just eggs and toast."

"Bias doesn't make me wrong."

Her laughter was soft, a pleasant counterpoint to the serenity of the morning. Tyler returned to his laptop, the smile lingering on his face even as his eyes turned cold, calculating, as they scanned the paragraph he'd just written.

The tranquility shattered as his phone vibrated violently on the desk. The harsh, insistent buzz cut through the calm like a razor, jolting both of them. Tyler's hand shot out, flipping the phone over to check the screen.

WILLIAM GRAYSON.

The name glared back at him, and a flicker of irritation crossed his face. He set his jaw, casting a quick glance at Emily. She arched an eyebrow but said nothing, returning to whisking the eggs.

Tyler inhaled deeply before answering, masking his annoyance with a carefully measured tone.

"Hey, Dad," he said, keeping his voice light.

The response on the other end was anything but. William's voice came through in a frantic, trembling rush.

"Tyler—Tyler, you need to listen to me. You're not safe. None of us are safe. He's coming. He's—he's coming after us."

Tyler's posture straightened, his fingers curling tightly around the phone. His heart remained steady, but he allowed his expression to shift into one of feigned concern.

"Dad, slow down," Tyler said, his voice steady, even soothing. "What are you talking about? Who's coming?"

Emily, sensing the tension, turned off the stove and leaned against the counter, her arms crossed. Her wide, curious eyes locked onto Tyler's face. He caught her gaze and raised a finger, silently asking her to wait.
On the other end, William's voice cracked.

"The Inked Reaper!" William nearly shouted. "He's not just targeting random criminals anymore. He knows about me—about us. Tyler, he's sending a message. I can feel it."

The weight of the words hung in the air. Tyler's lips pressed into a thin line as he stood and began pacing.

"Dad," Tyler began, his tone measured, "you need to breathe. What makes you think he's coming after us?"

There was a crash on the other end, followed by a muffled curse. Tyler's grip on the phone tightened.

"Tyler, the photos," William said, his voice breaking. "The damn photos! He knows about your mother, about me. He's taunting us. Playing some sick game, and I'm not going to let him win."

Tyler closed his eyes briefly, inhaling slowly to maintain his composure. The corner of his mouth twitched—a faint crack in the facade that he quickly masked.

"Photos?" Tyler asked, feigning confusion. "What photos, Dad?"

A heavy silence fell on the line, punctuated only by William's uneven breathing.

"The ones left at the scenes," William whispered. "I've been looking at them all morning. It's subtle, but the hints are there. He knows about her, Tyler. He knows about your mother."

Across the room, Emily mouthed, What's going on? Tyler shook his head slightly, his eyes narrowing.

"Dad," Tyler said firmly, "you're letting this case get to you. The Reaper doesn't go after innocent people. He's methodical—every victim has been a criminal. You've seen the patterns."

"What if I missed something?" William shot back, desperation creeping into his tone. "What if he thinks I'm part of the system he's fighting against? What if he comes for you? Or Emily?"

The mention of Emily sent a ripple of genuine anger through Tyler, though it never reached his voice.

"Stop," Tyler said, his tone sharp enough to cut through William's rambling. "You're not one of the bad guys, Dad. You've spent your entire life fighting for justice. The Reaper knows that."

"You don't know that," William countered, his voice barely above a whisper. "You don't know how these people think."

Tyler allowed himself a faint, sardonic smile. "You'd be surprised how much I know." Emily tilted her head, her concern deepening as she watched Tyler's expression darken briefly before softening again.

"Listen, Dad," Tyler said, his voice returning to a calm, reassuring tone. "You're spiraling. You need to step back and breathe. The Reaper thrives on fear. Don't give him the satisfaction."

William's breathing slowed, the frantic edge giving way to exhaustion.

"You're right," William murmured after a long pause. "You're right. I'm sorry, son. I didn't mean to unload on you like this."

"It's okay, Dad," Tyler replied. "That's what family's for. I love you. We'll get through this."

"I love you too," William said softly before the line went dead.

Tyler lowered the phone and stared at it for a moment, his expression unreadable. Then, he took a slow sip of his coffee, turning toward Emily.

"Is everything okay?" she asked, her voice gentle but laced with worry.

"Yeah," Tyler said, his tone weary. "Dad's just stressed about this case. He thinks the Reaper might be targeting our family."

Emily's eyes widened, her hand flying to her mouth. "Oh my God. Do you think he's right?"

Tyler shook his head. "No. The Reaper doesn't deviate from his pattern. Every victim has been a criminal, someone who deserved it. Dad's just tired."

Emily stepped closer, brushing her fingers through his hair. "Still, if you need to take the day off to help him, I'd understand."

Tyler smiled up at her, his expression warm. "I appreciate that, but I've already got a meeting with Jerry today."

Emily hesitated, her brow furrowing. "You sure? Your dad seemed pretty upset."

"He'll be fine," Tyler said, standing and kissing her cheek. "I think I managed to calm him down."

"Alright," Emily said, though her concern lingered. "But promise me you'll call if you need anything—or if your dad does."

"Promise."

Emily smiled faintly, squeezing his arm before heading to the bedroom. Tyler watched her go, the warmth in his eyes fading as a cold, calculating expression took its place.

He turned to the window, staring out at the sprawling city below.

"Don't fear the Reaper, Dad," Tyler murmured to himself, his voice laced with quiet menace. "Fear the man who hides in his shadow."

FRACTURED SHADOWS

The faint hum of the refrigerator was the only sound in Kate's dimly lit apartment. She sat at her modest kitchen table, an untouched glass of red wine beside her laptop. Her fingers hovered over the keyboard as she scrolled through the case files. The harsh white glow of the screen highlighted the exhaustion etched into her face. Lines of text blurred together, but her mind refused to rest.

Kate leaned back, rubbing her temples. "Just one more file," she muttered, trying to convince herself that one more piece of data would reveal the key to the Inked Reaper's identity.

A sharp knock on the door broke her concentration. She froze, her heart skipping a beat. No one ever came by this late—at least, no one she expected.

Her gaze darted to the handgun resting on the counter. She rose cautiously, her socked feet silent against the floor. Grabbing the weapon, she tucked it into the waistband of her jeans and approached the door.

"Who the hell is knocking at this hour?" she whispered to herself.

She peered through the peephole. Jerry West stood outside, shifting nervously from foot to foot. His face glistened with a sheen of sweat despite the cool night air. Kate cursed under her breath.

Sliding the deadbolt, she cracked the door just enough to glare at him. "What do you want, Jerry?"

Jerry's eyes flickered toward the hallway behind him. "Kate, let me in. Please."

Kate's lip curled. "What part of 'don't show up unannounced' did you not understand last time?"

"I know, I know," Jerry stammered, running a hand through his disheveled hair. "But this is different. It's serious."

"Everything's 'serious' with you," Kate snapped, her hand still gripping the edge of the door. "You're paranoid."

Jerry's tone dropped, pleading now. "Kate, I think I'm being followed."

Her annoyance wavered for a moment, replaced by wariness. "Followed? By who?"

Jerry leaned closer, lowering his voice. "Tyler Grayson."

Kate blinked. "Tyler?" She snorted, shaking her head. "You've lost it. Tyler's a kid."

Jerry's face darkened, his voice gaining a desperate edge. "He's not just a kid, Kate. He's the Reaper."

Kate stiffened. "Get out of here with that bullshit."

Jerry shoved his foot in the door before she could slam it shut. "I'm not crazy! I've been watching him, Kate. The way he moves, the things he knows. It all fits!"

Her voice was low, dangerous. "You're accusing the son of one of the best detectives I've ever worked with of being a serial killer."

"Yes," Jerry said, his voice trembling but firm. "And you know I'm right."

Kate stepped back, letting the door swing open. "Fine. You have five minutes. Prove it."

Jerry stepped inside, his movements erratic as he pulled a crumpled folder from under his arm. "Look at these," he said, spreading a series of photos and clippings across her table. "Every crime scene. The poems. They all tie back to Tyler."

Kate's eyes flicked over the evidence. Her expression remained neutral, but her mind raced. Some of the connections Jerry pointed out were tenuous at best, but others... others made her pause.

"Even if this is true," she said slowly, "you have no hard proof. And without it, you're just another conspiracy theorist with a vendetta."

Jerry slammed his hand on the table, making her flinch. "You don't get it! He's going to kill me, Kate! I've gotten too close."
Kate crossed her arms. "And what do you expect me to do about it?"

"Help me," Jerry pleaded. "You're the only one who'll listen."

Kate shook her head, exhaling sharply. "If Tyler is who you say he is—and that's a big if—you think confronting him is the answer?"

Jerry's voice broke. "I don't have a choice."

"Then you're already dead," Kate said bluntly. She stepped toward him, her voice softening. "Jerry, listen to me. If Tyler is dangerous, you need to disappear. Leave town. Lay low."

Jerry shook his head violently. "No. I can't run. Not from this. If I run, he wins."

Kate's patience snapped. "Then what? You want me to stick my neck out for a theory? Risk my career? My life?"

Jerry's shoulders slumped. "I just... I just need someone to believe me."

Kate stared at him for a long moment before turning away. "Go home, Jerry. And stay away from Tyler."

Jerry stood there, looking like he wanted to say more, but the steel in her voice left no room for argument. "Fine," he muttered, heading for the door. "But don't say I didn't warn you."

When the door clicked shut behind him, Kate let out a shaky breath. She sat down at the table, staring at the scattered clippings. For the first time, doubt crept in. Could Jerry be right?

Jerry trudged toward his car, his head down. The streetlights cast long, lonely shadows. He climbed into the driver's seat, fumbling with his keys.

Across the street, Tyler sat in his car, watching. His face was calm, but his eyes were sharp, calculating.

"So Jerry's gone to Kate now," he murmured. "Interesting move."

He watched Jerry drive away, his mind running through possibilities. Kate wasn't one to entertain conspiracy theories, but Jerry was persistent.

"If he convinces her..." Tyler's grip on the steering wheel tightened. "That would be inconvenient."

His gaze shifted to Kate's apartment. The light inside flickered as she moved through the space. Tyler leaned back in his seat, a small smile playing on his lips.

"Let's see how far you'll go, Kate." He started the engine, pulling away from the curb. In the distance, the city loomed, its lights blinking like stars against the darkness. Tyler's mind was already working, planning his next move.

AN ARCHIVIST

The air feels heavy under the muted glow of the moon, its pale light barely illuminating the quiet suburban street. A breeze rustles the overgrown bushes, casting long, shifting shadows across the cracked pavement. Tyler Grayson's car sits idling a block away, far enough to blend into the background but close enough for his keen blue eyes to remain locked on Jerry's house.

Inside the car, the cherry-red glow of a cigarette flares as Tyler takes a slow drag. The ember highlights the sharp angles of his face, his jaw clenched with quiet intensity. His mind is sharp, focused, calculating.

The Passenger stirs within him, its presence a subtle vibration that thrums through his consciousness. Its voice, smooth and menacing, slithers through his thoughts.
"He's hiding something, Tyler. You can feel it, can't you? Justice demands we see."

Tyler exhales a plume of smoke through his nose, his gaze narrowing as Jerry appears under the faint light of the porch. A satchel hangs from Jerry's shoulder, clutched tightly to his chest like a lifeline.

Jerry glances over his shoulder, his movements jerky and anxious. His eyes scan the street, but his paranoia doesn't land on the shadowed vehicle where Tyler waits, silently observing.

"Not the front door, Jerry?" Tyler mutters, his voice low and gravelly. "What're you hiding down there?"

The Passenger hums approval. "Patience, Tyler. Let him show us."

Jerry crouches by the cellar doors, his hands fumbling with a key. The lock clicks, and he quickly pulls the doors open, vanishing into the dark void below. The heavy clang of metal echoes faintly as the doors shut behind him. Tyler crushes the cigarette into the overflowing ashtray, his smirk hardening into a cold, predatory expression.

"Alright, Jerry," he mutters. "Let's see what skeletons you're keeping in your closet."

The street has fallen into an oppressive stillness, the only sound the faint chirp of crickets hidden in the grass. Tyler waits, motionless, his eyes glued to the cellar doors.

Finally, they creak open. Jerry emerges, his satchel now bulging slightly at the seams. He locks the doors with trembling hands, casting another nervous glance around before scurrying to his car.

As the taillights disappear down the road, Tyler's fingers flex around the steering wheel. The Passenger whispers eagerly. "He's alone. Vulnerable. Take your time, but don't waste it. The abyss waits for no one."

Tyler steps out of the car, his movements calculated and soundless. The chill night air brushes against him as he approaches the cellar doors.

Tyler crouches by the cellar doors, inspecting the lock. A smirk tugs at his lips. It's cheap, almost insultingly so.

He pulls out his lockpick set, his gloved fingers working with practiced precision. The lock gives way with a faint click. Tyler pauses, his sharp hearing picking up the faintest of sounds—a dog barking a few houses down, the distant hum of tires on asphalt.

Satisfied the coast is clear, he pushes the doors open, the hinges letting out a soft groan.

The smell hits him first—a cloying mix of damp earth, mildew, and a faint metallic tang that sends a shiver of recognition down his spine.

The staircase descends into near-total darkness, the beam of Tyler's flashlight cutting through the oppressive gloom. The air is heavy, each breath thick and stale.

His footsteps are measured as he moves down the narrow stairs. The first thing the light catches makes him pause.

Photographs. Hundreds of them.

They plaster the walls, chaotic yet meticulous, like a deranged mosaic. Tyler's flashlight sweeps across the faces, and his stomach tightens.

It's his work. Every victim, every carefully staged tableau, captured in high-definition clarity. The poses, the poems—every detail meticulously documented.

Tyler steps closer, his eyes locking onto a photo of a middle-aged man sprawled on a wooden floor, his limbs contorted unnaturally. The poem he left behind is visible through the photograph, the ink smudged but unmistakable.

"Son of a bitch," Tyler mutters, his voice barely audible.

"Admire it," the Passenger purrs. "He's your greatest fan, Tyler. An archivist of your symphony of justice."

Tyler clenches his jaw, his flashlight sweeping across the rest of the wall. Each face stares back at him, lifeless and grotesque.

"One hundred thirty-three kills," he murmurs. "Documented. Archived."

His light lands on a small table in the corner, cluttered with notebooks and papers. But at the center of the chaos sits a pristine notepad.

Tyler picks it up, flipping it open to reveal a scrawled note:
Password: Mortem133
Address: Pyrework Coffee
He chuckles darkly, the sound low and humorless. "Pyrework Coffee. Real subtle, Jerry."

His flashlight catches another glint. Beneath the desk, a folder peeks out. Tyler kneels, pulling it into the light.

Inside are detailed notes about him—or, at least, what Jerry thinks he knows. Schedules, psychological profiles, and crude attempts at predicting his next moves.

Tyler lets out a low whistle, flipping through the pages. "You've got no idea, Jerry. But you've got my attention now."

The Passenger's voice coils through his mind. "He's clever, but not clever enough. And now he's yours, Tyler. A gift waiting to be unwrapped."

Tyler carefully places everything back where he found it. With a final, sweeping look at the room, he turns back to the stairs, the weight of the Passenger's presence urging him forward.

The street is silent as Tyler slides back into his car. The Passenger's voice is quiet now, content, its dark satisfaction pulsing in his chest like a second heartbeat.

His phone buzzes, the screen lighting up with a notification. Pyrework Coffee flashes across the display, the address pinned on the map.

Tyler chuckles, starting the engine. "Guess it's time to pay a visit."

The taillights of his car fade into the darkness, leaving Jerry's house shrouded in unsettling silence.

SHADOWS UNVEILED

The rumble of Tyler's car engine reverberated down the quiet street as he pulled into the small parking lot beside the café. The night air was crisp, with the faint scent of rain lingering from earlier in the evening. Tyler killed the engine, his eyes immediately locking onto a car parked just a few spaces away—a sleek, dark sedan he knew all too well. Jerry's car.

Tyler's mind raced. Why would Jerry be here, of all places? His jaw tightened as a mixture of curiosity and anger bubbled within him. He stepped out of the car, his boots crunching against the gravel, and adjusted his leather gloves. The café was mostly dark, save for the soft glow of a single light above the entrance.

Walking toward the door, Tyler glanced through the windows. The café appeared empty. Tables were neatly arranged, and the counter was clean, but there was no sign of Jerry. His sharp instincts, honed over years of meticulously orchestrated plans, told him something was off. He pushed open the door, the bell jingling softly.

The air inside was still, almost too quiet. Tyler's eyes darted around, his senses on high alert. Suddenly, the faint sound of movement from the back of the café caught his attention. He took a cautious step forward, his hand instinctively brushing against the inside of his jacket where he kept a small knife—just in case.

"Jerry?" Tyler called out, his voice low and controlled, masking the tension in his chest. No response.

The sound came again—quieter this time. Tyler's eyes narrowed as he moved toward the source, his footsteps silent. He reached the door leading to the café's back exit and paused, listening.

On the other side, Jerry West stood in the alley, his breath coming in quick, shallow bursts. His heart raced as he glanced around nervously, clutching a folder tight against his chest. When he heard Tyler's car pull up earlier, he'd felt a chill run down his spine. There was no way Tyler could've known he was here—could he?

Jerry swallowed hard, his journalistic instincts warring with the survival instincts that screamed at him to leave. He couldn't risk confronting Tyler. Not now. He shoved the folder into a bag slung over his shoulder and darted down the alley, leaving his car behind.

Back in the café, Tyler opened the door to find nothing but an empty alley bathed in dim yellow light from a flickering streetlamp. He frowned, scanning the shadows for any sign of movement. The faint scent of cigarette smoke lingered in the air—fresh.

He was here, Tyler thought. But why run?

Tyler lingered for another moment before stepping back inside. His gaze fell on Jerry's car through the window, a small smirk forming on his lips. "You left in a hurry," he murmured to himself. "What are you hiding, Jerry?"

Later that night, Tyler stood outside a run-down industrial building on the outskirts of the city. The location had come to him through a combination of careful research and a hunch—Jerry's movements had been erratic lately, his focus shifting to darker stories, ones that intersected with the Inked Reaper's kills. Tyler had followed the breadcrumbs, and they'd led him here.

The building loomed like a monolith, its windows boarded up, graffiti scrawled across the cracked walls. The faint hum of machinery in the distance provided an eerie backdrop to the silence surrounding the structure.

Tyler's steps were deliberate as he approached the side entrance, a crowbar in hand. He jimmied the door open with practiced ease and slipped inside, the faint creak of the hinges echoing through the cavernous space.

Inside, the stench hit him first—a vile mixture of sweat, urine, and something metallic. His nose wrinkled as his stomach churned. The dim light from a single bulb hanging from the ceiling illuminated a sight that made his blood run cold.

Children.

Dozens of them, chained to the walls and lying on the filthy floor. Their faces were pale, their bodies bruised and emaciated, except for one—a boy who appeared to have been fed more than the others, his face swollen with fear as he glanced at Tyler.

Tyler's fists clenched, rage boiling under the surface, but he forced himself to stay calm. He knelt down in front of the children, his voice soft but firm.

"I'm here to help," he said, his eyes scanning their faces. "But I need you to tell me something first. Did you see anyone here? Anyone who did this to you?"

The children exchanged hesitant glances, their fear evident. Finally, the boy who had been fattened spoke, his voice trembling. "There were two men," he whispered. "One with glasses... he was here a lot. The other... he was scarier. He... he laughed when he hurt us."

Tyler's jaw tightened. He pulled out his phone and showed the boy a photo of Jerry. "Was this one of them?"

The boy nodded quickly, tears welling in his eyes. "Him. And the other man... his name was Edward. They said it sometimes."
Jerry and Edward.

Tyler's suspicions solidified. Jerry wasn't just digging into dangerous stories—he was a part of them. And Edward... the name was new, but Tyler would find him.

"You've been so brave," Tyler said, his voice softening as he reached out to gently pat the boy's shoulder. "The police will be here soon. You'll all be safe."

He stood, his mind racing as he moved to a dark corner of the room. Pulling out his burner phone, he dialed a number he'd memorized but never saved—an anonymous tip line for the police.

"There's a building on West Elm," he said when the line connected. "Children are being held there. Send a team now."

He hung up before the operator could ask questions, his heart pounding as he turned back to the children.

"You'll be free by morning," Tyler promised, his voice steady despite the storm brewing inside him. "But I need to go now. Stay together, okay?"

The boy nodded, his small hand gripping the chain that bound him. Tyler lingered for a moment, then slipped back out the way he came, the weight of what he'd seen pressing heavily on his shoulders.

As he drove away, his grip on the steering wheel tightened. Jerry was no longer just a nuisance. He was a threat. And threats needed to be eliminated.

SHADOWS FROM THE PAST

The lamp's soft glow painted the room in golden hues, the light spilling over the worn coffee table and the array of books stacked neatly by the corner. Emily Taylors sat cross-legged on the couch, a mug of tea balanced precariously on the armrest. Her hazel eyes flicked to the wall clock. It was nearing midnight. A thin tension hung in the air, the kind that comes with restless thoughts and unanswered questions.

A sharp knock at the door shattered the silence. Emily jumped, her heart racing as she glanced at the door and then back at the clock. It was late—too late for casual visitors. Setting the mug aside, she rose cautiously, the floor creaking softly beneath her bare feet.

Peering through the peephole, she saw William Grayson, his disheveled appearance starkly at odds with the meticulous detective she knew. His shirt was wrinkled, his tie hanging loose, and his eyes—bloodshot and filled with something she could only describe as desperation—sent a chill down her spine.

Opening the door, she offered him a tentative smile. "William? It's late. Is everything okay?"

William didn't answer. Instead, he stepped past her, his movements quick and agitated, as though driven by some unseen force. He paced the room, running a hand through his graying hair.

"Nothing is okay, Emily. Nothing." His voice cracked with exhaustion.

Emily closed the door behind him, watching him with a mix of concern and curiosity. "What happened? Is it the case?"

William stopped mid-step, his hands trembling as he clenched them into fists. Turning to face her, he seemed to weigh his words, struggling to speak.

"The Inked Reaper," he said finally, his voice barely above a whisper. "He's getting closer. Closer to Tyler. Closer to my family."

Emily's stomach dropped. She had followed William's cases for years, but there was something different about this one—something that felt more personal. She stepped forward, her gaze steady. "What do you mean? What's he done?"

William's laughter was bitter, hollow. "He knows things, Emily. Things he shouldn't know. Things no one should know."

Emily reached out, placing a gentle hand on his arm. "William, calm down. Take a breath."

"Don't tell me to calm down!" William snapped, his voice sharp enough to make her flinch. He immediately recoiled, shaking his head. "I'm sorry. I just... you don't understand what this means."

Emily took a step back, giving him space. "Then help me understand. Tell me what's going on."

William sank onto the couch, his shoulders slumping under an invisible weight. He rubbed his temples, his hands trembling. "He knows about Tyler," he muttered, his voice barely audible.

Emily frowned, moving to sit beside him. "What do you mean? What does he know?"

William looked at her, his eyes haunted. "He knows Tyler is my son. That's bad enough. But there's more." His voice broke, and he buried his face in his hands. "He knows about... about the thing I've buried for years. Something only Tyler and I know."

Emily leaned closer, her voice soft but insistent. "William, you're scaring me. What secret?"

He shook his head violently, refusing to meet her gaze. "I can't... I can't say it out loud. Not even to you. But if the Reaper knows, then he's been watching us. Watching Tyler."

Emily's mind raced. The Inked Reaper had already proven himself to be a master manipulator, but this—this was something more sinister. She reached for William's hands, her grip firm. "Listen to me. Tyler is smart, William. He's resilient. He's your son. Whatever this is, he can handle it."

William pulled his hands away, standing abruptly. "You don't get it, Emily! This isn't just about him being strong. This is about a predator circling my family." He began pacing again, his movements frantic. "I've dealt with killers my whole life, Emily. I know how they think. This one... he's different. He's methodical, precise. He gets inside your head. And now, he's inside mine."

Emily rose, stepping into his path and forcing him to stop. "William, you can't let him win like this. That's what he wants, isn't it? To make you doubt yourself? To make you afraid?"

William stared at her, his jaw tightening. "It's not just me. It's Tyler. He's already been through enough, and now this... this monster has him in his sights."

Emily placed her hands on his shoulders, grounding him. "Then we protect him. We protect each other. That's what families do, right?"

William's expression softened, but the fear in his eyes didn't fade. "You don't understand, Emily. The things I've done to protect Tyler... the decisions I've made... they're not enough anymore."

Emily tilted her head, studying him. "What are you saying?"

"I'm saying I've failed him." William's voice cracked, and he took a step back, his eyes filled with regret. "And now, I might lose him."

"No, you won't," Emily said vehemently, shaking her head. "Not if you keep fighting. You've solved cases no one else could, William. You can solve this one too."

"It's not just a case, Emily." William sank back onto the couch, his shoulders slumping. "It's my life unraveling."

Emily sat beside him again, her voice gentle but unwavering. "Then let me help you keep it together. You're not alone in this, William."

"I'm not sure how much longer I can hold on, Emily." His voice was barely a whisper.

"Then lean on me. Lean on Tyler. You've got people who care about you, William. Let us help."

A tense silence fell between them, broken only by the distant hum of the city outside. Finally, William straightened, wiping his face. "Thank you, Emily. I mean it."

Emily smiled softly, though worry lingered in her hazel eyes. "Anytime."

As William rose to leave, Emily watched him with a growing sense of unease. Whatever secret he was hiding, she knew it was bigger than he was letting on—and more dangerous.

THE JUSTICE OF THE VOICE

The phone booth was a relic of a bygone era, its glass walls streaked with grime and etched with years of graffiti. A faint smell of rust and mildew lingered in the air, mixing with the damp chill of the night. Tyler Grayson stepped inside, closing the folding door behind him. The faint squeal of the hinges barely registered as he turned his focus to the task at hand.

The receiver was cold in his gloved fingers as he lifted it to his ear. He exhaled softly, his breath fogging the glass in front of him. Outside, the streetlights buzzed faintly, their orange glow casting long shadows across the deserted street. The world felt eerily still, as if holding its breath for what he was about to do.

His blue eyes, sharp and calculating, darted over the keypad. He dialed a number with deliberate precision, each press of the button releasing a muted beep that echoed faintly in the confined space. Tyler's heartbeat remained steady, his mind focused.

He leaned back slightly, the phone pressed against his ear, and stared out into the empty night. The silence stretched, the only sounds the distant hum of the city and the faint crackle of static on the line. Then, a click.

"County Sheriff's Department, what's your emergency?"

The voice on the other end was calm, professional, and alert. Tyler's lips curled slightly at the edges—this was the moment. His voice, carefully altered with a faint rasp, emerged low and deliberate.

"There's a café on the outskirts of town. Pyrework Coffee," he began, his tone measured as though weighing each word.

There was a pause, just enough to add tension, before he continued.

"There's something going on in the back room. Kids being trafficked."

The words hung in the air like a loaded weapon. Tyler could almost feel the dispatcher stiffen on the other end of the line. There was a sharp intake of breath before the voice returned, tinged now with urgency.

"Can you confirm what you saw? Are the children still there?"

Tyler exhaled softly, the sound controlled, calculated. His gaze shifted, briefly catching his own reflection in the glass—a shadowed figure with piercing eyes that seemed to cut through the dark.

"They're there. I saw them," he replied, his tone as steady as stone. "It's a small operation, but they're holding them in the storage area. You'll need to move fast."

The dispatcher hesitated, the crackle of the line betraying their momentary scramble to process the information.

"Sir, can you provide your name and location? We'll need—"

"No names," Tyler interrupted, his voice firm and unyielding. "No location. Just send someone."

The line went silent again, the tension palpable. Tyler could hear faint voices in the background, the sound of keys clicking as the dispatcher relayed the information to units. When the voice returned, it was professional but strained.

"Understood. We'll have units on it immediately. Thank you for reporting this."

Tyler didn't respond immediately, his grip tightening on the receiver as his mind churned. He wasn't here for gratitude or validation. The Passenger, the ever-present shadow within him, murmured softly, its voice a low whisper in the recesses of his mind.

"Justice takes many forms, Tyler. Tonight, it moves through you."
He let the words settle, their weight both comforting and chilling. Justice wasn't blind, not tonight. It saw the darkness, and it would cut through it like a blade.

Without another word, Tyler hung up the receiver. The faint clatter as it hit the cradle echoed in the booth, a sound that seemed to linger as he stepped back.

Outside, the world was still again, the quiet pressing against him. Tyler adjusted his gloves, his movements methodical. He glanced toward the street, his gaze scanning the empty expanse before him.

He didn't wait to see the flashing lights or hear the wail of sirens that would soon cut through the night. This wasn't about being a hero or seeking acknowledgment. It was about ensuring that monsters met their end, one way or another.

As he stepped into the shadows, the glass door of the booth swinging shut behind him, Tyler disappeared into the night, leaving behind only a faint chill in the air and the promise of reckoning.

NO SECOND CHANCES

The basement reeked of decay. Each breath Tyler took was tainted with the acrid stench of mildew and the metallic tang of fear. The faint hum of the single lightbulb above flickered intermittently, casting elongated shadows across the walls. It was the kind of place that stories whispered about—the kind of place no one came back from.

Tyler stood over the man strapped to the cold, metal table in the center of the room. His black gloves creaked as his fists tightened at his sides. The man, mid-thirties with greasy brown hair and hollow cheeks, squirmed against his restraints. His muffled cries seeped through the damp cloth gag stuffed into his mouth, but the sound was pitiful, weak.

Tyler tilted his head, his blue eyes cold and unyielding as they traced the contours of the man's face. Sweat clung to the man's pale skin in rivulets, dripping onto the metal beneath him, mixing with his tears. He stank of desperation, and Tyler drank it in, his expression an emotionless mask.

"You know," Tyler began, his voice calm, almost conversational, "it's funny."

He leaned down slightly, his face illuminated by the erratic light above.

"You thought you could just... do what you did. Hurt them. Break them. And get away with it."

The man whimpered, his pleading eyes darting around the room, looking for something—anything—that might save him. Tyler followed his gaze, smirking when it landed on the door.

"Nobody's coming," Tyler said, his tone matter-of-fact. "The cops? They wouldn't get here in time even if you did manage to scream loud enough. Not that they'd care about a guy like you."

The man's body jerked against the restraints, his muffled cries becoming more frantic. Tyler let out a low chuckle, devoid of humor.

"You thought they'd save you, didn't you? Maybe you'd lawyer up, spin some sob story about your rough childhood or how you had a moment of weakness."

Tyler straightened, his hands clasped behind his back like a professor delivering a lecture.

"But that's not how this story ends. Not for you."

He turned to the small, cluttered table at his side. Among the neatly arranged tools—a roll of duct tape, a length of rope, a jug of water—his hand hovered over the jug. Tyler's fingers curled around its handle, and he lifted it slowly, deliberately, savoring the growing panic in the man's wide eyes.

"You see," Tyler continued, stepping back toward the table, "I'm not like them. I don't believe in second chances. Especially not for someone like you."

The man shook his head violently, his muffled pleas escalating.

"'It wasn't my fault,'" Tyler mocked, mimicking a whiny tone. "'I didn't mean to.' You know, that's the kind of garbage you'd say in court. Play the victim, act like you were misunderstood. But you weren't misunderstood. You were calculated. You chose to do what you did."

With one swift motion, Tyler tipped the jug, pouring the water over the cloth gag. The man convulsed instantly, his body arching against the restraints as water seeped through the fabric and into his mouth and nose. Gasping and gagging, he thrashed wildly, his muffled screams a mix of desperation and terror.

"What's the matter?" Tyler asked, his tone mocking. "Having trouble breathing?"

The man's chest heaved as he tried to expel the water, his struggles growing more frantic.

"You didn't care when they were gasping for air, did you?" Tyler hissed, leaning closer.

For a moment, he considered letting the man drown. It would be easier—quieter. But no. This man deserved worse. Justice wasn't just about death; it was about fear, regret, and making them understand the weight of their sins.

Tyler yanked the cloth back, allowing the man to sputter and cough violently. Water dripped from his face, pooling beneath his head. His breaths came in wet, ragged gasps.

"Pathetic," Tyler muttered, tossing the cloth onto the table.

The man tried to speak, his voice hoarse and broken, but his words were unintelligible. Tyler crossed his arms, tilting his head as he studied the pitiful creature before him.

"You know what the real tragedy is?" Tyler asked, his voice soft, almost kind. "If I hadn't found you, the system probably would've let you off easy. A few years, maybe. A slap on the wrist. And then what? You'd go right back to doing what you do."

The man's head lolled weakly, his lips trembling as he attempted to form words. Tyler leaned down, his voice dropping to a whisper.

"But me? I'm not so forgiving."

The faint vibration of a phone shattered the moment. Tyler straightened, his expression shifting from cold focus to mild annoyance. He pulled the phone from his pocket, the name on the screen flashing brightly in the dim room.

DAD.

Tyler sighed, swiping to answer.

"Hey, Dad," he said, his tone light, casual.

"Tyler." William's voice was sharp, laced with urgency. "We found something. You need to get down here. Now."

Tyler's eyes flicked to the man on the table. He was barely conscious, his chest rising and falling in shallow breaths.

"What's going on?" Tyler asked, forcing a note of curiosity into his voice.

"It's the Pyrework Café," William continued. "There's something here you need to see. It's... big."

Tyler's jaw tightened, but his voice remained steady.

"I'll be there soon. Just... gotta finish something up first."

"Don't take too long," William said, his tone insistent. The line went dead.

Tyler slipped the phone back into his pocket, his expression darkening. He turned back to the man on the table, who was trying weakly to lift his head.

"Looks like our time's up," Tyler said, his voice tinged with disappointment.

He grabbed the cloth and shoved it roughly back into the man's mouth, silencing his feeble protests. Then, with one smooth motion, Tyler pulled a knife from his pocket. The blade glinted in the flickering light, sharp and precise.

"Goodnight," Tyler said simply.

The blade sliced through flesh, the sound wet and visceral. Blood sprayed across the table, splattering Tyler's gloves and jacket. He stepped back, watching as the man's body convulsed once, twice, then stilled.

Tyler exhaled, steadying himself. The Passenger whispered its approval, but Tyler ignored it. There was work to be done.

He grabbed a roll of thick black trash bags and duct tape from the corner. His movements were methodical, almost clinical, as he wrapped the body, layer after layer, ensuring nothing would seep through. The tape sealed the package tightly, a grotesque gift to the grave.

"Let's clean you up for the trip, huh?" Tyler muttered.

Hoisting the body onto his shoulder, he carried it out to his car.

The night air bit at his skin as he stepped outside. His car was parked just outside the basement's entrance, its trunk yawning open. Tyler heaved the body into the trunk, the sound of it hitting metal echoing in the stillness. He wiped a speck of blood from his sleeve, adjusting his jacket with precision.

"Time to play the good son," he said under his breath.

Sliding into the driver's seat, he started the engine. As the car rumbled to life, Tyler's gaze flicked to the rearview mirror. The faint wail of distant sirens reached his ears, but he didn't look back. He never did.

YET ALONE A KILLER

The lake lay still under the silver glow of the moon, its surface like polished glass. The gentle lap of water against the hull of Tyler's speedboat was the only sound, apart from the low hum of the idling engine.

Tyler stood at the bow, his figure silhouetted against the faint shimmer of moonlight. Draped over his shoulder was the tightly bundled body of his latest target, wrapped meticulously in thick black plastic and secured with layers of duct tape. His breath was steady, his striking blue eyes focused on the dark water below.

He adjusted his grip on the body, speaking softly to the lifeless form. "What a waste," he muttered, shaking his head. "All that effort to ruin lives, and for what? This?"

With a grunt, he heaved the bundle over the side. The body hit the water with a loud splash, disturbing the tranquility as ripples radiated outward. Tyler didn't flinch. He stood there, watching as the package sank, its dark outline swallowed by the inky depths.

"Goodbye," he said coldly, stepping back toward the boat's controls.

The engine roared as Tyler pushed the throttle forward. The boat surged ahead, slicing through the water like a knife. The wind tugged at his hair and jacket, but his focus remained on the horizon.

Unknown to him, a figure stood at the distant docks, cloaked in shadow. Jerry West watched Tyler's boat speed away, his sharp eyes tracking its path across the water. His jaw tightened, a mix of anger and determination etched onto his face.

"Got you, you son of a bitch," Jerry whispered to himself.

Tyler tied his boat securely to the dock, his boots thudding softly against the wooden planks as he strode toward his car. The docks were eerily quiet, the occasional creak of wood or distant hoot of an owl the only sounds accompanying his footsteps.

The faint scent of saltwater and gasoline lingered in the air. As he neared his car, parked under the shadow of an old shed, Tyler's instincts flared.

"Going somewhere?" a voice cut through the silence.

Tyler stopped mid-step, his hand hovering near his jacket pocket. Slowly, he turned to see Jerry West step out from behind a stack of crates. The older man's posture was rigid, his expression grim.

"Jerry," Tyler said smoothly, slipping his hands casually into his jacket pockets. "Didn't expect to see you out here. What brings you to the lake at this hour?"

Jerry's jaw clenched as he closed the distance between them. "Funny. I was about to ask you the same thing. Late-night boating trip? Doesn't exactly scream innocence."

Tyler tilted his head, a faint smirk playing at his lips. "Sometimes a guy just needs some fresh air. You know how it is."

"Cut the crap, Tyler," Jerry snapped, his voice low and filled with venom. "I know what you are."

Tyler's smirk faded, his expression hardening. "And what's that?"

"A killer."

The word hung in the air like a thunderclap. For a moment, neither man moved. Tyler's icy blue eyes narrowed, his smile returning but colder this time.

"That's a pretty bold accusation," he said, his voice calm. "You got any proof, or are you just fishing for a reaction?"

Jerry's hand twitched toward his jacket pocket, where a small recorder lay hidden. His lips curled into a snarl. "I've been watching you. The late nights, the places you shouldn't be. You're sloppy, Tyler. And I've got enough to bury you."

Tyler took a deliberate step forward, his hands still in his pockets. "You've been watching me?" He chuckled, the sound low and mocking. "Wow, Jerry. Didn't know you cared. Kinda creepy, though, don't you think?"

Jerry's face darkened. "You think this is a joke? You think you're untouchable? I'm going to make sure everyone knows what you really are."

Tyler's eyes gleamed with something dangerous as he closed the gap between them. He dropped his voice to a near whisper. "And what is that, Jerry? A genius? A perfectionist? Someone who's always ten steps ahead while you're fumbling in the dark?"

Jerry's nostrils flared. "You're nothing but a coward who hides behind his little games. You think you're clever, but I see through you. You're not as smart as you think."

In one swift motion, Tyler's fist shot out, connecting with Jerry's jaw. The impact sent

Jerry stumbling backward, his foot catching on the edge of the dock.

"Careful there," Tyler said mockingly, shaking out his hand. "Wouldn't want you to take a swim."

Jerry's arms flailed as he lost his balance. With a loud splash, he hit the water, disappearing beneath the surface.

Tyler walked to the edge, crouching down to peer into the lake. Jerry resurfaced, coughing and sputtering, his arms flailing as he tried to stay afloat.

"Wow, Jerry," Tyler called out, his tone dripping with sarcasm. "Didn't peg you for the swimming type. Guess we all have hidden talents."

Jerry glared up at him, his teeth chattering as he struggled to tread water. "This isn't over, Tyler," he rasped. "I'll—"

"Save it," Tyler interrupted, standing and dusting off his hands. "Next time you want to accuse someone of murder, maybe don't do it near the water. Looks bad for your credibility."

Jerry continued to cough, clinging to the dock's edge as Tyler turned and strode back to his car.

Tyler slid into the driver's seat, slamming the door shut. He glanced in the rearview mirror, catching a glimpse of Jerry hauling himself out of the water, dripping wet and seething.

Tyler smirked to himself. "Should've stayed out of it, Jerry."

The engine roared as he sped away, the tires kicking up gravel. The docks faded into the distance, but Tyler's mind was already racing.

"Time for damage control," he muttered under his breath.

Back at the docks, Jerry collapsed onto the wooden planks, his breaths coming in ragged gasps. His jaw throbbed, and his clothes clung to his shivering body. But his eyes burned with determination as he stared at the retreating tail lights.

"This isn't over, Tyler," Jerry growled, his voice hoarse but resolute. "Not by a long shot."

SHADOWS AND CHAINS

The stillness of the night was shattered by the symphony of chaos at Pyrework Café. Red and blue lights flashed in rhythmic patterns, casting fleeting shadows across the narrow street. Uniformed officers cordoned off the area with yellow tape, their voices sharp as they directed bystanders to keep their distance.

Inside the perimeter, federal agents and local detectives moved with purpose, barking orders and comparing notes as the harsh beams of floodlights illuminated the grim reality of the scene. Evidence bags lay spread across hastily arranged tables, and the faint scent of stale coffee lingered beneath the sharper, metallic tang of blood.

Tyler parked his car a block away, blending into the shadows of a nearby alley. He stepped out, closing the door with deliberate softness. His usual air of composure remained intact, but his sharp blue eyes darted methodically across the scene, cataloging every detail.

"A circus," he muttered to himself, his voice low. "As expected."

As he approached the edge of the yellow tape, an officer moved to intercept him. Tyler didn't flinch, maintaining his calm as the officer frowned at him.

"Back up, kid. This is a crime scene."

Before Tyler could respond, William Grayson's voice cut through the noise.

"That's my son," William called out, his voice authoritative despite the weariness in his tone. "He's clear. Let him through."

The officer hesitated before lifting the tape. Tyler ducked under it smoothly, straightening as he locked eyes with his father.

William's face bore the marks of exhaustion—lines deepened by stress and sleepless nights—but there was a flicker of relief in his expression as Tyler approached.

"Thanks for coming," William said, his voice quieter now.

Tyler nodded. "You sounded urgent. What's going on?"

William gestured for Tyler to follow him, leading him through the bustling crime scene. Tyler's eyes swept over the evidence as they passed: chains hanging loosely from rusted hooks on the walls, burner phones neatly cataloged in plastic bags, and a stack of fraudulent government checks being examined by an agent.

William's jaw tightened as he spoke. "It's worse than I thought. Seven kids, Tyler. Seven. Chained up like animals in the basement."

Tyler's heart clenched, but he kept his expression neutral, his tone matching his father's seriousness. "Are they okay?"

William let out a heavy sigh. "Physically? Maybe. Mentally? God only knows. CPS is taking them now, but... I don't know if they'll ever be okay."

They passed a line of officers escorting the last group of children toward waiting vans. Tyler's sharp gaze caught the chubby boy he'd encountered earlier. The boy's wide eyes darted around nervously until they locked with Tyler's. For a split second, the boy's lips parted, as if to say something.

Without breaking stride, Tyler raised a finger to his lips in a small, deliberate motion.

"Shhh," he whispered under his breath, his voice too soft for anyone but himself to hear.

The boy froze, his small frame trembling before he nodded slightly and looked away. Tyler's pulse quickened, but he buried the reaction under a mask of calm as they reached the evidence table.

Chains, bloodied rags, and plastic-wrapped burner phones lay neatly arranged, illuminated by the harsh glare of a portable light. Tyler picked up one of the evidence bags containing a phone, turning it over in his hand.

"What about the blood?" he asked, his voice steady.

"All theirs," William replied grimly. "Nothing from whoever did this."

Tyler placed the bag down, his mind churning as he surveyed the table. "No prints, no DNA. It's meticulous. Whoever ran this place knew exactly what they were doing."

"That's what worries me," William said, rubbing the back of his neck. "This wasn't some random operation. It was organized. Clean."

Tyler's eyes drifted toward the café itself, its once-inviting atmosphere now marred by the chaos. He noticed a door leading to a back room, its lock hanging broken.

"What's back there?" he asked.

"Storage room," William said, following his son's gaze. "Mostly empty."

Tyler led the way, stepping carefully into the room. The space was stripped bare, save for a few overturned chairs and a faint bloodstain on the floor. He crouched beside the stain, running a finger just above the surface without touching it.

"Any leads?" he asked, his tone curious but detached.

"Nothing solid," William admitted, his frustration palpable. "The burner phones don't lead anywhere, the checks are stolen identities, and the hard drive from the security system is missing. Whoever did this covered their tracks so well it's like they were never here."

Tyler straightened, brushing off his knees. "So no faces, no names. Just ghosts."

William exhaled sharply. "Damn it, Tyler. These bastards didn't just hurt those kids; they made a mockery of us. They knew we'd find this place eventually, and they made sure there was nothing left to find."

Tyler placed a hand on his father's shoulder, his touch firm but reassuring. "You'll figure it out, Dad. You always do."

William's tense posture softened slightly as he met Tyler's gaze. "I hope you're right. Because if we don't..."

He trailed off, glancing toward the CPS workers loading the children into vans. The chubby boy lingered at the edge of the group, his gaze finding Tyler one last time before he disappeared into the van.

Tyler turned back to the crime scene, his eyes scanning the details with renewed intensity.

"You good here?" William asked, his voice weary but resolute.

"Yeah," Tyler said with a nod. "I'll stick around, see if I can piece anything together."

William clapped his son on the back before walking away, his shoulders hunched under the weight of the case.

Tyler stood there for a moment, his calm exterior concealing the storm brewing within.

"No prints. No hair. Just ghosts," he murmured, his voice barely audible.

His eyes drifted toward the remnants of the café, now hollow and lifeless under the floodlights.

"But even ghosts leave shadows," he whispered, his lips curling into a faint, knowing smile.

As he turned back to the evidence, the chaos of the crime scene faded into the background. Tyler's mind was already racing ahead, calculating his next move in the intricate game of predator and prey.

FUCK

The front door swung open, and Tyler stepped in, his shoulders slumping under the weight of exhaustion. Before he could take another step, Emily appeared in the hallway, rushing toward him with the force of a small storm. She threw her arms around his waist, pressing her cheek against his chest.

"There you are!" she said, her voice a mix of relief and exasperation. "I was starting to think you were never coming home."

Tyler let out a tired chuckle, the sound barely audible as she pulled back just enough to plant a soft kiss on his cheek. Her smile, warm and reassuring, lit up the room like a lighthouse piercing through a storm.

"I missed you," she added, her hands still resting on his arms.

His expression softened, and he leaned down to press a kiss to her forehead. "I missed you too."

Emily studied his face, her brows furrowing with concern. "You look... drained. Was it that bad?"

"Worse," he admitted, his voice low. "But I'm home now."

Her smile returned, a touch brighter. "Good. Because I'm not letting you out of my sight for the rest of the night."

Tyler chuckled softly, reaching up to ruffle her hair. "Deal."

The dining room was bathed in a soft glow, the flickering candle on the table casting dancing shadows on the walls. Tyler sat across from Emily, their plates laden with breaded pork chops, mashed potatoes, and steamed vegetables.

He took a bite, savoring the familiar taste, and set his fork down with a small nod.

"You've outdone yourself. Again," he said, the faintest hint of a smile tugging at his lips.

Emily grinned, leaning forward slightly. "Well, someone needed a pick-me-up after the day you've had."

Tyler leaned back in his chair, exhaling deeply. "You're not wrong. Today was... something else."

Curiosity flickered in Emily's eyes as she tilted her head. "What happened?"

Tyler smirked, his expression lightening with a mischievous edge. "I finally got Jerry to back off."

"Jerry? That reporter guy?"

"Turns out he's not just a reporter. He's a fed."

Emily's eyes widened. "A federal agent? Are you serious?"

"Dead serious," Tyler replied, a glimmer of satisfaction in his voice. "And let's just say it only took breaking his nose to make him reconsider following me around."

Emily clapped a hand over her mouth, stifling a laugh. "You broke his nose?"

"Sent him flying off the dock," Tyler said, his grin widening.

This time, Emily couldn't contain her laughter. It spilled out of her, warm and infectious, filling the room. "I would have paid good money to see that."

Tyler reached across the table, taking her hand in his. "It felt pretty damn good."

They shared a quiet moment, their laughter subsiding into a comfortable silence. Emily leaned forward, her voice softer now. "Well, here's to you, my hero."

"Hero, huh?" Tyler echoed, his smirk returning. "I'll take it."

They both laughed again, the heaviness of the day momentarily forgotten as they continued their meal.

The air in Tyler's study was thick with tension. He sat hunched over his desk, a notebook open in front of him and his laptop casting a cold light against his face. His fingers drummed against the desk, his mind racing.

"Jerry," he muttered under his breath. "Kate. The trafficking ring."

He closed his eyes, inhaling deeply as fragments of the night replayed in his mind. The crime scene. The terrified boy. Jerry's unexpected appearance.

His eyes snapped open, the pieces clicking into place with an almost audible force.

"Kate's been investigating me," he said, his voice rising. "Paying Jerry to keep tabs on me."

He slammed a hand on the desk, the sharp sound cutting through the quiet room.

"But Jerry..." Tyler's voice dropped, his jaw tightening. "He's tied up in this. The burner phones. The government checks. He's not just watching me."

His eyes widened as the realization hit him.

"He took that kid," Tyler whispered, the words barely audible. His voice hardened. "He's going to sell him."

Pushing back from the desk, Tyler stood abruptly, his chair scraping against the floor.

"Not on my watch," he said, his tone resolute.

Tyler strode into the hallway, his movements swift and purposeful. He grabbed his car keys from the hook by the door, the metallic jingle breaking the silence.

"Ty?" Emily's voice called from the living room, tinged with confusion.

She appeared in the doorway, her arms crossed as she studied him. "Where are you going? It's late."

Tyler paused, his shoulders tense. "I... I'll explain later."

Emily stepped closer, her brows knitting together. "Tyler, you're scaring me. What's wrong?"

He hesitated, his hand gripping the door handle. "I can't stay," he said finally, his voice firm. "Don't wait up."

Her voice rose, panic threading through her words. "Tyler! Talk to me! What's going on?"

But he didn't answer. The door swung open, and Tyler stepped outside, disappearing into the night.

Emily stood on the porch, her arms wrapped around herself as she watched his car speed away. The engine's growl faded into the distance, leaving her in a chilling silence.

"Be safe, Ty," she whispered, her words lost to the night.

The city's empty streets stretched out before Tyler, the streetlights casting ghostly shadows across his face. His hands gripped the steering wheel tightly, his jaw set.

"I'm going to stop him," he said, his voice filled with steely determination.

The camera pulled back, showing his car disappearing into the distance. The city lights flickered behind him, swallowed by the dark as the haunting quiet of the night took over.

A RUSH INTO THE UNKNOWN

The hum of the engine reverberated through the cabin, blending with the faint static of the radio he hadn't bothered to turn off. Tyler's hands gripped the steering wheel tightly, his knuckles ghostly white under the dim glow of passing streetlights. His jaw was set, his eyes flicking between the darkened road ahead and the rearview mirror.

"Where the hell are you, Jerry?" he muttered, his voice low but brimming with frustration.

His fingers drummed against the leather wheel as his thoughts churned like a storm. Images flashed in his mind—Jerry's mocking smirk, the chubby boy's terrified eyes, the hastily scribbled notes and maps pinned across Jerry's cellar walls.

"You've got a spot," he hissed to himself. "Everyone has a damn spot. A safe house, a meeting point... something."

The faint thrum of a passing car snapped him back to the road. Tyler clenched his teeth, narrowing his eyes. His pulse quickened as he recalled the detail he'd overlooked earlier—the circled address in red ink, screaming at him from the chaos of Jerry's hideout.

"The address," he said, his voice barely above a whisper. His fingers tightened on the wheel as the memory sharpened.

Then, like a dam breaking, it hit him.

"The other address!" He snapped his fingers, the sound sharp in the confined space. "Like a goddamn beacon."

Without hesitation, Tyler yanked the wheel to the left, making a sharp and illegal U-turn. Tires screeched against asphalt, and an angry honk from a passing car barely registered in his ears.

"That's it," he muttered, pressing the gas pedal to the floor. The car roared forward, its speed mirroring the frantic energy buzzing under Tyler's skin.

The house was as unremarkable as Tyler remembered it—modest, with peeling paint and a porch light that flickered like a dying firefly. It stood in eerie silence, the surrounding neighborhood dark and lifeless.

Tyler pulled into the driveway, his headlights casting long, distorted shadows across the front of the house. He left the engine running, the low rumble filling the air as he stepped out.

His boots crunched against the gravel as he approached the door. Each step felt heavier, his breathing growing shallow. He didn't knock. He didn't wait.

With a swift, calculated motion, Tyler slammed his shoulder into the door. The wood splintered with a deafening crack, the force sending it swinging inward.

The house was a shell of itself. The walls, once plastered with photos and chaotic scrawls, were stripped bare. The air was stale, the faint scent of sweat and cheap cologne lingering like a ghost.

"Come on, Jerry," Tyler muttered, stepping inside. His voice echoed in the empty space. "You've got to leave something behind."

He moved with purpose, yanking open drawers and cabinets, rifling through their contents. Empty. All of it. The frustration simmering beneath his skin threatened to boil over.

"Damn it!" He slammed a drawer shut with enough force to rattle the entire desk.

He turned toward the kitchen, his movements growing frantic. Boxes, cupboards, even the fridge—nothing offered the answers he sought.

"Where is it?" he growled, his voice rising. "Where the hell is it?!"

A sudden, shrill ring cut through the silence. Tyler froze, his head snapping toward the sound.

"A phone?" he whispered, his pulse quickening.

The noise led him to a pile of discarded papers on the floor. Tyler dropped to his knees, shoving them aside until his hand closed around a cheap flip phone. The screen blinked with an incoming call.

He hesitated for only a moment before pressing the green button.

"What?" he barked.

"I thought you'd never pick up."

The voice was distorted, masked by static, but Tyler's sharp ears picked up the faint hum of an engine in the background—and something else.

A child's muffled scream.

Tyler's heart skipped a beat, his grip tightening on the phone until his knuckles ached.

"Who the hell is this?"

"You want to see the kid again, don't you?"

His blood ran cold.

"Where?"

The voice on the other end chuckled, low and taunting.

"The cabin. Off the highway, near the zoo. Be quick."

The line clicked dead. Tyler stared at the phone in his hand, his chest heaving.

"The cabin," he whispered.

The map app on Tyler's phone loaded slowly, the small red marker taking its time to appear on the screen. His fingers drummed impatiently on the wheel.

"Cabin... highway... zoo," he muttered, repeating the words like a mantra.

Finally, the marker appeared, blinking in a remote area surrounded by dense forest.

"There you are."

He tossed the phone onto the passenger seat and started the car with a roar. The tires spun against the gravel before catching traction, propelling him onto the road.

As he sped toward his destination, his phone buzzed. Emily's face appeared on the screen, her bright smile a stark contrast to the storm brewing inside him.

Tyler's hand hovered over the phone, hesitation flickering in his eyes.

"Not now, Em," he said, letting the call go to voicemail.

The phone buzzed again almost immediately.

Emily.

"Damn it," Tyler muttered, slamming his hand against the wheel. He didn't answer.

The highway was nearly deserted, the rhythmic flash of streetlights illuminating Tyler's car as it cut through the darkness. His mind raced, the pieces of the puzzle finally snapping into place.

"Jerry," he muttered. "The trafficking ring. The kid."

His fingers tightened on the wheel. The image of the terrified boy burned in his mind, fueling the fire that had been smoldering for far too long.

"This ends tonight," he said, his voice low and resolute.

The GPS chimed, announcing his exit. Tyler veered onto the ramp, the tires screeching as he took the turn too sharply. The road ahead was darker, the streetlights replaced by the oppressive shadows of looming trees.

The dirt road ended abruptly, opening into a small clearing. The cabin stood ahead, its dilapidated form cloaked in darkness. The air was thick with tension, every sound amplified in the oppressive silence.

Tyler killed the engine and stepped out of the car. The faint crunch of gravel under his boots was the only sound as he approached the cabin.

NO TURNING BACK

The gravel crunched beneath Tyler's tires as he crept along the dirt road, his headlights dimmed to avoid alerting anyone to his approach. The cabin emerged from the dark, a hulking silhouette against the faint silver light of the crescent moon. Two vehicles were parked in front of the rundown structure: a rusted sedan that had seen better decades and a black SUV with its windows tinted.

Tyler killed the engine fifty yards back, sliding the gear into park behind a dense thicket of trees. His hands gripped the steering wheel so tightly that his knuckles burned white. He stared at the cabin, watching shadows shift behind the dimly lit curtains.

In the window, a hulking figure moved, hoisting something—a small, limp body—over his shoulder.

Tyler's stomach twisted. His jaw clenched so hard his teeth ached.

"They're dead," he muttered to himself, his voice low and venomous. "All of them."

He leaned over, popping open the glove box. The cold steel of his revolver glinted in the moonlight. Four bullets rested snugly in the cylinder—four chances to end lives that didn't deserve to exist.

He clicked the cylinder shut, tucking the weapon into his waistband. His heart thundered in his chest, but his breathing stayed measured. Tyler wasn't nervous. He wasn't scared. He was ready.

Opening the door slowly, Tyler slipped out into the night. His movements were silent, practiced. A predator stalking prey.

A man stood just outside the cabin, leaning against the porch railing with a cigarette dangling from his lips. He took a long drag, the ember glowing bright orange before he exhaled a cloud of smoke into the crisp night air. He was armed, a Glock holstered lazily on his hip, but his posture screamed complacency.

Tyler circled wide, sticking to the shadows of the tree line. His steps were soft, calculated. The man didn't notice him until it was too late.

The revolver pressed against the back of the man's skull.

"Don't fucking move," Tyler growled, his voice low and sharp.

The man froze, his hands instinctively going up. The cigarette tumbled from his lips, landing in the dirt.

"What the fuck—who are you?!" the man stammered.

Tyler grabbed the back of his collar, yanking him down from the porch. The man stumbled, almost losing his footing, but Tyler didn't let up, shoving him toward the woods.

"Walk," Tyler ordered.

The man tried to turn his head, to get a look at who was behind him, but Tyler slammed the butt of his revolver into the base of his skull. The man let out a sharp grunt of pain, staggering forward.

"I said walk. Unless you want a bullet in your goddamn head."

They reached the creek, the sound of rushing water masking their footsteps. Moonlight reflected off the rippling surface, casting ghostly shadows across the forest floor.

The man tried to plead, his voice shaking. "Look, man, I don't know who you think I am—"

"Shut up," Tyler snapped, shoving him to his knees. "How many kids? Huh? How many did you ruin?"

The man's voice cracked. "I don't— I don't know what you're talking about—"

Tyler laughed, a cold, humorless sound. He knelt down, his mouth close to the man's ear. "Wrong answer."

He didn't give the man a chance to beg. The gunshot echoed through the forest, sending a flock of startled birds into the night sky. Blood sprayed across the rocks and water as the man's body collapsed into the creek. The current carried him downstream, leaving a crimson trail behind.

Tyler stood, watching the body disappear into the darkness. His hand was steady, his breathing calm.

"One down."

The gunshot drew attention. The cabin door flew open, slamming against the wall as a second man stormed out, shotgun in hand. He scanned the woods, his eyes wild.

"Who's out there?!" the man barked, his voice echoing through the trees.

Tyler crouched behind a tree, his revolver at the ready. He watched as the man stepped off the porch, his boots crunching against the gravel.

"Think you're smart, huh? Hiding out there like a little bitch?" the man taunted.

Tyler's lip curled into a snarl. He stepped out from behind the tree, just enough to draw the man's attention.

The shotgun blasted, bark exploding from the tree as the buckshot missed Tyler by inches. He ducked back, his heart pounding.

"Missed me," Tyler called out, his voice mocking.

The man growled, stalking closer. "Come on out, asshole! Let's see how tough you are!"

Tyler didn't let him get closer. He lunged, grabbing the barrel of the shotgun and twisting it upward. The man fired again, the shot going harmlessly into the sky. Tyler drove his knee into the man's stomach, making him double over, then slammed his elbow into the side of his head.

The man stumbled, but Tyler didn't relent. He wrenched the shotgun free, flipping it around in his hands. Before the man could recover, Tyler swung it like a bat, the butt of the weapon smashing into his jaw. Teeth and blood sprayed from the man's mouth as he crumpled to the ground.

"Wait!" the man gasped, holding up a trembling hand. "Please—"

Tyler pumped the shotgun, aiming it at the man's face.

"Begging? That's rich," Tyler sneered.

The blast was deafening. Blood and bone splattered across the dirt as the man's head exploded. Tyler tossed the shotgun aside, wiping a smear of blood from his cheek.

"Two down."

The cabin was silent as Tyler approached, his revolver drawn. The dim light inside flickered, casting long shadows against the walls. Tyler could hear movement—a chair scraping, hurried footsteps.

Then, car doors slammed. Engines roared to life, and the two vehicles peeled out of the driveway, their tires kicking up gravel as they sped away.

Tyler growled under his breath. "Cowards."

He slipped inside the cabin, his eyes scanning every corner. The air was thick with the stench of cigarettes and beer. The small living room was empty. So was the kitchen. Tyler's frustration bubbled over.

"Where the fuck are you?" he hissed.

A door creaked behind him. Tyler spun, his gun raised.

Jerry stood in the doorway, adjusting his belt. His eyes went wide when he saw Tyler.

"What the—"

Tyler didn't let him finish. He grabbed a plate off the counter and hurled it, the ceramic shattering against Jerry's head. The man staggered, blood dripping from a fresh gash on his forehead.

"You," Tyler snarled, advancing on him. "You piece of shit."

Jerry stumbled back, raising his hands. "Wait! I can explain—"

Tyler slammed him against the wall, pressing the barrel of his revolver under Jerry's chin.

"Explain this," Tyler hissed. "How many kids did you sell, Jerry? How many lives did you destroy?"

Jerry whimpered, sweat pouring down his face. "I—I didn't—"

Tyler pulled a rag from his pocket, soaking it in chloroform. Jerry's eyes widened in panic.

"No—no, don't—"

Tyler pressed the rag over Jerry's mouth and nose, ignoring his muffled protests and flailing arms.

"You're going to pay for every single one of them," Tyler whispered, his voice ice-cold. "Every. Single. One."

Jerry's struggles weakened, his body going limp as the chloroform took hold. Tyler let him collapse to the floor, standing over him with a look of pure contempt.

"And this," Tyler said softly, "is just the beginning."

WHEN THE KILLER IS UNLEASHED

The cold night air bit into Tyler's skin as he leaned against the back of his car, his arms crossed. His breath formed visible clouds that hung in the air like ghostly remnants of the man he used to be. The chaos of the last few hours still hummed beneath his skin, but now it was silent. Still. The fire inside him had quieted to a dull, simmering rage.

He stared at the cabin, its dark windows reflecting nothing but the empty stretch of woods that surrounded it. The place was eerily quiet now, like a predator lying in wait, patient and hungry. The flickering lights inside had long since gone out, and only the shadow of the house remained—a silhouette against the star-streaked sky. It seemed like a metaphor for the world Tyler had found himself in.

A world where things weren't ever quite as they seemed.

His gaze shifted to the ground. Jerry's body lay in the dirt, sprawled like a ragdoll discarded after a brutal game. Blood pooled around his head, the dark crimson stark against the pale earth, a fitting end for a man whose sins ran deep. Jerry was unconscious, but Tyler had no doubt that when he woke, he wouldn't be the same. Not after everything that had happened. Not after Tyler had finally dragged him from the shadows where he'd hidden so long.

Tyler's hand reached instinctively to his waistband, checking the gun that was still tucked there. The weight of it was comforting, a steady reminder of the power he wielded. A power he could never turn off. Not anymore.

His phone buzzed in his pocket, snapping him from his thoughts. He glanced down at the screen. William.

He hesitated. His thumb hovered over the green answer button for a second too long. His pulse quickened—his father. The one person who still had the ability to pull him back. But could he? Could William ever understand how far Tyler had fallen?

He pressed the button, dragging in a breath before raising the phone to his ear.

"Hey, Dad," Tyler said, trying to keep his voice casual, but it came out more strained than he intended.

"Tyler," William's voice was filled with a mix of relief and frustration. "Where the hell have you been? I've called you three times today."

Tyler's eyes moved once again to the cabin. His jaw tightened. He didn't need to look to know what was happening inside. But he did anyway. The air was thick with the smell of blood, sweat, and something else—something darker.

"Sorry, I've been busy," Tyler said, keeping his voice steady, though his words tasted like ash in his mouth.

"Busy?" William's tone turned skeptical, and Tyler could hear him shifting around, probably sitting down in his office chair. "I hope this isn't about another signing or some media stunt, because I need you to be careful, Tyler. Things are getting messy out here."

Tyler's stomach twisted. He could hear it in his dad's voice—concern, but there was something more. Something sharp. Suspicion? Or was it just his imagination?

"No, Dad," Tyler replied, his voice dropping slightly, his gaze narrowing. "It's nothing like that."

A sigh came from the other end. William's frustration was palpable, but it was tempered with a sense of helplessness. "Look, I didn't call to hound you. I just wanted to check in. You've been distant lately. Your mother used to—"

Tyler cut him off before the words could go any further. Before the weight of them could pull him under. He didn't need to hear about his mother right now. Not with everything that was happening.

"Dad, I know," Tyler snapped, a little too harshly. "And I appreciate it. But right now, I've got something in front of me I have to handle. If I don't, it'll ruin everything I've worked for."

The silence on the other end felt heavy, as though William was weighing his words, trying to read between the lines. Tyler's pulse drummed in his ears. His fingers tightened around the phone, and he could feel the thin veneer of control slipping. The walls were closing in. There was no turning back now.

"What do you mean?" William's voice softened slightly, the suspicion still there, but tinged with concern. "Is this about the new book?"

Tyler's lips curled into a faint smirk, but there was nothing light about it. "Something like that."

He could hear William exhale on the other end, a weary sound, as if the weight of their entire strained relationship was suddenly crashing down on him. Tyler's throat tightened.

"Alright, fine," William said after a beat. "Just… be smart, okay? I can't clean up your messes anymore."

Tyler's eyes drifted back to Jerry's body, lying in a crumpled heap like the trash he was. His mind flashed back to the blood and the fear in the men's eyes. He could still hear the sounds—the pleading, the begging. They had all thought they could get away with it.

They were wrong.

He straightened, brushing his fingers along the edge of the trunk, feeling the cool metal beneath his fingertips.

"Don't worry, Dad," he said quietly, almost to himself. "I'll handle it."

The silence on the other end stretched out. Tyler could hear his father's faint breath, as if he was trying to gauge whether his son was serious or not. Tyler wanted to scream. He wanted to tell him everything—the whole damn truth. But he couldn't. Not now.

"Alright," William finally grunted, his tone resigned. "Call me when you're free."

"Will do," Tyler replied, his voice like stone.

The line clicked off, and Tyler stood there for a moment, his phone still in his hand. The weight of the device was oddly comforting—almost a tether to his old life, to the part of him that was still human. But even as he stood there, staring at the cold night, a part of him knew: that version of him was slipping away.

Tyler slammed the trunk shut with a sharp clang. The sound echoed through the woods, cutting through the stillness like a warning. He stared at the cabin again, his hand still wrapped tightly around the phone. He couldn't explain why, but it felt like it was daring him to go back inside. To finish what he had started.

No turning back now.

Tyler's mind flashed to the faces of the men he had killed. The bodies of those they had hurt. The lives they had ruined. His heart was a ticking time bomb, each moment pulling him closer to the inevitable explosion. There was no more reasoning, no more restraint. He was a force now. The Inked Reaper wasn't just a name—it was who he was.

He could feel it now. The anger, the fire, the rage that had been bubbling beneath the surface for so long, rising up like a flood. And for the first time in a long time, it felt right. All of it.

Tyler's hand went to his waistband, his fingers grazing the cold steel of his revolver. It was still there. He wasn't alone in this. He had the power to shape the world around him, to wipe it clean of the filth he had spent so long hunting.

But even as he took that breath, ready to move forward, a small part of him—the part that still remembered who he had been—whispered in the back of his mind. What happens when there's nothing left to kill?

He pushed the thought aside, his mind steeling itself. He had no time for doubts. He had a job to finish.

With one last look at the cabin, Tyler turned on his heel and stepped into the darkness, ready to take on whatever came next.

The basement of Pyreworx Cafe was suffocating, its thick air clinging to the skin like damp cloth. The walls were made of rough-hewn stone, dripping with the moisture of the earth itself. The only light came from a flickering bulb overhead, casting erratic shadows across the room. A low hum of distant machinery vibrated through the floors, the only other sound breaking the stillness.

But it wasn't enough to drown out the quiet, oppressive silence in the air. The chains hanging from the walls, rusted and twisted, swayed ever so slightly, their metal links clinking with a soft, chilling rhythm that cut through the tension like a whisper in the dark.

Tyler stood motionless, his eyes fixed on Jerry's unconscious form sprawled across the cold concrete floor. Blood, dark and thick, had matted Jerry's hair, pooling beneath his skull where the gash from earlier had left its mark. The man was broken, a shell of the monster he had once been, but Tyler knew better than to assume he was finished. Not yet.

Tyler crouched beside him, his eyes cold and calculating, his face a mask of unreadable calm. The only sound was the occasional groan from Jerry's body, the dull thud of a distant door creaking in the cabin overhead.

"Poetic, isn't it?" Tyler whispered under his breath, the words barely more than a breath of air.

The chains—the very same chains that had been used to imprison others, to make them feel small, helpless—would now serve to bind Jerry. He couldn't help but marvel at the irony of it. He had spent so long hunting men like Jerry, monsters that hid in the shadows, preying on those who couldn't protect themselves. But now, in this small, dank room, the tables had turned. Jerry was the prey, and Tyler was the hunter.

He reached for the first chain, his fingers brushing against the cold metal. It was heavy, unwieldy in his grasp, but it didn't faze him. His movements were steady, practiced. He wrapped the chain around Jerry's wrist, testing its weight, making sure it would hold. Then, with a deliberate click, he locked it in place.

The sound was sharp, almost too loud in the stillness, and it reverberated off the stone walls, a reminder of the trap he had set. Tyler stood, his back straight, and wiped his hands on his jeans.

"Not yet," he muttered, almost to himself, as he grabbed another chain from the pile.

With each movement, he grew more focused, more certain of his actions. There was no room for hesitation here. Jerry's other wrist was soon bound, the chains tight and unforgiving, pulling his arms toward the stone walls that seemed to close in around him. Tyler paused for a moment, surveying his work, his eyes calculating. Jerry was helpless now. Bound. Vulnerable.

The satisfaction was almost palpable, a tingling sensation running through Tyler's veins. He couldn't help the small smile that tugged at the corner of his lips. This was what it was all for. Every hunt. Every decision. This moment right here.

But there was more to be done.

Tyler reached into his pocket, his fingers brushing against the rope coiled tightly within. It was strong, sturdy, designed for this very purpose. He pulled it out, the fibers whispering against the air as he unraveled it. Jerry's legs were next. With a swift, practiced motion, Tyler wrapped the rope around Jerry's ankles, securing it with a series of tight knots that would leave him no room to move.

The room was still. No more sound. Only the drip of water somewhere deeper in the bowels of the cafe, each drop falling at a rhythmic, almost mournful pace. Tyler stepped back, surveying his work with a sharp, assessing gaze.

Jerry lay there, stretched out, his body forced into an unnatural position. The chains bolted into the walls held him tight, while the rope kept his legs in place. Tyler was thorough, always precise. He had no tolerance for failure. And Jerry wouldn't get the chance to escape. Not this time.

Tyler's eyes narrowed as he studied Jerry's face, the slow rise and fall of his chest, the trickle of blood from his forehead, staining the cold concrete floor. He wasn't dead, but he wasn't far from it, either. The agony would come soon enough. Tyler could feel it in his bones.

He turned and walked across the room, dragging a chair from the corner. Its legs scraped against the concrete, the sound so sharp it felt like it could pierce through the very walls of the basement. Tyler didn't flinch. Instead, he slid the chair into place, right in front of Jerry. He spun it around, straddling it, his arms folding over the backrest as he settled into his seat.

The moment felt suspended in time. The silence was thick, suffocating, and Tyler let it settle around him. His eyes never left Jerry, his gaze unwavering, even as Jerry shifted slightly on the floor, a faint groan escaping his lips. Tyler didn't react. He was patient.

He could feel the weight of Jerry's presence, even in his unconscious state. It was like the man's soul was already caged in this room with him. Tyler leaned forward, his face inches from Jerry's, his voice low and measured.

"You'll wake up soon," Tyler whispered, the words almost a promise. "And when you do... we're going to have a nice, long chat."

He could hear Jerry's breathing becoming a little heavier, a little more erratic, as if the proximity to consciousness was dragging him closer. The quiet drip of water was the only other sound that accompanied them, falling in its own steady rhythm, as though the world was holding its breath, waiting.

Tyler leaned back in the chair, folding his arms across his chest. His gaze never wavered from Jerry's face, watching for any signs of life, any hint that his victim might be coming around. The room felt colder now, the air growing heavy with anticipation. Each passing second seemed to stretch, as though time itself was stretching itself out to meet the inevitable.

A faint groan escaped Jerry's lips. It was barely audible, but it was enough to send a shiver down Tyler's spine. His eyes gleamed with an almost predatory light as he leaned forward again, watching with intensity as Jerry's eyelids fluttered. The storm was about to break.

Tyler sat there, waiting. His pulse matched the rhythm of the dripping water, slow and steady. The calm before the storm. The silence before the inevitable explosion.

And when Jerry's eyes finally opened, dazed and disoriented, the first thing he saw was Tyler's cold, calculating gaze.

Tyler didn't speak at first. He simply stared. He could feel the power shift, the weight of his actions settling over them both. Jerry's body trembled slightly, the shock of what was happening just beginning to register in his mind.

He opened his mouth to speak, but Tyler held up a finger to his lips, silencing him before he could utter a sound.

"You'll speak when I'm ready," Tyler said, his voice quiet but firm.

The storm was about to come. And when it did, Jerry wouldn't know what hit him.

A LEGACY OF SHADOWS

Jerry West's head throbbed like a drumbeat, an unforgiving rhythm that pulsed through his skull. The sticky warmth of blood matted his hair and streaked down the side of his face, dripping onto his shirt. He groaned, his fingers twitching as he came to. For a moment, he was disoriented, the world around him a haze of flickering shadows and muted, metallic sounds.

When his vision sharpened, the reality of his predicament crashed over him like a wave. His wrists were shackled to a thick metal pipe bolted into the wall behind him, the cold steel biting into his skin. He tugged instinctively, the chains rattling with an eerie clang. Panic seized him, constricting his chest like a vice. His breath came in shallow gasps as he scanned the room. The dim light flickered above, a single bulb dangling on a frayed wire. Its erratic glow illuminated the cluttered back room of the Pyrework Café.

Jerry recognized the place. He'd been here just hours ago, thinking it was another dead-end lead. Now, it felt like the walls were closing in, the space stifling and airless.

The sound of approaching footsteps pulled him from his thoughts. Each step was deliberate, measured, the echo bouncing off the walls and growing louder with every beat. Jerry's muscles tensed, his body instinctively bracing for what was to come.

From the shadows emerged a figure, calm and composed, his movements smooth and unhurried. Tyler Grayson. He looked almost serene, a black notebook in one hand, his other tucked casually into the pocket of his jeans.

"Hello, Jerry," Tyler said, his voice cool and unbothered, as though they were meeting for coffee rather than a confrontation in a makeshift dungeon.

Jerry's instincts kicked in. He surged forward, yanking at the chains with everything he had. The effort was useless. The restraints held firm, pulling him back with a jarring force that sent a fresh wave of pain shooting through his wrists.

"Let me out of here, you sick bastard!" Jerry snarled, his voice hoarse.

Tyler didn't flinch. Instead, he crouched just out of Jerry's reach, resting his forearms on his knees. His head tilted slightly, the barest hint of amusement playing on his face.

"Such a weak, pathetic little kitty cat," Tyler mocked, his tone light, playful even. "Look at you. All claws and no bite."

Jerry glared at him, his breathing ragged. "You're not getting away with this. Someone's going to find you, you son of a bitch."

Tyler straightened, the faintest smirk tugging at his lips. "You know, Jerry, I've heard that line more times than I can count. And yet"—he spread his arms wide, gesturing to the room—"here I am. Untouched. Unstoppable."

Jerry spat at him, the glob of saliva landing inches away from Tyler's polished boots. Tyler regarded the act with a raised brow, then chuckled softly. He rose to his feet and strode over to a nearby table cluttered with various objects—a roll of duct tape, a few knives, plastic sheeting, and a half-empty bottle of water. Tyler picked up the bottle and took a slow, deliberate sip, his eyes never leaving Jerry.

"You think you're in control," Tyler said finally, his voice laced with mockery. "The brave federal agent. The hero of your own story." He stepped closer, his tone dropping to a whisper. "But heroes, Jerry... heroes die just like everyone else."

Jerry recoiled, his eyes darting around the room. He spotted a toolbox in the corner and a stack of coffee bean bags piled against the wall—nothing remotely useful. His mind raced, trying to piece together an escape. Tyler followed his gaze, his smirk widening.

"Looking for a way out?" Tyler taunted, shaking his head. "There isn't one. I made sure of it. You're not leaving this room, Jerry. Not alive, anyway."

Jerry's jaw clenched, his breathing growing heavier. "You're going to screw up," he growled. "Guys like you always do. Someone will stop you."

Tyler threw back his head and laughed, the sound rich and genuine, as though Jerry had told the funniest joke he'd ever heard.

"Stop me? Oh, Jerry." Tyler crouched again, his face mere inches from Jerry's. "Who's going to stop me? William? Kate? Some other faceless drone in a cheap suit? They're chasing shadows, all of them. They don't even know where to look."

Jerry's heart pounded as Tyler rose to his full height, pacing the room with the measured grace of a predator circling its prey.

"You want to know the truth?" Tyler asked, his tone taking on a theatrical edge. He stopped abruptly, turning to face Jerry. "I killed them. All of them. Every single one of those 146 rotting bodies you found in that cavern? That was me. Every slice of skin. Every shattered bone. Every scream of terror."

Jerry's stomach churned, but he refused to look away. "You're a coward," he spat. "Hiding behind your little games, your masks. You think this makes you powerful? You're nothing but a twisted, broken freak."

For the first time, Tyler's expression faltered. His smirk faded, replaced by something darker, more menacing. He turned away, his back to Jerry, and let the insult linger in the air.

Slowly, he turned back, a chilling grin spreading across his face. "Twisted? Broken? Sure, I'll give you that. But a coward? No, Jerry. A coward hides from what they are. I've embraced it. I've become it."

Jerry's eyes widened, a flicker of realization dawning. "You're insane."

Tyler stepped closer, his voice dropping to a near whisper. "No, Jerry. I'm inevitable."

Silence hung heavy in the room, broken only by the faint drip of water from a leaky pipe. Tyler crouched again, his tone soft and almost conversational.

"You know what they say about curiosity, don't you? It killed the cat. And here you are, poking your nose where it doesn't belong. Thinking you're clever." He leaned in, his voice dropping to a sinister whisper. "You're not clever, Jerry. You're just another ink stain on my page."

Jerry tugged at the chains again, his breathing frantic. "You'll slip up," he said, his voice rising. "Someone will stop you. They always do."

"NO ONE WILL STOP ME!" Tyler roared, the sudden outburst reverberating through the room. Jerry flinched, his body instinctively recoiling.

Tyler inhaled deeply, composing himself. His smirk returned, colder this time. "The Inked Reaper isn't just a name, Jerry. It's a legacy. Long after you're gone, long after your body's rotting in the ground, I'll still be out there, cleaning up the messes your precious system can't touch."

He turned back to the table and picked up a small knife. The blade gleamed under the flickering light as he twirled it between his fingers, his movements almost casual. He glanced at Jerry, his expression unreadable.

"You're going to die tonight, Jerry," Tyler said matter-of-factly. "And when you do, no one will even remember you existed."

Jerry's chest heaved as he struggled against the chains, his face twisted in fury and desperation. Tyler watched him for a moment, then set the knife down and grabbed the bottle of water again. He splashed some onto Jerry's face, eliciting a strangled cough.

"Thirsty? No? Shame," Tyler said with mock concern.

Jerry glared at him, his voice low and venomous. "You'll burn for this."

Tyler crouched one final time, his face inches from Jerry's. His voice dropped to a near whisper, chilling in its calmness.

"Maybe. But not tonight."

With that, Tyler straightened and walked to the door. He flicked off the light, plunging the room into darkness. The sound of his footsteps faded into the distance, leaving only the faint rattle of Jerry's chains and the echo of dripping water.

The silence was deafening.

CHAINS OF INK

The room hummed with a stillness that felt alive, thick with anticipation and dread. Tyler leaned casually against the rusted counter, the dim light above throwing erratic shadows across his face. His smirk didn't fade as Jerry thrashed weakly against the chains holding him to the wall. The older man's breath came in ragged gasps, the sharp scent of sweat and blood saturating the air.

"I could've ended this hours ago," Tyler said, his voice soft and conversational, like he was discussing the weather. He flicked a fleck of something unseen from his sleeve. "But there's something poetic about watching someone realize they've lost. Seeing that hope drain from their eyes... It's like the perfect closing line to a story."

Jerry's eyes darted to the floor, where the greasy knife lay just out of reach. Tyler followed his gaze, his smirk widening.

"Go ahead," Tyler taunted, stepping aside with an exaggerated gesture toward the blade. "Pick it up. Try something stupid. I could use the laugh."

Jerry hesitated, his heart pounding against his ribs. His fingers twitched, and before he could second-guess himself, he lunged forward, his wrist twisting painfully against the chains as he grabbed the knife.

The move wasn't quick enough. Tyler's boot crashed down on Jerry's hand, sending a sharp jolt of pain shooting up his arm. The knife clattered to the ground, and Jerry let out a muffled cry of pain.

"Really?" Tyler asked, shaking his head in mock disappointment. He crouched down, his face inches from Jerry's, and lifted the knife with two fingers. "This? You thought this would save you?"

Jerry glared at him, defiance burning in his eyes despite the fear that quaked through his body. Tyler examined the blade like it was a relic in a museum, running his thumb along its dull edge.

"Do you know what makes a knife like this dangerous?" Tyler mused, his tone calm, almost instructional. He flipped the blade in his hand and gestured vaguely at Jerry's face. "It's not the sharpness. It's not the design. It's intent. You don't have it, Jerry. You never did."

Tyler rose to his full height and stepped back, tossing the knife onto the table with a loud clatter.

Jerry shifted, pain lancing through his wrists where the chains dug into his skin. "This... isn't over," he muttered, his voice trembling but resolute. "Someone will figure you out. You're not invincible."

Tyler tilted his head, his lips curling into a smile that didn't reach his eyes. "You're right, Jerry. I'm not invincible. But I am careful. I plan ahead. Unlike you, scrambling for answers you'll never find."

He turned his back to Jerry, pacing slowly across the room. His fingers trailed over the surface of the table, lingering on a collection of neatly arranged tools: pliers, scalpels, a length of chain coiled like a snake.

"Edward, though," Tyler said, his voice thoughtful. "Now that's interesting. Who is he, Jerry? A friend? A partner? A ghost from your past, maybe?"

Jerry's silence spoke volumes. Tyler glanced over his shoulder, his dark eyes narrowing.

"Oh, come on," Tyler said, stepping closer. "You've been screaming his name like it's some kind of shield. 'Edward will stop you! Edward knows everything!'" He mocked the words with a sing-song lilt, his smirk twisting cruelly. "But here you are. Alone. Chained up. Bleeding. Tell me, Jerry—where's Edward now?"

Jerry's jaw tightened, his lips pressing into a thin line. Tyler crouched down again, his movements slow, deliberate.

"I'll find him," Tyler said, his voice dropping to a whisper. "And when I do, maybe I'll let him know how bravely you fought to keep his name safe. Or maybe I'll just let him join you."

The flicker of defiance in Jerry's eyes flared to life. "You don't know a damn thing," he spat, his voice shaking with anger.

Tyler chuckled, the sound low and cold. He stood, towering over Jerry as his smile faded into something darker.

"I know enough," Tyler said flatly. "I know you're not leaving this room. I know Edward's name isn't going to save you." He leaned in close, his breath hot against Jerry's ear. "And I know that every scream you swallow, every tear you hold back, only makes this more satisfying for me."

Jerry flinched, his chains rattling as he pressed himself against the wall.

"You don't have to do this," Jerry whispered, his voice cracking. "You can let me go. Walk away. This doesn't have to end like this."

Tyler stepped back, his expression softening into something almost sympathetic. "Oh, Jerry," he said, shaking his head. "It was always going to end like this. You just didn't realize it until now."

He moved to the table and picked up the roll of duct tape, tearing off a strip with an agonizing slowness that made Jerry's stomach churn.

"You've been chasing me for how long now?" Tyler asked, his tone light, conversational. He pressed the tape over Jerry's mouth, silencing his protests. "Two years? Three? It's almost poetic, don't you think? You were so close. And now you're here. The final chapter."

Jerry screamed against the tape, the sound muffled and desperate. Tyler tilted his head, watching him struggle.

"I'll make sure they find you," Tyler said, his voice soft. "But not too soon. You'll be part of the story, Jerry. A monument to persistence."

He turned back to the table, his shadow stretching long and jagged against the walls. His hand hovered over the tools, and his lips curled into a smile as he picked up a pair of pliers.

The light flickered, the shadows seeming to twist and writhe. Tyler's voice cut through the oppressive silence, calm and final.

"Goodbye, Jerry."

The light flickered again.

And this time, it didn't come back on.

THE LAST NAME

The room was colder than ice, the kind of chill that seeped into the bones and lingered, refusing to let go. The flickering fluorescent bulb cast erratic shadows on the cracked concrete walls, each stutter of light slicing through the darkness like a taunt. The metallic tang of blood mixed with the sour stink of sweat filled the air, making it almost suffocating. The atmosphere wasn't just bleak—it was oppressive, a weight pressing down on everything inside.

Jerry dangled from the chains, his feet barely grazing the floor. His wrists were raw and slick with blood where the metal cuffs had chewed through the skin, and his shoulders sagged under the strain of his own weight. His face was a swollen mess, one eye nearly shut, his lips cracked and crusted with dried blood. Yet despite the obvious agony, there was a fire in his eyes—a stubborn, burning defiance that refused to die.

Tyler, leaning lazily against the workbench, seemed unfazed by the scene. If anything, he looked bored, like a predator waiting for his prey to exhaust itself. He held a scalpel in his hand, turning it over idly as if inspecting its craftsmanship. The blade caught the intermittent light, gleaming dangerously.

Jerry's voice came out rough, barely more than a whisper. "Say something." He coughed, blood flecking his lips. "You're just going to stand there? Or are you too much of a coward to face me?"

Tyler didn't respond immediately. He flipped the scalpel one last time before setting it down with a soft clink on the workbench. His movements were slow, deliberate, as though he had all the time in the world. Finally, he straightened and took a step forward, his boots clicking against the concrete. Each step echoed ominously in the room.

"A coward?" he mused, his voice low and calm. "That's... new. Most people like to go with 'monster.' 'Psychopath.'" He smiled faintly, his teeth white and gleaming against the dim light. "But coward? Hmm." He tilted his head, considering. "Do you really believe that, Jerry? Or are you just trying to provoke me because you know you don't have much time left?"

Jerry clenched his jaw, his breathing labored. The chains creaked as he shifted, testing them, but they held firm. He gave a bitter laugh that turned into a rasping cough. "You're hiding," he spat. "Behind this whole act, behind your stupid little games. Real men face their enemies head-on. They don't chain them to a wall and pretend they're in control."

Tyler's eyes narrowed slightly, but the faint smirk remained. He stepped closer, his shadow looming over Jerry like a dark specter. "You know what I think?" he said softly. "I think you're scared. Scared of what's coming. Scared of what it means if you're wrong."

Jerry barked out another laugh, though it sounded weaker this time. "Wrong? About what? That you're just another psycho with a God complex? Please. You think you're untouchable, but people are catching on. Kate's catching on. She'll—"

"Kate?" Tyler interrupted, his tone sharp with mockery. He laughed—a sharp, biting sound that echoed off the walls. "Oh, Jerry, you're still clinging to that fantasy, aren't you?"

His demeanor shifted slightly as he walked to the workbench, running his fingers lightly over the array of tools laid out in meticulous order. A pair of pliers, a scalpel, a bone saw. Each one gleamed in the harsh light, as if freshly cleaned. He picked up the pliers, turning them over in his hands like he was appraising a fine piece of art.

"You really think Kate's going to come storming in here, guns blazing, to save the day?" he asked, his tone light and conversational. "Kick down the door just in time to whisk you away to safety?" He glanced at Jerry, one eyebrow raised. "Is that what you're holding onto? That little shred of hope?"

Jerry said nothing, but his jaw tightened, the muscles in his face twitching. Tyler's smile widened, as though he'd found a chink in the armor.

"She's not coming," Tyler said simply, his voice cold now. "Do you know why? Because she doesn't even know you're gone. There's no trail, no breadcrumbs. You didn't tell anyone where you were going, did you? Thought you could handle this yourself. Thought you could be the hero." He paused, letting the words sink in. "And now, Jerry, here you are. Another name on my list."

Jerry's breathing quickened, the chains rattling as he struggled against them. The panic was starting to creep in, evident in the way his movements grew frantic. "You're wrong," he growled. "She'll figure it out. She's too smart for you."

Tyler's expression darkened, the smirk fading. He crouched down in front of Jerry, balancing easily on the balls of his feet. Their faces were inches apart now, Jerry's ragged breath mingling with Tyler's calm, even exhalations.

"Too smart?" Tyler echoed, his voice low, almost a whisper. "You think she's smarter than me? You think she's going to piece this together in time to save you?" He tilted his head, studying Jerry like one might study an insect pinned to a board. "Let me tell you something about Kate. She's predictable. She's just like you. A cog in the machine. Spinning in the same direction as everyone else."

Jerry's eyes burned with fury. "She's going to bury you," he spat. "She'll figure it out, and when she does, she'll put you in the ground where you belong."

Tyler's smile returned, colder this time. He stood, towering over Jerry, the pliers glinting in his hand. "You're adorable," he said softly. "Truly. But let's be clear—you're not a hero. You're not even a threat. You're just... in the way."

He turned, walking back to the workbench. The sound of the tools clinking against each other as he selected something else filled the room. This time, it was the scalpel. Tyler held it up to the light, turning it slowly. The blade was so sharp it seemed to hum with lethal potential.

Jerry's breath hitched. He thrashed harder now, the chains rattling violently. "Wait," he gasped. "We can work something out. I can help you—"

Tyler glanced over his shoulder, his expression unreadable. "Help me?" he repeated, his tone laced with amusement. He walked back to Jerry, crouching again. "You've already helped me, Jerry. You gave me everything I needed." He leaned in closer, his voice dropping to a whisper. "And now, you're done."

The scalpel gleamed as Tyler raised it, the light catching on the blade one last time before it descended.

THE FINAL WORDS

The room was a symphony of despair, the cold air thick with the metallic stench of blood and sweat. A single bulb swung lazily from the ceiling, casting sporadic light that painted monstrous shadows on the stained concrete walls. The space felt alive, as though it fed on the suffering that unfolded within it, devouring every scream, every sob.

Jerry hung limply in the center of the room, his arms stretched above him, chains cutting into his wrists like cruel jewelry. Blood trickled in thin, crimson rivulets down his forearms, dripping in rhythmic splatters onto the floor below. His head lolled forward, chin brushing his chest, his breaths shallow and uneven.

Across from him, Tyler Grayson stood with a predator's stillness, his shadow stretching long across the room. He rolled up his sleeves, each movement precise, methodical, as though preparing for an art project. His face was devoid of emotion, yet his eyes betrayed something darker—a quiet storm brewing behind a mask of control.

Tyler broke the silence first, his voice calm and steady, cutting through the oppressive quiet like a blade. "You know, Jerry, I never thought it would come to this. You and me, here, like this." He gestured vaguely around the room. "It's poetic, don't you think? The hunter becoming the prey."

Jerry didn't lift his head. His lips, cracked and coated with dried blood, twitched faintly, but no words came. Tyler frowned, his head tilting slightly, like an artist disappointed in a half-finished piece.

"Nothing to say?" Tyler continued, his voice softening, almost teasing. "No final words, no clever quip? I thought you'd be more... spirited."

Jerry finally stirred, his voice barely more than a whisper, hoarse and raw. "Go to hell, you bastard."

Tyler chuckled, the sound low and almost warm, though it carried a razor's edge. "Already there, my friend. And you're coming with me."

Before Jerry could respond, Tyler's fist slammed into his stomach. The blow landed with a sickening thud, forcing a sharp gasp from Jerry's lips. His body jerked violently against the chains, the metal groaning under the strain. The sound reverberated in the small room, a cruel echo that seemed to mock him.

Tyler leaned in close, his lips brushing against Jerry's ear as he spoke, his tone mockingly tender. "That's more like it. See, Jerry, this isn't just about killing you. No, no, that would be too easy. Too merciful." He stepped back, pacing slowly, his hands clasped behind his back like a lecturer preparing to address his class. "You wanted the Inked Reaper, didn't you? You wanted to see the monster up close." He turned, his eyes locking onto Jerry's with an intensity that could shatter glass. "Well, here I am. Take a good, long look."

Tyler reached for the workbench, his fingers dancing over the array of tools until they settled on a jagged piece of metal. He held it up to the light, inspecting its edge with almost reverent care. Turning back to Jerry, he smiled—a smile devoid of warmth, devoid of humanity.

"Let's make this memorable, shall we?"

Without hesitation, Tyler slashed the jagged metal across Jerry's chest. The wound wasn't deep, but it was deliberate, calculated to inflict maximum pain without hastening death.

Jerry screamed, the sound raw and guttural, reverberating off the walls like a dying animal's cry.

"That's the sound I've been waiting for," Tyler said, his eyes alight with a twisted glee. He wiped the blood from the blade onto his sleeve, the crimson stain spreading like a dark flower. "You've got a good set of lungs, Jerry. Let's see how long they hold out."

Jerry's chest heaved as he fought to catch his breath, his voice trembling when he finally spoke. "You're... a coward," he rasped, each word a struggle. "You hide behind this... this mask. You think you're in control, but you're just a scared little boy pretending to be a god."

Tyler froze mid-step, the smile sliding from his face like a mask discarded. For a moment, his expression was unreadable, a blank canvas. Then his eyes darkened, and the air in the room seemed to grow heavier.

"Scared?" he echoed, his voice low, dangerously calm. "Oh, Jerry. You have no idea what fear really is. But don't worry—I'll show you."

He set the jagged metal down and reached for the pliers. The tool felt cold and heavy in his hand, a perfect extension of his intent. He moved toward Jerry with the grace of a predator, his movements fluid and precise. Gripping one of Jerry's fingers, Tyler clamped the pliers around the nail. He didn't rush—there was no need to. The anticipation was half the fun.

Jerry's eyes widened in realization, his breath hitching. "Wait—" he began, but the words died in his throat as Tyler yanked the nail free with a sickening crunch. Jerry's scream tore through the room, raw and visceral, a sound that seemed to rip at the very fabric of the air.

Tyler stepped back, examining the bloodied nail held delicately between the pliers. "There," he said softly, almost tenderly. "That's fear. That's the sound of your soul breaking, piece by piece."

Jerry's head sagged forward, his body trembling. "You're... sick," he choked out, his voice barely audible. "A monster."

"Monster?" Tyler repeated, a flicker of amusement returning to his face. "Maybe. Or maybe I'm just the result of a world that loves monsters. A world that creates them, nurtures them." He crouched down, leveling his gaze with Jerry's. "I'm not the disease, Jerry. I'm the cure."

Jerry's body slumped further, his strength fading with each passing moment. Tyler stood, wiping his hands on a rag, his breathing steady and controlled. But there was something else—a faint tremor in his fingers, an almost imperceptible crack in the veneer.

"I didn't want it to end like this," he said softly, his voice tinged with something resembling regret. "You were a good adversary, Jerry. A worthy opponent. But in the end..." He paused, his eyes distant. "The game was mine."

With one final motion, Tyler reached out, his hands gripping Jerry's face. He forced the man to look at him, their eyes locking in a final, silent exchange. Then, with a brutal twist, the sickening crack of Jerry's neck breaking shattered the silence.

The room fell deathly still. Jerry's body hung limp in the chains, his head lolled to the side, his lifeless eyes staring into nothingness. Tyler stepped back, his chest rising and falling as he fought to steady his breathing. He reached up, unfastening the chains, letting Jerry's body collapse to the floor in a lifeless heap.

The weight of what he'd done pressed down on him like a lead blanket, but Tyler didn't allow himself to linger. His movements were mechanical as he began the grim task of dismembering the body, each cut precise, each motion deliberate. Blood pooled around him, soaking into the cracks of the concrete floor, but he didn't flinch.

When the work was done, he stood over the remains, his hands trembling, his face pale. He wiped his face with the back of his hand, smearing blood across his cheek like war paint.

"I'm sorry," he whispered, his voice barely audible, as if the words were meant for himself alone. "Truly."

The silence that followed was deafening, the room now a mausoleum, a shrine to the horrors that had taken place. Tyler turned, his shadow stretching long and dark behind him as he walked toward the door, leaving the carnage in his wake.

EVERYTHING AT THE END OF TIME

The lake stretched into the horizon, a mirror reflecting the cold, pale light of the moon. The air was thick with silence, the kind that pressed against the ears and refused to let go. Tyler Grayson sat at the stern of his small motorboat, staring down at the bundle wrapped in tarp at his feet. The faint hum of the engine had long since faded, leaving only the gentle lapping of water against the boat to fill the void.

The bundle was still, its edges bound tightly with chains that gleamed under the moonlight. Dark, uneven stains had seeped through the fabric, a silent testimony to the violence that had preceded this moment. Tyler's gaze was steady, his face devoid of emotion, but his mind was anything but calm.

He reached into his jacket, pulling out a battered pack of cigarettes. The action was mechanical, like a habit ingrained so deeply it no longer required thought. The click of the lighter broke the silence, and the flame briefly illuminated his face. In that fleeting moment, his features appeared almost angelic—smooth, youthful, unmarred by the horrors he had wrought. But his eyes told a different story.

They were empty, devoid of warmth, and yet brimming with something far more unsettling: clarity.

Tyler inhaled deeply, the ember glowing as he did, and exhaled a plume of smoke into the night air. It curled and twisted, dissipating into the darkness like a ghost.

"I'm a serial killer."

The thought was as clear and undeniable as the cold air biting at his skin.

"That's the truth I live with, the truth I've accepted. The world sees Tyler Grayson, the boy wonder. The prodigy. The perfect son. The loving boyfriend. But they'll never see this side of me. The side that hunts. The side that kills."

He reached down, his hand brushing against the bloodied tarp. The sensation was familiar, almost comforting. His fingers closed around the edge, and he began to drag the bundle closer to the edge of the boat.

But then he paused, the weight of his own thoughts halting him.

"Jerry's gone. That should feel like a victory. Like relief. But it doesn't, does it? No. It feels... hollow."

He leaned back, the cigarette dangling from his lips. His eyes drifted to the horizon, where the sky met the water in an endless expanse of black.

"Sorry, Jerry," he murmured aloud, his voice barely above a whisper. "You were good at your job. Too good."

The words hung in the air, unanswered.

Tyler reached for the chains coiled beside him, their links cold and heavy in his hands. He began to loop them around the bundle, his movements precise and methodical. Each knot was a finality, a closing chapter.

As he worked, his mind wandered.

"Jerry was a problem. Always poking, always prying. He was too curious for his own good. And now he's here, wrapped in tarp and ready to disappear. But what about the next one? And the one after that? They'll come, won't they? There's always another."

The final knot secured, Tyler paused, staring down at the lifeless bundle. For a moment, he thought he saw movement—a trick of the light, a ripple in the fabric—but he dismissed it. He knew better.

"Jerry," he said softly, almost conversationally, "you always talked about justice. About truth. You were relentless. It's why I had to do this. You understand that, right?"

The bundle didn't respond.

Tyler exhaled slowly, flicking ash from his cigarette into the water.

"You almost had me," he continued. "I'll give you that. But almost doesn't count. Not in this game."

He dragged the bundle to the edge of the boat, the vessel rocking slightly under the weight. The water below was impossibly dark, its surface broken only by the faint ripples caused by the boat.

"This is it," Tyler muttered. "Goodbye, Jerry."

He heaved the bundle over the edge. The chains dragged it down quickly, the splash muffled, almost apologetic. Tyler watched as the ripples spread outward, then faded, leaving the water still once more.

For a long moment, he simply sat there, staring into the abyss.

"It's done. It's over. But why does it feel like this isn't the end?"

The ride back to shore was uneventful. The motor's drone filled the emptiness left behind by the act, but it wasn't enough to drown out the thoughts swirling in his head. As the small dock came into view, Tyler's hands tightened on the steering wheel.

He killed the engine and secured the boat, his movements efficient but heavy with the weight of what he'd just done. His boots thudded against the wooden planks as he stepped onto the dock, the sound echoing in the stillness of the night.

By the time he reached his apartment, his clothes reeked of cigarette smoke and lake water. The door clicked shut behind him, and the familiar confines of his room did little to ease his nerves.

Later that night, Tyler sat at his desk, staring blankly at his phone. The faint hum of his desk lamp filled the room. The shelves around him were immaculate, each book perfectly aligned. It was the only semblance of control he had left.

The phone buzzed, jolting him from his thoughts. He glanced down at the screen.

The sender: Tony.

Tyler's brow furrowed. Tony was an old classmate, someone he hadn't spoken to in months. He opened the message, his chest tightening with every word.

"I know your second life. We need to meet ASAP."

His heart sank.

"Tony? No. This can't be. He doesn't know. He can't know."

Another buzz.

"Don't make me come to you."

The room seemed to close in on him. He stood abruptly, the chair scraping against the floor. His mind raced, searching for an explanation.

"No," he whispered, shaking his head. "No, this isn't real."

The phone buzzed again.

"The lake was a mistake, Tyler. You should've burned him."

Tyler's stomach twisted into knots. His throat tightened as he reread the message.

"How? How could he possibly know? I was careful. I was—"

Another buzz interrupted his thoughts.

"Don't act surprised. You're not as invisible as you think. I'll be in touch soon. Sleep tight, Reaper."

The words sent a chill down his spine. Tyler stared at the screen, his hands trembling. For the first time in years, Tyler Grayson felt the cold grip of fear.